AF444624

QUEST

C.N. EISENBRUCH

TO

SETH

the inspiration

Table Of Contents

I

A Beard Quest

There are probably worse things to grow up without, than a beard. Like parents. Or any member of your natural race for that matter. But McKenna, not overly burdened with filial responsibility or kinship with anyone who wasn't a *duergi*, honestly believed the greatest tragedy in life was her smooth, stubble-free chin.

It's not like the *durgir* of Clan Hammardin held it against her. But it was a deeply cherished belief that a beard brought morality, and strength, and truth. Without one you were just a callous youth unworthy to strike the iron within the mountain.

She looked up from the neat piles of slate stacked before her, some carved with runes and some painted in gold filigree. There were vellum scrolls and the occasional book or two littering the shelves of the library, but durgir preferred to work the stone. You were more likely to take care of your words when it meant ten hours with a chisel and hammer to carve them.

The gritty tapping of coarse iron on brittle slate echoed in the otherwise silent chamber. Few durgir spent their days, as she did, buried in ancient texts to the god Malfaestus. Those in her company wore braided beards tucked into belts around their shortened stocky waists and were swathed in the fine robes of the monks of Malfaestus.

"Eh, Gripple, can ye be louder then?" She heard another duergi complain, and smothered a smile.

"Ah could, but that would be rude." The unaffected Gripplewith continued pounding away at her slate, pausing for a moment to dust the flakes from her coarse brown beard.

"McKenna, ye tell 'er to hush then. I kin barely read as it is," bemoaned Argellin, his red face crinkling with a roguish wink at the monk whose long limbs, hunched over the low shelf of stone dug from a pit in the floor that served as a desk, betrayed her heritage more than her lack of beard ever could. McKenna, when she stood (which was rare; the girl spent more of her time than she cared to admit in the dusty library) easily brushed the low ceilings of their underground home with the crown of her coiled and braided locks.

The monk winked back. "'Tis no' the noise keepin' ye from yer readin', Argle, and ye know it. Ye've never been the studyin' type."

"Compared to you, girl, none o' us are the studyin' type. Ye ever get out o' this library?"

"I do fer a spar. Care to take a break?" The bridge of her nose wrinkled in a challenging smile.

Gripple muttered under her breath. "Books and beatin's. Back in my day, tha's all it took fer the monks of Malfaestus." She cast a sideways glance at the unbearded woman idly unfurling a scroll. "Leave the lass be, Argle. She'll find 'er way soon enough."

Biting her lip and pretending not to hear, McKenna's eyes travelled to the scroll she unraveled. Like most of the texts in the pile surrounding her, it featured the old stories of ancient durgirn heroes who all had one thing in common - they had all embarked on a beard quest.

"The quest to find yer beard," Pabble, the head priest of Malfaestus and the closest thing to a parent McKenna ever had, would say to the durgirn novitiates, "is a dangerous one. Some of our clan's greatest Jaerls have gone on such adventures, though it's been centuries since the last."

The young novitiates would chuckle, elbowing one another or twirling the scraggly fluff that adorned their own chins. The older masters scolded them with stern eyes beneath heavy brows that always softened when they spotted the unbearded figure sitting upright among her stocky peers. Though tough as the mountain and mithril they mined, all the members of the clan that lived in Mount Oer had soft spots. And for the monks of Malfaestus, that soft spot took the shape and form of the tall girl left among them when she was only a babe with nothing but a pretty blanket and a curious silver mirror.

Sighing with frustration and unable to concentrate with the steady tapping of Gripple's dictation ringing in her ears, McKenna uncurled herself from her nook and decided if she couldn't wheedle any of the novitiates into a spar with her, she'd just train by herself. It wouldn't be the first time.

"Malfaestus," she whispered, bringing the resin-coated wood of the quarterstaff she'd grabbed from the training rack close to her face and taking a deep breath. Exhaling a simple chant that fired the runes inked upon her sable skin she began a series of maneuvers, relaxing into the flow of the exercise with the same calm concentration she experienced while reading in the library or polishing the bright crystals and gems that decorated the High Altar to the Secretkeeper - Malfaestus, god of the durgir. Many times before had she lost herself for hours in this martial meditation and now, quite easily, she did again. Though the sun's glare crept its way in through skylights vaulted high into the carved ceiling, it came and passed without her really noticing.

Noise broke through her reverie. Over the resounding thumps of her polearm striking the burlap dummies, she heard raised voices echo through the stone hallways. Not that this was a particularly uncommon occurrence - durgir weren't quiet - but the tone caught her attention.

Rarely were voices raised in fear in the stronghold of Mount Hammardin.

The smoke of the mines stung her sensitive eyes that never seemed to adjust either to the dimness of the caverns nor the constant streams of soot and fire that poured from the kilns fired below. She followed the echoing sounds, padding softly and alert for danger. These voices in particular, belonging to the Trade Guild, were even more interesting. The Trade Guild, unlike the rest of their secretive and xenophobic clan, were the only durgir from Mount Oer who ventured into the rest of the realms of Faie to deal with the other races and guilds that populated it. *Hope it en't another daemor...*

"There mus' be somethin' wrong on the road. Nary a single keg since Red Solstice," someone moaned, their youthful tone carrying through the stone hallway.

"Get yer mind off yer drink! The ore from Bristendine's near gone, and not a brick's come to replace it in moons," grumbled a sterner voice she recognized of Hammardin Pock, a clan elder.

She peered around the cavern's opening, taking stock of the group gathered before her in the imposing stone hall. Members of the Guild made up most of the assembled company, joined also by Pabble, whose steady sense and magical knowledge made him an irreplaceable boon to such enclaves as these.

Grumbling voices spoke words too low for her to hear for a moment, til the first speaker's carrying tones rang out again.

"Aye," groaned Garble, the youth who'd bemoaned the lack of mead that normally flowed with abundance among the mines. "No envoy from Bread Basket in over two moons. An' Pock willnae let the guild go'n investigate."

"Tisn't our route to walk now, Garbleton Disgeld," Pock's voice was deep and resonant, and he spoke with authority unused to any challenge.

Pabble's voice joined his. "Hammardin Pock is right. We've agreements wi' the *asafolk* o' Beausun. To set a band o' durgir upon the road now could mean war."

McKenna's eyebrows raised in surprise. Though the durgir mingled little with the asafolk to the south, she'd no reason to suspect enmity among their people. Certainly not to the extent the elders seemed to be implying.

Again their voices lowered, and as McKenna knew better than to be caught eavesdropping she made no effort to inch closer than the solid marble column she stood behind. Sounds such as "Malfaestus" and "nobles" made it to her ears and she lost the train of the conversation in trying to recall what nobles were. By the time she picked the thread of the conversation back up, the voices began to raise again until Hammardin Pock gruffly called them to order with a terseness little heard among the sedate clan. A few mutinous whispers briefly followed, but then no further dissent broke the silence.

The mood had darkened perceptibly in the smoky cavern, the elders turning dour glances upon one another. Pabble sighed.

"Tisn't our route to walk," he repeated Pock's words firmly. "The guild can set upon the Low Road at Yellow Solstice - no sooner. That's the agreement."

Garble and the younger clerics cast each other dissatisfied glances which were not lost on McKenna. If she didn't know any better she would be almost certain that Garble planned to set out anyways - permission or no.

Hammardin Pock sized them up silently. Hammardin Pock did most things silently - and slowly - reminding McKenna of the restlessness she always felt among her kin.

Would it kill them to think quicker'n the drip of limestone, she thought to herself. Seeing that none of the others meant to try and challenge the elders, she snuck off back down the catwalk through the mines to the library.

The only thing McKenna wanted more than a beard, was a quest. A desire she thought she hid rather well from her kin, despite the fact she wore her yearning on her face and with every unduergilike move she made during the interminable years of her novitiate. And despite as much proof as she could pull from texts and old stories to bolster her claim to a beard quest, she knew nothing would convince her clan to grant her one if leaving the mines meant disturbing the carefully guarded peace and neutrality of the duergir.

"Ye mean she's among the books again?" A voice carried itself through the meandering stone halls of the chapel carved deep within Mount Oer.

"Where else would she be? Not one ter watch rocks grow," was the reply, the shrug in Argle's voice as clear as the exasperation in Priest Pabble's.

McKenna pretended to ignore her mentor's knock on the sturdy bookshelves, just as she pretended to ignore him as he quietly and slowly sank beside her on the stone floor. However, Pabble had always been much better than her at this game, as evidenced by the fact that very few minutes went by before she snorted in disgust and turned away from her book to regard him, confusion and frustration keen on her usually bright and inquisitive face.

"Somethin' eatin' ye, girl?" The warmth of his smile dissolved the tension within her, and drew a crooked smile in response from the corner of her mouth.

"I err...overheard some talk. From the traders," she admitted. "That we're no allowed ter leave the mines, less it's fer trade, and only after the Solstice."

"Ah. An' it got ye thinkin' maybe that's why yer unfair Papa Pabble won't let ye go on yer beard quest, then," he guessed, with a knowing twinkle in his eye.

She realized he must have known she was there, and let her overhear on purpose. Exhaling slowly, she realized the punishment could have been worse.

"Maybe. Would be a convenient excuse," she countered. "Since ye won't tell me what the real reason is."

"The real reason is summat even I don't know entirely. An' that's the truth," he said softly and earnestly. "But it's not to be ignored ye simply have no been ready fer it - nor ready ter leave the mines, let alone under the conditions of a beard quest."

"I can take care of meself!"

"That's not the point of a beard quest," he reminded her pointedly, "and ye know it. Taking care of yerself ain't yer weakness."

"You mean ye don't think I kin get along with *faiefolkr*." She smoothed a page of the tome open before her, one of the rarest in the library. This was written not by durgir, but in a flowing script that read in the language of the *ilvir*. It had taken McKenna most of her novitiate to learn how to read ilfish text. Ilvir had never once been to Mount Oer, and no Hammardin duergi (living, at least) ever visited the vaulted glades of their forest home in Meliamne, as far south as Mount Oer was north.

"Ye think ye kin learn folk outta books, then, girl?" He replied, and though his eyes were smiling his brow was heavy.

"Don't see why ye can't, exactly," she muttered, flipping the pages of the massive tome idly, to an illustration of the pantheon. Portraits painted of the legendary Sh'nia and Atosa, the realms' patron goddesses, were faded in ancient ink. On a page opposite,

in fresher tints, lay the Secret Keeper - Malfaestus, god
of durgir and the metals beneath the mountain. Flanking
him on either side were the two *aesir* gods: Bahamut, the
magnificent golden dragon, and the ivory scales of Sanct
Germain.

"Jest 'cause durgir don't know how ter make friends,
doesn't mean I won'. We been buried in these mines fer
too long, Pabble. There's more to the world than this,"
she waved her hand at their surroundings, with the other
firmly pressed against the book before her.

"They've no space fer the like o' us. We do 'em a
service, we trade and we don't bother one another.
Knowing," he raised an eyebrow at the book she
so aggressively gestured to, "innit the same as
understanding. And *that*," he said, a fierce edge to his
tone that McKenna knew not to challenge, "is a lesson we
learned from asafolk."

Her voice grew quiet. "Is that why ye said they'd
bring us war?" she asked, fingers tracing along the blades
of swords held by paladins in the shadow of their great
god on the page.

"Mebbe I exaggerated a little, but..." he trailed off,
and again that sensation of darkness - almost fear -
descended upon his brow as he spoke. "There've been
whispers, lass, and whispers are more'n enough to keep
us from gettin' involved. The realms ain't what they used
ter be, and it's not fer durgir to solve problems they didn'
cause."

A faint scent wafted past. Cordite, the smell that
accompanied crushed rock, and the heady aroma of
incense. A general bustle at the altar alerted them
both that they were no longer alone in the library and

McKenna closed the book, stacking it neatly with the other texts on the desk where she sat.

"I'm going. With or without the gods, I'm going because I must."

He stared at her, his serene expression a mystery. She realized the runes on her skin had begun to fire, flickering in patterns too fast to catalyze any spells. But that is not what he noticed. It simply distracted her from seeing what he saw. An aura, a glow that enveloped her and spoke louder than any mere god could.

He knew then that there was nothing more he could do to stop her.

"Just... wait," he said, emotion catching in his throat and making him sound gruffer than usual. "I have summat for ye, but it ent ready yet. I'll bring it to ye, and then-"

But he was cut off by the sound of durgir chanting at the altar. The novitiates had retired to their evening studies. With another last look and a smile at the girl, her legs crammed awkwardly in the bench carved under the table, he sighed and left.

—

In the ensuing weeks McKenna spoke little to Pabble or any of the other novitiates, burying herself in tomes and hoping for a clearer picture of the relationship between durgir and those who lived in the wider realms of Faie. But she could sense the tension in the mines growing heavier. One bright winter morning - the first morning of winter, in fact, the day of White Solstice and her own, vaguely acknowledged birthday, Pabble appeared in her chambers with a gift.

"Promise, I en't here to try'n talk ye out o' anything," he began, patting down the dust from his long robes in an attempt to not quite meet her eye.

"As if ye could," muttered McKenna, but she smiled at the durgirn priest anyways and invited him in.

"I know no one's been able to stop you yet, but I figured ye should a' least take this," he said, pushing aside the long black beard tucked protectively around a small bundle in his belt. Sitting down on the end of a bench, he hesitated as though unwilling to hand over the package.

McKenna took it from him and unwrapped it. A bright gleam of rhoditum, with an edge of what was unmistakably mithril. It resembled a blade, but that was all.

"I thought we weren't allowed weapons?" she said, confusion blended in her voice.

"Ye're not. But technically, this en't a weapon yet," Pabble replied, sounding a bit anxious. "It's jes' the head. You'll have to find your own shaft, but once ye do, this'll be the finest guisarme ye ever held."

"I believe you. I didn't even think we could make mithril into weapons anymore," McKenna said appreciatively, as she saw the unmistakeable striations and color banding that marked the blade's composition of invulnerable and magical mithril.

"Tha's jest what we tell the ilvir to drive the price up," he winked conspiratorially. "But ye're right, this is very, very old. Still good though, for all that."

"Jes' like me Pabble," McKenna teased back. She was going to miss her calm, sturdy mentor. His temperament and pensive wisdom set him apart from most of the blunt, burly durgir of her clan, which made him perfect as the head Priest of Malfaestus. A subtle power seemed to always cling to him like the shalesoot that clung to the miners. She studied him for a moment, the black dusty beard twisted into his girdle, the fine, but well-worn robes draped over his stocky figure.

"I'll find me truth, if'n I dig it from the ground bare-handed," she said, putting a hand on his shoulder. "I want ter know, but more'n that I want ter *seek*. The quest promises more'n the reward."

He smiled as he looked up at her, but the smile faded with a sigh.

Dew-bright eyes lined with age watched his adopted child inscrutably, his heart full of misgiving. Raising McKenna as a duergi meant many things - and not a single one of those things was he free to share with the bright-eyed and eager monk who stood before him. Just plain unfair, he thought it. Swallowing such blasphemous thoughts, he could only offer a silent prayer that disguising McKenna's quest as one that had her searching for her identity may actually be more on the mark than she realized.

"The less I know you know, and the less you know I know, the better," he answered with a shrug. McKenna's brows drew together in a comical expression of bewilderment and Pabble allowed himself a laugh.

In the head priest's long life, he'd seen many heroes

leave the halls of Hammardin to find what lay beyond the secrets kept beneath the mountain. The curious balance of magic and physics, the discordance between the very real existence of beings on the Material plane and the ephemeral Celestials that guided them, required constant interference by those brave enough and connected enough both to gods and mortals to maintain that balance.

And here she stood, his girl, his ward, without even knowing what mantle it was she prepared to don. Unfair put it too mildly.

No matter what obstacle you put afore her, she'll leap it wit' room to spare. None else can touch her with blade or thought. Would she could even have a rival, she'd be more like to treat them as a treasured friend. Her passion and empathy run deeper than the veins o' mithril in this here mountain. But by the gods, she's a complete innocent. Let this quest simply be the adventure she seeks, the glories and the challenges bedamned.

"This be the one thing I can give ye, on'y what ye can take from the mountains. Make yer preparations swift, then, lass, and off with ye into the world." With those words, he rose and made his way out.

"Pabble?" Her voice reached him just before leaving.

"Yes, child," he replied, turning in place to answer one last question.

"Have I really got to be naked?"

II

Influences

A tall, fair woman stalked back and forth. The surface of the wide, shallow dish set before her emitted sparks of silver and green light that reflected off the satin shine of her moon bright hair. A proud mouth, pursed in dissatisfaction, boded ill for any foolish enough to disturb her. But of course the *ilvir* of Meliamne, especially those who resided here in Tirre Lunir, knew better than to interrupt a sorcere in the throes of a summoning.

Whispers seemed to emanate from around the room, curses and inquiries cast from the spell-bound pool of liquid light. She didn't bother with a response, instead continuing to pace along the dais in front of the bowl. Every rune marked on the floor with precision, every line and crystal emanated the power she had imbued over months of preparation. Methodically, she checked every single one against a tome propped open before her.

A door to the Abyss was no simple feat. Lesser sorceres died in the attempt to summon even an imp or kvetchling. She knew, for she'd watched them perish, torn apart by stinking smoking claws in the blink of an eye before the more learned mages present could bind the monsters and put an end to the carnage. For reasons unknown, the denizens of other planes always desired to walk upon those they did not inhabit, and sorceres- like the woman pacing before the glowing gate- simply channeled their considerable skill and magical attunement to bridging that gap as frequently and as carefully as possible in exchange for knowledge and power promised by the creatures from the Abyss. Provided, of course, that they could control them. But she was confident in her abilities and knew her casting to be completely foolproof.

Katarin never made mistakes.

She watched with the same dissatisfied look as the shimmering light began to congeal and darken. Finally, the head and shoulders of the *daemor genirae* Makarh emerged, only to stop short as though iron bands had arrested his momentum.

He chuckled and stared the sorcere down. "Your bindings are uncomfortable as ever, Katarin."

The largest and most formidable of all Abyssal creatures, summoning a *daemor* required near preternatural ability and a host of high ranking sorceres. Nothing daunted, Katarin - Third Sorcere of the Guild of Moonbow, and possessed of talents even beyond the most practiced and accomplished of her class - preferred not to share these opportunities for gaining otherwise unattainable knowledge with others despite the enormous risk. And so far, she remained unmatched.

"Have you found the mirror?" she demanded, wasting no words bantering with the tricky Abyssinian. Truthfully, she found the words of daemor grating as the harsh strike of iron on wood, and she much preferred the soft, pensive whispers of the dead who made their home in Hel - yet another plane that abutted the Material, and one much harder to traverse. But the dead couldn't see as far as Abyssal creatures, and she needed a clarity beyond mortal comprehension.

"Yes," he replied with equal brevity, offering no further clarification than a sinister grin.

"And?" she urged, scratching a thin nail along the shaft of a scepter marked with glowing runes. *This is why I hate working with daemor. Worthless and crafty without even the saving grace of being disposable. You never know when one you cross may come back for revenge.*

Makarh winced as the gesture flicked his essence to the raw. "You know that's no way to treat a guest. I cannot reach the mirror. My banishment from this plane has not yet been lifted by the one who inflicted it. You will have to send some of your less powerful consorts to acquire it. My time here is up," he spit the words as he attempted to struggle again with the bonds that held him.

"Not yet," she whispered in a tone nearly as fiendish as the daemor's own. "I did not ask you to bring it to me, so do not waste my time with your complaints. You cannot tell me who holds it- the mirror's power prevents that- but you know where it is. Tell me that, and I shall release you... and send whomever is foolish enough to keep it from me to you, for punishment," she growled. *What a waste of my summoning. Makarh grows more irritating with every visit... that paladin must have really done a number on him.*

His face broke into an evil grin. Influencing asafolk was almost too easy. "I suppose until I can consume your soul, another will have to do. The mirror has been one of the secrets kept locked beneath the mountain. I was only able to discover it because, for reasons unknown, it seems to have suddenly left."

Her face remained impassive at the expurgated response, while Makarh shifted once more against the

iron grip of her spell. Without a blink, she released him—
and the daemor disappeared in the quintessential clap of
brimstone and flame.

The secrets kept locked beneath the mountain. A ringing
chord, accompanied by words sung in holvir voices.

Mount Oer, she mused to herself. It was far, but it was
a start.

Katarin took a seat carefully before the large, open
fireplace. The summoning of daemor spirits often took
enough energy to put sorceres into a near-comatose state
for a day or more, but she remained resilient as ever to
the sap of arcane energy. Nevertheless, she wouldn't
push herself farther than necessary, and saw no weakness
in sitting for a moment to compose her spirits. The safety
of her chamber's defenses provided her ample security
should she choose to rest, but the knowledge was too
new, too fresh, for her to set aside just yet. Discovering
the mirror's location in the duergin stronghold confirmed
a suspicion she'd held for years.

"Twins," she murmured under her breath, waving
a hand in front of her as though to imagine its duplicate
attached to another.

The firelight danced before her, reflecting off the pale
white wood of her chamber walls and the crystal panes
of glass that rippled overhead, a domed observatory
glowing in the light of the moon. Not for anything would
Katarin forget what brought her here, nor for a moment
could she ignore the call of destiny that granted her
such unparalleled power. And yet, were the daemor's
words to be trusted, all that stood to be destroyed by
the interference of a single, providentially discovered
being who seemed to appear out of nowhere. She would

suspect divine intervention were she not entirely certain that the only divine power capable of such manipulations currently rested, impotent, at her utmost control.

As she sank deeper into cushions of rich damask, composing her energies after the difficult casting, she felt her consciousness begin to ebb and flow like the fabled tides of the Unnamed Sea. Regulating her breath, she loosened her taut limbs and slipped into a trance, a relief from her persistent and rigid discipline. Thoughts pooling on the edges of her consciousness spilled forth into a flood, a deluge, mighty and roaring and filled with voices. So many voices.

A forbidden spell, a holvir story. Moon-bright hair of a little princess, raised by adoring ilvir, growing like a flower amidst this ancient race. Beloved for her heritage, and the immortal blood of a goddess that flowed through her mortal body. Voices, theirs, promising her devotion.

Voices, louder, insistent, promising her power.

Katarin felt again the stirrings of consciousness. With a wave of a thin, be-ringed hand she cleared the runes from the dais. The shallow bowl, emptied of its potion, she returned to a wardrobe. Locking the doors, she swept away to a desk, bare but for a single notebook. She opened this and scanned a few pages, then snapped the book shut and began an incantation.

Suddenly the turbid shape of a man began to appear before her in the room. Within the span of a breath he stepped through the shimmering portal she summoned and swept off his hat, bowing low before her.

"Katarin. To what do I owe the pleasure?" he began, his deep voice possessing a magic of its own.

"Your reputation, Razan. What else?" she bantered back, relaxing slightly.

The statuesque assassin always seemed to put her at ease, a feeling most would not share in the least. Even the fellow members of his guild, enthralled as they were by his leadership, tempered that adoration with a healthy dose of fear. Katarin, however, admired the crafty guild Master, and what Katarin admired, she could respect to the utmost. Many times had she interacted with him and his band of assassins, the lesser guild Onyx Blade, in their capacity as the hired guard for the more influential Guild of Moonbow. But beyond that- and, perhaps, beyond a few tempestuous personal encounters- she found the man useful for more than just his skill. Certainly his physical appearance left little to be wished for. His murky, soulful eyes were always hinting at secrets impossible to unlock, and he had a dark clear skin cut into powerful jaw and lithe, competent muscles.

"It is ever at your service, Princess," he replied, arching a delicate eyebrow and curling the corners of his sensual mouth. "I would hope I haven't given you reason to doubt it yet."

"Yes, yes, you're very good at what you do. Don't make me pamper your vanity," she shot back with a playful grin. How much easier it was to talk to him than daemor.

"If it wanted pampering, I'd know better than to seek that here," he chuckled, settling comfortably into a settee turned toward her imposing figure.

The voices in her head always grew quiet around him. The man exuded an aura of otherworldliness that muffled the influences constantly vying for her attention, and entranced the sorcere almost as much as it enraged her. While she struggled daily against the physical limitations imposed by her mortality, despite her divine heritage, he seemed to flow effortlessly between the martial physics of the Material plane and the magical mysteries that moved within it. She had reason to question his own heritage - and she had knowledge enough of his temper to know better than to actually pose those questions to him. Though she felt he trusted her beyond even the lieutenants of his own intensely loyal guild, there were some secrets that simply couldn't be shared.

She could hear the whisper of souls as they danced before death. His remained tantalizingly mute.

Though all traces of her summoning had been completely effaced, leaving the room as innocuous as any other, he again arched a delicate eyebrow and seemed to sniff out the essence of daemoric energy. He fixed her with a quizzical look, one she could tell meant to be sympathetic, but simply irritated her.

"You may be good at what you do, but you don't know everything, Razan," she responded to that look defensively, a sullen edge to her musical voice. He pursed his lips but said nothing.

"If it makes you feel any better, it was a complete waste of my time. I need your services anyways, to fill in the blanks that worthless creature left in my questioning," she wheedled, internally cursing the silent judgement she'd been met with. *He always does this. He knows I'm a sorcere, why does he have to treat me with such disdain every time I perform a summoning? Such insolence... and presumption.*

He sighed, a curt laugh escaping under his breath. "This won't be the first time I'm sent to clean up after daemor. And, Princess," he added, with a sudden urgency adding ardor to his tone, "I never doubt your prowess, either. You mistake me. I just…" he cast a look to the empty brazier, and in the depths of his dark brown eyes a brightness kindled, glowing the hue of freshly spilled blood. Her breath caught in her throat at the sight 'til he turned and regarded her with the candor and affection he seemed to reserve only for her. "I'd hoped you had a… warmer need for me, is all," he finished, leaning toward her and turning the full power of those expressive eyes to her cold and pensive face.

She felt a familiar burning, urgent sensation deep within her breast but smothered it. This quest was too important to waste even a moment- and she knew longer than a moment would be wasted should those impulses override her judgement. She ran a finger along the scepter she had used to control the daemor, choosing her words as carefully as if she'd been speaking to Makarh again.

"I seek the possessor of an item- a mirror," she mused, staring into the crest of the scepter while being deliberately obtuse.

"Certainly you need no mirror to prove your ethereal beauty," he supplied after a pause, with a raised eyebrow conveying a world of meaning.

"No mortal in all the realms can use that mirror. But it's not for mortals," she began, then hesitated. Ever distrustful, she disliked giving more information than the barest necessity, but she needed the assassin to be armed with every possible advantage.

"I need this mirror to defeat a god."

—

"You look horrible. Princess summons that bad?"

Deirdra's laconic voice shook him from his reverie as he stepped from the portal, his heeled boots ringing loudly on the inky obsidian floor. Hearing her voice, he quickly mastered his expression into one of languid amusement.

"Jealousy doesn't suit you, *Altennette*," he replied, using his second in command's title as a reminder of her rank. While he allowed his subordinates a surprising amount of license, he knew better than to allow too much familiarity.

She sensed the rebuke and said no more, retreating into the shadows. Heels still ringing on the stone floors, he made his way through the labyrinthine structure to his sumptuous quarters as deep underground as Tirre Lunir was tall.

Ignoring the untidy stacks of missives and packages littering his rather shabby oak desk, he dug around in a drawer instead to pull out an envelope, stained the colour of fresh blood and sealed with a five-pointed sigil stamped deep in wax.

They have absolutely no subtlety, he rued, sliding a painted fingernail under the wax seal that had remained unbroken since the letter was delivered... Razan genuinely couldn't remember how long ago.

The letter was from his mother. Razan despised his mother.

He hadn't reached his age in this profession without uncommon edge in more than just the physical. Born with an innate affinity for the arcane, he was originally marked on a path to priesthood. A great and renowned cleric his mentor, the wealthiest guild in the oceanside city of Lianor his allies, there was nothing holding the boy back from greatness.

Except for the tiny insignificant fact that Razan hated magic.

Ethereal beings plagued his dreams; spells and incantations interrupted his daily routine. His everyday life succumbed to a narrow, predetermined path with each footstep marched along by powers he could not control. What else could a precocious, charismatic, disillusioned child do but chafe and struggle against the bonds that held him? It wasn't his fault his mother was a slut and his cleric mentor an infidel. Nor was it his problem that his family chose to sate their lust for power and intrigue by mating, both figuratively and physically, with daemor. So, Razan did what any self-respecting independent young boy would do. He ran away to join the Onyx Blade- a travelling guild of godless rogues.

The same guild, or rather, their children and consorts all, that he led to this day. By growing up among them and proceeding to a coveted seat of power that none so qualified as he could hold, he dragged the reputation of Onyx Blade from local infamy to a notoriety that contracted them to guard the most prestigious sorcere's guild in the southern realms of Faie. On their behalf, his guild of assassins and fighters had dealt in intrigue, the subtle balances of power and eminence tipping one way or another by various quests and objectives that put his rigorous and strategic mind to the test.

Razan may have hated magic, but he couldn't deny it had its uses.

Sinking gracefully into a luxurious couch and pouring himself a glass of murky, aromatic liquor, he sighed and opened the letter, brows furrowed as he analyzed the spidery writing on the page. He snorted, and flipped the paper over once, before rolling his eyes and using the sharp edge to slice the side of his hand, drawing blood.

He pressed the wound to the page. It glowed for a moment, then caught fire.

Well. At least I know the invitation hasn't expired.

The ashes disintegrated, immolating to the point the entire letter simply disappeared. No mark, neither physical nor magic, remained.

Hmm. Perhaps they do know subtlety after all.

"Hel's portal," he breathed into one of the bangles resting upon his arm. The bangle chimed twice in agreement. His dark features furrowed into a scowl, but the chime's clear note lingered in the air.

What could Katarin be playing at, he wondered to himself. An accomplished sorcere in her own right, he had to acknowledge that before now she had never exhibited the lust for power that some of her more ambitious compatriots often betrayed. In fact, he often wondered how such a sedate, cold individual as herself had managed to advance so far as she had, despite her prodigious skills. One did not simply command power as a sorcere. Power controlled you, demanding more and greater sacrifice of one's mortality, and dignity, and desires with each summoning until the user was next to a

Abyssinian themselves. That is, unless they got eaten first. But Katarin, he thought to himself with a rakish grin, was *quintessentially* mortal.

Her words and her command unsettled him. But none knew better than he that to unravel the truth of a falsehood, one had to simply follow its orders to precision. And that, he thought as he stood and donned his cloak and wide-brimmed hat, was exactly what he planned to do.

Alone.

III

A Little Help

Of course, the panther didn't just appear from nowhere. Even in Faie things like that didn't happen without a reason. However, as it would be strange and slightly disconcerting for a hero to wander aimlessly and indefinitely around an empty forest completely naked, the monk knew that she had to start working on generating her own reasons for things to happen.

McKenna knelt at the timberline. The thin, invisible boundary marked the end of Mount Oer and the beginning of asafolk territory. The Bread Basket, they called this region; and if it once had a different name everyone had forgotten it. She sucked in a deep breath, feeling, with her devout attunement to her honored god, the shift in magic that separated duergi from aesir. But chanting still came naturally, and slipping into a profound meditation even more so.

The chanting started to echo. From her perch she could see the trees begin to sway, feel the gravel shift against her bare thighs, and hear the wind off the sea come barreling through the mountains faster and easier than the rail carts full of ore that trundled up and down along the coastal Low Road. A taste of it, salty tang; and bitter, metallic blood. Her meditations brought her peace, and Malfaestus was bringing her a fight.

She exhaled long, slowly, feeling the air pass from her naked torso into her broad chest and out through her full, pursed lips.

"Respect yerself. Honor yer practice. The gods on'y take ye so far," McKenna mimed the words her mentor used to parrot every blessed day. She missed him already. "And most importantly, know yer purpose."

My purpose, she thought as she peered into the setting sun, surveying the valley below. *Dunno if I have a purpose for this, really. I'm naked, I'm starving, and I'm carrying a useless piece of pointy mithril. I guess my purpose is to find some clothes*

Mornings dawned bright and clear in the valley pass that lay in the shadow of Mount Oer. She woke on this one to something new, something different. The sound of carts rumbling through the rocky mountain pass.

It's about time, too, thought McKenna in relief as she regarded the long-awaited envoy of traders from the south. *I wonder what kept 'em - maybe I'll ask.*

As she approached, she noticed a dark shadow stalking the envoy. Not that she could see it, exactly; she sensed it, in the bristled pikes and alert eyes of the durgir traders, in a tumble of scree that slid without warning off a cliff. She felt a humming along the shaft of her makeshift guisarme, the runes on her skin thrumming in sympathy.

This shadow was her boon - an answer to her prayers.

Suddenly a shout, and the fierce knocking of shields locked together, echoed across the valley. A shape flitted from the trees to the caravan, and then back again with such speed it appeared as nothing more than an uncanny darkness against the brightness of the morning. The screech of its claws as they raked the metal of the shields rang in her ears - and then, it let out a wild yowl that drowned the valley in its ferocity.

A dire panther.

She'd never seen one, of course. Dire animals were a figment of myth, or so the stories told her; massive and brutally intelligent versions of their dumber, smaller counterparts, created entirely by the heathen Sh'nia-worshipping druids of Gamor. Dire animals were said to possess the soul of the druid that created them, letting the enchanter live a second life as the beast they most revered. And yet, despite myth, despite legend, despite *logic*, here one was in the wilds of the north, chasing down a caravan of surly traders fighting their way along the rutted and root-ridden High Road.

If this was meant to be her first challenge, she began to appreciate why the gods were loath to let her roam free at all.

The staccato orders shouted out by the durgirn soldiers were drowned in the whine of adamantine as their shields shifted like a living wall, repelling each strike of the massive beast. In lockstep coordination each durgir advanced and retreated, protecting the inner ring of wagons and traders. Quickly, McKenna realized they couldn't do much more than defend from the beast. They hadn't the strategy or the weapons to attack it due to its speed and sheer size. The dire panther, in some uncanny way, seemed to know this and focused on exhausting their efforts and getting those shields to drop even the tiniest bit with the weight of its overwhelming bulk.

Recognizing their weakness, McKenna tightened her grip on her guisarme and advanced slowly. The craftsmanship of her makeshift shaft, crudely carved from a branch and marked with runes storing power and spells, would face its first test today. She knew, as well as the panther, that to lower those shields even for an instant would bring a deadly opening for the panther's attack. But the monk never fit in the shield wall, and therefore focused all her training to the offensive. Her long weapon, paired with her extensive limbs, kept attackers too far to need a shield for defense.

Hoping to pass by unseen, McKenna tried to keep a wide berth of the trading party- but unfamiliar with the cat's uncanny sense of smell, failed to hide her scent. Sensing a new and, as it thought, unprotected foe, it turned and yowled, leaping full over the trade wagons and into the trees above. McKenna gave chase, a net of woven vines looped around one hand and the guisarme perfectly balanced in the other. The durgir all turned in bemusement to see what had startled the cat- and suffered the same shock it did.

"Are ye plannin' o' chasing that panther with a stick- are ye *naked*?!" one cried as she dashed past them.

"Yeah, the cat's still wearing my clothes!" she shot back laughingly.

The lithe, dark shape flitted quickly in and out of McKenna's vision. She whispered a prayer to Malfaestus and stroked one of the runes on her skin, and the brightness of the sun dimmed as a glow lit itself around the panther. Her endurance was her one advantage. She could tirelessly stalk the creature, never pausing nor letting it pause for rest, and now she could see it clear as a beacon no matter how far it got nor how dense the forest around it. Their deadly dance ranged the width and breadth of the valley floor, a ceaseless game of hunter and prey.

Stalking a dire panther, naked, in the High Road ter Bread Basket. This is not how I expected me quest to go.

Her efforts began to pay off. The panther, annoyed at this sudden reversal of the natural order of things, made to give up in disgust. There were other, easier targets that would make a tasty enough snack, and it had no idea what it was doing this far north anyways. It turned toward the banks of the river, seeking a spot to blend into the camouflage which nature so thoughtfully provides its creatures.

McKenna knew better than that, though. The runes - ancient spells that had been passed from duergi to Hammardin duergi for generations, honoring the god Malfaestus - firing along her skin helped keep her apprised of the monster's every movement. The Secret Keeper had granted her this boon and she was not about to waste it. Motionless, she waited for the dire panther to brood over a small pool before making her first strike.

She was an instant too precipitate. The panther, catching her scent by a shift in the wind, pivoted and screamed another feral cry that nearly killed the heart within the monk. Wincing at the sound, she set her teeth and muttered an oath to Malfaestus. She could only hope the spell would work. Facing one of her peers in the sparring dorms deep within Mount Oer, with a bevy of clerics and healers just on the other side of the complex, was quite a different matter to facing several hundred pounds of pure muscle while alone and naked in the woods. The creature hissed as the magical dweomer shimmered against her dark skin, lashing its tail and swiping a massive paw at her face. Not wanting to take the god's gift for granted, McKenna dodged, diving into a roll that brought her closer and off to the side of the wild beast.

It screamed again, pivoting in place with the preternatural strength granted to Sh'nia's fabled dire beasts. Nothing daunted, McKenna shifted her position and tossed her makeshift net off to its side, to drive it toward her or entangle its powerful limbs. The panther leapt away and managed a swipe at her unprotected chest, but using the cat's momentum, she rolled into its grasp- grunting at the rake of adamantine claws across her shoulder and back- and thrust her guisarme deep across its throat.

The shot told.

Fight a dire beast, completely naked. Yes, this is a completely normal and natural tradition, she thought exasperatedly to herself as the weight of the dead cat bore her down, limp against the shaft of the guisarme that, in testament to her craftsmanship, had withstood the strike to the panther's heart. But honestly, she didn't even have time to feel the pride of success. Feeling the monster's blood spill and mingle with her own, she slumped weakly and lowered its lifeless body to the ground. Strangely, while she knew the claw marks torn across her back should have at least rendered her unconscious, she could feel the soft flesh begin to tighten and knit of its own accord. Whispering a prayer of thanks to Malfaestus, she cut the heart from the panther and buried it deep within the soft soil by the stream. Though the god never required nor particularly cared for blood sacrifice, she owed it to the animal to leave part of it with the realm from where she took it. With a start, she felt a soft tug against her soul, a brush against it from one passing on to the next realm.

Shivering, she stood up to shake off the sensation - and nearly immediately buckled from the strain. Though her oath clearly worked, rendering her skin harder than twice cured leather, the wound ran so deep even the prayer she offered struggled to finish healing it. Not wanting to rely entirely on the god's benevolence, she began to search the banks for inglefoss to press into her deepest scratches. It wouldn't heal her, but it would stop the bleeding.

Exhausted, she hid the panther's limp remains in the roots of a tree and dropped in place in a bed of moss, blacking out quicker than the panther's strike.

—

"McKenna, what in the blazes brought you all the way out here?"

Pabble's face swam before her. She bit her lip.

"I was followin' the sounds, Priest. They ask me to come find them," the girl replied, her voice quiet but firm.

"Sounds? Them? Who do you mean, child?" His own voice lowered, as he bent to look her in the eyes.

She pointed to the tattered remains of rope beside a deep, uncovered chute. The cairn before them laid unbothered for decades, a silent tomb for some unlucky travelers who sought secrets they had no right to know.

"They're sorry. They're real sorry," the girl tugged on Pabble's robes, startling tears in her own amber eyes. "They just want to go home, Pabble, can I please? Can't I send them home?"

Home is Hel, child, they whisper, the mournful sounds of souls as they dance in life before death. *The doors are closed, we cannot get in.*

—

Waking to the soft drip of dew falling from the treetops, she rose and stretched, shaking the vestiges of the already fading dream from her consciousness. The wounds on her back twinged in discomfort, but the moss and prayer had done its work well. Her blood had ceased to flow from the fresh and healing scars. She could hear Pabble's chiding remarks- *heedless, foolhardy, taking on a dire panther what were you thinking you fleshy young mongrel.* A rueful grin flitted across her features at the thought of just how deserved those criticisms from her patient and exasperated mentor would be.

Staring at the mass of lifeless monster before her, she sighed, puffing that stray lock of hair from her face again. *Now I've got to reduce ye to somethin' useful. I was better off in chapel.*

Preparing the pelt for tanning- now that would be a process, she knew, that could take a moon or more. Tapping a thoughtful finger to her still-hairless chin, she groaned when she realized what the day had next in store for her. If she listened through the stillness of the forest she could even still hear the echoing sounds of those traders, rumbling their way along. So, once she'd scraped the last of the muscle and sinew from the panther's skin, she brought it back to her makeshift camp and draped it from the branches of a willow tree to dry. Carving runes of deception around the base of the tree- to thwart any sticky fingers or curious animal marauders- she set off to find the durgirn party. Luckily, she still had the net she used to trick the panther, and she draped herself in it hastily. It wasn't the most effective cover, but indeed, durgir have little shame. If she caught up to the traders, she could get rid of the panther's ivory teeth in exchange for coin. Food was plentiful enough in the valley for those who knew how to catch it, but McKenna needed to continue on her journey. Her next stop would be in the village of Hanthor, and the first tavern she could reach.

Taverns held faiefolkr, and faiefolkr provided quests.

"Besides," she mused to herself as she leapt fleetingly across the forest floor, "I'm supposed ter be a monk, not a barbarian."

The durgir hadn't so much as crossed from the valley to the switchbacks by the time she'd caught up to them. She felt surprised they'd even made it as far as they did. The root-covered and rutted valley floor punished wagons, and theirs groaned under the weight of its load. Approaching their party, she greeted them from the path.

"Well met, fair traders. On the path to gates of Mount Oer, I see?" she cried, still at a bit of a distance from their cart.

"Are ye a proud ilvi, then? To be standin' so far!" one chided, though well aware of her predicament. You don't quickly forget a naked warrior screeching through the treetops.

"Come now, no need to banter! A better sight for sore eyes as yours will be the mead halls of Hammardin!" she shot back with a wink.

The durgir chuckled amongst themselves, and one, black beard shining in the midday sun, stepped apart from the rest. "I'm not sure we'd agree on that- we caught a bit of what ye're hiding when ye passed by with the cat, an' our eyes are less sore than dazzled!" he replied with a saucy guffaw. "Did ye catch the beast?"

"I did indeed. A bit too fresh for the wearin', but time will cure tha'. Happen ye have a use fer its teeth?" she inquired, unfolding a leaf to display the range of glossy ivory fangs. The shortest matched the length of her index finger.

The black-bearded duergi nodded. "Would never waste any part o' such a magnificent animal, and teeth are fair hard to come by. Besides, you've done us a favor doing away with the pest. How plan ye to do the exchange?" he countered, a saucy, yet sympathetic, grin on his face.

McKenna laughed and shed her mock modesty. "In person, as all compacts between duergi should be," she replied, waltzing up to him.

The net did enough to hide the most obvious bits and her dark skin did the rest, but still, durgir are curiously helpful to heroes on quests. As she approached him, he shed the cloak he wore and offered it in one hand with the bag of coin in the other. "Raqim," he introduced himself with a handshake. "Take both, my lass, for sure'n you'll need them before long."

McKenna felt a surge of gratitude, and homesickness, at his gesture. As she reviewed the party silhouetted against the horizon, she sighed with longing for the warm hearth and home she'd left behind.

The durgir, though similar in stature to those of her clan, were clearly distinguishable as none other than their southern cousins of Bristendine. McKenna took stock of their softer beards, slimmer forms, and finer garments suitable for those who trade in goods, and not in brawn. They begged her to join them for dinner, and she accepted gratefully, with a rueful grin at the thought of the panther.

I bet if it'd just asked politely they would've shared with it too, she thought to herself.

"Ye're from the mines then, lass?" Raqim asked with a raised eyebrow.

"Aye. A monk of Malfaestus, on me beard quest," she replied proudly, puffing out her chest a little.

"Ah, ye're Pabble's girl then," he chuckled knowingly, and the suspicious looks on his companions' faces suddenly vanished. "Am a good friend of the priest's, though I've never had the pleasure o' meeting his bairn."

She grinned cheekily. "I didna leave the chapel fer much."

"And how be yer travels thus far?" he asked, leaning back with a long pipe between his teeth.

She looked up for a moment, to choose her words with care. As familiar as she was with the twinkling of precious stones in the deep caves, still more brilliant was the gem-encrusted river of sky that flowed inkily above her. A new moon did nothing to dim the brightness of more stars than she knew to count, and their soft light blended the shadows of tree and rock beyond her makeshift camp. The quiet hum of insects, sharp trill of owl, and keening squeaks of bats filled the air, Faie's own hymn to the ancient goddesses that shaped it.

"Like nothin' I've ever known. O' course, to ye all who've seen the length and breadth of Faie, it may seem like nothin' to be wandering jes' the valley before Bread Basket," she offered meekly.

"Assam here's not been further than the Bristendine gates afore this trip, lass," Raqim nodded at a surly duergi seated cross-legged on a stump beside them. Assam snorted. "We all be gettin' our starts somewhere."

"Well this is a start and then some. O' course, I knew the rules, but…" she laughed at herself, indicating to her scantily clad form. "Naked. Why naked?" The mental image of sturdy, surly durgir ransacking this primal forest wearing naught but their worldly selves made her laugh, especially in comparison to the stark contrast of her own slim shape.

The durgir laughed, the sound echoing among the rocks on the switchbacks. "Ye do know the last beard quest were hundreds of years ago? Mebbe back then they liked the thought o' a nice, healthy breeze round the nethers."

"Ah had to deal with more'n breezes," she scoffed. The memory of uncomfortable beds of leaves, frigid baths in half-frozen streams, and tenday after tenday of working at her net and her guisarme's shaft with naught but her hands and sharp stoneshale made her shudder. "If it weren't for ye, and that cat, I'd be half feral by now."

To that they raised their mugs, dipping their beards in the foam. McKenna had to make do with one of her braids.

As the durgir began to swap tales of their first beards,

another memory tugged at her, like the sensation of the panther's passing soul had the day before.

The *nommir* were mystics, mystics who could see within minds, and read secrets and thoughts tucked deep inside them. It was a deeply personal and almost uncomfortable experience, having your mind read by a gnommi, but one was willing to do it anyways to learn what one would otherwise keep hidden.

It felt like that, only she was the one reading the mind of the stranger, the trespasser in this unknown folkr's hidden soul.

But that's impossible, she thought to herself with a shake of her copper curls. Souls couldn't walk the Material plane - they found their home in the realm of Hel, beyond the Doors of Death carefully guarded by Atosa and her shepherds. She wanted to shrug off the feeling but it persisted, nagging at her even as she had no idea how to address it.

"What do you want?" She begged exasperatedly, not expecting a response. And there was none.

Even the forest had gone silent. Uneasy, but not willing to give up on her quest so easily or even tolerate the idea of retreating back into the mines, she shook herself off and settled into a deep meditational prayer, summoning composure and commanding her senses to rigid discipline. *It's just the unknown. I do not understand it, but I will not fear it. I will not let that master me.*

Raqim peered at her keenly, breaking through her reverie. She shook her head to clear it and smiled.

"So, what brings you along the High Road?" She

asked, keen to change the subject. "Would explain why we've no had any traders these past few moons, if all ye get stuck on roots and monsters," she chided.

The duergi prodded the fire thoughtfully. "Ye're not far off, girlie. We normally make the passage through Illusen, to the east of here, on the rail carts of the Low Road. But we found our way..." He trailed off, casting an uneasy look at his suddenly grim faced partners.

"Barred," one replied gruffly, with a sideways glare at McKenna.

"Tha's an understatement, Jefir. They blew up the rail," replied Assam.

McKenna's jaw dropped. "Sure'n ye jest? What manner of affront is this?"

Jefir shuddered, but didn't carry on. Raqim leaned back, putting a hand to his hairy chin. "Couldn' tell ye. When we tried ter ask, we got turned away at the road."

"Paladins," spat Assam. "'Twere never easy to deal wi' the folk o' Beausun, and now they be gettin' their gods involved."

"Paladins? In Illusen?" She asked in confusion. Illusen, though a town of asafolk who worshipped the good god Bahamut, had no godly guild. They were a simple coastal town of builders and traders, the perfect combination for the ambitious venture that was the railway. Fresh were the texts that recalled the glorious truce of duergi and aesir that built a better, faster route to the lofty peak of Mount Oer.

And yet, for seemingly no reason, they blew it up.

"They weren't from Illusen. I'm guessin' they come from Lianor and that great guild there. But we're traders, not warriors. We'd not the numbers fer a fight. We turned around and decided ter come up the High Road instead."

"So, how'd you find out they blew up the rail?"

"Some folk from the town... they came ter find us. Tol' us how it were," Raqim offered hesitantly.

"Ye're sandin' it too smooth, Raqim," interrupted Assam, as the duergi beside him nodded, his black brow lowering in anger. "They told us we weren't welcome. No duergi need apply. That our railway were a violation o' the natural order, and the asafolk had no need fer our trade nor our company."

"They... they're mad at the durgir? They wanted to break our treaty? But we've no done any wrong ter them!" McKenna cried.

"It were more like... fear, to be honest with ye," offered Raqim, and McKenna had to admire his calm wisdom and empathy. "Not of their own will would they bar us. But we weren' there for a fight, and there's nothin' like fear to breed anger," he shrugged, another glance passed to his perhaps not so easygoing companions, whose dark and kindling expressions McKenna keenly perceived.

She pondered that, suddenly aware of how she must have appeared to these rebuffed travelers. Turning toward the duergi on the stump, she nodded deeply, thanking him wordlessly for helping her - a complete stranger - despite what they had so recently endured. He grinned, clapping a hand to his chest and nodding back.

Duergi honored duergi.

Illusen turning away durgir. That's… not promising, she thought uneasily to herself as she made her way back to camp. *Hanthor's closer to the mines than Illusen, but not by much. Easy enough ride for a sentry. And if they see me, coated in runes of the durgirn god, I might as well just stay in the valley and hunt more panthers for all the good I'll get from there.*

Shaking herself from her reverie and setting her mouth in a determined line, she banished the misgiving. *Not all durgir're the same. Not all asafolk're the same. As I wouldna want to be judged by those I call my brothers, so I shouldna judge those who done me no harm.* Racial divide or not, she was on a quest, and to give up in the pass, mere steps from her home, would be foolish beyond compare. She stood up and, thanking them for their food and company, headed back to her camp under the willow.

Pockets lined the cloak Raqim had given her. Legs curled in the moss, McKenna browsed them languidly, wondering if they had anything useful tucked inside. She stroked the bevelled edge of something hard and metallic. Frowning, she pulled the object free - a mirror, glassy and sparkling in the hazy midmorning light

She gasped. She knew this mirror. *But how?*

Carved along the mirror's frame were, for lack of any better word, runes. Not quite a decorative pattern, and yet she knew without knowing that the symbols spelled words and the words, meanings long lost to time, were once known to her. Her own face, still beardless, flashed in its otherwise unassuming surface. And she swallowed heavily as it tugged at her, demanding recognition she was loath to pay.

But how did the Bristendine durgir get you? She mumbled to herself, with an uneasy feeling the coincidence of where she found the mirror was the mirror's fault, and not the Bristendine duergi's. The pocket held no other object, and the others lining the spun woolen cloak gave up no further treasures.

Just this mirror. This mirror she had clutched in infant hands, reflecting the surprised faces of durgir as they beheld the tiny babe holding it on a wintry White solstice night, so many years ago.

"That is another day's problem," she told herself decisively, and tucked the mirror back into the cloak.

Another tenday, and then another, passed uneventful. She scoured the valleys for adventure, a need to hone her skill with the guisarme- and a little fear of the unknown influencing her, guiding her aimless ramblings. No party followed the first, and one day while idly fishing in the creek she realized she was waiting. Waiting for another party, another monster, or even a glimpse of her own clan setting out on the road, meeting her, knowing her, welcoming her home.

It was then she picked up the pelt, reduced it to something decently wearable, and finally turned her steps out of the valley toward Hanthor.

IV

A Holvir's Tale

The guards at the doors of the Guild of Moonbow looked incredulously at the bold little *holvi* standing before them.

"You want to… speak to a sorcere?" one repeated slowly in disbelief.

"Yeah, just any old one. We're not picky," said Ginni nonchalantly. Asafolk, ilvir, it didn't matter - none ever took *holvir* seriously, so in turn they tended to treat the world with the same mocking disdain. "We were told by our Pasha that our information is of interest to them, from this guild in particular."

The guard stared bemusedly at his companion, who shrugged. How could a holvi be of interest to the guild? "Unless you know who expects you, we're not letting you pass."

Ginni Willow squinted at the guard, while her partner, Tjena Oak, just rolled their eyes. "Is there like a sorcere's directory or something? Anyone tasked by a god or goddess or whatever to help holvir? Nomads? Bards? Faiefolkr who live in the Naijor?"

"Did you say Naijor?"

A voice from behind made them all start. The guards suddenly snapped to attention - Razan stood before them tapping his chin lightly while appraising the holvir.

"That's a fair bold claim, considering no one… *lives*… in the Western Desert," he said simply, a light emphasis on the word giving it ample meaning.

"We were from the border. Between Styckes and Mount Cerbium," offered Tjena, as Ginni was too busy gaping at the figure Razan cut to be the first to answer.

He was quite a spectacle. The perfect tone of his figure, as though hewn from stone by a sculptor with second sight, lay open to the best advantage by clinging leggings of some oily, iridescent material and a tight vest strapped by a harness that seemed to serve little more purpose than showing off every inch of his powerful physique. At least, Ginni couldn't see any weapons hanging off it.

"*Were?*" he queried in response.

"Banished. I got blighted," answered Tjena.

Ginni offered no corroboration, but did finally close her mouth. They didn't know how the imposing aesir would react to the presence of blighted holvi, and by the rapt attention paid from the guards, this one obviously had a decent level of importance. But they had sworn to tell their story to only the one who could help them, and Ginni could tell they had only piqued this man's curiosity, and not his sympathy.

"Interesting," his musical, amused tone set the holvir more at ease. "Blighted at the border of Styckes. Well, luckily for you," he said, while turning to the guards and chiming his bangles, "I know the exact sorcere for you to speak with. No directory required."

At the sound, the guards selected a key from a large ring and fitted it to the lock in the door. With a faint purple flash, the door vanished and a hallway appeared. Razan beckoned them forward.

"Katarin's quarters are directly ahead of you. Make your story as interesting as possible, and maybe she'll help you," he nodded towards the *naiti* slung across Tjena's shoulder. "She does have a soft spot for music-shame you can't travel with a harp."

With that, he nodded to the two guards, and with another chime of his bangles swept away from the group.

Completely unnerved, but unwilling to ignore the clandestine stroke of luck, Ginni and Tjena grabbed hands and stepped forward through the portal. Their nerves weren't much soothed when it suddenly blinked out of existence and left nothing before them but an ornate door gilded in silver and runes.

"Do uh… do you think we knock?" whispered Ginni.

"It is not recommended," said a voice surrounding them.

The door stayed firmly shut, so Ginni assumed the sorcere - Katarin, he called her (if that's who was speaking) - used an amplification spell to throw her voice. Ginni grinned to herself. Even the most novice bard could play at that game, and she was far from a novice. Holvir were little folk, taking up little space and thought little of, but for their uncanny knack for the arts that brought beauty and life to the realm of Faie. Ginni was a singer - and she was a master of her craft.

She threw her own magical lilt through the barrier, a
song and a query blended harmoniously and lending the
spell its own impenetrable charm. "A door is a powerful
tool- but it's only a temporary barrier at best. We were
directed to you, with a song or two to tell our tale, and we
would be grateful for your audience."

A charming laugh echoed back and the door before
them vanished. A warmly lit chamber beyond beckoned
as invitingly as the woman's laughter, and the two holvir
made their way forward.

Katarin sat before the fireplace. She looked almost
girlish, curled on the sofa with her feet tucked under her.
She motioned the holvir towards an ottoman, but they
chose instead to stand opposite her seat. It was a dance; a
test, one the holvir couple had taken many times before.
Holvir did not sit, like equals, among the more powerful
races.

There wasn't even a pretense of equality here in
the beautiful chambers of the illustrious sorcere. And
her enigmatic smile did not set them at ease. "I've.
never had an amplification spell cast so cleanly past my
enchantments before. You must have powerful voices."

"We do indeed, Princess," replied Ginni, scraping a
deep curtsey beside Tjena's low half bow. "I believe I'm
correct in understanding you are the Princess Katarin, of
the Guild of Moonbow?"

Of course, Faie had no real royalty. "Princess" was
just an affectionate title given by the ilvir of Meliamne to
their precious charge. Bards had performed many lays
about lances born by knights of Bahamut and shattered in
honor of the ethereal lunar beauty, much to the chagrin of
the noble golden girls who shone with the blessings of the

aesir gods and not the strange and ancient Atosa.

Ginni knew, because she'd written some.

Katarin peered more keenly at the couple before her. Holvir laid flattery on with a trowel. They had to, in order to have any attention paid to them, and most had no ego to speak of. But that didn't prevent Katarin from appreciating the compliment to her notoriety. "Powerful bards with extensive knowledge of legend. To whom do I owe this pleasure?"

"We are Tjena and Ginni," responded Tjena in harmony with Ginni, strumming the *naiti* and coaxing from it an accompanying tune that blended with their voices, "holvir on a journey from the wastes of the west, to find a cure for blight in exchange for news of the dangers lurking under the border of Naijor."

Katarin smothered her surprise. No one but her should know of those dangers. No one living, anyways.

"Who opened my portal to you?" She asked, leaning a little forward with a long fingernail pressed to the tip of her chin.

"Oh... He didn't give his name. Seemed important though, the guards kinda just stood at attention when he showed up and let him do whatever he wanted," Ginni replied, somewhat nervously.

That didn't narrow it down for her - the guards served many masters in the guild tower.

"He walked with a bit of a swagger," Tjena offered. "Wore heeled boots and bangles that could... talk?"

Razan. So he's returned. Yet with nothing to report...
Her brow furrowed. Still, he had no way of penetrating
further into her plans than she wished him to - the
encounter with these holvir must have simply been
coincidence. She bade them continue with their story.
"Never mind - he's not important. Do go on."

She relaxed into the couch. There was nothing they
could tell her she didn't already know, she was sure of
it. But the night was lonely and Tjena's naiti, a curious
stringed instrument shaped like a long, flat box, was
making the unmistakeable thin wavering notes of a harp.

Ginni's voice, that could swell to a din and be heard
in the farthest reaches of camp, faded to a whisper.

"The rain before had been nothing compared to
this," she began in a song- why say what you could sing,
Ginni always believed- "one could tell in a moment. The
creek, swollen and breaking the banks of every branch,
deepened to the waist. The distant thunder at erratic
points in the run forewarned of the miniature rapids and
infinitesimal waterfalls, picturesque in their tiny beauty.
The running water trickled softly like a lullaby, and the
haze lit by a late-afternoon sun gave everything the aura
of a dream."

The aura of a dream - Ginni shivered in
rememberance. The painting of her subtle words could
not disguise the truth. These holvir had encountered
magic. And to the beleaguered and oppressed race, magic
meant death.

"We traveled alongside it, exploring anywhere we
could plant a solid foot," she continued with a twist of
her wrist, her fingers mimicking the flow of water as she
described their descent along the riverbed - the ancient

Styckes that bordered the wastelands of Naijor. "The dancing faeries were thick, their colorful lights a rainbow in the air. As we crossed through Styckes, the barren glen that desert winds and harsh suns had previously lain to waste now resembled a glorious haven, with bullrushes and wheatgrass swaying in the soft wind."

"Styckes?" interrupted Katarin. She knew well of the ancient river, and the mysterious power it drew from Faie. "You mean you crossed it?"

"Of course we did. It… something called to us. We know it was wrong, but we…" Ginni trailed off, casting a glance at her blighted partner.

The music in her voice died at the sight of Tjena's face. They shouldn't have gone down there in the first place. And yet, getting out of trouble was something the two had always been particularly skilled at.

So what made this time any different? She thought despairingly to herself.

"We found ourselves facing three tunnels," she continued dully. "And Tjena took off into one before I could stop them. When we entered, all light, all warmth, all hope, was blotted out in an instant. Our only conscious understanding of the world around us was the sound of water rushing 'round our feet. The depths of existence, it… she… she seemed to call to us. Irresistible! Who can turn a deaf ear to the words of the Faie Mother?" she challenged, clearing her throat and throwing back her proud little head, her voice grew stronger again.

"The whispers are stronger to the ear that knows how to listen," hummed Tjena. An old bardic mantra. The true mark of the artist; knowing that they are not just a voice, but a vessel for those with none to sing through them.

"I didn't want to let them go," Ginni said, gesturing to Tjena, "but as much as I couldn't begin to stop them even less could I let them go alone. The homeless souls that wander the chasm did warn us, almost... forbidding us from going in. But how can one forbid what another is unable to resist?"

Katarin started, sitting up in her chair. Homeless souls. *So it has begun. The Doors of Death are closed, and they cannot get in.*

"Then, out of nowhere, we reached the end of the tunnel and finally, something dispelled the gloom. It looked like... like some kind of abandoned grotto. The moss-draped trees that hung from above and the crumbling stoneshale walls would not have looked out-of-place in one of those godly guild graves in Lianor. It wasn't 'til then we realized, the Faie Mother had no voice here. The Faie Mother had been calling us back, trying to save us, but..."

She trailed off, wincing. Then she swallowed. "But he was stronger. His calls were insistent, his dread horrors what nothing could ever compel me to recount." She shivered, a dead, haunted look occupying her normally bright and lively eyes. She turned to Tjena, her love, her partner through everything, and threw her arms around them, clinging desperately to they who she had nearly lost. After a moment, she composed herself and continued.

"I was scared. I let myself get lost in my fear, I lost sight of Tjena- and in exchange," she swallowed a watery sob, and even Tjena's firm shoulders tensed, "Tjena lost their sight. A cry from the heart- my heart we share beating within their chest- and in answer a fiendish, musical laughter piercing the air that lay pulsing with the eerie agonies of souls neither alive nor dead."

When they reached the curse of the blight, Katarin felt the whispers that never quite left her alone grow insistent, demanding her attention. While they sang of a faceless terror and a void harboring a horde, she realized the holvir had been sent here - to help her with the placement of a powerful artifact furthering her ambition. The charming music kept her from focusing too much on where these ideas came from - they could have belonged to the voice, they could have belonged to the holvir, or they could have been the subtle stirrings of her own subconscious, eager as it was to achieve her goal and seek her rightful place among the pantheon.

She knew what had caused that chasm. It is the edge of world, above the doorway that leads to Hel. The only way to cross it is to die.

What else could lie beyond the desert?

"It is a dangerous path you two walk, and you've already suffered such tragic pain," she began. "Are you sure, truly, that you want to return home?"

Tjena's shoulders slumped, and Ginni hesitated before speaking for her beloved partner. "Home is where we are," she said simply. "But it's Tjena's sight- and blight- that we wish to be cured. Holvir and curses… we don't mix so well," she offered haltingly. "We have no gods like you, to pray to and provide guidance and divine cures. When we're blighted, we kind of just…"

"Wither and die," finished Tjena bluntly.

Katarin knew even without the whisper's insistence that she would help these two. She also knew she could probably just cure the blight here- it was a simple enough countercurse. But the whispers insisted on requiring an advantage- one she surely couldn't understand right now, but knew would have significance in the future.

Many of her decisions in life had played out like this, slow, subtle, deliberate, yet unclear.

She bade the holvir to sit again, and this time they did. "I do have the power to cure your blight. But I need two things. One that will help you, and one that will help me."

Ginni and Tjena looked at each other with an amused expression. Pretty typical exchange from the larger races. Certainly not unexpected, requiring mutual benefit to justify philanthropy.

"Of course. More than, you know, the information we just provided?" Ginni suggested anyways. The mystical cadence of her voice had faded, and she spoke with the familiarity that came most natural to her.

"Yes. In order to perform the countercurse, I need the curse's… trace. Blights always leave a trace behind," Katarin ad-libbed. In truth, curses left no such thing- nothing tangible, anyways- but she had no reason to fear the holvir would sense any incongruency nor be left empty-handed. A trace would appear, so the journey seemed not wasted. "And to find this trace, I will give you a tool."

She stood up and went to the brazier, where, buried in the vestiges of ember and ash from her previous sorcery, she found a small, bright glass orb. Retreating to her desk and reviewing the notebook again, she whispered a short incantation into her palm where the orb rested. It flashed briefly, and she tucked it in a small velvet pouch, enchanted so that its contents were untraceable and undetectable but to the bearer.

Meanwhile Ginni and Tjena had reclined in their seats, Tjena gazing blankly in the direction of the fire, Ginni analyzing Tjena's face. She hummed softly to catch their attention, and they strummed the *naiti* lightly in response. The pair often communicated like this, their musical notes and sounds as good as speech to the souls tuned in every way to one another's thoughts and emotions.

You think she's telling the truth? Seems a little too easy, Ginni insinuated towards the thoughtful Tjena.

Don't know why she would be lying, honestly. She's a princess. She already has everything she could ever want, they assessed summarily.

Ginni had to admit they had a point. These two dealt easily with the other races because they so intrinsically understood the motivations of individuals. Considering how base holvir were in general and these two- cursed, outcast, and self-sufficient- in particular, it really benefited no one to take advantage of them.

Plus, they had no other option.

Should we tell her about the empty towns? Tjena queried, raising a thoughtful eyebrow.

Ginni shivered. She didn't want to tell anyone about those haunted spaces. She didn't want to think about them ever again.

Hmm. Dunno why she would care, really. Not like Meliamne has any jurisdiction over Beausun.

They fell silent for a moment, before Tjena picked up their musical conversation again.

Doesn't it seem rather… Tjena trailed off, puzzling over something, *crowded, to you?*

The forest, you mean? Ginni replied. *Not more than usual, asafolk come here all the time, and if they're still building those towers…*

But Hand Over Fist doesn't live here. Not like Onyx Blade.

The asafolk guild had a unique reputation. They travelled extensively, and scrupled not to form alliances with any guild regardless of race or religion. They were builders: if it needed building, they would come.

At this point Katarin had stepped forward and offered the pouch to Ginni. "Bring this to where you encountered the blight. When you're close, the trace will make itself apparent to you. Bring the trace back to me, and I can use it to restore your sight and lift the curse."

She felt a quick surge of pity as she watched Ginni tie the pouch to her belt and stroke Tjena's arm in one swift, almost subconscious motion. It was a struggle to govern the emotion- it welled up from within and surprised the normally selfish sorcere. Suddenly struck by a fierce headache, she grimaced and sat down quickly.

Ginni noticed the woman's discomfort but said nothing. Together, they stood and bowed. "Thank you eternally, most gracious Sorcere," they chimed in unison.

"Hopefully when our quest is complete, we'll have a new ballad with which to charm you," Ginni trilled before the two backed out of the chamber.

Katarin nodded, waving them off. She inexplicably craved Razan's company, but if he decided to send the holvir to her instead of coming himself, clearly there was something he didn't want to share. She was unsure if the rush of emotion she felt at the thought was anxiety on behalf of the danger he may be in- or annoyance that he could so easily avoid her.

"If only he knew..." she chuckled to herself. "He'd probably make fun of me."

V

She Meets The Rogue

"Well... fer certain is no' the pretties', but it covers the important bits, and that's what matters."

Desperate to hear sounds other than the chuckle of kobolds in the undergrowth, McKenna had picked up the habit of talking to herself. She paced resignedly before her reflection in a still pool. If she listened closely, she could hear voices - the loud, carrying tones of asafolk, with their hard consonants and nasal vowels - as they left the fields for the day and headed back into the safety of the village. She had to give them credit despite the jarring nature of their speech. It was their language, after all, that the rest of the races had adopted as the common tongue across Faie.

"Alright. No more excuses then, I guess," she swallowed and swept the duergi's cloak around her and slung the guisarme over her back, completing the meager outfit she'd managed to scrape together during her weeks in the wilderness. "Time ter find me beard."

If she were being honest with herself, the prospect seemed almost overwhelming.

Stories'n legends can on'y take me so far, she reminded herself, reverting back to mental soliloquy instead of verbal. *I mustna allow meself to let narrow-minded stereotypes cloud me judgement. I'll take faiefolkr as I find them. I know the spirit of adventure lies in all our deepes' natures. If nothin' else,*

When she left the mines, a crisp chill had the land wrapped in its icy grip. Now the days were longer and warmer, and the budding trees that covered the rolling hills of the mountain valleys unfurled emerald leaves. She reckoned White Solstice and Green had passed by now, welcoming Yellow in all its golden glories of bounteous growth and brightness of day. A moon lit the twilight sky. She could see it, just beginning to wax full, hovering still above the horizon and challenging the brightness of the waning day. While the monk knew she would miss the wild lonesomeness of the open valley, she turned her steps toward the brackish path that led from the forest to the upper road leading into Hanthor.

Smoke curling in plumes along the horizon met her gaze. Those she passed took in her massive form kirtled in the pelt of a dire panther and kept a wary distance, even though she greeted all she saw with a smile. She'd never met an aesir, but even if she had, the physical attributes they shared in common wouldn't have clued her in to her own ancestry.

Tall for a duergi, that's all. Tall for a duergi and late for a beard. It happens ter the best of us.

Despite her abrupt appearance, the townsfolk mostly paid her no heed. A settlement like this, on the outskirts of more bustling strongholds such as Hammardin's in Mount Oer to the north, or Lianor's great walled city to the east, often attracted travellers both solitary and en masse. Nothing daunted and driven by the pangs of hunger, she continued her confident stroll down the main road into the village toward a tall, tipsy wooden structure unimaginatively referred to as "Hanthor's Inn".

She stepped boldly into the inn's smoky and delicious-smelling tavern, quickly scanning the room for an open bench. Starving was no exaggeration. Even the raucous laughter and noise of the bar's patrons couldn't drown out the rumble in her stomach.

Lucky I were able ter find traders for those panther teeth, she thought with relief, patting the small pouch filled with more than enough coin for whatever was giving off that heady aroma. Strictly speaking, she didn't have to eat. A true Master of the monk class could go days without sustenance, if they meditated enough. But food had ever been her comfort and her weakness. She continued through the crowd, her height attracting notice- and her polearm almost immediately repelling it. Finally, through the haze that dimmed the room, she was able to spot what looked like an empty seat and plopped down with a sigh of satisfaction.

"I wasn't expecting company, but I guess that doesn't necessarily mean I'll turn down yours," chuckled a low voice at her elbow.

McKenna started and turned toward the sound. There was a man seated at the table, his chair pushed back enough to slip into the shadows of the corner in which they were situated. He may have managed to avoid notice by the tavern at large, but McKenna, nothing daunted, leaned forward to observe him. Though no coat of arms or deity's symbol marked his rank, she could tell he was no ordinary bar patron. The man's aura shone brighter than any she'd seen before. Eyes so deeply gold as to be almost black stared bemusedly (and slightly blearily- the tankard on the table before him was empty) back at her, his high cheekbones framed by locks of soot black hair. She could see the hilt of a sabre at his hip (*But…why is he wearing it at the table?* she wondered to herself) and the arms crossed over his chest were protected by a fine, sturdy black maille made of mithril. She gasped at that.

"Like what you see?" he grumbled, raising an eyebrow at her thunderstruck expression.

"There's enough mithril in yer armour to clothe a king, and yer jest... hangin' out at a bar in it?" she gaped, ignoring his tone.

"What are you talking about? Mithril's common enough, if you have the right job," he remarked, settling back into his seat after lifting up his tankard and realizing it was empty.

"And what job could that possibly be? Unless ye be Guild Master or paladin... I've ne'er seen such well-crafted garb."

He inhaled sharply, casting a keener glance meant to size her up more thoroughly. "Well, you're right in one. Or I guess, right in none, since I'm neither anymore," he muttered coolly, digging a nail idly into a groove on the table, picking at the wood grain as carefully as his words. The boards were clean, but shabby and well-worn.

McKenna started in surprise. The idea of just deciding to one day stop being a monk literally struck her dumb for a moment. "Ye... ye quit bein' a paladin? Ye left yer guild? How's that even possible?"

He didn't answer right away, not that she really expected him to. A low grating sound came from the empty tin mug as he twirled it idly against the wooden table, as though he wished he were still drinking it instead of talking to her. Coolly taking stock of the runes on her arms, the carefully braided and coiled locks of her hair, and the polearm casually slung over her shoulder, his response fell just short of bitter.

"Is the pot calling the kettle black, now? Or do monks of Malfaestus often abandon the mines of Mount Oer and strike out into the heart of Beausun?"

"Huh. I guess ye have me there." But this was different. She had every intention of returning, once her quest was completed, once her beard was grown.

Or did she?

"That question was rhetorical," he replied with a smirk. "I wouldn't have told you the truth if I didn't think that you were on the same path. But," he stared into the empty mug sadly, heaving a sigh, "it is a long, long story."

She laughed, taking the hint. "It sounds like one worth telling, my friend. But firs', I see yer dry, and I'm dying," she said, taking the hint and plucking the empty mug from his grasp before turning in her seat to squint into the crowd. "Now where's the server?"

She spotted a harried-looking waif attempting to carry mugs larger than his head between two long packed tables. His patrons didn't make it easy, either. They kept throwing back their heads in laughter or benches in anger into his path. After watching him drop a third cup of ale she rolled her eyes and got up to get to the bar.

"If I watch ye spill one more drop o' good drink I'm going ter pick ye up and bodily carry ye ter the next table," she sighed exasperatedly.

The bartender chuckled good-naturedly and shook

his rag at the emaciated server. "From the size of her, I'd believe it if I were you."

He gulped. "W-what can I bring you?" he stammered.

McKenna smiled, and pointed behind the bar. "Whatever's stewing in that pot," she squinted, her mouth watering at the smell, "and two mugs of whate'er it is ye keep spilling."

He nodded nervously and turned away. The bartender saw the mistrustful look she gave him and laughed, pouring two mugs right out to take with her. "The finest mead this side of Bread Basket. I'm sure you'll appreciate it more'n this lot," he thrust his chin out at the crowd of aesir farmers with a wink.

"We been dyin' fer mead in the mountains. Many thanks," she replied, dropping an extra coin on the bar.

"Alright. In exchange fer drinking this, ye get ter tell me where ye got that armour," she said as she sat back down at their shared table, tossing the mug toward him. The tin added a metallic flavor to her sips of mead, and she pursed her lips and frowned. It made her pace herself, more effectively than the unobtrusive fired clay steins common to Mount Oer's mead halls.

He caught it and downed half in a gulp. "Fine, but when I buy the next round you get to tell me how you recognized powder-coated mithril chain in a smoky pub."

She took her seat and he began.

"I am Seth, disgraced paladin of Bahamut. I've been raised my whole life to follow my god. One day he turned around and told me to go somewhere else."

Bahamut is an old, old deity of the wind-whipped Eastern Plains of Beausun, the first of the new gods who rose up to usurp the old goddesses. His scales are brighter than the grain and his wisdom goes deeper than the Material plane. His followers, a goodly company, hail from across the wide expanse of Faie, most from the populous realm of Beausun. Some of the land's bravest feats of championship and daring owed their attribution to his most dedicated- the Guild of Tooth and Claw. Whole families and villages would sponsor the strongest and the best of their youth for a chance to bring their homelands fame and fortune by joining the prestigious guild. And it was from one of these, deep in the central plains, that Seth had begun his hero's journey.

"Prophecy chooses all Bahamut's paladins, and our village's soothsayer decreed that a man born at sunset and woman born at sunrise would bear the next at high noon on the brightest day- Bahamut's feast day."

"You?" suggested McKenna.

"Aye, I," poetized Seth. He sighed and looked tragically into his once-more empty mug, and McKenna cleared her throat suggestively while nudging her own. About to rise and seek a refill, the sublime sight of two full drinks descending upon the table arrested him.

"Looks like ye kin complete a trip after all," laughed McKenna at the youth, beset on all sides by demand for similar services. "Eh, here, now quit your whining Set-"

The rogue clapped a hand over her mouth and scowled darkly at the young server. "Our thanks, boy," he grumbled meaningfully.

The boy gulped and cast a concerned look at McKenna, then vanished back through the thinning crowd.

She mumbled behind the rogue's restraining grasp, and he withdrew his hand. "Smart. I would've bitten ye in another second."

Seth shrugged, took a hearty swig and continued his tale.

"The most promising paladin my village had seen in living memory! I was quickest with the lance, noblest with the sword, harmonious with the wildest steed," he chanted, with a roll of the eyes so violent they nearly made McKenna dizzy. "From a babe my masters trained me to think the pinnacle of the aesir's life were the adventures he conquered, and I believed nothing as strongly as the truth Bahamut spoke. The riches of the land were for those strong, and just, and devoted enough to deserve them- and that one's unfailing duty was to serve and protect those who couldn't."

He took another drink, and added, "Whether they liked it or not."

McKenna raised an eyebrow at that. "I thought Bahamut's paladins followed the letter of the law to the utmost. For sure'n such a fair dragon doesn't tolerate those totalitarian acts it sounds like yer mentionin'?" she queried, wondering if her own study of the just and unequivocally neutral Malfaestus had led her astray in her knowledge of the general pantheon.

Seth hesitated before speaking. A long pause preceded his next words, and McKenna could discern he was picking them with extreme care. "A god can be and say whatever his followers choose, if they are beings with soul and power of cognitive choice. That's the... risk, I suppose, of granting mortals the protection of your immortal name. How they choose to wield it... may be something you no longer control."

It were more like... fear, the Bristendine duergi had said, of the villagers in Illusen who barred the normally free passage of the durgirn envoys.

Were guilds interfering with the free folk of Beausun? What could they possibly have to gain from blocking the trade route between Hammardin and Bristendine?

He grimaced at the shock that crossed her face. From the runes crossing her skin to the simple garb that clothed her, he had guessed that she too derived power from a deity, and so the disgust she expressed didn't surprise him. "To disobey the god to whom ye owe yer power, yer importance... it's madness! Why would the Guild of Tooth and Claw do such a thing?"

Seth's face hardened. "It is not so uncommon," was all he would venture.

She felt a whisper of magic shiver through the runes on her guisarme, the near-perfectly healed wounds on her back, and the pelt girdled about her waist. It was completely alien to her nature, the idea of thwarting a deity's core alignment in a bid for personal gain. The goodly pantheon of gods that ruled Faie shared its power freely with the beings that roamed over, in exchange for something as simple (in her mind) as devotion and thanksgiving. In McKenna's meditations, the whispers of the gods were always winsome- as though they too wished to walk the realms they governed, vying in any way to share the essence of mortality.

His action earlier suddenly made sense though, and she felt ashamed for almost betraying his name to a stranger. The zealots who follow such powerful guilds treat abandonment tantamount to murder. By leaving his guild, no matter his motivation, he became a target for any seeking favor with Bahamut by disposing of him as a traitor.

Seeing Seth's expression, however, she chose not to press the issue. "I admire ye, fer seein' past the lies of those who would so deny Bahamut his true nature. An' I admire the strength of yer resolve to break with them. Whether it comforts ye or no, I know yer god will see and thank ye for it."

He seemed unlikely to respond for a time, so McKenna summoned another round. A few more drinks helped to put the rogue back at ease, and the night wore on. For her first time in what asafolk tried to pass as a mead hall, McKenna admitted herself to being fairly impressed. Durgir liked to imply that an aesir couldn't finish a draught without swinging a fist after, but the patrons of Hanthor belied the stereotype for the most part. Hardy farmers, hunters, and traders all, none appeared to have physical reputations worth establishing or protecting in such a remote place as this.

"So then, what's next fer the rogue Seth?" followed up McKenna, unwilling to let the opportunity to potentially join a quest pass her by.

Luckily, he didn't disappoint. "Just more or less of the same, I guess," he replied, stretching his arms behind his head and leaning back with a sigh. "I still have my sword, so I use it whenever someone has enough gold to make it swing." He shrugged, casting a furtive glance around the tavern. "I've been following bands of… marauders, from town to town, picking up the bounties sponsored by magistrates."

He took another swig of the fresh round of ale before them. McKenna debated digging deeper into the nature of his quests, but opted instead to focus on the philanthropic. Championing the defenseless sounded exactly like what she should be doing. Her very chin prickled at the thought of righteous battle against godless bands of who-knew-what threatening the lawful balance of the goodly societies. It certainly sounded a far cry better than challenging the might of one of Faie's largest and strongest guilds, or untangling sordid trade disputes. And maybe she could even restore the good faith between the asafolk of the northern villages and her durgirn family. She stroked her chin thoughtfully, thankful again that her first encounter with unpredictable aesir society hadn't ended in disappointment.

Seth seemed likely to slip into deep, impenetrable reverie (or coma, thought McKenna, counting the empty mugs scattered haphazardly across the table), so she kicked at his shin under the table and favored him with a jocular smirk.

"If ye kin finish this mug I leave ye alone. If ye can't, and I do, I get to join ye on yer next quest," McKenna dared.

"I don't even know your name!" he shot back, making no move for the drink before him.

McKenna shrugged, swiped it up, and downed it to the dregs. "McKenna o' Clan Hammardin, my lord," she snickered with a courtly- and perfectly sober- bow.

He groaned and rolled off the bench.

Ah well, bet the floor's cheaper than a bed!

VI

The Plot Thickens

Morning found the mismatched pair, neither worse for the wear, on the road. Seth, mouth set in a hard line, had clearly found it easier to keep the monk around than try to leave her behind. He'd made something of an attempt when dawn's light finally overcame the strength of sleep- but McKenna clearly wasn't lying about her durgirn heritage. That, or the sheer size of her assisted in the dissipation of alcohol. She easily paced him as he made his way from the tavern, chuckling good-naturedly as he held his fuzzy head.

"Do ye carry yer armor on yer travels, then?" she asked, raising an eyebrow as he shouldered a bulky pack after buckling on his sabre. He snorted.

"No, I have a horse. So good luck trying to keep up," he said, making his way down the high street towards a public stable.

Fog dimmed the brightness of the day's break, fingers of mist softening the rigid, dark forms of buildings and early farmers heading out from the safety of the town's walls to the tilled land beyond. It was a sweet, quiet morning- one that reminded McKenna how good it was to be out of the dim smoky darkness of the mines. She shivered, the air brisk against her skin despite the thick fur pelt she wore wrapped about her form.

As they approached the stables, she noticed a large

party bustling outside. McKenna beamed in delight, recognizing the stocky forms as they came in sight- another travelling party of durgir, and of her own clan, no less.

"Hail, McKenna! Still cannae believe Pabble cut them apron strings," jockeyed a beetle-eyed duergi, the wiry bristles of her beard twitching into a smile.

McKenna clapped her on the back. "I cut them meself, good Gimble. Time for my beard!"

"Aye, yer beard quest!" chimed Gimble's party in glee.

"Ye'll be needin' a horse, then? Ye've not made it far, by my reckoning," Gimble added.

"If'n ye can spare one," McKenna grinned wickedly in the hapless Seth's direction, who rolled his eyes and disappeared into the stables. "Where be ye off to, then?"

The jovial tone sank, and a hushed sadness pervaded the group.

"Home, the only place left ter go. The mead's gone, lass. We've no' got a barrel for moons. The elders sent us to Hoplin ter find out why, and..." she trailed off with a sniff.

McKenna remembered the plight of the Bristendine traders, and pursed her lips. "They run ye out too?"

"There weren't no one tae run us out. We heard from the traders what come up through the High Road, an' made sure ter steer clear of Illusen. But it didnae matter - the farms are gone. All of 'em, a heap o' ash and dust.

This side o' Bread Basket be all that's left, it appears. You'll learn more, on yer travels, I'm sure," she sighed, "but we're returnin' to the mines ter see what the clan will do abou' it."

Shocked, McKenna covered her hand with her mouth. *Wonder if the marauders Seth's been chasin' down come from there. Guess I'll find out,* she shrugged her shoulders philosophically, waving as the group departed in return to Mount Oer.

A short time later found their small party heading south- McKenna perched atop a placid white mule who she'd named Clopalong and Seth astride a powerful golden destrier. The monk couldn't help but comment on the horse's appearance.

"Sure'n he's a bit flashy for someone trying to keep no profile," she bantered to the surly fighter. He just shrugged.

"Bahamut gifted him to me. Kurya. I could never ride another steed," was all he offered in return.

They continued along in silence, the mountainous forests giving way to undulating plains. Mount Oer loomed behind them, still visible in the distant north, but McKenna looked resolutely ahead to the road that grew wider as they travelled south into the populous realm of Beausun. She patted Clop's flanks appreciatively as it stepped quickly along the path that grew incrementally less rocky and more hard-packed. Mules were known more for their endurance than their speed, but Gimble had a spare set of quickstep horseshoes they'd brought for trade. Even Kurya, unsettled and marginally offended by the swift-moving pack animal, had sped up and would huff in annoyance every so often as she kept pace.

Otherwise the silence grew a little unsettling, especially as McKenna began to notice they had abandoned the main road and swerved west, along a tiny track through the brush that she would never have even noticed. Though she'd no reason to believe Seth regretted being so chatty the night before, she discovered he had absolutely no intention of continuing to be so. Or he only talked a lot when he was drunk.

Realizing he seemed unlikely to overcome his reticence on his own, she took it upon herself to strike up a conversation. "So tell me, to what adventure do we ride this day?"

He shook himself out of his reverie, casting a hooded glance in response to her eager tone. "I guess I shouldn't be too resentful of your company, especially since I may be about to lose it. A horde of *ilmaurte* moved this way over the last few weeks, and I've been quested to destroy it."

McKenna nearly fell off Clop. "Excuse me, a horde of *what*?" she stuttered.

"Ilmaurte. Undead. The ensorcelled remains of decay and death, on the march to obliterate the goodly realms as we know it," he returned, deadpan.

"Oh no, I heard ye, I was just hopin' ye were kidding."

He snorted, but to her surprise, didn't lapse back into silence. "You're right to be skeptical. You're not the only one. They're the stuff of legends, villains of folklore, that don't belong in modern society. Unfortunately that doesn't matter, since they are in fact here."

McKenna couldn't believe what he was saying.
In the myths of Faie, there did tell a legend of restless
spirits who managed to slip past the goddess Atosa and
her shepherds, drawn forth by powerful incantations of
mages on the surface world. But the evil intent needed
to perform such spells simply didn't exist in the realms
anymore.

Then again, she had been learning much more than
she cared to know about the subtle duality of guilds.
Necromancy wasn't far removed from this martial
proselytism they engaged in, if Seth was to be believed.

"At any rate, I have no idea how large this particular
swarm may be. I've managed to dispatch a few here
and there in my travels, but I worry that these isolated
towns may prove a different story," continued Seth. "So
I can understand if you decide to decamp and quest...
elsewhere."

She raised an eyebrow at that. "Sure'n you're not to
be calling me a coward," was all she replied.

Seth just shrugged again and continued on. "I wanted
to check in on the town they're supposedly terrorizing
first," he said, picking up the pace of their journey. "We
still have a good twoday's ride ahead of us."

She cast a look over her shoulder, squinting first at the
paved road that vanished into the horizon behind them,
then at the narrow, difficult path they rode on.

"Err, does that happen to be because we're no' on the
right road?"

He sucked in a breath. "All roads pass through

Wheelspoke," he replied cryptically.

It was an old expression, written on almost every aesir map of the region. And it was true. Wheelspoke was a populous city founded in the direct center of Beausun, the major roads to every realm in Faie passing through its carefully guarded gates. But though the expression commonly meant "the road will always lead you where you need to go", she thought that maybe it had a meaning a little bit more personal to him.

"I take the side roads to keep that low profile," he said, tugging a lock of Kurya's mane with a raised eyebrow and a self-deprecating smirk. "But do be cautious. This is orgir territory too. Or it would be, if Beausun recognized the rule of any but their own," he said with something of a sneer.

"Orgir! Ye mean there're still tribes o' them in Faie? I thought they were all..." she trailed off awkwardly.

History was not kind to Faie's native race, and even the neutral monks of Malfaestus could little compliment them, or equivocate about their fate as they were mercilessly marched out of the realms by asafolk.

"Massacred? Not quite. Not for lack of trying, don't get me wrong." Though Seth's words were almost comically heartless, McKenna could see his face grow pale, lips thin over gritted teeth. "But they have places to hide where even asafolk cannot reach, and they dance with death in such a way that we could never truly destroy them."

McKenna swallowed uneasily. *I think I owe Pabble an apology. He were right. Readin' history outta books is nothin' to livin' with it in the real world.*

Though he observed her keenly, she simply spurred her mule onward to match his pace.

As darkness fell, they felt it prudent to build camp. Seth hopped off Kurya's back and stretched, grimacing at the weight and restriction of his armor. Loosening the supple gorget from around his throat, he tossed it with his mailled gauntlets into a dusty pile next to his pack. McKenna looked askance at this.

"And I thought it were only monks who didna appreciate armor," she joked lightly.

"Hmph. I could throw this into a pit of vicious hyverines and it'd come out without a scratch. Dropping it on the ground won't do anything to it."

"What's it made of then?" She was curious, and though only the adopted daughter of craftsfolk knew how to admire good workmanship.

"Dragon hide."

"Eh? What kind of a lie is that then? There be no dragons!!"

In answer, he simply shucked off one of the pauldrons buckled around his torso and tossed it to her, before dropping the other into the pile. She caught it, stunned at the lightness and flexibility of the material. It moved like the softest leather, but she could feel the tension and a strength that could be matched only in the strongest ores; like adamantine or plantinium. At first glance the armor appeared black, but it seemed to reflect a dull, burnished gold in the light.

"Ok, I'll bite," she laughed, running her fingers along the patterns like scales embossed in the plate. "Where do ye get dragon hide then?"

"From dragons. There may not be dragons anymore-but there were. And when there were, paladins of Bahamut made armor out of them."

"You mean ter tell me the *Golden Dragon*'s most devoted followers hunted dragons fer their armor? Seems... cannibalistic."

"Dragons aren't all good." He knelt to dig into his pack, sighing in relief. He still wore his mithril hauberk, but under it a simple linen tunic and black leather breeches. "Kind of a matter of principle that the bad ones are taken care of by the good ones though."

"So this..." she held up the pauldron, gesturing towards the rest of the armor now piled in the dirt, "Ye must not be the first ter wear it?"

"No. It's had several owners before me," he replied nonchalantly, tossing a few apples from his pack to Kurya before biting into one himself. Kurya snorted, and Seth shot him a challenging look. "All dead."

"Tha's cheery. Did any die wearin' it then?"

A gleam of amusement twinkled in his gold eyes. "At least two."

The absolute stillness of the surrounding landscape encouraged them to think they were enough alone to build a fire, and Seth unfurled a small bedroll from his pack. He had the grace to look slightly bewildered as McKenna simply sat cross-legged on the ground, the only object in her possession the fine handmade guisarme.

"Is there any particular reason you've got absolutely no provisions?" he couldn't help but ask. McKenna laughed.

"'Tis the nature of a beard quest. You're sent out into the realms with naught but your worldly self. I was stark naked when I left Clan Hammardin." She laughed at the completely baffled look on his face. "No' as bad as it sounds. Durgir are all manner of helpful. It's part of the quest ter trust yer brethren and be not too ashamed or proud to ask for help." She gestured at the cloak enveloping her form, provided by the first trader band she encountered.

"You mean to tell me you walked up to a band of durgir completely naked and asked for a cloak?"

"Aye."

"And the pelt?" Seth seemed almost afraid to ask.

"Fought a cat."

"You fought a *cat*?"

"Aye."

"Naked?!"

"As the day I was born!" cackled McKenna as the stoic fighter laughed, staring at her in disbelief. "That's why they gave me the cloak you see here, and coin for the mead that so graciously put you under the table. The panther had been stalking 'em fer miles and I killed it."

The exchange seemed to be wearing on Seth's reserve. Quite a genuine smile left from his unexpected laughter lit up his hawk-like features, and McKenna paused to note how well the expression suited him.

Sparks from their fire flickered and dissipated into the brisk night air. The remainder of a modest repast lay beside her- a crumbly loaf of bread bought from the inn as they packed up in the morning, and one of the tin mugs (shamelessly stolen) of fresh spring water. Seth offered her portions of his own dried meats and fruits, but she declined it with a smile- they'd hunt something down in the morning.

Their calm camaraderie deepened with the night. McKenna hadn't expected conversation with other races outside the durgir to be so easy, especially not with this reserved ex-paladin. Yet she sensed too that he normally wouldn't be so open, and that her nature seemed to soothe him somehow. She leaned her curly head on her knee as she listened to him talk about his quests across the prairie and regaled him with the tale of her own departure from Mount Oer.

"Stands to reason then you'd be crazy enough to face the undead with a stranger," he said, in a softened tone.

"Ah, c'mon, ye're not still a stranger when ye've broken bread and spilled the mead!" She cried, her wide smile contagious enough to creep onto his own face, and he laughed outright. "No beard quest is ever completed alone. Defeats the purpose, ye know? If ye could've grown a beard on your own in the first place, ye wouldna needed ter leave home."

Seth seemed to accept this. "I guess it's not too far off from being chosen by some prophecy and sent to a guild to make your destiny," he mumbled, tension returning slightly to his form.

"There's a hell of a difference, if'n ye ask me. It's choice, innit?' she countered thoughtfully, leaning back and digging her elbows into the soft dirt. "I chose to leave. Did you choose your path, then? Did ye want to be a paladin?"

His gaze, turned toward her, was unfathomable. It almost made the monk self-conscious. She decided not to press the question, contenting herself instead with the peace surrounding them.

It didn't last long though. A hush descended, and suddenly they discovered they had been surrounded in the night. A dark form stepped closer, growling harshly. "You are bold to laugh as you light ground on our land, asafolk."

Seth sprang to his feet, hand to the hilt of his saber. McKenna stood also, peering into the gloom. "An' who might you be, to call this land yours?" was her imperious, yet inquisitive, reply.

"Those who find every inch of it snatched from beneath them, one step at a time. You will leave, and not meet Atosa this night," replied the figure.

Sensing the rogue was reaching the edge of his restraint, McKenna swiftly dumped a bag of sand over the firepit, extinguishing it utterly. She stepped forward, whispering a prayer to Malfaestus while using her god-given powers to discern who had accosted them. A silvery aura lined the five standing before her, and their silhouettes became clear.

Orgir.

She swallowed, thinking quickly. Seth's armor was still in a pile on the ground, leaving him almost defenseless. But she decided to put her studies to the test, hoping they could avoid combat, hoping her knowledge would outweigh experience.

"As yer goddess Atosa would... grant us passage into the realm of death, so too would our... spirits thank ye for it," she replied haltingly- a simple orgirrish greeting, one of the few she'd been able to learn.

The band seemed taken aback by this. The shadowy figures cast sideways glances at one another, pushing out their full underlips as they pondered the pair by the fire. "An aesir would know us?" said one, with more curiosity than hostility.

"Aesir?" She repeated in confusion. "Nay. Jes' a durgirn monk, with me directionless guide," corrected McKenna. But she kept the formality in her words and tone as she continued. "We go at dawn, and will grant this land to yer goddess, though you wouldna grant it to us."

She hadn't noticed the aura surrounding her own figure as she spoke with the orgir. Even if she had, she wouldn't have understood the effect it had on them. Without a word, they vanished back into the murky darkness. McKenna suddenly realized how tense she had been, and as the adrenaline left her body she slumped to the ground. Seth dropped instantly beside her, slipping a skein of water into her hand.

"How did you know what to say?" he asked as she took a deep draught.

"It's me business to know the realms," she replied. "I studied with the most learned of our race- and didn't have much else to do besides."

He seemed to accept her answer, and chose to remain seated beside her. McKenna could sense he finally seemed glad for her company, instead of resigned to it. She was thankful for that.

"We needn't pass from here. They know we're harmless now," she said. "Probably shouldn't light that fire again though."

Seth agreed, but refused to sleep before her. She assumed again her meditative pose and drifted into the night.

VII

We Meet The Holvir...
Er, Again.

"I guess we bury ourselves in more ways than one," she said thoughtfully, as they rode over a low ridge toward a scrubby copse of forest below. The silence was starting to drive her crazy. She was determined to break through the obstinate silence of the rogue at any cost. "The Clan hain't heard of ilmaurte. Good thing too, else I'd never'd been allowed to leave," she mumbled under her breath.

He snorted, but her chatter elicited no other response. She groaned audibly.

"I been listening ter nothin' but the sound o' me own thoughts fer moons," she wheedled desperately, spurring her mount to amble alongside his. Kurya looked askance at the plebeian mule, but slowed his pace of his own accord despite the firm press of his rider's heels in his flanks. "Please use yer words, rogue, I'm desperate."

Seeing his horse had no intention of moving any faster, Seth sighed and turned his gaze on the monk. She smiled brightly, encouragingly, and he felt his reserve begin to melt away. He paused for a moment, but she could tell he was simply searching for the right words to use instead of pursuing his policy of not using them at all. "It hasn't been happening for long. Most reports pinned them as bandits. Some towns still won't even accept the truth of what they are - usually the ones they've left alone, for one reason or another - but I've been taking quests to dispatch them long enough to know better."

It was hard to imagine roving hordes of undead roaming the landscape unrolling before her. She looked and looked again at everything surrounding her - emerald green leaves still clinging staunchly to high limbs, the unspun burnt gold of grain bleached by the sun, and the low waters of a lazy river feeding the great basin from the permafrost capped peaks to the north.

"They seem to be travelling from the west," Seth continued. "No one has traced them far enough to pinpoint their exact origin. But I'm almost certain they do not exist of their own accord. They're being summoned, and whoever's summoning them must be a powerful necromancer," he said.

"Somethin's off, now" mused McKenna, "Atosa's not sealin' 'em back up? Seems unfair to let the mortals do it when it's literally her only job."

Seth deliberated for a moment. "You're not wrong. The gods and goddesses usually let us make our own way, but this is beyond mortal control. Either she is blind to it, or worse, unable to stop them." He paused, then continued. "Maybe it's a test for her children."

"Ye can't be serious," laughed McKenna. "That's a myth. She didn't have mortal children, it was jes' a metaphor."

The rogue took in the posture of the woman beside him, opting to say nothing more. He had his suspicions about this clandestine durgirn monk, especially after the events of the night before, but her utter surety in her existence brooked no argument.

She saw his pursed lips, the thoughts dying before he could speak them. So she pushed him again. "Penny for yer thoughts, then? Say 'em out loud, ye were doin' so well."

He smiled. A genuine smile, she could tell, not simply the self-deprecating kind he seemed to reserve for anything that resembled a compliment.

"She does, actually. Have children… or, one child, at least. The ilvir have been hailing her as a princess for decades now, so either she's an extremely lucky charlatan or the true offspring of a celestial deity."

"Who are you talking about?" queried McKenna amusedly. "Didna' realize there was any royalty on Faie."

"Princess Katarin. Or rather, nowadays, Katarin, Third Sorcere of the Guild of Moonbow," he replied nonchalantly. "I guess I'm not surprised you haven't heard of her. Ilvir and durgir aren't exactly friends, are they?"

She laughed outright at that. "Okay, that one is definitely a myth. Durgir and ilvir do business all the time. But have you seen a duergi's legs?" she bandied jestingly. "They aren't up for walking much, let alone a hundred leagues ter Meliamne. An' ye could as much get a duergi ter swear off mead as ye could to use a portal. When we trade, we meet in the middle. Sometimes Bristendine, sometimes Wheelspoke."

Seth flinched almost imperceptibly and changed the subject abruptly. "What's the metaphorical child of Atosa, then?"

McKenna paused, measuring her words before responding. The texts were old that mentioned Atosa, because the funeral rites of durgir were methodical, arduous, and completely engrossing of all who lived in Mount Oer. The race lived so long that the death of a duergi- almost exclusively by illness or accident, never old age- heralded a celebration of their history with the clan and a festival of learning and joy, grief and antipathy, and an almost catastrophic level of alcohol consumption. Atosa featured very little- most of the time, not at all- in the passage of a duergi's soul into the afterlife, as they took almost as long to reach it as they took to live in the first place.

"She left behind her, in the mortal realm, the true understanding of how to celebrate death, and the reminder that all life leads to the same end," she said finally, coming out of her reverie. "She birthed the idea among the soulful races that we should respect death, not fear it."

The rogue, astride his ambling steed, nodded thoughtfully but made no other comment. Kurya nickered under his breath, casting an expressive glance toward Seth, who chose to ignore it. Silence stretched onwards again with them along to the horizon.

Farms and other signs of habitation now dotted the surrounding landscape. They stopped earlier this evening and decided in favor of another fire, clear of orgir territory and certain of being along the outskirts of the scrubby forest that bordered the town towards which they headed. McKenna put her guisarme to good use swiping fish from a brook nearby, as Seth unloaded crudely wrapped rations and fashioned a quick cookout. The two relaxed, enjoying the dying light of another day.

But it appears smoke attracts more than just territorial orgir. McKenna and Seth, instincts honed for danger, sprang to alert as the clear sound of footsteps reached them.

However, they found themselves braced against nothing. Two holvir, brazenly attracted to the light and smell of burned fish, stepped carefully into the clearing.

"Hi hello, yes, we're strangers right now!" a frank voice met their ears. "But we don't have to be, because you have food, and we have song, and also," her belly rumbled in harmony with her voice, "hunger."

With that she approached them calmly, wrist outstretched and palm out, while the other hung back hesitantly. Neither had weapons drawn, but while the lead-most holvi wore an expression of (delirious?) nonchalance, her companion's wary look seemed more appropriate to the situation.

"I'm Ginni, and this is Tjena-" she began-

"Tjen" interrupted the other holvi.

"Okay, so, today you're Tjen. Anyways. Now we have names!" Ginni smiled broadly, exposing her wrist and wiggling her fingers in invitation for a greeting.

McKenna stepped forward and grasped her slim paw. All (okay, most) of the tension had gone out of the clearing by now.

"I guess it's nice to meet you. I'm McKenna and this is... ah..." she cast an uncomfortable look at Seth, while Ginni peered at her questioningly, looking at the dark fingers wrapped around her tiny ones in slight confusion. "Well, last time I tried to give his name without his permission, he punched me."

"Seth," he stated plainly. "You could've lost an arm, waltzing into a strange camp with your guard down and goodwill outstretched like that."

"It looks like I'm about to lose an arm after all. Why are you grabbing me like that?" she asked McKenna, cautiously raising their clasped hands.

"Err... it's a handshake. Ye don't do like that in the south?" McKenna replied uncomfortably, dropping the holvi's hand in embarrassment.

"I'm thinking we do it wrong... 'in the south'," Ginni's equivocal tone, charismatic and soothing, calmed the monk. "A handshake. I like it. I should visit the durgir more often."

Tjen crept closer to Ginni, and there would've been something almost protective about the gesture had Tjen not been so patently expressionless. It didn't escape McKenna's notice. In fact, as she peered more closely at the reserved holvi, she could tell that they were blind.

"Ye should. But, what, err, brings the two of you out here?" she said, gesturing towards the fire and, more importantly to the holvir, the crusty remains of a couple large and fatty trout.

"Oh, you know, bard stuff. Tjen and I are really very good musicians." said Ginni breezily, grabbing for a fish.

Tjen took advantage of Ginni's distraction. "Village elder made us leave. It's not uncommon, where we're from."

Ginni butted in. "Yeah, and it's not like Tjen could go on their own. I mean, just look at them!"

"You fell into a puddle this morning because you were yelling at a bird."

"That. Is. Irrelevant."

McKenna smiled, enjoying their chatter and their camaraderie. It sure was a change from the taciturn Seth. She cast a sidelong glance at his long figure flickering in the firelight. He too seemed at ease; a good sign from the distrustful rogue. Catching her look, he raised his shoulders in a near imperceptible shrug, maintaining the silence that seemed most natural to him. The gesture itself broke the bounds of his normal reserve, a sign he may be choosing to soften to more than just the strangers. Perhaps he'd begun to invest some trust in her, after all.

"We're traveling back actually, from Meliamne," Ginni said, after swallowing a mouthful of trout. "You wouldn't happen to be heading towards Styckes, would you?"

"Styckes?" McKenna raised an eyebrow. According to the texts that mentioned it, the river Styckes once ran the length of Faie from the boundless desert into the sea along its eastern border, before drying up centuries ago. Even the riverbed itself had been mostly effaced from the plains, though a large portion made up a major pass leading from Wheelspoke to Lianor and the eastern cities of the coast. "That's a real place?"

"Sure is. Sometimes pretends to be a river, runs into that great chasm by Naijor. Full of all sorts of fun and exciting stuff."

"Like…?" McKenna responded bemusedly.

"Why in the world do you want to go there?" interrupted Seth. "Everyone knows the water of Styckes is cursed. And if you were banished, why would you go back?"

"A sorcere needs us to pick something up- I dunno, I wasn't really paying attention. Folk always want something in return when you ask for favors," replied Ginni evasively.

Observing the holvir keenly, Seth chose not to interrogate them further. McKenna hoped the rogue was simply showing signs of sympathy. Further study of Tjen discovered the truth to her as clearly as a physical deformity. Tjen wasn't just blinded. They were blighted, by a heavy, impenetrable curse. Little wonder they were kicked out of their clan, despite their clandestine nonchalance about the whole situation. The wave of sympathy that rushed over McKenna threatened to choke her, but she shook back the emotion and smiled reassuringly.

"Well, I can't exactly speak for Seth, but if you want a companion once our quest is complete…" she trailed off and looked at him searchingly.

He jerked his head noncommittally, then sighed. "The horde is moving from the west, or so the rumors say. I suppose having guides along who know the area could prove useful," he eyed them meaningfully.

"Oh. Yeah! Guides, of course, definitely. I fully intend to walk you directly into the chasm. I'll even draw you a map," replied Ginni sarcastically.

"Gods, Seth, you know you can travel with someone without needing some kind of exchange?" McKenna interrupted exasperatedly.

"What! They wanted our protection, I'm just making sure it's justified," he responded defensively.

The monk eyed him searchingly. So much for trust. "She didn't ask for our protection. She just asked if we were going there. Sounds like they just need a little companionship is all, right, you two?" She turned to them with a warmhearted smile, the kind holvir never seemed to get from asafolk.

"Uh… uh…" Ginni stammered, almost beginning to blush.

"You must be really pretty. She's always tongue-tied with the pretty ones," mused Tjen aloud.

"Shut it! Am not! I just… she's an aesir-"

"Duergi," Seth corrected before McKenna could react.

Ginni squinted her eyes at the monk briefly, then rolled them. "Whatever. Not a holvi. As in, you know…" Ginni floundered, finding it difficult to give a voice to the prejudice that blanketed holvir history.

"Greater than?" finished Seth, with a strange look in his eye.

"Seth! What is wrong with you?" McKenna leapt to her feet, completely baffled by the rogue's distressing treatment of the destitute bards. "Am I missing something? Why would holvir be less than asafolk, or durgir?" What was she missing, in this strange world where everyone lived side by side, and yet seemed to hate each other for no reason? "You're *faiefolkr*, aren't you?"

Tjen put a hand on McKenna's knee, turning their sightless eyes toward the monk. The gesture was oddly soothing - and McKenna realized again, perhaps her studies hadn't been so thorough, after all.

"You can't blame him," they said softly. "It's just the way things are."

An uncomfortable silence succeeded their words. *I left the mines to find answers. Instead I'm faced with more and more questions.*

Casting an expressive and apologetic look at McKenna, Seth's pensive voice relieved the silence. "She can't blame me, you're right. But she can expect better of me." The rogue came and knelt before the two holvir. "I welcome the chance to travel together, and to prove my respect for you and the holvir is no less than the respect I have for my own."

The quizzical look McKenna cast caused a soft blush to creep up the rogue's neck. "You don't have to look at me like that. I mean it," he stammered under his breath.

"I know you do. That's why I'm looking at you like this," she replied with a grin as the blush slowly faded.

"Fantastic! In exchange, you get the bountiful pleasure of our company- music included. We are bards after all. Tjen, whatcha got for these folks?" trilled Ginni, her voice subtly shifting from spoken word to melodic song.

Tjen strummed their strange stringed instrument, coaxing out the purest tone imaginable. The forest's rustle died down and the fire's glow illuminated the two holvir, settled pleasantly into their element- the harmony of song and storytelling.

"For time eternal in realms of Faie
Two sisters guard as night and day
While Sh'nia, the eldest, granted the breath of life
Young Atosa was left to soothe death's strife
Beloved Sh'nia beheld her gift
As jealous sister proposed a rift
The reaper of souls sought mortality
To live among those who hid from she
Who would guide their souls from mortal plane
To seek the gift of life again
A mirror, by ilvir in secret held
The corporeal gift of body meld
For three days and nights did Atosa gaze
Until a mortal form for her would raise
Elated, Atosa found a gleeful home
In song and dance, in life and love
Two children born of her heavenly soul
Twin spirits extend her mortal role
Blessed Sh'nia in vain did try
To gift both life to Faie's beings and let them die
'Dear sister, I need you by my side
Restore balance to our work's divide.'
Knowing now her subjects loved her true
As much as they loved her sister too
Atosa returned to her Celestial throne
Leaving one child with tree, one child in stone
Ilvir and durgir each blessed with one
Child of Moon, and Child of Sun."

The children of Atosa. Here it was again. "Convenient

subject matter. You sure you weren't spying on us?" McKenna said, raising her eyebrow at Seth.

He just chuckled, reclining against his bulky pack. "See, I told you," he said in a friendly rumble. "Children."

McKenna shook her head in bemused disbelief, scattering more chips on the fire. "I still say it's a metaphor."

The growing darkness deepened around their camp. Tjen stared, unseeingly, into the heart of the fire's glow- absentmindedly strumming the *naiti* which echoed almost feral sounds of woodland charm. But despite the soothing melody, a sensation shivered its way through McKenna's spirit, a deep and loathsome foreboding that alerted her to danger before her sight did.

"Ginni," said McKenna suddenly. "Do you two know bardic spellcasting?"

Ginni's eyes widened as she switched her gaze from Tjen to the monk. "Uh, in a… sense… why do you ask?"

In one swift movement, Seth had spun into a crouch, dragging his heel through the dirt in a wide arc that kicked up his sabre into his waiting grasp. Unsheathing it, he dove into a roll towards Kurya, who had reared up as though to smash his powerful hooves through an unseen foe- which made itself seen, soon enough.

"Because we're going to need it," McKenna finished, flourishing her own guisarme and drawing a brand from the fire.

VIII

A Scourge Unknown

Ranged among the trees shambled ragged, haunting figures. As they shifted from ephemeral to corporeal, McKenna had no doubt these were the ilmaurte of which Seth had warned. It was difficult to count their number— harder still to even really recognize the forms for what they really were, so unnatural, so appalling was their mere existence. Seth had charged the vanguard while astride Kurya but his sabre, and the destrier's pounding hooves, seemed to have little effect. McKenna assumed his prayers to Bahamut were not fully formulated, and she hastily began chanting, calling on numinous protections of her own against this immaterial foe.

A sound shimmered through the clearing, soft and powerful. A clarion call that rang as though it were the voice of a blessed Celestial itself. Music in durgirn halls sounded of winding horns and guttural groans, the crash of stone on stone, but this was something entirely new, entirely different. The purest tones imaginable, woven through by the golden thread of the naiti's perfect pitch. If nature had a noise made music, it would be the sound singing itself from the powerful holvi's throat and her companion's instrument of string and wood. Ginni, accompanied by Tjen, began a ballad to inspire courage. The ephemeral tones sang in McKenna's blood and fired her runic protections faster than she could call down oaths.

She surged forward at the phalanx that crept up from

behind, swinging both blazing brand and guisarme. The fire seemed to drain the ilmaurte's inertia, slowing their momentum enough to dismember with the blade. But their corporeal forms simply shifted and manifested new limbs to advance the attack. Frustrated, McKenna called upon the god Malfaestus, striking her palm across the flat of her blade and lighting the runes with deific power. It seemed to work; with every new strike, the undead assembled more and more slowly until finally there remained naught but piles of smoky detritus littering the clearing.

Not sure what power Malfaestus has over the dead… must be the effect of divinity over malevolent evil, she thought to herself uneasily, ignoring the shivers that ran down her spine at the incessant sensation of souls tugging against her own.

McKenna could hear the scream of Seth's mount over her shoulder, and she turned to see the horse leap from a crowd of the clawing, moaning horde… without a rider upon its back. She shrieked in fury, then turned her own momentum to rush to the prone fighter's aid.

The holvir were faster. Taking refuge as close to the fire as they could possibly stand, Ginni's voice became a battering ram. Wave upon wave of sound crashed upon the shuddering undead. Her song couldn't destroy them, only push them back from the prone form on the ground. McKenna spotted a golden glow around the fallen fighter and realized he had managed to enact a spell of protection. Swinging her polearm with wild abandon she reaped the ilmaurte like so many sheaves of wheat, forcing them further and further back from the warrior.

Seth stood timorously, his breathing ragged, and aimed a small hand crossbow at the horde. With each piercing shot, the ilmaurte began to slowly dissipate. McKenna kept them back with wide sweeps of her guisarme as he continued to try and pick them off one by one. Bolts, blessed by Bahamut and doused in the waters of Styckes, destroyed the enchantments that bound the undead souls to their borrowed bodies.

Suddenly McKenna felt a sharp pain blaze along her forearm. She had swung too wide and a bolt grazed her flesh, drawing a stinging line of dark blood along her skin.

The ilmaurt it hit burst into a pyre of smoke, and in an instant, evaporated.

Shocked, she stared at Seth, who stood open-mouthed at what he'd just witnessed. McKenna glanced slowly at her bleeding arm, then back to the remaining horde. Acting on impulse, she rubbed her palm across the gash, then smeared the blood along the flat of her blade. In one swift motion, she raked the guisarme through a line of advancing undead.

As the blade rent the air, so too did it raze the ilmaurte.

One by one they dematerialized, reanimated corpses decomposing almost before they hit the ground. The only imprint left was the shifting mass of tetherless shivering souls hovering desperately above their desecrated remains. McKenna felt them dragging, trying to cling to her. The whispers of death rang in her mind and soul, but she knew not how to respond to their desperate plea.

Suddenly, the purest, sweetest note cleft the night sky - a cleansing rain, a dancing sunbeam, a breath of spring air. A suggestion of purpose, of destiny, of forgiveness and homecoming all in one. Ginni held the note impossibly long, while Tjen, face screwed up in concentration, drew a small bow along the strings of their instrument that seemed capable of almost every reverberation. And one by one, the souls answered their call. As the sounds spread through the clearing they shivered out of existence, purified by the holvir's sweet song.

And in that moment, the haft of her guisarme exploded.

Seth shouted, but more from shock than pain. The splinters bounced harmlessly off his armor, and luckily the runic protections McKenna had activated on her skin protected her too. The blade spun helplessly in the air for a moment, before tumbling to the ground. As she knelt to pick it up, she noticed a burnished brown mark across the flat of the blade - her blood, staining a metal that should repel all impurities.

"I'm assuming it was not supposed to do that," Seth commented, his eyes wide as he regarded the plain spearhead she was studying in her hands.

"Uh, no. But I guess that's what I get fer using a stick I found in the woods as a weapon. Hopefully this town o' yers has a smithy."

"I didn't mean the shaft. I meant the blade," and he pointed to the grim streak of blood, still bright, across both the mithril edge and iron forte. "Mithril doesn't stain - look, the undead left no trace whatsoever - and yet it's still covered in your blood."

She tried rubbing it with the palm of her other hand, and the edge of her pelt, but it was no use. "Guess I'll have ter ask the smithy about that too."

He regarded her for a moment, his expression inscrutable. She thought - hoped, maybe - that he'd question her more, but he simply shrugged and moved away.

They returned to the campfire and the holvir. Tjen remained seated, rubbing rosin on their bow. Ginni, a little out of breath, ran up to meet the two.

"Okay, maybe I've done that before. I think. At any rate it worked and that's what matters!" she said gleefully, before taking note of McKenna's gashed arm and the generally tousled appearance of Seth. "Um, your horse will come back, right?" she said, while dousing a cloth in an aromatic solution from a flask at her side and offering it to him.

Seth took the rag and issued a low, piercing whistle. A whinny answered his call, and the riderless horse loped into view. He nudged the pack on the ground, from which Seth pulled a golden apple and offered it with a chuckle.

"Kurya always comes back," he winced as he dragged the sodden rag across his injuries. The horse blew a breath into his hair, settling down around him before crunching the apple.

"Anyway, what took them out so fast? It looked like one minute you guys were overwhelmed, the next they just disappeared," asked Ginni, as she stroked the ointment from her flask along McKenna's arm. McKenna took out a small patch of inglefoss and handed it to the holvi, who gently started packing it along the wound.

Seth raised an eyebrow at McKenna. "That's a great question, monk-without-a-beard. How did you manage to do that?"

"Beats me. You're the one who sniped me with a crossbow," she shot back, sticking her tongue out at him as Ginni bandaged the wounded arm. "I just saw the spray of blood and kind of… panicked." She drew the blade into her lap, grimacing at the rusty red streaks dried along the mithril.

"You mean to tell me your blood dispels ilmaurte?" chimed in Tjen. "That's… morbid."

The monk chuckled uncomfortably, not really trusting herself to answer. The idea of her blood having any kind of power at all gave her chills. Wrapping the cloak tighter about her, she felt the sharp beveled edge of the mirror dig into her side. She slipped her fingers into the pocket and stroked it, but shook her head and withdrew her hand. Tonight was not the night to solve that enigma.

A lethargic silence descended upon the four. The stars, as if to make up for the swift descent of darkness that arrived with the undead, sparkled brilliantly and vibrantly among the heavens. Ginni, finished with her ministrations and waving off McKenna's fervent thanks, shuffled over to the fire and laid her head in Tjen's lap. The blinded bard stroked her hair absentmindedly, smiling at the touch of their loquacious counterpart. "I guess I'm lucky this blight doesn't seem to affect our music," they mused. "Those songs seemed stronger."

The little vocalist kissed their open palm. "Your bow draws quicker than any druid's I've seen, that's for sure," she said.

Tjen plucked the naiti, reverting to the holvir couple's unspoken language of music. *"Why'd we help them? Why didn't we just run?"*

Ginni hummed back under her breath. To the others, it sounded like a melancholy whisper of the wind, nature's music dancing among the boughs of the fir trees. *"We need them. I know we'll need them. Besides, what if there were more out there? We wouldn't last a minute against an ilmaurt, let alone a horde."*

A shiver passed through Tjen's small frame, and they curled tighter around the holvi in their lap. *"Need them, huh?"* Their tone chastised their partner. *"Guess McKenna should've saved her breath. Seth was right."*

The music died down as the wind itself picked up. The stiff branches swayed and creaked, and the darkness hung heavy outside the fire's warm glow. Ginni frowned, as something like guilt began to steal its way into her. She didn't owe them anything - but that woman had a draw to her that Ginni couldn't ignore.

She felt Tjen stroke a lock of hair from her forehead, and smiled despite herself. *"We'll be fine, you and I, love."*

We're always fine.

Meanwhile, McKenna had drawn herself up into another meditative pose. She heard whispers again- the sounds of voices unfamiliar- and screwed up her face in concentration to listen. But the harder she tried to hear the fainter and fainter the voices grew until they finally went out altogether. She sighed and felt the tension, from the spell and the battle, slowly dissipate from her nerves, sinew, and bone.

Staring deeply into the fire's dying glow, Seth seemed wound so tightly that he could spring apart at any moment. She offered him a wan smile when his gaze wandered aimlessly across her line of vision, shaking him from his reverie.

"We should get some sleep," was all he said, before pulling the roll again from his pack and slipping into it. A guard seemed pretty pointless, and no one volunteered to be one. The aura of dispelled ilmaurte saturated their entire camp, repelling any who may have still been in the area and also infusing their environment with a high key sense of danger that would ward any other malicious intent away. McKenna, after another look at the holvir couple dozing before the fire, took a deep breath and relaxed into meditation, her chastened spirit seeking guidance from the Celestial Plane.

IX

Coventries And Witches' Deeds

Dozens of robed figures filled the amphitheater atop Tirre Lunir, seating themselves upon benches made from branches suspended among the sylvan city's tallest trees. A faint thrum of magical energy filled the space and multi-hued light glowed in strange and wondrous patterns. The gentle glow of the moon illuminated the area, activating enchanted glyphs and wards surrounding each seated sorcere. In times of greatest need, Atosa herself had been known to bless their seances.

But of late, the goddess had been ominously silent.

Razan lingered near a knot of lesser mages huddled together, their low, hushed tones still discernible to his keen ears.

"Barra and Olearia have already withdrawn the bridge," said one, and while he spoke in a cold, dispassionate tone Razan could sense in it the hint of fear he couldn't quite mask.

"But they have contracts with the guild too," complained his novitiate, her narrow face pinched with worry. "Are they defaulting?"

The others muttered angrily, their thin eyebrows drawn together and long fingers clutching the shimmering cloth of their ritual garb in irritation.

"Everyone knows ilvir contracts with asafolk are non-binding," he hissed in reply. "And we seem to be overrun with asafolk lately."

Feeling their eyes turn towards him, Razan slipped through the benches and out of sight.

Overrun with asafolk.

The aesir assassin couldn't ignore the implications. No longer could the powerful realm to the south turn a blind eye to the rumors of ilmaurte roaming and terrorizing their northern neighbors. Even now the groves overflowed with refugees from across Faie, and while dire need and desperation drove the differing clans together, already the close quarters and foreign climes alienated each and made them more than restless.

Asafolk are only as good as their gifts, he thought to himself. The Meliamne clans would make alliances, so long as they were the ones reaping the greatest benefit. As soon as the scales were tipped, the ilvir had no more use for anyone else.

A glittering pair of amethyst eyes broke into his reverie. He looked up, spotting Katarin seated among the sorceres in the stands above him. She smiled and fluttered her long fingers at him, and Razan had to appreciate her cunning as he moved to join her. As Third Sorcere, she could take a seat at the podium, drenched in dazzling moonlight and magical power. But she chose not to put herself on display, sitting instead among the peers whose respect and love she'd long earned as their beloved princess.

Choosing to stand among them meant fewer daggers pointed at her back.

She perched her head on his shoulder, purring seductively and suggestively in his ear. "I appreciate that you didn't ignore the summons."

He reached back to twine a lock of her hair into his grasp, divining the subtle hint in her otherwise innocuous comment. "Don't worry. I won't lose my lead," he replied in his deep, measured drawl. Katarin rolled her eyes and draped herself more comfortably over Razan's back. He settled into her, surprised at the normally aloof princess's public advances. A few faces turned towards them, but the obvious (and perhaps, the hidden) members of Onyx Blade standing guard kept them free from anything more than idle curiosity.

"Those holvir were a nice distraction. I'm assuming you plan on telling me what they were distracting me from," she replied, arching a delicate brow.

"Perhaps I thought you were simply in need of some music," he responded lightly.

But his face grew dark, and Katarin could feel tension in his frame as it rested against hers. When she was sure no one paid them any attention, she ran her teeth gently against the top of his ear, thrilling to the instant sigh and melting response she felt in the assassin's normally languid form.

He rolled his eyes, continuing to look away from her and into the crowd. "Fine. My mother didn't send her compliments, so I thought I'd make up for her lack of manners."

He chose his words wisely. A dawning look of comprehension replaced the imperious curiosity that dominated her face, and she relaxed perceptibly. There were some secrets even she didn't dare force from the assassin.

His tie to the Cult of Naszer was one of them.

A low, clear sound suddenly rung out among the treetops, silencing the group almost instantly.

"It is known that we gather infrequently- even less so when not for casting a great spell." The magically amplified voice carried to every member present belonged to Mirai Mistmoon, their Grand Master and First Sorcere of the Guild of Moonbow. She had features lightly marred by the ravages of time surrounded by a corona of dark, silver streaked hair. The diminutive, unassuming woman maintained a neutral posture and expression as she stood erect upon the podium before them. "However, the threat to our realm has grown too great to be further ignored by us. Below us huddle the hungry, the shaken, the homeless of Faie- and we stand now with purpose to aid in ridding them from this scourge, before our own homeland is so blighted."

An interesting approach, thought Razan. He didn't expect the appeal to sympathy from the Grandmaster. Not to this crowd, at any rate.

A figure close to the dais stood up, and the Grand Master waved for the man to speak.

"Our divinings have encountered whispers," he began, with a voice similarly magically amplified to reach all in the area, "that a dangerous force is behind the horde. These are not merely bands of escapees suddenly drifting through the planes between Life and Death. They are being summoned here, by a being with power that grows greater each day."

Murmurings began to ripple through the clearing. They had all heard rumours. They were sorceres, after all. Many were the whispers of stirrings from the deeper planes. Katarin observed the speaker and his entourage narrowly, noticing with comfort that Razan was clearly doing the same.

"Now they… should definitely not be here," she hissed under her breath. He returned an almost imperceptible nod and his bangles chimed lightly, blending with the whisper of the wind in the tree boughs. Figures began to melt into the shadows, completely camouflaged by the shifting light of the moon through the trees above.

"A being with power enough to summon the dead? Surely this is impossible," questioned someone from the crowd near Katarin. "There is only one master of Death, the great goddess Atosa."

A stirring rustled through those who sat near the standing speaker. "But where is Atosa!" they cried. "Why does she not answer our calls? Why does she let the lost wander so?"

Katarin stood up and clutched at Razan's shoulder, her hostile gaze trained in their direction. Though she knew every single member of the Guild of Moonbow, these figures were strangers, never seen before in their hallowed precincts. The Grandmaster Sorcere was quicker to retaliate.

"You forget in whose presence you stand, accuser,"

she chastised, catching Katarin's eye but focusing her words on the black-robed figure. "We all speak to the goddess; there is but one who can speak for her."

Those seated around the princess stirred, their impassive faces turned in challenge toward the huddle of unknown interlopers and their fingers twisted against their chest in a ward of protection. There were no bonds of family among the ilvir; especially none here in Tirre Lunir. Alliances were mutually beneficial and nothing more. But Katarin's place among them was unique. They adored their princess, and revered her as the blessing left behind by their beloved goddess. The devoted loyalty shown by them touched the sorcere, and she knew she must make an example of those who would so defy her status. She simply needed the right opportunity - and it was, finally, here.

"I speak not for my mother," spoke Katarin humbly, as she slowly sank gracefully back to her seat with a flash in her eye. "But the gods have ever let us make our own way," she continued, remaining seated and not bothering to amplify her own voice.

The speaker, his long black robes bearing a vaguely familiar sigil of emerald and silver, rose and extended a long, accusatory finger towards Katarin. "And what way have the gods laid open before you? Who stands to benefit most from Atosa's disappearance?" he hissed.

The gathering surrounding Katarin rippled in shock, but the speaker continued before they could retaliate. "We belong to the Ward- we whisper the secrets of the dead back into the world they have left behind. Atosa has always favored the witches, always listened to our prayers, and yet now she grows silent as her flock wanders dangerously among us."

Finally Katarin recognized the group and the sigils
they bore on their robes. Witches of the Ward- an ancient
tribe of asafolk from the wastelands that bordered Naijor.
Witches never joined sorceres' coventries. They were
almost always at odds with the ilvir who drew power
from alternate planes. They often accused the Guild of
paying lip service to the blessings bestowed upon Faie
by Sh'nia and Atosa, while accepting with their other
hand the blasphemous and frankly appalling blessings
gifted by the neodivinity of their eastern kin. The witches'
presence here at Tirre Lunir, the Guild of Moonbow's
sacred stronghold, stood testament to the instability of
the time. She turned involuntarily toward Razan, who
stared impassively at the witch who spoke. Seeing his
concentration eased Katarin's mind. She knew that look.

Where Razan had eyes, Razan had blades.

Emboldened by this, she rose from among the stands.
Though she had every eye in the gathering trained upon
her, none but the gaze of the witches were in the least
hostile. This guild had raised her, from precocious child
to master of her craft. She did not lead them- indeed,
the guild acknowledged no leadership but that of the
Grandmaster Sorcere, and that mostly only as a formality.
But they recognized her blood and her birthright. And
it was this very birthright she stood to claim. Prompted
by the whispers of her own hubris, those voices that
promised power, she threw back her shoulders and
amplified her voice with the same spell she used on the
holvir, speaking with authority and grace.

"I do not speak for my mother," she repeated, "but
I am my mother's child. If this is true what you say, that
Atosa no longer holds her throne in the realm of death,
then I stand to assume that mantle. I propose," she said,

sweeping her arms wide, "a seance. To summon the immortal spirit of Atosa and to determine her path."

Those words whispered in the back of her mind were reassuring. No call would answer the seance. Only the silent nomination of her rightful place.

"And if the goddess remains mute?" Mirai's face was inscrutable as ever; neither challenge nor sanction in her silver blue eyes.

"I will do what is necessary to rid our lands of the scourge of undead, who wander lost among us. I will possess the mantle of goddesshood, and I will shepherd the poor souls myself."

Those seated nearest to her- the family, for lack of better term, who had so reared this princess, touched a hand to the guild sigil at their throats. The motion was a pledge to defend their princess' right to this challenge, and their devotion to seeing it through. At the sight, the witches stood in a body around the one who spoke for them.

"Our goddess will rise and defy such pretensions," he spat. "We will restore Atosa and demand an inquiry to the nature of the hordes that have risen. Should those be traced to you," he continued in a hiss, "we will strip you of your birthright."

"Begone, Witch. You hold no sway here to make such baseless accusations," spoke Mirai warningly. Her patience for the interloping trespassers was at an end. She waved a beringed hand and the dazzling light of a moonbeam struck the group, who vanished without a trace.

A stunned silence met the clearing for a moment. Katarin remained standing, and all attention had pivoted from the Grandmaster Sorcere's forceful ejection of the witches to her resolute expression in the face of such a challenge.

Those who had pressed the sigil remained inert, their hands at their throats. This display impressed those who remained skeptical. To have inspired such unequivocal support from so many was no small feat in this place where allegiance to personal advancement reigned supreme. In the time since Katarin's arrival she had carved her own place among them, a force of personality established by accomplishment as much as by birth. None rose to defy the challenge brought to the witches- honestly, it meant little to any of them, after all. Mirai spoke again, interrupting the silence.

"Third Sorcere. The guild recognizes your claim," she said, waving a hand to a scribe who had diligently noted every word. "In three moons, should the goddess remain silent, Moonbow will honor your ascension. Let us hope," her hard eyes glittered for a moment, "that it will put an end to the scourge in Faie, allowing our... visitors... to return home."

Low murmurs began to stir in the canopy. Mirai rose, the sorceres upon the podium rising with her. One by one, they filed out, followed casually by the rest of the guild members in attendance, who either dispersed back to their towers or lingered among the stands, speaking quietly amongst themselves. Razan flicked his wrist and his entourage melted from view, as Katarin stood and swept off amongst her apprentices.

Making as though to follow her, he instead lingered by a tightly knotted gathering of lesser mages who still remained, whispering uncomfortably to each other and casting fearful glances around the clearing. Some caught Razan's eye and subsided into silence - but one, a tall, good-natured looking ilvi, raised an eyebrow in notice of the silent assassin, beckoning him over.

"'Three moons', she says. What is with these sorceres and their arbitrary declarations? What possible import could 'three moons' have anyways," the ilvi, a round-faced and smiling mage by the name of Illin, sighed and rolled his eyes. "We didn't even get a chance to make our proposition, Master Razan. There was no point in coming here after all, there never is."

Resigned looks met his statement - Razan, sympathetic to their complaint though bristling at the slight against Katarin, simply shrugged. "Three moons is Red Solstice - the perfect time for an ascension. You can't deny the power of a Solstice, nor our Grand Master's decision to call upon it."

"No, and I don't care about it, personally," Master Illin replied with brutal honesty. "I'm just annoyed her grandstanding took attention away from our real purpose here - the fate of the refugees. She and those ridiculous witches - our ancient goddess has no domain over the living asafolk who are stuck in Meliamne, with no shelter and no purpose, so why waste our time?"

"Mistmoon shouldn't have tried to engage the whole guild," agreed Razan. "But whatever it is you're planning, you'd have better luck with the Choirmaster of Meliamne. It's a waste indeed to rely on the gods," he said with a hiss of distaste, "especially when it is only mortals who suffer."

"You're probably right," Illin replied with a mournful

sigh, standing slowly from the bench and waving his fellow mages off. "We won't get anything done sitting around here, that's for certain. I'll get an audience with the Choirmaster, and hopefully, with the help of Hand Over Fist..." he trailed off, gazing into the distant lights of refugee camps scattered among the trees, "well, if we can't return them to their homes, perhaps we can help them make some here."

"I wish you luck with that," Razan said emphatically, exchanging friendly bows with the mage before turning to depart for Katarin's lofty tower. Her declaration, though not unexpected, did make the assassin uneasy.

And he didn't like the tinge of fear that crossed her face when confronted by the Witches of the Ward.

X

Last Breath

Stepping from the swirling darkness of his transportation spell into the moonlit apartment, Razan could see the sorcere pacing distractedly before the embers of a dying fire. She turned to regard him briefly, rearranging her features from ones of distress to her normal imperious reserve.

"Are you off again, then?" She asked dismissively; unwilling to betray how deeply she needed the comfort of his presence.

"Unless the Princess has other need of me," he responded lightly, idly spinning the bangles that hung loosely on his wrist.

Katarin felt suddenly winded. Though she knew she had comported herself with dignity and persuasion, the effort to do so left her breathless. Razan stayed silent, watching from the corner of hooded eyes for her next move.

"Witches of the Ward, indeed. As if they had any idea of the will of Atosa, or the shadow she casts," she murmured inconsequentially.

"Perhaps Atosa did no one any favors, living among us as she did," needled Razan with a smirk, thinking of the mages and their disdain for the ancient rites that surrounded a goddess who cared little for them. "If anyone chooses to interpret her visitations as anything more than those of an aloof, unattainable deity reminding the flock of her inexorable reign, they're fooling themselves."

Katarin shot him a withering look over her shoulder. "Surely the life of Razan would be simpler had I not been born," she sniped back at him.

He didn't answer her with words - not at first. In swift strides he closed the distance between them and kissed her, grabbing her face with a hand so practiced in the art of death, yet so soft in the act of love.

Every inch of defiance melted from her in an instant. He felt the insistence with which she met his caresses and broke from her, eyeing her questioningly, not bothering to keep the spark of desperation from burning in the depths of his eyes and the rasp of his breath.

"Would you rather I said no?" She murmured, eyebrow raised defiantly.

"I wouldn't let you," he growled, burying his face in her neck and his teeth into her collarbone.

She tried to stifle a moan, in an attempt to depress his cocksure attitude, but she just couldn't help herself. It felt so good. Her cries drove him crazy, and she felt him tighten against her, pressing harder, diving deeper with each measured stroke.

They lay tangled among silken sheets in a pool of moonlight, utterly spent, clinging to each other. She turned, and murmured something into his shoulder. He grabbed her chin - softly this time - and told her to repeat herself.

"So you didn't mean I shouldn't have been born," she grumbled, realizing how childish the words sounded even as she said them.

"I meant," he said, reaching to take her pale hand, "you are not beholden to your mother any more than they pretend to be. Your accomplishments and your destiny should be your own. Why follow in her footsteps when all you have to look forward to is lip service like theirs?"

"They are not just her footsteps, Razan. They are mine," she countered. "These paltry... these *mortal*," she spat the word with distaste and rose from the bed, donning a shimmering robe that did nothing to hide the alluring charms of her body, "achievements… what are they worth? What do these faiefolkr," she said, contemptuously sweeping a long arm out towards Meliamne and the realm beyond, "mean beyond death? They are nothing, and my goal," her amethyst eyes, piercing into his very soul, locked with his, "is everything."

He bit back a sigh of frustration. Always she reminded him of mortality, decrying its weaknesses while paying no heed to the freedom it promised. His history had ever been a mystery to everyone who knew him. Despite the passing decades, few had confidence enough to question why the inscrutable assassin never aged.

The raised flesh of the cut on his hand had nearly disappeared. Razan regarded it idly as he dressed, one of the many marks his family inflicted upon him. *She knows not what it is she demands*, he thought to himself. His putrid and daemoric ancestry cursed him with the very gift she so desperately sought. He lived eternally among the mortals of Faie, his blood outwitting the ravages of time.

Nothing but blade or banishment would grace him with the chance to meet Atosa's shepherds.

He turned his face back to the sorcere, and while he feared her fanaticism, he had to admit the scintillating light of power and ambition that emanated from her both humbled and aroused him.

"Who is it I'm seeking, Katarin?" He asked bluntly. Though he had his suspicions, he wanted to hear it from her.

She turned cold twilight eyes on him, that saw not the man before her but a destiny that lay hundreds of leagues away.

"My sister, Razan. My sister, appearing from who knows where, alongside the undead, and possessing the only artifact with the power to raise them," she whispered, words from another source spilling from her roseate lips. "That mirror can summon Atosa - that mirror can destroy her. I am the only one with the knowledge to wield it. The only one," she emphasized, her slim fingers curling into claws, "who deserves to possess it."

He swallowed hard, observing her narrowly. *So the game has changed.*

"My mother abandoned her flock once. It is my duty to be sure she does not do so again," she continued. "First the mirror comes, threatening to undo all I have accomplished. And now these... these Witches..." she seethed.

"I will find your mirror, Katarin, if I have to pry it

from your sister's undead fingers," he promised, disliking the expression that curdled the loveliness of her face. "But what harm does this strange cult pose? You saw Mirai, and how summarily she dealt with them–"

"They broke into our home, challenged my birthright," she hissed quietly, still not quite meeting his gaze. "They pose every danger, Razan, and their *seance*," she fair spit the word, as though the taste of it were bitterroot, tart and vile, "could unravel the very fabric of the pantheon. You know it, and yet you hesitate?"

A deathly silence pervaded the room, as cold as the shafts of moonlight filtering through the crystalline dome above.

"Do you want me to kill them, then?" the query was blunt and harsh.

"Of course." The reply was calm, innocent, and devoid of warmth.

"What else are you good for?"

—

Howls on the wind, no more than sound. Blood that drenched the soil; rich, futile. One by one the witches fell to whispering blades; hands clenched to throats sliced clean, lungs pumping air and mithril, drowning in flesh and the soft voices of spirits as they cleaved unto death.

Few ever tried to tame the heartless wasteland of Naijor. Tonight, it claimed victim after victim, the desiccated dust uncharacteristically drenched, not with water, but with lifeblood. As his followers fell one by one around him, the black-robed figure that had so hurled the challenge stood chanting desperately, clinging to the souls surrounding him that sought release, using every ounce of his spellcasting ability to reach his long-silent goddess. The darkness of despair descended; each star, as it winked out of existence, mocked him for his futile faith. Still he prayed, even as he felt the blade slide through his chest, as his own blood and bile surged to choke him and the very breath in his lungs expired.

"Atosa's… will," his final whisper, lost itself to the night.

The silent assassins had regrouped a short way off, wary of the stench of death. They stood silent, waiting for their leader to speak. Razan, with lips pursed, listlessly twisted a bangle around his wrist. Finally, he acknowledged his band, locking eyes with his dark, angular lieutenant Deirdra, her hands resting lightly across the pommels of two sheathed blades.

"All dead," she barked in response to his mute inquiry.

He looked over the few other blades ranged before him. Their tension in the wake of this massacre was palpable. Though the chaotic group had committed deeds far worse than punishing an unwarranted and illegal invasion of the most private and sacrosanct pavilion of Tirre Lunir, Razan always balanced them on the edge of neutrality. He understood that each trained killer had their own motivations, and their own morals.

With a sympathetic smile, he signaled to release them. Each pulled a black glass bead from pouches slung on their hips, and with a swift motion smashed them to the ground, vanishing into the darkness that burst forth. Each would find a reward beyond what he promised them, and such wealth would buy silence greater than fear or respect could do. Hopefully, it would also buy drink potent enough to wipe the less savory memories of this night from their minds, and he could use them again. Until then, he could only accomplish his next move alone.

Surrounding the massacre, the guileless ilmaurte stood still, gazing upon the bloodshed with unseeing eyes. They waited to feast upon the prospect of death, perfectly inanimate, as ordered by the enchantment compelling them.

A moonless sky, draped with clouds torn to pieces and flung across the heavens, drifted deliciously above him. The silence grew deafening. On this, the edge of the civilized realms, such loneliness and despair prevented even grass from growing. Life had no place here- the pitiful remains of the witches' corpses stood testament to that undeniable truth. Razan looked impassively over the scene, his own path marked out clearly. And he would walk it, one step after the other.

As though any mere durgirn woman, digging herself from the dirty mines, could control the withered spirits and animated corpses of the undead. The assassin buried his face in his hands briefly, hating that he would not only let Katarin stoop to such heinous acts, but perform them for her.

And with a single ominous chime of his bangles he too dropped a black bead and spirited away from the deathly scene.

The undead descended, and as they feasted, their

horde grew.

XI

The Edge Of The World

Up before dawn, for once McKenna wasn't the first to rise. Blinking the dew that had settled overnight from her eyes, she spotted the holvir leaning against one another before the ravages of campfire, toasting their hands and bits of fruit bread over the still-warm ashes. Ginni smiled at McKenna, then raised an eyebrow at the lump of sleep roll that contained Seth. McKenna rolled her eyes and scoffed.

"He was like this the first morning we woke together too. Though at least then he had the swallowing of a fair keg of mead to excuse him. Not sure what it is now," she said, with no attempt to lower her voice. A grumble was the only response offered from the bedroll.

McKenna laughed and unwrapped her hair from its protective silken wrap. She tousled fingers gingerly through her textured hair, as carefully braided as any duergi beard. The night's dew nearly soaked the wrap, but it kept her locks smooth and almost completely dry. Which was lucky, she thought with a pang, because there were no duergi around to help her re-braid them. She was on her own.

With a smirk, she shook the dewy material over the recumbent form still tucked firmly in the bedroll, causing him to groan again and retreat even further into its depths. Even Tjen and Ginni decided to join in the fun, sending small pebbles sailing from the direction of the fire. Finally, after a few minutes of pestering, the groggy Seth emerged from his cocoon to glare at them all.

"Did it occur to any of you," he hissed in annoyance, "That fighting off a horde of ilmaurte while invoking the protection of the god I forswore would be a bit of an exhausting effort?"

"Oh hush, it didn't seem to hold any of the rest of us back," taunted Ginni, stuffing some of the fruit bread into his hand as he plopped down beside her at the edge of the fire, rubbing his eyes and yawning. "We're all outcasts in some sense of the word. Just eat and be merry already."

The strange scattering of the pebbles caught McKenna's attention. She picked one up and flicked it directly at the bedroll, then watched in fascination as it simply soared past.

"Wha- how?? How did it do that? What happens if I-" she reached for the lacing on the side, then suddenly found herself slammed to the ground, breath knocked out of her as though a dragon's tail had whipped into her stomach.

"Yikes! What in the realms? Seth, did your bedroll just attack McKenna?" yelped Ginni.

No response but a muffled chuckle issued from the rogue. McKenna stood and dusted herself off, staring wide eyed from Ginni to Seth. "Did you see that? What just happened?"

Seth slowly shook his head and ran a hand through his tousled black hair. "Blessed bedroll. Gift from my god. Stole- ahem, *had*, a certificate, at some point…" he rifled in his pack, then pulled out a tightly furled scroll. "Ah, here it is."

This bedroll, lined with the still-shimmering shed scales of the Dragon God Bahamut is one of the most curious of the many blessed objects bestowed upon his followers. It is said that it was granted in a time of great need, when a young champion of the order cried out to the deity for but a little more time. While it can be neither stored, nor summoned, it is said that it still exists in the world to this day, protecting those who need it most from the wrath of their assailants.

Ginni snorted, then laughed outright. "Oh, 'a little more time'? I've heard that story. You mean to tell me this bedroll makes you invulnerable? Why would you ever get out of it?"

"To exact vengeance on those who throw rocks at me while I'm in it," he responded, with a meaningful look. Ginni had the grace to look abashed.

Once fast was broke and camp dismantled, the party headed further into the forest, aiming for the town that lay nestled in its heart. They passed no one on the main road- unnerving, but unsurprising given the circumstances of the night before. Finally, a curious clock tower and industriously smoking chimneys appeared abruptly on the horizon, heralding their approach to Ljotebroek; a frontier city known for being the last town at the edge of the world.

Life stirred into view around them. Asafolk moved in small, huddled groups or remained behind windowsills and doorways with eyes and emotions guarded. A small militia, queuing up after a long night of vigilance, appeared as they rounded a corner and found themselves in the town square. The villagers, though wary, made no move to drive the party away. Ginni stepped forward quickly, wrist exposed in the universal expression of goodwill and neutrality.

"We've just made it through your woods, good faiefolkr, and instead of being stuck in them again for the night we'd much prefer a bed within your borders. That something we could possibly make happen?" She queried to the nearest, a tall and strapping older man with peppered black and silver hair.

He paused to observe her narrowly for a moment, and McKenna tensed, unsure of his intentions. He did not lower his weapon.

"I suppose you could, if you tell us how it was you made it through that forest in one piece," he replied. The militia behind him stirred lightly; tired from their night of vigilance, but alert for any danger posed by these strangers. A few wrinkled their noses at the holvir, elbowing each other and sniggering, but while the reaction bewildered McKenna, she held her tongue.

"It wasn't as easy as it should have been, I'll say that much, good Sir… errr…" Ginni trailed off leadingly.

"Rowan. Just call me Rowan, of Ljotebroek," he finished gruffly.

"Ljotebroek? Why does that sound so familiar…" McKenna trailed off, staring again in awe at the marvelous clock tower standing sentinel in the center of the square.

Rowan gave the monk a quick once over. Some durgir rolled runes in bowls. Mckenna preferred to sink them into her skin. The corners of his eyes crinkled, a shadow of a smile on his gaunt face.

"Many have heard of our town at the edge of the world, though few of your kind tend to visit. Hail, duergi of Hammardin," he replied with a courtly bow.

"Hang on. You know she's a duergi?" questioned Seth quickly, his own eyes narrowed.

"We recognize our own," he replied lightly, turning away from Seth with a scowl at the holvir. "And who might you two be, then?"

"Well met, Rowan of Ljotebroek! I'm Ginni Willow," she said, she and Tjen twisting into the formal courtesy holvir often displayed toward more powerful asafolk. "And my partner Tjen; bards who are most willing to tell you the marvelous tale of our current possession of every limb in exchange for the hospitality of your fair town."

"Hospitality, you say. You may ask for it, but you're not like to get it here. Those two may pass," he said, with a nod at Seth and McKenna, "but we allow no holvir here. Either you leave, or we arrest you."

Before McKenna could react, Seth grabbed her shoulder, willing her to stay silent. She realized her intervention would only cause more problems, but the look on her face caused a flicker of unease in the aesir's, who had the decency to look abashed.

"I will let your companions speak for you. In the meantime, you will wait in the clock tower," he amended. Two armed guards suddenly flanked the holvir. Ginni sucked in a breath and simply marched forward, followed by Tjen.

"Don't - they know the risk, they will be unharmed, so long as we say nothing," hissed Seth in McKenna's ear. Her knuckles whitened as her hands curled into fists, and she felt a knot in the pit of her stomach warring with her impulse to take after the holvir, to yell at Rowan, to demand an explanation.

One breath, two. She exhaled and smiled tightly.

"I can only assume, from the looks of you, that you have a reason for such company. But I am not the one to tell that story to. Go to the Magis," Rowan said, and McKenna could see in the depths of his eyes an almost sorrowful expression. "You'll find 'em at the smithy. Start there, and I'll take care of the rest of your party. They will be treated fairly… until we have reason to treat them otherwise."

Rowan beckoned to a small urchin nearby, who darted up and grabbed at Kurya's bridle.

Seth made a distressed noise in the back of his throat (Kurya's noise was louder) but McKenna stepped between them.

"Fine. I'm sure this young lass will show us where to meet you," she smiled at the girl, who'd stepped back at the horse's whinny and was now eyeing the animal with misgiving and disgruntlement.

"Never met a steed with so few manners, for sure," was all she said in reply.

"Well, you know what they say, a horse is only as good as its rider," mused McKenna, hoping Seth would take a hint.

He didn't. "Horses don't need manners, faiefolkr need sense. Show me where to take him, I'll handle the lead."

Rowan looked askance at the fighter's tone, but said nothing further. Following the holvir, he disappeared into town, and the two remaining had nothing to do but follow their guide with Kurya and Clopalong in tow.

The girl kept a wary distance from the temperamental steed. Seth chirped under his breath to guide Kurya along and McKenna walked with her mule between them. The strangeness of everything frightened her more than she cared to admit, and almost without thinking she reached for Seth. She placed a hand gently on his shoulder and, surprisingly, felt all the tension suddenly leave it. He exhaled and gave her a rueful grin.

"I'm still not so used to having a companion on my travels. It appears, neither is my horse," he patted Kurya's flank and he swished his tail discreetly. McKenna stifled a laugh.

"Well, I never had an aesir companion before, so I guess we're even. Ye're nae so different from the durgir. We may no' share much, but we hide even less," she mused. "An' no' of me clan would watch as innocents get taken again' their will."

"It's strange to me when you talk like that, you know," he replied. She looked up at him perplexedly. "You speak as though you really think you're a duergi."

"But I am!" She replied. "Jes' because I'm taller doesna change the fact Pabble raised me from a babe, and Clan Hammardin is as durgirn as ye can get."

"But… didn't you have aesir parents?" he persisted.

She felt a strange twinge at that, the same she felt every time she looked upon an aesir. While she recognized their features as her own, there was a distinct otherness she felt that couldn't just be in relation to her upbringing in the mines. Asafolk were so deeply preoccupied with the present, with an awareness of their fleeting mortality to which McKenna just couldn't seem to relate. For her, life stretched on in waves of conquered goals and quests, and time was nothing but a construct she measured against those she walked among. Durgir, with their centuries-long lifespans, may have inspired that feeling, but even they had a narrow focus on their life's work she could never settle to. Her aspirations were as immortal as the glory of her pursuits. She cast a sidelong glance at her partner, who stared at her repentantly.

"It's not my place to pry. I just… recognize your need to find a place, and hoped that knowing your roots may help," he hesitated, and seemed to lose conviction even as he spoke.

She shrugged, not quite sure either of them were able to dive into this conversation. It was clear he had his own horrors, and the fact he had to leave the god he'd followed for so long shook him to the core. So far as McKenna could tell, Seth's resolve was his deepest and strongest trait- and the distinct lack of faith he had in his ability to guide himself threatened to undo him. But for all that, she found she was glad to have joined the disgraced paladin.

Having reached the stable and tied up Kurya and the patient Clop with enough feed to drown them both, they turned and walked in the direction pointed out by their youthful guide. McKenna dismissed her with a coin, and she made off without another word.

"Don't worry about Ginni and Tjen," he added. "It may sound bad to you, but they're definitely used to this by now. Holvir have a reputation- whether an earned one or not, I will not say. But they'll be safe here," he said, casting a glance at the curious architecture and intricate environment around them, "I'm sure of it."

Ljotebroek proved an industrious town indeed, though somber in its aspect. Streets paved with smooth stones ran in front of crystal-glazed shop windows, most boarded up, but some bright and inviting. Most faiefolkr in the streets chose not to linger long, entering buildings with purposeful and grim expressions and hustling out in small knots, as though fearful of travelling any distance alone. Dominating all the shops along the street appeared the smithy, shadowed only by the clock tower as the largest building in the district. And if appearances were any guide, the busiest.

"This may sound like a stupid question," McKenna turned, slightly embarrassed, toward Seth. "But me weapon's broke. Usually I jes' go ter the clan smithy an' they give me anything I need, but I'm assuming...?" She tossed the pouch of coin she'd gotten in exchange for the panther teeth nervously in her hand.

"Yes, you can barter anything for enough coin. A smithy's no different from a bar for that," Seth actually grinned reassuringly. "But if you need my help, I can negotiate for you. Focus on the holvir and I'll get your blade repaired."

"Negotiatin' ain't a thing I'm particularly good at," she admitted with a guilty laugh. "Never one to keep

things I don' want, like money, when others be havin'
a better use for it." She tucked the pouch back into the
pocket of her cloak with a sigh of relief, and together they
marched purposefully for the black metal building.

XII

Of Gods And Men

A facade of stone, latticed by strange black metal woven and twisted impressively over doorway and windows, housed a billowing fire and a team of sweating, bemuscled apprentices wielding all manner of hammer and anvil. Some patrons stood around on the open porch front of the large building, speaking in low tones and casting terse glances around them. Their stares followed McKenna and Seth, who continued purposefully through the entrance.

The blacksmith was the happiest person anyone had ever met. He laughed when he talked, and Yori was always talking. His forge rang out, with words, with bells, with clanging metal. Sometimes one would think he belonged in the past, the blacksmith- with his ancient iron anvil and his accordion bellows. He waded through his grim faced apprentices, clapping them on the back with a hearty greeting as deep as the sound of ringing mithril. Most just shook their heads and kept working, tucking cheeky grins back in place. A couple greeted him back with a jibe or a clasp of the hand.

As McKenna and Seth watched him progress through the shop, they were suddenly arrested by the appearance of a matronly woman who manifested almost out of thin air.

"You two seem lost. What brings you here?" she asked simply.

The blacksmith's wife spoke with the lightest hint of an accent. Which was strange, because no matter who you asked- unless you asked herself- the blacksmith's wife had always lived here. When anyone did ask her, she would look at them with that sad smile in her eyes and say she hadn't- with a lift of the eyebrows- *always*. But no one listened, because everyone remembered Michelle.

McKenna held back, unwilling to jeopardize Tjen and Ginni's safety with any ill-timed words. Clearing his throat, Seth approached the woman. "A magistrate commissioned my partner here to get rid of some ilmaurte we're told have been plaguing the life from this town. We came to report our findings," his steely gaze matched the woman's own, "and collect our bounty."

Before McKenna could remonstrate for not mentioning their friends, a boisterous voice appeared over the woman's shoulder. "Bounty! Now that word we be using little here. Who'd you say sent you?"

Yori had made his way toward their little gathering, interested in the newcomers- a rare occurrence in these dangerous times. He slung an arm around the broad shoulders of his wife, who rolled her eyes and smiled at her nosy husband.

"Magistrate. I'm assuming Lord Timmett, since he's the only one of them who went with the last party. Unlikely to return, just like the rest," Michelle said, addressing Seth while wrinkling her nose, "so your bounty is back where you picked up the quest, I'm afraid."

Before the surly rogue could respond, McKenna hastily intervened. "I assure you, we fought them as much in self-defense as we did in response to the quest. We could hardly expect compensation for protecting our own selves, now could we, Seth?" she said, glaring at him. If this was his idea of negotiation, maybe she didn't need his help after all. Ignoring her tone and flashing a warning look at her, he intervened once again before the woman could respond.

"Such a town as this would be worth preserving anyways. I guess we were lucky we managed to save both," he said in a neutral tone, "along with the help of two holvir, who are now in custody of your guardsman, Rowan."

"You mean to tell me Rowan sent you here?" Michelle replied, arms still crossed over her chest. "To ask us what he should do with some holvir?"

"Yes. He told us to find the Magis, and that they would, err, decide on the fate of our *friends*."

Some of the angry tension crackling at the ends of McKenna's wiry coils dissipated at the word, and she began to trust Seth's judgement a little better. The woman's keen gaze passed over her, and her eyes narrowed.

"Yori. What have you to say of these two... and their, friends," she remarked quietly, rolling the word on her tongue with distaste.

The blacksmith had been quiet up to this point, eyeing the monk inscrutably and completely ignoring the banter between his wife and Seth.

"Who be you, then, lass?" He said, not unkindly.

"Err, I'm McKenna, of Clan Hammardin," she stammered.

"Hammardin! Why, you're tall for a duergi, no? Have you swung the hammer, then?" He asked, with a squint at her sizable muscles.

"No sir. A simple monk," she replied, surprised by his knowledge of durgirn cant. Swinging the hammer was an initiation for the smithy's apprenticeship, a highly coveted honor and sign of strength among durgir. "On a beard quest, along which I found my partner here."

Seth stepped forward with a small nod towards the pair. He cast a hooded glance at McKenna, then drew in a breath. "A quest which led us to your gates, where swarmed a horde of ilmaurte. And as much faith as I'm sure you have in your garrison, they'd be nothing but pools of blood come morning had we not been there. With our friends," he insisted again, "who apparently need your blessing to continue through town."

Michelle made no reply, and Yori just laughed. "Aye, lad, save your formality then. We turn away none of our own, and if the lass speaks for them holvir, I suppose they'll cause no trouble. Go on then, Michelle, go find Rowan and tell 'em the holvir mean no harm."

She shot him an acid look, but didn't argue, and swept past the monk and the rogue without a word.

"Aye, forgive my wife, then. She puts up with worse from ol' Yori," he said, with a grin, "and she's none too fond o' the little folk. What brings you here, then, child of the Secret-Keeper?"

"Well, other than getting our friends free…" she

trailed off, with an uneasy look at Seth. Instead of crossed arms, he leaned against the railing that separated the heated kilns from the raised raise at the entry of the lobby, and favored her with an encouraging smile. "I… err… broke me weapon. Was wonderin' if ye might be able ter help with that."

She carefully unclasped her guisarme from around her chest and removed the wrapping from the blade. At the glint of mithril, the smith gasped aloud. "It's my blade. I got some… err… a mark on it, that won't come off. I don't want it ter dull, but I haven't the tools to whet it. Just the coin to pay to have it done," she said, reaching for the dwindling substance tucked into her cloak. Before she could pull it out though, Yori stopped her with a hand on her elbow.

"There's no coin could put a price on the workmanship of Malfaestan mithril," he murmured. His eyes had widened to the size of coins. A few of the apprentices around them had caught sight of the precious metal too. One, a woman shrouded in a black apron with her mane of grizzled white hair bundled haphazardly on top of her head, gaped openly, her toned arms suspended above her head mid-swing.

An unsightly rust-coloured streak still marred the smooth surface of the guisarme. She offered it to the blacksmith, who took it reverently. He drew a thumb along the flat of the blade, his rough and hardened fingerprint finding no purchase along the slick and level metal. He handed it over to the woman, who took it with an awed look and began to inspect it herself. "Mithril doesn't stain. What made this mark? It looks like…" he began.

"Blood. Err, my blood, to be exact," finished

McKenna, peering at her inquiringly.

"Berta's the expert when it comes to Malfaestaen metal," added Yori, with a deferential nod toward the apprentice, who blushed at his praise.

"Mithril absorbs the properties of all it encounters. It can't be damaged or cursed, the metal simply takes hold of anything inflicted and either assumes it or dispels it. Blood would normally face the latter fate. Your blood must have some kind of… of magical property that the mithril recognized as more powerful than its own, and assumed it," explained Berta, as she continued to inspect the weapon.

"I may have… accidentally shot her with a crossbow. The blood coated a quarrel and the next ilmaurt it hit dispelled instantly," replied Seth. "After she saw that, she improvised."

Yori laughed. "You shot her with a crossbow? Aren't you partners? Why would you go and do a thing like that?"

Elbowing Seth in the arm, McKenna laughed too. "Well, it's lucky he did anyway. We were barely holding our own, there were so many. But after I rubbed some of my blood onto the guisarme, they went down like chaff."

"You shot her with a crossbow and in return she saved your life. I'm thinkin' ye're to owin' this monk more than you know," chuckled Yori. "Berta's right. This mithril now possesses whatever magic you have in your blood, so even once we restore it to its natural shine and sharpness, it should have the same effect. Uncanny. And here we thought you lot were simply lucky to have made it through those woods alive."

Seth raised an eyebrow, then looked down at his own saber. McKenna caught his gaze. "Don't you even think about it!" she gasped in mock outrage.

Missing nothing, Yori turned a shrewd look on the rogue. "You saying your blade is made of mithril too? And yet the pair of you come to shake down a poor town for its meager lyra? For shame, for shame!" he cried jestingly.

"The bounty is forfeit, we promise," Seth bowed, extending his wrist in a gesture of peace. "Now, where might we find our companions, and take lodgings for the night?"

Michelle reappeared at the entrance. Her mouth was still set in a taut, grim line, but she eyed the two with a frank and unstudied appreciation.

"I'll take you. Easier to walk through town as strangers with me by your side," Michelle replied. She kissed Yori, who had joined the older apprentice in examining McKenna's guisarme, on the cheek. Then, dusting her hands on her voluminous skirt, she led them from the building onto the high street.

A martial sense of alert readiness pervaded the whole town, with few people standing idle on the streets and almost all the shops closed. The scourge of undead clearly had an impact on Ljotebroek. But its remaining citizens appeared either foolhardy enough to face it or resigned enough to their fate.

McKenna matched her stride to that of their guide. "What keeps the rest of you here? It sounds as though many have already fled," she inquired of Michelle.

"Sheer stubbornness, for the most of us," bluntly replied the stalwart aesir.

Her gait marched with purpose. McKenna sensed no fear from her, and she could easily imagine her capable of her own quests and adventures if given the chance.

"This is your home, isn't it? If you felt you could protect it, leaving would be too much to bear, I suppose," offered Seth from the rear.

Michelle grinned. "Caught me," she admitted. "Those that stayed behind, they're the original settlers. We built this place with our hands. Stands to reason we can defend it with them, too."

The words were simple enough, but McKenna was shrewd enough to read between them. A town like this built in a single generation stood as no simple feat. The blacksmith's shop, though a wondrous work of art on its own, wasn't the only prestigious and architectural marvel boasted by this town on the outskirts of the realms. The clock tower, towards which they progressed, stood out as another impressive feature. Storied buildings of brick and stone surrounded it, all woven with the same curious metallic latticework.

"Explains why you wouldn't be quick to honor stranger's words of bounty. I'm assuming the magistrates who fled aren't particular favorites?" he pressed on.

The woman laughed outright at that, her lined features brightening perceptibly. McKenna could see the martial spirit flash forth and yearned to know more about this particular aesir's history. Though she was unsure of a polite way to go about and ask, and was still slightly distrustful of the way they treated the bards.

"No. Lord Timmet Smith is a flighty coward. He always has been. The nobles who left first were the ones with debts, the rest their squeamish followers. We've no time for folk like those," she spat.

Seth chuckled. "Aye, you wouldn't. I know their kind. Evangelizers, preying on the citizens of Faie almost as virulently as the horde. Between the two, I'd rather the ilmaurte myself."

McKenna twisted her face in confusion, but before she could make sense of the ideas dawning on her they had arrived. The clock tower stood over a large wooden building, carved with runes familiar to the monk.

Rowan stood outside, and with a curt nod Michelle departed, leaving them to the guardsman's care.

"Come. Your friends are inside. Should you wish to stay, you're welcome here," he said, fitting a key to the metal door of the clock tower.

"Err, as guests, or...?" McKenna queried, eyeing the metal bars with misgiving.

"Yes, as guests. You have to understand this - Ljotebroek is on the highest alert right now. If it's true you made it through an ilmaurte horde, then you'll quickly figure out why. It is as much for your safety as it is for ours that you stay here," and McKenna, though full of the tension of their unexpected encounter, could still sense the integrity and the honesty with which the man spoke. She said nothing in return but simply nodded her head and, in an imitation of the gestures she'd seen before, exposed her wrist to Rowan. He smiled, genuinely, and closed and locked the door behind them.

XIII

People Are People

"Well. That could've gone worse," breathed Seth, for once the first to speak.

"Ye're telling me. Now where be our friends?"

The interior of the clocktower displayed the most curious design for a building McKenna had ever seen. A spell of silence had been cast upon each and every moving component, rendering the space that should be full of a normally unendurable cacophony silent as a tomb. Every artistic stroke of metal, wood, and stone had a place in the vast mechanical infrastructure, a modern marvel of ingenuity and magic.

"Not magic," Seth said suddenly. McKenna gave him a confused look- had she spoken out loud?

"How did you do that?" Incredulity tinged her laugh as she raised an inquiring eyebrow at him.

"Do what?" he responded innocently.

"Read my mind!"

"I'm not reading your mind, I'm reading your face. It speaks louder than words sometimes, did you know that, monk," he explained. "You're easier to read than a book."

She pursed her lips, forced to accept his explanation,

and turned away, deeply investigating the curious contraptions and vaguely familiar markings and construction of the metal.

Suddenly a voice rang out, unhampered by the spells of silence cast on everything else.

"Not magic, huh, Seth?"

"Ginni!" cried McKenna, kneeling down and sweeping the holvi into a fierce hug.

"Woah! Woah. What is this, what… wow. Okay," dithered Ginni, pressing her own arms lightly around the woman's shoulders. "You alright there?"

"I was worried about you! Is that… is that weird?" McKenna said somewhat defensively, releasing Ginni from their embrace.

"No! No. Not weird at all. Definitely not weird. Yeah being arrested was uh… was for sure the weird part in all this. Uh, right Tjen?"

Tjen sidled up to McKenna, and she reached out to guide the holvi to her side. "What Ginni means to say is she's not used to anyone worrying about her, because worrying about her is pointless. She does what she wants whenever she wants to regardless of any consequences."

"HEY! That's only… mostly… true…"

"And of all the jails we've been in before," Tjen shrugged, ignoring Ginni's stammered protests, "this one is for sure the nicest. But thanks for the rescue."

Sitting back on her heels, McKenna could only nod.

There was so much about these realms she was only beginning to understand, and she realized there were some things that may never become clear to her.

"As long as you're okay. I'm sorry for getting you into this," she said, with a sincerity that shocked the holvir yet again, "and I promise to get you out of it. Now," she sprang back to her feet and returned to studying the intricate clockwork and its curious spells, "what did you mean about this not being magic, Seth?"

"Divine power takes many different forms," he replied evasively.

"Divine… listen to yourself. It's *science*," Ginni groaned exasperatedly, disappointed in his answer. "Technology developed beyond the reach and the skill of the pantheon. Mechanical wonders like this are invented every day, by holvir, by asafolk, by mortals - not gods."

"And it's comments like THAT, Ginni," muttered Tjen, "that get us thrown into jail."

Ginni rolled her eyes. "Asafolk can be so stubborn sometimes. We're in a modern age. Magic does nothing but segregate us- force us to one god or the next in the struggle to outdo each other. It's just ridiculous."

"It's our way, Ginni," admonished Seth. "Stronger souls than yours have perished for what you're saying."

Her little nostrils flared in frustration, but she held her tongue. They followed McKenna into an open foyer, surrounded by alcoves and room after room. The furniture ranged haphazardly from rows of wooden pews to luxurious brocade couches. The whole space appeared to be some kind of common area used by the townsfolk for gatherings- lecture, convention, or even celebration. McKenna was surprised that they'd been left entirely to themselves in this empty space. Until she remembered Michelle's words about the fleeing populace. *They must not have much time or motivation to gather anymore*, she mused to herself.

As they entered a room filled with bunks, a curiously familiar wall of books met her eye. All were religious texts, but with bindings marked in runes she knew better than any other.

"Malfaestus! These asafolk worship the durgirn god?" cried McKenna in excitement.

"From the workmanship of the metal, you couldn't tell?" scoffed Seth jovially. Ginni snorted loudly and threw up her hands.

McKenna turned a renewed gaze at the wonders around her. Sure, durgir mined ore, but they used it for tangible goods to trade and barter. Occasionally a duergi would create a work of art- a statue or a mechanical trinket- but durgir treated metal as a tool. Uncut gems and chiseled stonework more commonly adorned the halls of Mount Oer than filigree and architecture. The frugal people deemed it a waste to use metal on anything not weapon, tool, or armor. She peered at the runes inscribed in the mechanics of the clock tower, trying to decipher their purpose. Suddenly, Yori's question about wielding the hammer took on a new meaning.

"It's like they worshipped Malfaestus and then… stopped. Like they found a better god, or tool, or whatever. I can't really understand it. This whole place," she said, sweeping her arms wide, "they built it to honor the god. But that is no longer its purpose. These runes haven't attuned to Malfaestus in years."

"Not to distress your orthodox soul, but they probably found truths deeper than the ones the pantheon provided," explained Tjen. "Their blacksmith and their farms and their education- it's all based in the understanding of physical and mechanical powers controlled by mortal, and not by god."

Seth grunted in contradiction. "Some may have pursued that. But our talk with- what did Rowan call them? The Magis? makes me think otherwise. They followed Malfaestus until other religions came to crowd them out."

Tjen bit their lip and raised an eyebrow at the mechanical wonders around them. Seth laughed.

"Okay, perhaps a bit of both. I speak from experience though, you know, and not just bias. Guilds can be… invasive," he sighed bitterly.

"Think of how much nicer this place would be if they'd been left alone," mourned Ginni.

McKenna shook her head in disbelief. "So… if they aren't ruled by guilds, or by gods, why did they treat you like that? Why put you in jail, when you didn't do anything wrong?"

Ginni looked at Tjen and shrugged. "Same reason you got mad at Seth for. Asafolk just don't like holvir. They think we're a bother mostly, homeless vagrants who do nothing but sing and paint and play all day."

"That doesn't seem fair," McKenna huffed, but the bard just shrugged and sat down on one of the poufs.

McKenna joined her, stretching her long legs out across the floor. *And I thought the durgir's trouble with Illusen was bad. How in the world could an entire people be judged by their ethnicity?*

Normally when faced with an incomprehensible problem, she consulted Malfaestus. Digging around in the pockets of her cloak for a little hammer talisman she whittled, she instead pulled free the mirror.

"Where'd you get that?" asked Seth, kneeling down next to her.

She studied it for a moment, unsure of where to begin. "I've… always had it, I think. I lost it years and years ago, but in the early days of my quest it suddenly… reappeared."

"Those runes…" he trailed off, eyebrows knitted in sudden consternation. "I feel like I've seen those before. May I?"

As she was handing over the mirror, a knock sounded at the door. "Sorry to interrupt, but word came from the blacksmith's shop. You seem to have a weapon ready?"

Rowan's voice echoed through the building, and they soon saw him follow it to the doorway of their room. "I recommend going after it sooner rather than later. We have to keep a curfew, so everything but the tavern shuts down before nightfall." He turned toward the bards. "Speaking of tavern, our last musicians lit out a couple weeks back, and we've been sore lacking in the song department since then. Sure you'd pick up a bit of coin, if you come with me," he offered with a sympathetic grin.

Ginni could tell he was trying to extend a sort of

peace offering for his earlier actions. Though he acted a little uncomfortable around the holvir, he seemed more keen to make them welcome than she'd expected.

I guess wiping out a deadly horde of undead is one way to earn a welcome, she thought to herself, studying him as she and Tjen stood to join him. The lines on the man's face were deeper than nature would warrant. *He's not a warrior by choice it seems. None of them are.*

"You've got us for the night, then," she flashed her crooked grin at the militia master, then turned and waggled her fingers in farewell to the others. "You kids don't go killing any more ilmaurte without us."

McKenna felt slightly nervous letting them go again, especially after their earlier experience. She looked a mute inquiry at Seth, who knitted his brows but shrugged.

"We did just meet them after all. They seem capable enough to make it around on their own. It's you, novice, that I'm more worried about," he chuckled jocularly. Sticking her tongue out at him, McKenna wrapped up the mirror and stood, taking another cursory glance at the runes lining the walls before heading back out into the twilight streets.

XIV

Fade Into Darkness

As they walked up the high street, the sun's dying light reflected off the crystal windows and puddles in the road, illuminating each and suffusing the air with a faint golden glow. McKenna loved seeing the many faces the world wore outside of her cavernous home. The contrivances and architecture of hardy asafolk impressed her with a sense of awe and respect, and she was amazed to see the ways in which the different races performed the same tasks, living in the same realm and yet in such a different world.

Of their personalities she could not say much. Most wore forbidding expressions thinly masking fear, others a resigned hardiness not unlike that of durgir. She hoped asafolk weren't always like this- that it was simply the grim specter of the undead horde holding the natural joy and optimism of the quixotic race hostage.

"You seem pretty grim yourself, though," she meditated aloud, elbowing the taciturn Seth as he walked in silence beside her.

"What? What's that even supposed to mean?" he cried, shaken out of his reverie.

"I'm just musing on what kind of beings you asafolk are. Everyone we've met so far seems so… severe. It's unnerving, is what," she replied, eyeing him keenly.

"We're not all born of the same mother, McKenna. Everyone has their own approach to danger and fear," Seth had an edge to his voice that surprised the monk. Was she being insensitive?

"Sure'n I know everyone's got their differences. That's not what I really meant. It takes all kinds to make a world now, doesn't it?" Her face lit up in a calm devotion as she spoke. The comment seemed to disarm him, and her simple, candid appreciation of this new world around her gave her far more license than he would normally give anyone else. He simply shrugged and smiled in response.

"You're really something else, you know that?" He smiled begrudgingly, his eyes on her peaceful face.

"There's something in everyone, I think," she replied. "There's something in you, though ye hide it to the best of your ability."

He blushed, then sighed. She didn't let him slip into a reverie, and instead, slipped her arm under his.

"Dunno how long it is you've walked this path o' your own, rogue," she said, squeezing him. "But I'm here, if it helps. Sometimes an audience is all it takes."

He stared off into the horizon, but McKenna could tell he wasn't being silent intentionally, just searching for the right words. "It hasn't been long. But it's been long enough to learn the consequences of..." he swallowed, suddenly deadly serious.

Their gold draped palls. The low, winding horns.

She waited as he trailed off, twisting his middle and

index finger as though spinning a ring that no longer sat there. A master Paladin, abandoning the most powerful guild in all the realms. A sudden realization struck her.

"Ye weren't the only master ter quit, were ye?" Her voice, full of concern, roused him.

One by one they depart for noble quests.

One by one do they return, at noble rest.

He winced, his normally smooth, severe features twisted in unfathomable agony.

"I can't explain it. Not yet." He breathed heavily. He looked at her, noting that she still kept a firm grip upon his arm. Her amber eyes were inscrutable.

"There are many things I could say to you right now, I'm sure," she took a measured breath, choosing her words carefully. "But none of them are really what you need to hear. I'm listening, Seth, I see you. I believe you. And your god, I promise," she spoke urgently, remembering a golden glow surrounding the man amidst a crawling mass of ilmaurte, "I promise he sees you too. The gods know of our strife, and will help us face it. Come what may."

There was a measure of empathy and deep, unequivocal kindness that radiated from her like a dweomer. He began to understand the strength of her conviction, her absolutely surety in herself and the identity that adorned her. The ever-present tension within him began to slowly unravel in her presence, under the influence of her calm touch.

"I'll find the words for it, I'm sure. I'm... out of

practice." She was relieved to see that haunted look had faded, and smiled reassuringly. "Never been much of a conversationalist, even in the best of times. And these have definitely not been the best of times."

"Ye'll get plenty o' practice with me. I never shut up," she said with a laugh.

The impressive smithy rose up before them. The patio outside had mostly cleared of lingerers, testament to the setting sun and Rowan's warning. McKenna hallooed from the yawning portal before them, and the wizened older woman who had taken her guisarme waved them over to the anvil.

"Yori left me to you- Berta, at your service," she greeted, extending a gnarled hand with a grip of adamantine. "It's a beauty, to be sure," she said, uncovering the polearm. "Ol' Yori worked his bit of magic, sure as the sun shines. He decided to give it a little… something extra."

Both McKenna and Seth gasped in surprise. What had once been a fine mithril blade fixed atop a crude wooden shaft now stood transformed into a flawlessly balanced guisarme, the long pole cast from the same curious black metal that lined the buildings of the town. She ran her fingers along the coarse, grippy material, feeling the grooves of runes and scrollwork filigree worked into its length in imitation of her old staff. The runes had been artfully engraved by a skilled hand- one who knew the depths of Malfaestus's lore as keenly as any duergi. McKenna lifted it in reverence and each one flashed in recognition of the spellwork she maintained upon herself.

"It… it's perfect," she breathed, as some of the more complex and curious dweomers awoke in response to her reverent touch. She could almost feel the pull of the metal, as if it were a living, breathing being and not just a lifeless tool. A faint streak still dulled the perfect shine of the smooth mithril blade, reflecting the glowing red light of the forge.

"Boss got upset when the stain wouldn't rub out. Took it personal, that he did, on his skill," Berta cackled. "When he couldn't fix it he thought he'd disguise it, see? Put up a bit extra an' hope you wouldn't notice."

"I truly wouldn't have if you didn't point it out," McKenna replied, still reverently inspecting the fine weapon.

Berta laughed at that. "Of course you wouldn've. That's why I told you. He thinks he can get away with anything. Now, a wonder like this needs a name, my girl," she leaned in towards the monk encouragingly.

"*Laghrusse*," McKenna replied, stroking a symbol engraved close to the handle. A powerful bindrune, combining the natural strength and courage of the warrior with the intuition and compassion of the individual. A blade swung in righteousness is a blade that does no harm.

Berta nodded with a smile, the awe and joy in the monk's face the truest form of repayment any craftsman could receive. While she could sit and talk all night about the weapon's design and different functionalities, the boss and his wife had already gone to the tavern- and she thought perhaps the two of them should head off? It wasn't far, only around the corner. They couldn't miss it. McKenna thanked the apprentice profusely and, slinging the polearm over her back, followed Seth back out into the town.

Basins of pitch began to light in the distance, a glow carrying through the dim fog slinking across the quiet prairie. Not a leaf rustled on the trees. And in the village an eerie silence weighed heavily, broken suddenly by the dolorous din of the clock tower's chiming bell.

McKenna turned to Seth in surprise and confusion, and even he couldn't keep the rising fear from his face.

"They're back? But... how?"

Seth couldn't answer her.

"The militia. They've lit the beacons. That's not good." Michelle's voice rasped in warning. By this time they were joined by the Magis and Rowan, peering into the gloom at the sinister flicker of fire burning along the horizon.

"It's good they lived long enough to light them," replied Seth as he stood, tightening the belt holding his sabre to his hips.

The holvir had descended from the bar, Ginni approaching to cast a questioning gaze at McKenna. "I knew we got off too easily. I'm beginning to think maybe I should listen to my own songs and not join heroes on quests. Trouble always follows you guys."

"This isn't your fight, adventurers," Rowan began, but Ginni scoffed with a roll of her beguiling hazel eyes.

"Not our fight, but we'll fight it anyways." Tjen's words were accompanied by a complicated riff on the naiti, and the fog began to clear around them, offering a clearer view of the horde approaching. "None of us are like to hide in a barn as it burns down around us."

Another quick strum of the instrument and a cheerful warble from Ginni's throat, and weapons that lay heavy in tired yeomen's hands suddenly felt lighter, their steps surer, their eyes brighter. They could fight for one more night.

The militia master looked as though he meant to argue, but suddenly swallowed. Though distracted by the oaths she was whispering to her god under her breath, McKenna noticed a distinct expression of respect cross Rowan's face. Respect, and perhaps a measure of shame.

Good. About time they saw the holvir for who they really are.

Seth, whistling sharply, grasped the halter of his galloping steed as Kurya swept by him. Taking only a moment to call down an oath from her own god, McKenna followed behind, the Magis and Rowan in tow.

Quiet and calm stood the city streets. All doors barred, hiding townsfolk who resignedly doubted seeing the light of another day. A dull glow continued to bloom in the west. Fallow fields allowed an unbroken view of militia, armed with whatever they could carry, braced against a slowly advancing horde of undead.

"But the fire. Where's the fire coming from?" McKenna murmured, her question unheard and unanswered as the holvir wound up the power of their song.

Quicker than light, McKenna's runes fired in a spirited pattern, rendering her step light and quick and her skin hard as mithril. The metal pole of Laghrusse hummed in her grip, and she realized the finely tooled magics of the magnificent weapon were harmonizing perfectly with her own- a testament again to Yori and Berta's attunement to Malfaestus. She peered into the distance, seeing a golden figure flit to the front lines, the blur of the horse solidifying into a shimmering and impervious aura protecting the foot soldiers.

Their screams still carried to her ears, senses heightened by magic that felt the claw of deathly fingers into mortal flesh.

As she reached the line of undead, she quickly found herself surrounded on one side by a sickly wall of smoke and ash, on the other the pale and swollen faces of undead monsters.

"Time to put yer work to the test, Yori!" She cried as she braced against the muddy ground, slinging oaths and her bloodstained blade into the path of the ilmaurte. They advanced with more precision than the horde she'd faced in the forest. Some even bore weapons, weapons their senseless arms and sightless eyes knew how to use. And while they could sustain blow after blow from pike and axe, or battering shield studded with spikes, the yeomen who faced them were mortal and could not. The blaze, too, grew hotter, filling their lungs and eyes with smoke and ash.

Suddenly a loud, sucking sound rent the sky. The fire, swirling in a vortex that burned the air, had grown to a massive pillar. At its heart, an imp directed sparks and streams of the blaze to light anything it could reach around the monk.

McKenna felt her blood run cold. A daemor from the Abyss- its seething, hateful aura billowing forth like the smoke through the battlefield. A daemor, here, leading an army of ilmaurte.

She realized the daemor must be animating the ilmaurte, granting the reanimated corpses the unnatural affinity for battle they once possessed in life. The groans of dying soldiers rang in her ears, drowning out even the holvir's rousing song of battle, Kurya's pounding hooves as Seth swept through the ranks of ilmaurte, Rowan and Yori's barked commands as they tried to fruitlessly martial their defenses against the oncoming scourge. She could hear nothing but the sounds of dying. Helpless souls crying out, beating in vain against doors closed against them, severed from their hold on life and unable to find the sweet release of Death.

Sensing her distraction, the imp changed course. The swaths of tattered corpses, the animating spell upon them that unnaturally married departed soul to decaying body broken, alerted it to her power. It shrieked with fiendish ferocity and turned its swirling vortex of fire to bear her down.

Or would have, if a bolt of lightning hadn't gotten in the way.

Her ears ringing, McKenna spun in place, searching for the source of the godly power. Behind her, wielding a short, perfectly symmetrical blade, stood Michelle, her face bright with fury. A tattoo on her neck stood out in silver relief and the gentle waves of her almond hair crackled with energy.

Silver scales. A Master of Sanct Germain...?

"Monk! To me!" She shouted, and McKenna responded instantly to the martial command that rang in her tone. Flanking the warrior's left side, the two women quickly dispatched the remains of the imp, a lurid cloud of purple and black smoke enveloping the creature as its essence returned to the Abyss. With a grim look at McKenna, Michelle began to advance towards the line of ilmaurte still pushing against Seth's magical barrier.

However, they didn't stand a chance against the combined might of the magic of the gods.

Another hush, as loud as the silence before the battle, descended. All that remained were the scattered remains of both undead and aesir casualty, and a dense silvery haze. Untethered souls, hanging mournfully over the battlefield. Ginni's battle song, subdued into a quiet dirge, gathered the spirits as they clung desperately to the shred of Material magic her voice offered them.

"What now, monk of Malfaestus? Can you disperse of them?" Yori's voice for once lacked its normal boom. He breathed heavily, clutching his side with one hand and a hammer in the other, while watching the undulating spirits with a fearful expression.

"I... We did once, but..." For reasons McKenna couldn't quite explain, she was almost certain these souls were the same ones animating the ilmaurte that attacked them before. She shot Seth a nervous glance, and he slid off his horse to stand beside her.

"You know what they are, McKenna," he murmured in her ear.

"I don't know how. But I do," she replied back, frightened at the silver light of the untethered souls reflecting in his golden eyes.

"Then send them home."

It wasn't a command. She could hear the urgency, and the reminder that her identity was her own. No matter what unknown magics she controlled, or unknown destiny shrouded her future in mystery, she knew what she could do today.

She took a deep breath and stepped toward the pulsing mist. Though she could not see it, a purple aura shone around her entire body. Those alive on the battlefield stepped back almost involuntarily, feeling a draw their spirits couldn't ignore. The feeling that this woman's soul called to their own, promising them release, promising them freedom.

The siren song of eternal death.

But the untethered souls had no mortal body to hold them back. En masse, they slowly gravitated towards her, and she lifted her arms to greet them. She could almost feel it - fingers clinging to her own, sighs and soft thoughts of spirits who, though always longing for one more day among the glories and beauties of their world, knew they must return to the eternity to which they belonged. Without realizing what she was doing, she pulled the mirror from her side, holding it aloft toward them. Chanting issued from her lips, words she didn't recognize, a prayer to a goddess she barely knew, and one by one the souls faded from sight.

Then, of course, McKenna blacked out.

XV

The Old Town Road

"They were guided by an imp. Imps may be strong, but they haven't the power to summon the dead- let alone direct them in battle."

She awoke to the sound of Seth's voice closer than she expected it. Groaning and forcing her eyes open, his face swam into view, hovering just over hers on a long bench at the tavern's shared table.

"Uhm. Why am I in your lap?" She asked groggily.

The occupants of the table shifted uncomfortably. It was Michelle who finally answered. "None of us could... none would get close enough to carry you. Only Seth."

"That clears it up, love," interrupted Yori. He had his arms crossed tightly across his chest, but leaned toward them and winced slightly. Groggy as she was, McKenna could almost understand why. She felt again that draw of spirit plucking at her own, and impulsively shifted away from him. He leaned back toward Michelle, breathing a sigh of unmistakeable relief. "Dunno what it is about you, my girl, but you reek of death."

"So..." her head was swimming. She shut her eyes and took a steadying breath, then opened them again. "So how come I don't affect you?"

Seth shrugged. "Maybe I don't have a soul worth

stealing."

"You don't affect us either," piped up Ginni. "We don't have souls. But we're also extremely small, so carrying you was not an option. Sorry about that!"

Tjen snorted audibly, catching McKenna's huff with a shrug.

"You have a soul," she murmured weakly, looking up at Seth. She could feel it, too - now she knew what they felt like. But she knew, just as instinctually, that his soul was absolutely untouchable. Shaking her head, she slowly sat up, clutching the table for balance as the room spun around her.

"Okay. Well. I'm... I know that worked. Those ilmaurte..." she narrowed her eyes, as a swirling image - a great door of light, carved into a wall of stone deep underground, flashed before her eyes. "They're gone. From... here, at least."

"We owe you a debt, duergi." Michelle spoke solemnly, holding a fist over the center of her chest. "All of you. Our town would be yet another blot on the horizon, a forgotten relic of cinders and ash. Thank you."

McKenna studied her closely. The silver tattoo that still stood out in relief on her neck, under a lock of almond hair. "Ye look like ye have beautiful ghosts," she said simply.

Startled out of her composure, Michelle leaned forward. "What do you mean?"

"Ye know, tales. Stories worth telling, like ye were surrounded by folk of pride and strength who used ter call ye sister. Memories can be more hauntin' than spirits, as we say in the mines."

That broke her solemnity. She studied McKenna for a moment, then turned her gaze to Seth. Suddenly, McKenna noticed the parallels between the way the two held themselves, the reserve of their expressions, and she hazarded a guess. "Ye were a guild master, too, then?"

A silent acknowledgement seemed to pass from one to the other, and Michelle took a deep breath while still observing the disgraced paladin. "Not for a long, long time." She tucked the lock of hair behind her ear, exposing the tattoo emblazoned on her neck- the scales of Sanct Germain, balancing an eye and a hand. "But you're right. I was a cleric. Bit of a family thing, really. My sisters were all paladins, masters within the Guild of Golden Eye."

Yori gripped her shoulder. "The lass grew lost in a religious melancholy. She found her way here, just as baffled as you at the hardy asafolk building a town in honor of Malfaestus."

"But I lost all my powers," she interjected with a slow smile. "Sanct Germain... and his followers... have no use for tetherless moral quandaries, so they cut me loose."

McKenna cast a furtive look at Seth, who studied the woman silently. Again with the abandoning one's class. She wasn't surprised the god revoked the woman's powers. Clerics performed miracles in the name of their god, able to heal and influence all life within the realms of Faie. A powerful enough cleric could turn the tides of death. It almost made her uncomfortable on his behalf, but she realized anew how firmly and how devoutly he walked within the light of his chosen god.

*He says he abandoned his faith. He better tell his faith that,
then,* she thought with a cheeky grin.

"Forgive me if I'm being unfairly nosy. I sensed your
strength earlier, and it... well... it made me desperate
to hear the stories you have to tell," replied McKenna,
fervent light animating her eloquent eyes. Michelle
laughed good-naturedly at the innocent inquiry, abasing
her accomplishments until a determined look from
her husband encouraged her to speak. She had lived
in Lianor, apprenticed to a cleric of Sanct Germain, in
the same guild as all four of her sisters. As she grew in
strength alongside them, she found herself on quest after
quest in search of glory and tribute to the great god. Her
guild had been her life. Until she met Yori.

"Talk about your one-horse town. Ljotebroek's long
name outpaced its main road at the time. My sisters
couldn't believe I'd strike out from Golden Eye for
such a wasteland as this. But," her eyes misted over in
remembrance, "it was the desolation I craved the most. I
spent my whole life seeking glory for someone else, and
I couldn't even claim any of my own. Here, I was free to
build and fail for myself. That was worth more than any
god could ever give me."

Ah. There it is, McKenna thought to herself. *Just
because one has lost their way doesn't mean they have to
abandon everything that makes them who they are in order to
find it again. One can't punish their god for their own missteps.
One has to accept responsibility, and either grow from it, or
fall from it. Looks like she chose the latter. A shame, but then, it
seems to have worked out for her after all.*

Seth elbowed her under the table, a meaningful look
on his face. She quickly composed her features, realizing

he must have been reading her expression again.

"It helped she was hopelessly in love with yours truly," Yori boasted, planting a whiskery kiss on Michelle's forehead. The woman rolled her eyes at her incorrigible husband, unable to keep a smile from creeping into the corners of her face.

"So this town, your clan… it's an amalgam then?" queried Seth. "You have no one god? No guild alliance?"

"My forge will ever be a tribute to Malfaestus," he said with a toast of his foam-capped mug. "But we be a town of free folk, after all. Those who swing hammers in my forge pay homage to the secrets whispered beneath the mountain, and they do so on their own terms. The durgir may share few of those secrets, but the gods are public domain. We choose our following, so we choose our calling. But each and every one of us travelled here to get away from all that prejudice; your god, my god, the gods of our fathers. We wanted to live for the gods of ourselves. And our success spoke for itself, so we just let the gods go by the wayside, honestly. It wasn't until the clock tower got built that we even had a hall to worship in."

"Of course, that brought the vultures," Michelle interrupted with venom in her words.

A questing train from the Guild of Tooth and Claw descended upon the town some time ago, determined to influence what they interpreted as the "faithless" settlers to the light of the dragon god Bahamut. After they'd gone, wave upon wave of those who followed Bahamut's faith migrated, most doing their fair share of work but still managing to insinuate their religion into the secular little village. Finally, a united front of original settlers commanded the use of the clock tower as a means to share each other's culture and to ban all such discussion in the streets.

"The magistrates didn't like that. They come here to make us worshippers of Bahamut, stick their noses in everywhere. When the undead started pestering us, they claimed it was a visitation upon our sins. That we would either repent, or perish."

Seth convulsed in anger, gripping the table. McKenna easily understood why. It was the same story that had driven him from that very guild. A fresh wave of appreciation for the wandering rogue washed over her, for the determination that led him to abandon his livelihood in the face of these atrocities. To do so must have taken a strength of character that humbled her.

"At any rate, we didn't like that one bit. So we told them in no uncertain terms to honor our laws, or leave. The next time their guild came questing through here, ostensibly to drive out the undead, those that wanted so desperately to be evangelized left. And more have been leaving ever since," finished Yori, taking a deep draught from the mug before him.

"Wait. Lord Timmet followed the Guild of Tooth and Claw?" exclaimed McKenna, casting an uneasy look at Seth.

A thundercloud enhanced the rigidity of his features as the implications grew clearer. Timmet hadn't been trying to save the town. He wanted revenge on the deserting paladin on behalf of their disavowed guild.

Fire kindled in the depths of McKenna's amber eyes. So they wanted a fight, did they?

Yori, keen on her incensed expression, chuckled his heartiest. "Aye lad, I told you to keep the monk to your good side, didn't I? She'll have you thanking her again before long!"

—

A shaft of light, piercing through the oilcloth nailed over the windows of the clock tower, penetrated McKenna's meditations. She stretched slowly on the straw tick, rubbing her eyes as they adjusted to the dim morning glow. Seth was curled on a bunk beside her, frowning in his sleep. But the two holvir were awake, speaking in that unique musical language they possessed. McKenna smiled sleepily at Ginni, who hopped off her stool with a grin.

"Morning! So uh... about that whole escort-to-Naijor thing. You guys, uhm, you're still down for that right?"

Though the words were spoken lightly, McKenna didn't miss the sense of urgency in them, nor the sideways glance she cast at Tjena. By this time, Seth had woken up, and he studied the three of them silently.

"Yes." He yawned widely and stretched, but his gaze was clear and steady as he studied the bard. "That chasm you mentioned... I want to investigate it. I'm not asking you to take me into it," he said, raising a hand before McKenna could argue, "but if you could show me the way, I'd be grateful."

Ginni studied him for a moment. McKenna could almost see concern, and a haunted expression that had nothing to do with Tjen's blight or their shared experiences in Naijor.

What Ginni remembered were the towns full of ash and ghosts.

"You should probably know... what it is we've seen. Let's get on the road first, and I'll... I'll tell you everything."

The day was warm, and a peerless blue sky arced overhead. Their path had rejoined the major eastern route, a paved road winding through the golden grain out to the borders of the desert. Seth winced as they passed a signpost, pointing towards the west, that read "Wheelspoke".

The road, though clear, seemed little used this far east. McKenna had mounted behind Ginni on the mule, and Tjena clung behind Seth on Kurya. Before they'd travelled far, McKenna remembered what the bard had mentioned the night before.

"Excuse me, if this be a rude question. But that thing you said about... about not having a soul. Does that mean..."

"What? Oh, the soul thing. Yeah, holvir have no representation in the pantheon," Ginni turned in place to peer at McKenna, whose scandalized expression suddenly looked a little more familiar to the bard than the monk's usual peaceful confidence. "No god, no soul."

In truth, McKenna could only be shocked at her own ignorance of the blighted race. *So much for devout study of the pantheon.*

"You don't have to be so critical of yourself," Ginni replied, startled out of her usual singsong composure. It didn't take her long to realize that McKenna was simply a victim of her education, just like the rest of the world. "I didn't even think Hammardin durgir knew holvir existed. How could you know that about us?"

"I'm a monk. My whole life was spent studying our pantheon, and all the faiefolkr it protects," she replied with a shrug. "Kind of important to spreading the word of your god would be knowing who you're spreading it to, right?"

Ginni shrugged, but didn't argue. Seth chimed in. "Tooth and Claw never had much interaction with holvir. It seemed like every town we quested to was pretty much already clear of them. Any time we had some around, it never particularly… ended well. Mostly for them. I don't think they approve of paladin magic."

"It's true," Ginni spoke musically, the sound evoking the essence of a song despite the plain conversation. "About the magic. And the gods. And the paladins. Especially the paladins," she said with a shudder, and the whole party laughed. "And because of it, we can't abide with anyone in the realms. Inevitably, they all try to convert us. But how can you enforce faith on the faithless? We have no magic. We are built from Faie's bounty, the ground and the air and the water." Her voice plied the air, each pitch tuned to perfection, and McKenna realized it wasn't magic that enhanced Ginni's voice. Nature had simply fashioned her that way. "Our people are this world's finest artisans because they are so deeply attuned to nature and our natural existence. What need have we of the ethereal? Our bones are ours only until they return to dust. Why should we sacrifice them at the feet of impassive immortals who do not even see us?"

McKenna stroked the runes inked and carved into

her black skin, listening intently. Her connection with Malfaestus formed such a powerfully intrinsic part of her being, yet she still felt a potent curiosity and empathy for the nature of the holvi in front of her.

"We don't have gods or goddesses. We don't see Celestials. We walk among the faiefolkr, our feet step beside theirs, but we are almost as alien to them as the dead," she continued. "Our people cannot face the magic of the gods. The merest trace will infect us, will separate and banish the afflicted from their families, from their homes. Tjena and I are lucky. We're wanderers by nature instead of by nurture, and we would've left our village regardless if they pushed us out. Still, having the choice would've been nice," and a small discordant note broke her reverie.

"Ginni, the way your people are treated is appalling. There's no excuse for it, and you don't have to justify it, least of all to me," McKenna spoke feelingly, putting a hand on the little bard's curly head. "The gods exist to help light our way, to bless us with a better life if we want it. Or, to simply guide and protect what we already have. It is strange to me, to think of a whole race of intelligent beings left to walk this path alone. But strange shouldn't be a bad thing. If holvir don't feel abandoned by the gods, and find purpose without them, then who am I to judge how they live?"

A soft breeze brushed past the party, the whistling grain a soothing melody accompanying the monk's words. Ginni knew she meant them, too. As much as she didn't know how to respond in kind to this woman, who spoke her feelings outright without fear or shame.

Clearing her throat, she smiled at McKenna, a sympathetic expression of two faiefolkr meeting on terms of perfect equality. She waited for a beat, measuring the monk's silence, but faithful her next confession would be met with compassion and not with distrust. "Speaking of the dead, we've seen them up close too. That's what brought us out here," she said with conviction, the memory of the destroyed towns, the shambling figures. She motioned to Tjena with a sweep of her arm. "That's what happened to them."

Seth looked startled. "You've seen the dead? Not ilmaurte, but the actually dead?"

McKenna stared at him. "Uhm, not to be that guy... but what exactly is the difference?"

Seth shook his head slowly, unbroken gaze lingering on Ginni. "Ilmaurte would have left them in pieces. They must have encountered a Source." His look softened as Ginni's posture, tense as she expected contradiction, relaxed in visible relief that someone understood their predicament.

"A Source? You mean, a necromancer?"

"Not just any necromancer," replied Seth grimly. "The original source of death- a Lich."

McKenna blinked in confusion at Ginni, who looked at her and shrugged. "I know a lot of stories, but that one is beyond me."

"This is not a tale bards would tell. It's the same everywhere I've gone. As much as everyone resists the idea of a horde of ilmaurte, they flat out refuse to believe the idea of a Lich King. Our gods would never allow such a thing, they say. A few of us know better, but what good is the word of guildless rogues?" he scoffed. McKenna could sense his tension and tried to slip a comforting word into his painful self-abasement.

"For a guildless rogue, you do keep your word well enough, when that word leads you to adventure!" she ribbed, grinning straight into his face. He couldn't help but smile back at the comfort of her familiarity.

Ginni continued to speak lightly, her voice the bubbling of a meadow stream. "Urtha told us what it was we saw. She couldn't help us either. The orgir don't fear the undead. Their souls are too alien, too rich in Faie's blood, to be of any good feast."

"Urtha?" McKenna shifted in the saddle, remembering the figures illuminated by their silver auras leering at them through the darkness. "You met an orghi?"

Clearing her throat, she hummed a tune with an expressive glance at Tjena. The holvi plucked the naiti with one hand, the other still firmly clutching the pommel behind Seth.

"Guess it's time for that story we promised," she trilled in her musical voice.

XVI

Learning A Lesson

The savannah on the outskirts of Beausun is a wild place. Few pioneers are hardy enough to sustain life this far from the denser regions of civilization, but some asafolk- those who despised their own kind, or sought freedom from the bonds imposed by family or religion or both- made the wild scrub brush their home. While surly, they weren't as repulsive to the holvir as their eastern kin, and often offered hospitality in exchange for news of the broad world.

But for some reason, they were missing.

"Tjena… how long ago exactly was it since we came through here last?" She whispered, as they passed holes for campfires and the broken ground where canvas structures once stood. Ginni thought the settlement had actually come quite far in its development, the few times they passed through it. There were always new faiefolkr, she recalled with certainty.

Now there was nothing.

Beads of cold sweat stood out on the holvir's brows, and they walked surreptitiously, making themselves as unnoticeable as possible- a particular talent of holvir. The sensation of dread settled deeper, until finally Tjena stopped with a finality that Ginni recognized.

"We'll… we'll go around," she gasped. Shadowy

shapes had begun to make creep just out of view, and the deathly hush hung between them like a curtain. Turning instead down a path, little used, that led into a brook, the holvi pair waded in the water for as long as they could, until finally they could be certain they'd left the village far behind.

"What... what happened?" Tjena wondered aloud, once they'd camped again beside the main road to dry their feet. "That... all those asafolk. Asafolk don't just disappear."

The shadows lingered in Ginni's memory, pressing against the backs of her eyes, demanding recognition. She blanched.

"I... I hope they disappeared. Because I'm beginning to think the alternative is much, much worse." She looked around them, and then with a sigh of relief caught sight of a totem- a painted stone, lying on the side of the road, that nearly thrummed with magic. Ginni bent down and stroked it, humming a short melody. If there was anyone to tell about the missing villagers, it would be Kumbo's tribe.

"You are lucky you lost only your sight, young holvi," spoke Urtha, chieftainess of Tribe Akan, the largest clan that still roamed the Great Plains of Beausun. She had come at the call of Ginni's melody. The two wanderers had long ago struck up an unlikely friendship with the secretive orghi chieftainess, and many were the nights they'd spent at her fireside, spinning tales and sharing the exile imposed upon their races. "For it is souls this being devours, souls that should ascend to the Celestial plane and feed the new lives born on Faie."

"Eh, we're pretty small. He probably thought it

wasn't worth the indigestion," ribbed Ginni. Tjena cast a sideways glance at her, sensing the bravado that thinly masked the very vivid distress imprinted on the holvi by the vacant village, and gripped her fingers.

Urtha contemplated the two, and the threads of love that bound them. Her gaze softened, but she didn't respond in words.

A cloud of dense fog issued from her pipe, swirls and eddies showing the entranced holvir a series of mystical orgir visions. The wreaths of smoke twisted into forms, shapes of ephemeral wisps to represent souls that, once parted from their physical hosts, wandered aimlessly. Larger forms- the lithe, hulking orgir- surrounded them and guided them into a dance until, one by one, they dissipated. A large, purple plume- no doubt to represent Atosa- swept through, collecting the harvested souls.

The holvir felt humbled by the sight. It was very rare that orgir shared their visions with outsiders. Rarer still were the riddles they chose to tell actually intelligible. As the form that represented Atosa flickered, it suddenly burst into a shower of ash and sparks. And the souls, untethered, began to wail and congeal into a tepid slime that seemed to almost ooze through the air. An acrid rain in miniature, from the pipe's slowly dwindling cloud of smoke.

"You strange beings that will not stop moving. You ended up too close to the edge this time," muttered Urtha. Ginni blinked. Still trying to make sense of the vision before her, she missed the entire context of Urtha's statement.

Urtha gestured to a cracked vein in the ground before them. "And now not only has the *Likirricanthe* found a way out, but he's stopping anyone else who wants to come in."

"Likirricanthe…" Ginni rolled the unfamiliar orghirrish word on her tongue, "what is that?"

"Hmm. It is a being denied by those who speak the Common tongue. But in the more ancient words of the ilvir, I believe, they call him *Lich*."

"But Atosa," queried Tjena. "Where did Atosa go? She's the one who holds the Doors of Death. Is she back on the mortal plane too?"

Urtha chuckled before taking another deep drag. "On terms not her own, she has returned." She exhaled a fiery spray of ash that flickered like flames. Ginni and Tjena could feel the warmth, even brighter and stronger than that of a campfire. Without warning, she tapped the contents of the pipe onto the ground, grinding them out with the heel of her foot.

"I tell you enough for the ilvir of Tirre Lunir. I do not care for them- or you, for that matter- but we want back our souls. My people are shepherds," she said mournfully as she looked out over the horizon. "Without our flock, we are nothing indeed."

—

The little group went silent for a moment as Ginni's words reverberated in the air. "Anyways, it makes for one heck of a lay, doesn't it? The shepherd for lost souls... loses... the souls."

"I didn't know that about orgir," mused Seth while Tjena tuned their strings.

"I don't think anyone did, really. No one seems to pay much attention to them, except to get really, really mad when they won't share land. But I mean, if you've got gates to the Celestial plane to guard, makes sense really you wouldn't want anyone else anywhere near. It's part of a legend that Kumbo made a deal with Atosa," mused McKenna, recalling the spidery texts and illustrated pages she pored over as an apprentice. "Orgir can speak to the dead, so she borrows them from time to time as shepherds for souls. So it wouldn't make any sense for this… Lich… to feed upon them. They're too close to death as it is."

"You knew about that?" stammered Tjena, regarding the monk with newfound awe. "You really aren't kidding about knowing the pantheon."

Ginni gazed off in the distance, remembering their time spent with the chieftainess and her tribe. The nomads definitely had an otherworldly quality about them, and they could communicate beyond speech. She remembered asking Urtha questions that the woman would answer with little more than a riddle. She didn't feel like Urtha was hiding the truth; it was more like the truth was beyond mortal comprehension. She tried not to worry too much about it though. They had a duty, to their homeland and their people.

"I guess that explains why orgir are wanderers, like holvir," she wondered aloud. "She told us too that our best bet would be to visit Tirre Lunir and seek out the Guild. Sorceres have strange motivations. They're more likely to barter, if it means they get more knowledge or spellpower. Beats me how they get so strong as they do," she shrugged. She also placed a hand unconsciously on the pouch Katarin had given her. What knowledge could the pair be gathering for the enigmatic master?

"Sorceres use the power from alternate planes. They tap spirits, beings, and manipulate them into doing their bidding. Usually in exchange for a few moments spent on this plane. We are," grimaced Seth, "a particularly favorite place for daemorre. Their desire for material manna is insatiable."

He rubbed his cheek ruefully. McKenna noticed the faintest scar, really no more than just a slight discoloration, that contoured the bronzed ridge of his left cheek. Suddenly she recalled a moment of deep, staggering darkness, with the cries of her durgirn kin around her. Though tucked away in the chapel, she caught glimpses of a roaring and chattering creature that swarmed Hammardin's halls and rampaged with a might she had never seen before. She remembered creeping to the walkway above the mines, the large circular chamber showing a horrible sight - a pulsing red kvetchling, spined and bloodied and seething with a violent evil aura barely kept at bay by durgir knit tightly behind weapons imbued with the power and might of Malfaestus. She knew the daemor would be crushed utterly. And yet a penetrating and unshakeable sense of dread had sunk deep into her bones and left her a helpless, shivering little girl. Even with its power finally extinguished and presence banished from their mortal realm, the lingering essence of the daemor's pure concentrated hatred still remained. Pabble spent weeks with his initiates cleansing the halls and purifying the mountain's core again and again to rid their clan of its tainted presence.

"I've never seen a daemor," Ginni was saying in response to Seth. "We've visited the ilvir before, but only during Red Solstice when they were summoning a Celestial. Didn't stay long enough to see if it would work.

Ilvir love bards, but they've no use for holvir. Honestly, the feeling is mutual. We've no real use for them either. Or their trees, come to think of it. Too big," she said with a pout, stretching out to the tips of her toes as if to deny her diminutive stature.

Seth snorted at the petulant tone in her voice. "Don't worry, Ginni. Paladins of Tooth and Claw were never particularly welcome either. They've got a guild contracted exclusively for their protection, one," he growled under his breath, "that our guild has done its utmost to obliterate. Most are just hired swords, but they're best known for their assassins."

"Assassins? What? You can't be serious," McKenna cried.

"Sure. Onyx Blade, the largest guild of them I can think of. Used to find them skulking around on our quests, but they know better than to cross with us… unless conditions are perfectly favorable."

Assassins. What will they come up with next.

"I'm beginning to understand why Hammardin durgir don't wander around much," McKenna mused aloud. "Reading about all the different classes and races is all well and good, but this is a nightmare. *Assassins.* Faiefolkr, paid by other faiefolkr, to kill each other? What's the point? If you're dead, you can't mine the ore or drink the mead."

Ginni and Seth stared blankly at her for a moment before collapsing into breathless laughter. The monk blinked at her friends, reining up her steed before Ginni fell off it, and laughed too. "What? What did I say?"

"Oh, McKenna, you sweet beautiful summer child," gasped Ginni. "What it must be like to be so innocent."

Seth rolled back to a seated position, chest heaving. He wiped tears from the corners of his eyes as he cantered closer to clap the befuddled monk on the back. "You sure do have your priorities straight, is all I can say," he finally managed to gasp through fits of laughter.

She smiled at him, happy to see merriment shaking the stalwart rogue from his usual reserve. The journey through Ljotebroek seemed to have opened him up to their party more than any of their other adventures, and she guessed that the reminder of being hunted by one of Faie's most powerful guilds would bring down almost any walls among those he could trust to defend him. But she also noticed that after clapping her on the back, he had unconsciously let his hand linger there.

Sunlight shimmered across the bright grain, and pert crows cawed hoarsely from the wooden palings that lined the road. The dearth of travelers, on what McKenna knew to be an otherwise busy and populous highway, still proved slightly unnerving. And she found herself thankful for how easy it had been to fall in with a party of friends among whom she could travel. Especially considering the horrifying dangers they had already faced.

Pulling the cloak tighter around her shoulders, she felt the mirror slap against her thigh. She rolled her eyes. How could an inanimate object be so keen on making its presence known to her?

She slid it from its pouch, studying it offhandedly as Clopalong continued to trot at a sedate pace beside Kurya. A flash from its glassy surface brought her back to the moment, during their last battle, when the souls seemed to vanish within its depths. She scoffed at herself. It was just a mirror. It couldn't summon souls.

"Oh, you never got to see this, did you?" she said, as she realized Seth had slowed to see what had caught her attention. She wondered what he would make of the runes around its edge, and she saw again a flash of recognition and something she didn't understand cross his face as he caught sight of them again. He reached out silently and took it, puzzling over the flawless reflection.

They both had slowed to a stop. The road undulated along unbroken prairie, league upon league of golden grain as far as they could see. McKenna squinted into the vista, seeing if she could identify any recognizable marker. She knew that directly to the south lay Wheelspoke, so named for its cardinal roads leading to every major city in the realm, radiating outward from the city like spokes on a wheel. Far off into the east were the populous coastal towns; Lianor, and the durgirn trading stronghold of Bristendine among them.

However, their current destination and direction was the one she knew the least about. A haze of heat blurred the horizon, a reminder of the barren blankness that awaited. The desert realm of Naijor featured little in her studies, and not at all in her clan's dealings with the realms outside Mount Oer.

A bustle over her shoulder caught her attention. Seth had slid off his horse, and Kurya, unused to any rider other than his master, reacted by trying to dismount Tjena. The poor holvi barely clung to the reins of the bucking steed. McKenna swung herself off her mount and vaulted toward them, catching them just as they lost their seat.

"Are you okay?" She set the shaken bard upright, dusting them off. Tjena trembled a little and then nodded. She turned on Seth.

"What in the blazes were you thinking-" she started to shout, but stopped short at the look on his face.

He wore an expression of exquisite longing, his golden eyes fixed upon the strange letters McKenna had never been able to correctly translate. His hand shook as he dazedly met McKenna's curious glance.

"I haven't... seen these runes..." he stammered, shock electrifying every feature. McKenna, afraid to touch him, looked back helplessly at the holvir. Ginni slipped off the back of the mule and let loose a low trill, coaxing the calmest sounds from her flexible voice.

"Come back to us Seth," she intoned, gripping Tjena's hand. "Whoever it is you see in that mirror, the realities in truth stand before you, not behind glass."

Slowly the frenzied light died out of the fighter's eyes. He slumped visibly, and McKenna rushed to support his drooping figure. After a few moments, he shook his head.

"I- that was weird," he mumbled, a rueful grin on his face. "Where did you say you got this again?"

McKenna sat him down and offered a skein from her pack. He took a long, deep draught and shook his head again, trying to clear the visions from his mind.

"Tjena, I'm so sorry. I didn't mean to put you in danger like that. This mirror," he continued, offering it back to McKenna, "is no ordinary magical object."

"Pfft. I could've told you that," ribbed Tjena, harboring no ill will toward the apologetic fighter. "But now we're all curious. What did it show you?"

Seth took another deep breath, looking first at the holvir and then at the monk. "I can't really tell you what it says. But... I know where to go to find out," he said ruefully, absently rubbing the root of his index finger again. "And... it may very well be the key to undoing the curse that's animating the ilmaurte."

She realized he was right. The mirror hadn't dissipated the severed ilmaurte souls, like Ginni's song did. If the souls were, somehow, locked within the mirror, it meant they couldn't be cast again to reanimate the dead.

McKenna cast an uneasy glance over the holvir. She had promised to take them home.

"Oh, don't look at me. I'm just as invested as you are, and if this mirror keeps the ilmaurte at bay it would be nice to know how to use it." Ginni had easily interpreted her look. "Besides, I'm pretty sure we qualify as protagonists at this point, so what's a couple more days? Right, Tjena?"

Tjena just shrugged. But both their consort and the monk could see the eager curiosity expressed in the normally inscrutable musician's face. Blight bedamned.

McKenna turned back to Seth, an encouraging smile on her face. He had sunk back into a posture of indecision. Suddenly a flash of understanding struck the monk, and she understood the fighter's dread hesitation.

"You… Seth, do you have to go home for this?"

He groaned, an expression of acute misery upon his face. McKenna couldn't help but laugh.

"Come on now, sure'n it's not so bad as all that," she wheedled, not quite able to follow the myriad of emotions he showed.

"It's worse," he groaned again, putting his head in his hands. The monk, novice to the range of aesir expression and perfectly attached to her own homeland, didn't quite know what to do. She placed her hand on Seth's shoulder, and felt it tense quickly before relaxing involuntarily.

"If you were returning for the sake of restoring what you lost, you would be right to fear the journey," she offered. "You shouldn't have to prove anything to anyone. You're a work in progress and will never stop growing and improving, until you die. That's what being a person is. If they want to see only the result, and not be a part of the journey, they don't deserve you, or your confidence, and you don't owe them anything."

Ginni stepped into the breach, her small feet dancing lightly through the clearing as she sang a harmless ditty about a foolish dryad who had wandered too far from her tree, and the tree, heartbroken at the loss, had died. But she changed the ending. Upon her return, the dryad, instead of breaking her heart and dying too, wept bitter tears of repentance that watered the tree's lifeless roots with renewed strength and it came back to life, reborn by its dearest friend, who promised to never leave it again.

"I'm sure your leaving didn't actually kill anyone, so it can't be hard as that. But when foolish dryads leave home, they should know better than to dread the coming back," she chided.

A haunted look had flickered into Seth's face. But suddenly, he became aware of McKenna's reassuring touch. He scrutinized her for a minute before speaking.

"This mirror will cause you a lot of trouble. Are you absolutely certain you should bear it?" His gaze was fierce, almost savage. She quavered before it.

"To be honest with you, I don't think I really have a choice. But if I do, I will make it." Her eyes flashed back into his. "Tell me what this is, rogue, and I'll master it. Come what may."

"Well, that's all that sorted, right?" Ginni shimmied in anticipation. She loved adventure.

"It would be nice to know where we're going," encouraged Tjena.

Shaking the last of the mirror's effects from his normally stern resolve, Seth stood and faced the road before them. It led, McKenna knew, directly through the plains to...

"Wheelspoke."

XVII

Seth Goes Home

A driving rain pursued them, pushing back the setting sun and soaking the austere, searing landscape. Clouds rested atop the surrounding hills' misty peaks, supported by a high wind that held birds stationary above each crest. McKenna felt a pang of homesickness at the sight. The topmost point of Mount Oer was always invisible, due both to its height and its perpetual veil of fog and cloud, similar to the one rising above the hill they crested.

But it wasn't her home they headed toward. It was Seth's, and he looked more grim about it than she'd ever seen him.

She turned back to face the town they had reached, and the rain, as quickly as it had come, vanished. It almost seemed to break along the gated property of a manor, resting at the midway point of Wheelspoke's principal street. The town stood in stark contrast to Ljotebroek; no building taller than the manor lay along the soft, white dirt roads which though unpaved were smoothly uniform throughout the city. No manner of wondrous architecture or metalwork distinguished them. Long rows of neat farms tucked themselves within the boundaries of a few orderly creeks that trickled down from the hills, and up the high street ran a stately procession of wooden buildings with low, red clay tiled roofs. The monk had to blink for a moment, unsure if the vision were a reality or a mirage. Friendly-looking faces bustled purposefully; dogs, chickens, and the occasional goat wandered with spirit and vivacity. It looked picturesque enough for a novel.

A quick glance at her companions helped her get her bearings. Ginni and Tjena were nodding as they pointed out landmarks familiar to each other.

And of course, Seth's expression gave the impression that every building had been coated in blood and that horrifying ilmaurte instead of asafolk walked the streets.

"Is it… is this normal?" She whispered under her breath anyways to Ginni, still not quite trusting her eyes, as they made their way along the road and through the town's boundaries. Ginni gave a musical little laugh.

"McKenna, honey. Wheelspoke is literally the most normal town you can get in all the realms. Wheelspoke is the definition of normal. If you found the oldest dictionary on Faie and opened it to the word "normal", no matter the language, it would just have a freakin' picture of this town next to it."

"Huh," McKenna shrugged, dazzled and yet unsettled by the holvi's comment. "Guess all the aesir towns just tend to blend together to durgir. We know it's a place of importance for sure, all the roads lead through it, but I didn't expect it to be so…" she trailed off, looking at the landscape surrounding her.

Sentries regarded them with passive curiosity. They'd posted their horses just outside the city walls, opting to make the final approach on foot. They were still unsure of their welcome - and Kurya was a dead giveaway to his master's identity. Luckily, they seemed to be blending in with the normal stream of travelers who, despite the absolute dearth of them on the road so far, passed in abundance around the populous city.

"Impressive? Adorable? Magnificent beyond the Material and Celestial planes themselves? I have no idea how they get away with it - their Lady is a real piece of work, supposedly," Tjena snorted under their breath and raised an eyebrow expressively. "Guess they're on the guild's side. Look at them all; it's like there's no such thing as an undead horde. No other town so open as this could survive the advance of the ilmaurte without some heavy, heavy muscle behind it."

Seth cleared his throat and the three turned guiltily to regard him. He just rolled his eyes and continued to walk with purpose toward the imposing manor. McKenna wondered why, then assumed it must be part of the city's protocol. *It would make sense to have strangers hail themselves to the magistrate, especially in times like these.*

Gates suddenly arrested their procession, blinking into existence as soon as she had taken notice of the marvelous building. A path preceded them, and along that path a figure had appeared. McKenna turned a curious eye on Seth, who noticed the figure almost as soon as she did.

She thought the sentries hadn't noticed them pass - she realized quickly she was wrong. Several stood at attention beyond the gates, and a line flanking them appeared. She tensed, but though they bore weapons they seemed to stand more at attention to the woman approaching them than in any sort of aggression. The bards inched a little closer to her, Tjena shrugging as McKenna caught their eye - until turning their attention to Seth, who stood rigid at the gates, his teeth clenched so tight McKenna could almost hear them.

"Hello, Mother," he winced, as the willowy woman wound her stately way to the gates.

Her long black hair fluttered over tanned, velvet-clad shoulders, as ramrod straight as her posture. Seth's greeting was almost unnecessary. The resemblance between the two- even at the distance they were currently- was absolutely uncanny.

"M- your mother?!" stuttered McKenna anyways. "That's your mother. This is your estate? You live *here*?"

"Yes, she is my mother, and no, I don't live here, obviously, as you found me as far away as I could possibly get," Seth muttered darkly under his breath.

The monk and Ginni exchanged embarrassed grins. Tjena, lips pursed in a neutral expression, remained mute.

As the woman approached the gates, they shimmered and became translucent. Seth stepped forward, and the rest of the party followed suit.

These asafolk must have an incredibly strong connection with Bahamut, mused McKenna as she passed through the ephemeral vapour that still bore a faint resemblance to the crest of the dragonish god. *This is no simple protection spell.* She felt a twinge of sympathetic current through the runes on her skin as they came in contact with the dweomer. Honestly, such flashy magic didn't have much place in her practice- but she had to admit to herself that she was a bit impressed. The guards surrounding them saluted to the woman, and then marched back down the road to resume their posts.

"I am the Lady Arianna," she spoke, as soon as she

came close enough to be heard. Her voice had a firm, almost adamantine quality to it, and eyes the hue and dominance of thunderclouds threatening to break added to the illusion of her inflexibility. McKenna met her gaze fairly, but decided to keep her place a few steps behind Seth. *Lady. Of course his mother is the magistrate of this perfect town.*

Seth stepped back, in line with McKenna, and waved an introductory hand at the party. "Mother, meet McKenna, of Clan Hammardin, and holvi bards Tjen and Ginni, of no particular tribe," he spoke briefly.

"And it is ever a pleasure to enjoy your hospitality, my lady," offered Ginni as she and Tjen performed the standard curtsy offered by holvir to asafolk of rank. Lady Arianna's title indicated she was a woman of substantial property and influence, meaning her family most definitely patronized that very upscale-looking tavern further down along the road. Pleasing the lady of the land meant tips from her loyal bondsmen.

Her expression softened ever so slightly. "You may refer to me as Ari. As friends of my son, and from what I assume was the extremely tiresome cajolery you must have employed to bring him back here, I welcome and I thank you."

Cajolery? thought McKenna, remaining silent as she let the holvi's charisma work its magic. *And if she's so happy to see him, why did he have to leave?*

Ginni maintained her curtsy as she replied. "An honor for us, your Ladyship, that we accept as gratefully as the right to sustain your title when we speak of you. Though Ari is indeed a lovely moniker," she lilted charmingly.

McKenna cast a hooded glance at the bard. Ginni's tone reminded her of the exchange with the Magi woman. Though Lady Arianna had been perfectly cordial, it was clear the holvi would only trust her altruism so far. However, the monk had learned enough to hold her own tongue. Her companions seemed to be capable of making their own way, just as Seth had said.

Lady Arianna seemed familiar with this request made by the holvi, and nodded gently. Ginni, like many of her people, preferred to preserve and distinguish the line between her race and the others that always seemed to try so desperately to insinuate and indoctrinate them. Any form of familiarization- especially among those of power, as Ari clearly was- invited opportunities for subjugation as alien to holvir as it was inevitable of asafolk. The exchange honestly fascinated McKenna, and she felt a slight tension within her unwind as she studied the subtlety with which each navigated their spheres in this stratified society. *Still think it's appalling, to be honest, but what do I know. I'm just a duergi.*

Turning away after realizing she was unlikely to get any more familiar greeting from her son, Ari led the party into a pristine hallway. "While I do not hold any of you to our schedule," she said simply, "we will be dining shortly and, as that is the case, I must leave you here to finish my work. Make yourselves as comfortable as you prefer," and with that, she swept back through the corridor.

Once she was out of sight, Seth let out a mix between a sigh and a groan. McKenna just laughed.

"What are you doing slumming around with us? This place is a palace!" giggled Ginni shrilly, as she unwittingly perched on a cushioned sofa.

"It isn't a palace, Ginni. It's just a big house."

"Ah yes," she said faintly as she sunk into the plush divan. "A big house. Tjena, please help me, I'm most definitely stuck."

As Tjena trotted over to help extricate their hopelessly engulfed partner, Seth grimaced and paced the room. Signs of grandeur made little impression on McKenna. Her own chapel boasted some of the finest and most intricate filigree and stonework ever produced by her clan. But the space they found themselves in was surprisingly refreshing. Bearing clear signs of habitation, though also occupied by beautiful and curious and clearly costly things, it felt as though it had seen vigour and children and life. She took her own seat on a less dangerous divan, watching Seth with a bemused expression.

"Penny for your thoughts?" she offered, though not expecting much of a response.

"If he doesn't want it, I'll take it," quipped Ginni.

Tjena, however, offered Seth a sympathetic glance before strumming their *naiti* suggestively. "We should head to that tavern," they motioned. "As much as we'd enjoy dining with your...er...family, we could really use the coin."

Ginni bounced up. "Oh yes right, definitely. You two should both stay here. I can't imagine the need for any kind of bodyguards in this place. We'll be sure to pay our tithe or whatever, and slip in some *Streams of Silver*, that will keep the more devout happy."

McKenna nodded, still in thrall of the discovery of Seth's noble heritage and willing to trust her friends' good sense. "Alright. We'll try to join you up later. Have a mug ready, something tells me we'll need it."

"You'll need more than one," Seth grumbled from behind her chair, before exhaling deeply and sinking onto the seat beside her. "Also, Ginni, *Streams of Silver* is a Guild of Golden Eye ballad. You're better off with *Whispers of the Shiny Scale.*"

"Aye aye, it's your pub, you know best," she saluted before dancing out the doorway with Tjena following behind.

McKenna wanted to keep the banter, but something told her to wait until Seth spoke first. His gaze downcast, he took a deep breath when suddenly they were arrested by a boisterous noise from the doorway.

"Is it? Are you here? Are you here for real?! Bless Bahamut, Seth, welcome back!" cried a bright apparition from the hallway. Unable to really discern what spoke, McKenna suddenly leapt from the couch as the figure flung itself at Seth in a violent hug.

"I-can't-believe-you-came-back-where-did-you-even-go-what-were-you-doing-did-you-miss-me-I-bet-you-missed-me-I-can't-believe-you-left-me-alone-with-Mum-FOREVER-what-did-you-bring-me-oh-hey who is she?" gasped the girl- for McKenna was able to finally discern she was a girl, with pixiesh dark hair framing her deeply bronzed face- clinging tightly to a bemused and unruffled Seth.

"She, is McKenna. A duergi on a quest to grow a beard," announced Seth with the will-o'-wisp child in his lap. Her jaw dropped and she whipped her head around to stare at McKenna.

"He's having me on. You're gigantic! How could you be a duergi?" she said bluntly, her black brows knitted over her sparkling grey eyes.

McKenna couldn't help but laugh. Assuming by their interaction that she was his sister, she traced similar resemblances they shared with their mother. It really stopped short of physical, though. While their thin, wiry frames and straight black hair denoted a shared lineage, their expressions and attitudes were completely dissimilar. The girl's brazen, forthright speech and vibrant antics were nothing like the reserved and taciturn Seth. Without realizing it, she found herself recognizing within the child something of a kindred spirit. Confronted suddenly by a bright, wide grin, she discovered the feeling was mutual.

"Aye, I'm a duergi all right. Pabble used t'say I snuck in too many metal singings an' started ter grow with the ore, but who knows really," replied McKenna, emphasizing the drawl that of late had mellowed in the company of the aesir and holvir.

"I guess you don't see muscles like that on an ordinary woman," she sighed wistfully in response. "I'm Arya, by the way, since Seth is too good to introduce me, as he is the worst brother ever."

"Arya?" replied McKenna bemusedly. "Lady Ari and Lady Arya. Quite the combination."

Arya pulled a face, while Seth responded in mock gravity, "Don't refer to my sister as 'Lady'- not only has she not earned that title, she's made it abundantly clear she doesn't want it."

McKenna pondered that for a moment before brightening, recalling her studies of asafolk history and their curious politics.

"Oh, I guess that makes sense. Here in the southern realms, 'Lady' is really just a political position, isn't it?" queried McKenna.

"Exactly. Mother is a Lady because the city folk elected her. I mean, it helps she owns half the village… but she has worked her whole life for this city," the girl added fairly.

McKenna looked inquisitively at Arya, still perched on her brother's knee. "But you don't want to be a Lady? What would you rather do then?"

Arya leapt from her seat, brandishing a small foil strapped to her waist. "Why, become a paladin of course! Like Seth," she said, lunging expertly in an attempt to draw him into a duel. He rolled his eyes, but suddenly continued the roll with his body, landing near a display of varied weapons and drawing a foil from among them in one fluid motion.

Before McKenna could so much as gasp, the two swept into courtly bows, then thrust their foils at one another with lightning rapidity. A few quick ripostes and the point was his, but a couple return jabs showed his sister equal to the match. McKenna waited for the inevitable crash of priceless pottery as the siblings whipped around the room, but it soon became clear they knew every inch of their sporting ground better than she could have ever guessed. They seemed to anticipate each other's moves, and despite Arya's stature and age, McKenna honestly believed she might inevitably overpower Seth. The girl's infectious laughter filled the room, drawing forth a smile even from her brother. The expression, coming as it did on the heels of such distress, filled the monk's heart with a queer sort of joy.

However, after a few more minutes of balanced swordplay, Seth executed an impeccable and impenetrable offense that had his sister prostrate on the same divan that swallowed Ginni, where she too became stuck, laughing uncontrollably. Seth sheathed his foil back in the display and pulled her out of her predicament, and she seated herself on the edge of a harder chair next to McKenna while smoothing her tousled hair and panting to catch her breath.

McKenna couldn't help but be impressed. "I hope you get initiated into the guild soon. Your skills are almost unparalleled; I've never seen such swordplay," she said to the flustered girl, who blushed as she gasped.

"Unfortunately, her rascal brother has made it rather difficult for her to join one. Defection isn't looked very fairly upon," replied Seth, his mood starting to darken again.

Arya too sobered up at this, and for a while the silence of the room grew, amplified by both the volume of noise that preceded it and the heaviness of the subject that introduced it. Suddenly the protection spells and the wear of the room around them made more sense. Through the strength of their mother's force of will and the loyalty of her people alone, their family stayed safe. But to leave the safety of their village was to tempt fate, and so it was clear they were both under a form of self-imposed house arrest.

Lady Arianna must have a stronger connection to Bahamut than I thought, she mused. *The god's flagship guild could easily make short work of a place like this, but instead they choose to protect it?*

"No wonder you don't come back," she said under her breath.

"I can't. The greater my banishment from my family, the safer they are." Seth responded in kind.

"You must have really been telling the truth about the guild then. I mean, obviously your mother is still in the highest favor of Bahamut- which, considering her reception of you, means Bahamut doesn't condemn you for your actions." He flinched imperceptibly, casting a look at Arya, but McKenna missed it and continued, "Which should display a tacit condemnation of theirs... yet they still are able to wield the full might and magic of his protection? I don't understand!"

He took a deep breath, but before he could speak, Arya replied. "Bahamut is just a god. He doesn't live here like we do," she laid a hand on Seth's knee, swallowing before continuing, "These actions, the... the conflicts between his followers, and the actions they take in his name. He doesn't see those things, he can't know they happen. It's all just white noise."

Seth look at her, surprised, and she bit her lip and subsided. "Our family are devout and loyal followers of Bahamut. We've acted honorably and discharged his duties for generations. The Guild of Tooth and Claw is the same, more or less. But the finesses of aesir politics are too trivial for the gods. So, he grants protection to us both, despite our own personal... 'conflicts'," he finished, his gold eyes flashing.

Arya let out a quick sigh at his words, but quickly smiled again. "Anyways, as much as Seth likes to play the rogue, Mum is glad he came back. And so am I," she cried, wrapping her arms around him again.

Seth's expression, as normal, remained mostly inscrutable. McKenna could detect perhaps the faintest exasperation, but he belied the emotion by the physical nearness he kept to his sister. As much as he didn't want to come here and as loud were his protests against the loyalty he held for his family and homeland, she definitely sensed that he was still glad to be home with them.

"That dinner invitation wasn't exactly optional, I'm assuming," McKenna asked.

He looked at her in some surprise. After studying her for a moment, he seemed to be unsure of something, but shrugged. "Not for me, it isn't. Not if I want to get what we came here for, and also be allowed to leave."

McKenna didn't understand the look, but tried to meet it with enthusiasm. "I will never say no to a good meal, no matter the circumstances." Subconsciously, she stuck a hand in the pocket that held the mirror, running her fingers along the grooves of the runes carved in its bezel. "What is it you've got planned for us in the meantime?"

"Any visitations today, spitfire?" Seth asked his sister languidly, ruffling her hair.

"Why, avoiding Mother?" Arya's eyes danced in merriment. "You want Father's library, don't you. Should be empty, open hours for moderation with the public are over today," she said, mocking a pompous accent. "She'll be in the garden, I expect." With a roll of her shoulders, she drew forth her foil again, lunging lithely in place.

"Why don't you take that outside, you hellcat, and you can call us in when she's ready for dinner," suggested Seth.

Arya hesitated as though to argue, but Seth's eyebrow raised in an expression that made her think otherwise. Sticking out her tongue, she took off one way down the hallway, and with a roll of his eyes and a laughing shrug of his shoulders, he grabbed McKenna's hand and led her off down the other.

XVIII

Sparkling Domes And Dismal Tomes

As Arya disappeared outside, the monk and her host made their way to a conservatory-sized room. Vaulted ceilings of crystal and rhoditum illuminated the whole space with the glow of the late afternoon sun. Unlike the one they just left, this space was immaculate. Books lined the walls on organized shelves of such spotless cleanliness they looked freshly hung.

A dais rose directly across from the doorway, with a tall backless seat set upon it. Fine velvet carpeted the rest of the area, showing no wear or fading despite the many feet that must tread it back and forth each day.

But of course, as they advanced further, she could feel the light hum of magic that enhanced every inch of the imposing room.

Who needs a cleaning service or hardy furniture when you can just will your visitors to view whatever you wish them to, she thought to herself, wincing at the more dangerous implications of that thought. If this is where Lady Ari met with her constituents and mediated their struggles, her popularity suddenly made more sense.

"You're right, you know," came Seth's voice from the other side of the room, where he was nonchalantly browsing through the sizeable stacks of lexicons on the wall. "I guess I shouldn't be surprised you can sense it. She uses impression magic. Her charisma is undeniable- it really takes very little effort for her to… influence… the way people see her and her schemes."

"'Charisma', is it?" McKenna replied with a studied air of nonchalance. *Charisma sure is a word for it. These are almost Master-level magical manipulations.*

"Didn't work much for my father, who was about as charming as a bugbear," Seth continued, while McKenna activated a light dweomer to prevent the lingering spell from interfering with her focus. The room was positively saturated by it.

Despite her caution, she found herself drawn to a corner where soft light illuminated a painting mounted with prominence in an alcove.

"Ah, suddenly a resemblance I can trace between you," she quipped, as she stared at the large portrait of a man with wiry blond hair and piercing blue eyes. Any paternity in the man's stern visage was almost completely unrecognizable. His son inherited only the chiseled jaw, and… *aha, there's that grim look I know so well. It's like he's looking in a mirror.*

Almost compulsively at the thought, she drew the mirror from her pocket. It shimmered innocently, full of the soft light filtering through the glass ceiling and the man in the portrait before her. She'd never thought to use it for scrying before, but she felt a pull from the unassuming object she couldn't deny.

As its mercurial surface reflected his image, she could hear his deep, joyous laugh and the ringing of mithril against adamantine. Images flashed across the silver glass. A young man standing at attention before a cleric and being doused in holy water; tiger lilies clasped in his maille clad hands, laid in the lap of a tall woman with stormy grey eyes; the vision of a lance splintering a shield bearing the sigil of Sanct Germain; his arms around a woman holding a babe before cheering crowds, gold petals shimmering like scales in the air before them; the smile of a sunburned youth eagerly taking notes in a battered journal; a dimly lit office littered with stacks of books and papers covered in runes, scientific deliberations, and mathematics she'd never seen before; and finally, a muddling, swirling darkness punctuated by a sensation of desperation; but not fear, or pain. She almost couldn't place the feeling, until she remembered one particular day when, deciding to refresh herself on an older branch of magic, she couldn't recall the source of a philosophical theory and it led her down a week-long rabbit hole that left her more confused and frustrated than ever, until she gave it up entirely as a bad job. This man clearly devoted his life to study, and to the pursuit of higher knowledge. But he seemed to ignore the faithful and focus on the quantifiable; the scientific instead of the metaphysic.

A man so devoted to the gods, turning from them deliberately to seek other answers? His family, his life, his legacy revolved around the guilds and the pantheon. How could he possibly survive such dissonance with his sanity intact?

To her horror, if the spiral of his sinking consciousness she detected in her scrying was to be understood, he may not have.

She didn't notice Seth watching with an intense and inscrutable expression. As the images faded, she let out a long sigh, then started as she suddenly realized how near he was.

"He wasn't mad. He was a genius," said Seth softly. "He spent his whole life devoted to the martial law, and martial arts, of our culture and our time. He was a fearsome Lord of Wheelspoke and a devout follower of Bahamut."

"He would have made a splendid cleric," replied McKenna diplomatically, peering at the titles of the books around them.

"He kept to our family. He never needed to join the guild, or pursue becoming a Master." The rogue's reserve seemed fully shed before her for the first time, as he stared up at the portrait with an unmistakeable light of eager devotion in his eyes. "But when I was younger, I could tell there was more to him than what he showed the public. He knew I was a child of prophecy, that my destiny was set in stone as surely as his own, but regardless of that he still took time to teach me of things more powerful than magic, more complex than the gods."

Threw his child to the pressures of a life of prophecy and an upbringing within the strict confines of a guild, while also burdening him with truths he had no way to prove. How noble of him.

Her heart ached at the thought of the rogue growing up in such an environment. The manipulations of charisma and the burden of a knowledge even the most learned and ancient of Faie's societies hadn't quite figured out yet. Seth's strength of character, in the face of such influences, fascinated her. She felt almost bad about yelling at him for being rude to Ginni. Clearly, it was the least of the flaws in the education he managed to overcome.

"The clerics of Malfaestus always recognized the entire pantheon," she replied aloud, running her fingers over the spines of lexicons she recognized from her own studies. "Though devoted to the god that grants durgirnkind their magic over mineral, they understand there is no one god greater than another. Each has their place and their people. Malfaestus' followers study every kind of religion, ignoring evangelism for the sake of higher truths. Those who felt the calling would come. Those who didn't, or wouldn't, were already beyond his reach. Did your father… believe something similar, perhaps?"

"Bahamut, Sanct Germain, the gods of our fathers, are not so magnanimous," growled Seth. "My father grew up in the same narrow-minded culture that constricts all our race across the realms. You are either with us, or against us. There is no wisdom attainable that is not gifted by our gods. To borrow the texts and the discoveries of other faiefolkr- orgir, holvir, ilvir, durgir- is to deny your own heritage and turn your back on your people. That," sighed Seth, "is what drove my father to desperation. He couldn't escape his fate, and unfortunately, chose not to live long enough to see his son escape his."

His expression hardened as he studied the portrait. "Luckily my mother spun it as an accident. An act of heroism."

A sudden about-face, and his gaze locked to the seat upon the dais. "Lady Arianna is incredibly convincing."

The images in the mirror, reflecting the face of both father and son, faded slowly. Bowing her head, McKenna whispered a quick prayer of strength and peace to the tortured soul in whose presence she stood.

And a whisper of thankfulness, that the son he bore was able to free himself and follow his father's journey. That he would make it to the end, without the same tragic conclusion.

She took note of the book Seth was holding, a small, battered journal that seemed out of place when contrasted with the pristine spines lining the shelves around them. It was apparently the one he sought though, because he beckoned her out of the room and led the way to a well-lit, but far less imposing, office further down the corridor.

"This was my father's personal codex. He studied over a thousand languages dating far back into the origins of our realm. And he was able," Seth said as he scanned the pages slowly, "to collect around him some of the most brilliant and learned scholars of the time. Both as a patron of the arts and sciences, and as a leader of free thought. Thankfully for me, he was also a hobbyist calligrapher," and as he turned the beautifully illuminated pages of vellum, a warm smile lit his face. McKenna noticed some letters and words in the margins of the book, clearly written in a much different hand, and realized they were the notes of his son, presumably during late nights spent studying with his father collaborating in the same journal. The thought touched the monk deeply, and she watched Seth more reverently as he thumbed through the pages. He caught her recognition and chuckled. "My own handwriting is pretty poor in comparison, but it's nothing to my sister's."

Sounds started filtering through the hallways of the manor. Doors and footsteps, and the ringing bells of the household going about the task of preparing dinner. The noises broke the reverie, and Seth looked up with a rueful grin at McKenna. "I'm sorry… I think I wasted all our time. The Lady does not like being kept waiting."

McKenna laughed appreciatively and shook her head. "My time is yours, in your house. We can always work the runes on the road. But right now," and her stomach let forth a growl that challenged even the clamor made by dishes and chairs echoing through the house, "it's time to feast!"

Arya and Lady Ari were already seated by the time they made it to the dining hall. A plate of food stood ready at each of their seats- something McKenna was most thankful for, as she sunk gratefully into the chair Arya eagerly pulled out next to her. Seth took a seat at the bottom of the table, opposite his mother, as though keen to distance himself and hide among the few other household members who ate with them.

While Arya and McKenna chatted amicably about the lore of the dragon god Bahamut, analyzing differences between the aesir and durgir interpretations of some of his texts, Ari and Seth both maintained a determined silence. Evening dwindled into night, leaving only the four of them at the table. As Arya poured McKenna a glass of wine from a carafe while explaining how to pledge to the Guild of Tooth and Claw, Seth suddenly stood and made a motion to leave.

Arya pulled a face. "Already? But you just got here!" she cried.

Seth swept a burning look at the lady seated at the head of her table, sipping quietly from her goblet. She said nothing in return. "Since Mother has been bombarding me all night with her insinuations, I've decided it's time to go," he seethed.

McKenna's eyes widened in shock. She couldn't

believe how subtle Ari had been. But sure enough, she felt that familiar and unsettling thrum of magic weave its way about the room, with the heaviest concentration around her rogue son. The faintest traces of impression magic; a suggestion, a whisper, an inclination that nudged ever so invitingly. She took stock of their afternoon, wondering how else it had influenced their moves since arriving at the manor, and realized with horror that her compulsion led them to the alcove bearing the portrait of her husband. A reminder of the inevitable end should Seth continue to pursue his current path.

Breaking my own spell in the process… though I am far from Malfaestus' sight, here, thought McKenna, as she turned her focus back to enforcing the dweomers that resisted Lady Arianna's spells.

Ari kept her composure, but those adamantine grey eyes hardened perceptibly.

"Your returning is so timely, and surely you wouldn't leave us in a mess...again," She replied curtly, with the lightest emphasis on that final word. "Not when there may be a perfect opportunity to restore your favor and our family."

Seth stood up from his chair so swiftly it shot nearly across the room, toppling with a crash. "We came here to borrow a book, not to apologize or get swept up in your petty politics. You know what it will take for me to come back, and you refuse to pay that price."

Lady Ari's eyes widened and her mouth formed a hard line. "So you would abandon us here? Your sister, stuck in your shadow, unable to leave and discover her full potential?" she hissed through her teeth.

"Mother!" shouted Arya in outrage. "You're not being fair. You know I don't blame Seth, and he knows it too," she said, turning to her brother. "You know that, right?"

Seth's golden gaze stayed locked upon his mother's silver one. McKenna saw his jaw flex, as though he were holding back words desperate to escape. But he replied simply, "of course I know. Thank you, Arya. McKenna," he turned to her, and she rose from her seat. "Let's find the rest of our party."

McKenna followed swiftly behind him, pausing only long enough to rest a hand briefly on Arya's shoulder and exchange a powerful look of solidarity, while hating to leave her behind. She anticipated the woman that girl would become. And in that moment, she knew Arya could sense her admiration and was thankful for it.

As they made their way towards the magical gates, McKenna braced herself for the inevitable clash of the dweomer's protections and whispered a quick prayer invoking her own warding spell. But despite the potency of Lady Ari's undeniable connection to Bahamut, Seth merely raised his hand against the gate and it disappeared entirely without a trace. Shocked, the action reminded McKenna again of the grace of his god which Seth possessed. His aura flashed bright, and McKenna felt an ache of pride for the upright warrior beside her. Despite his feeling of betrayal, the death of his father, the imprisonment of his family, and the abandonment of his faith, he still walked in thrall of the god's goodly light. A child of prophecy, indeed. The golden dragon chose his champion well.

"I'd apologize for that, but I know you'd deny the obligation. So, instead, thank you," spoke Seth to her as they made it away from the estate. "For going through

it with me, and also for being nice to my sister. I'm glad
Arya has a better example set for her now than the one I
or my mother have imposed on her."

McKenna hesitated before answering, still seething at
the clean manipulation of his mother, but not wanting to
alienate him. After their shared experience, she felt more
than ever that he needed the support and the trust of a
peer, and she fully intended to be that person. "Arya is
her own soul. She needs no example- she's a testament to
everything that makes your people great. I can only hope
she finds her way out soon," she offered.

Darkness had fallen upon the town of Wheelspoke as
they made their way away from the manor. The moon's
silvery glow illuminated the horizon, accompanied by
the shine of windows and lamps lighting the road they
walked. At the end of it, a glowing building bustling
with the town's patrons beckoned to any wanderers on
the street. They stepped in quickly, greeted by the sound
of Tjen's curious stringed instrument and Ginni's sweet,
magical warble.

XIX

The Best Kind Of Bartender

The holvir were atop the bar, surrounded by empty glasses filled with coin and besotted men and women entranced by their song. It was a lovely ballad of the founding of Lianor, the undisputed capital of the Eastern realms and the largest aesir stronghold on Faie. There was no better tale of aesir might than this, the arrival of the nobles in their ships and the building of a skyscraping city of marble stone in the barren wastes of the plains by the sea, and the unity of the gods of the pantheon who blessed them with the physical and mental prowess necessary for such a feat. Despite Ginni's own obvious ethnicity she managed to infuse the song with a reverence and admiration of the short-lived asafolk, blended with a subtle acknowledgement for the other tribes who helped them achieve such a feat. That was the magic of the holvi's voice- she could not only remind her listeners of their greatness, but also their humility and patience for those tribes who surrounded the haughty and prideful race.

Tjen, mostly occupied with their instrument, made sure to scoop some coin from their overflowing cups to the till behind the bar. The easiest way to keep a stage-pay the landlord. Domnhall, the barkeep, was a strikingly handsome man who made his appreciation of the holvir musicians very apparent. He knew the benefits of having the talented pair keeping his normally boisterous patrons enthralled. Especially when he noticed the quiet entrance of the disgraced Seth accompanied by a woman whose reputation had begun to precede her in consideration of both the mystery of her existence and the proportions of her shape, reminiscent of the mystical giants. The Pike wasn't immune to the magics that Lady Arianna used to influence the behavior of her constituents, but no magic in the world could overcome the power of alcohol. Several dark dents in the walls and a suspicious sag in the center of the bar stood testament to fights of legendary proportions, and Domnhall was running out of mugs.

As Seth and McKenna took a seat in a corner, the barkeep whistled under his breath and nodded towards a couple sitting at the end of the bar. The man, thus addressed, raised his eyebrow as he scanned the room. Suddenly he shot from his seat, and the woman next to him let out a gasp and followed quickly behind.

"Unbelievable! The prodigal son has returned!" the powerfully built man thundered as he slid into a seat next to Seth. "I thought you made it pretty clear this place was dead to you."

The woman, petite and charming, laughed as she placed her partner's forgotten drink on the table in front of him, along with two new mugs she'd grabbed before following him over.

"Come on James, you know better than that- Seth couldn't abandon his soulmate forever!" she trilled with a giggle.

Seth just rolled his eyes before leaning over and embracing the man with a bear hug. "Katherine's not wrong," he replied with a smirk.

"Aye, yet you've already replaced me from the looks of it!" said James with a sigh, a rugged muscular hand over his heart as he scanned McKenna's form across the table. He noted the monk's absolute control over her posture- initially poised for conflict, then relaxing as the tone of the conversation shifted away from the dangerous.

McKenna grinned back. "I'm surprised Seth even has friends, since he has insisted in no certain terms on the exact opposite."

"I'm not sure 'friends' is really the right word for these two," piped up Katherine while holding out her freckled wrist in greeting to the monk. "Star-crossed lovers, kindred hearts estranged at birth, souls mated by the gods…" she trailed off as James and Seth rolled their eyes in perfect tandem.

McKenna laughed, appreciating the soft, clarion quality of the woman's voice. "Are you a bard, too?" she queried.

"What? This harpy? For shame. As if our villagers would tolerate holvir strangers if our tavern could host its own musician," responded James. McKenna winced at his dismissive tone and Katherine smacked him on the shoulder before turning her own on him, facing McKenna. "I deeply appreciate the compliment, but I'm just a healer. A cleric for the town, since no guild will have me," she sighed.

"She's an incredibly talented herbalist," offered Seth over the grumbles of his disgraced companion. "You spoke of metal singings- we have a similar treatment for our plants and animals."

Katherine's countenance, marbled by vitiligo, flushed with the praise. "It looks like you've been caught in the crossfire of some pretty powerful singings yourself," she offered to McKenna. "You're unfairly tall."

McKenna just shrugged her sable shoulders, taking a sip from the drink before her. "True, I'm the tallest duergi in my clan, but shockingly behindhand in beard growth. If only the gods were fairer," she rued.

Katherine and James blinked helplessly at that, while Seth just laughed.

"Anyways, introductions," he said. "McKenna, James, Katherine. James and I were born a day apart-"

"We used to joke it was our only day apart," interrupted the bear of a man with a hand clapped to Seth's shoulder.

"-and he's from a family of magistrates who help my mother run our village. We grew up and trained together, James my squire and I his knight." finished Seth, as the two men toasted and drank together.

"But you're not of the Guild of Tooth and Claw, is that right?" McKenna asked, addressing James with curiosity.

"Nope. No soothsayer would bother coming to my cradle when the Chosen One here was born the day before me. You don't have to pledge to the guild to be a squire- just, you know, be crazy enough to travel between Lianor and Wheelspoke constantly, with no benefit other than the honor of your noble knight's," he replied, with a wink.

"Yeah, no benefits other than access to the best education and martial instructors in all the realms without having to actually commit to anything," Seth jockeyed back.

"Makes… sense, I guess," McKenna responded hesitatingly. Their physical nearness to each other brought a heat to her face she didn't recognize and chose to ignore.

"And I had the insanely enviable task of patching them both up," quipped Katherine. "After the battles, that is. These two have absolutely no sense of self-preservation."

"I can only imagine," replied McKenna. The two men toasted again and took deep drafts from their mugs. "Those are our companions as well up there, by the way. Ginni and Tjen adopted us into their traveling party, and they're mostly responsible for why we're here."

James cupped a hand to his chin. "It would be like Seth to find himself in thrall of a couple holvir and a… duergi," he said, his eyes traveling along the runes inked into her skin.

McKenna wasn't quite sure how to read the comment, and it ruffled her slightly. Was he questioning her ethnicity, or judging her for it?

"Before you think my companion a hopeless bigot, I should probably explain," offered Katherine. "The eastern realms aren't very well known for their hospitality. Despite the lovely ballad your companions were just singing, they like to forget anyone but themselves built this society. That's the official line, anyways. Our plebeian selves try to be more disposed to humility and recognize

the soulful, regardless of who they are. It's just our Grand
Masters, and our Lords and Ladies…" she fumbled for
the right expression.

"Do not. They recognize only our religious and
physical superiority," finished James, under his breath.
"So, you know, we're just bigots on the surface. You don't
think the bar broke itself, did you?"

McKenna laughed at the sight of Ginni gingerly
avoiding the sag in the bartop while dancing. "Okay,
that's fair. Now I really feel bad for snapping at you,
Seth," she said, elbowing him lightly. He just smiled and
shrugged.

"Don't. I deserved it. We hide behind our veils here,
not wanting to stir the pot, not wanting to start anything
with people we know we can't sway, but that's really not
an excuse- and there's none at all for bringing the habit
with me on the road," he muttered under his breath,
still ducking his head slightly to avoid the looks of other
patrons.

A quick glance around the tavern explained their
discomfort. Every member aside from the pair on the
bar were aesir. And their holvir friends were clearly
only tolerated in their self-imposed servient position.
Placed on the bar, they showcased and even exaggerated
their tiny limbs and lack of stature, putting themselves
on display in an effort to give their audience the power
to judge them as they would. The act was Ljotebroek
all over again and it struck McKenna as a testament to
their unshakeable senses of self. Despite deliberately
prostrating themselves as lesser to those they travelled
among, they didn't let it weaken their spirit nor did they
hold themselves up to the mirror of public opinion. The
holvir simply were, regardless.

"Enough sacrilegious talk," enjoined Katherine. "How did you even make it through the horde? Last time we travelled to Lianor, it took a garrison from the guild to ensure we made it there in one piece."

"Oh, we've found them all right," replied Seth. "We travelled down from the north and took out a host of our own."

"How in the realms… a host of ilmaurte? By yourselves?" questioned James aggressively, narrowing his eyes again at the monk.

"Seth says he's been fighting them for a while now, but…" she trailed off.

"But I hadn't even made a dent until I met McKenna. We… discovered a neat trick that perhaps the durgir have been holding out on us."

She smacked him. "Don't you start. Durgir have more alcohol in their blood than magic, everyone knows that."

"Excuse me. Your what?? Did you say blood?" asked Katherine, her keen eyes suddenly trained to the newly healed gash across McKenna's shoulder. "Can I see that?"

"Sure. Don't worry, an ilmaurt didn't put that there, Seth did," she said, tilting toward the inquisitive woman who softly investigated the wound with all the expertise Seth claimed of her. Katherine snorted at her blasé delivery, while casting an expressive look at Seth.

"Not you, too. I got pinned by about seven of the damned things and she fights with a guisarme! You think those limbs are long, you should see them in action with a polearm!" he cried defensively. James wrapped a comforting arm around his shoulder and grimaced at Katherine, who simply laughed her musical laugh and continued to inspect the mark.

"Well, now I'm curious because if I know Seth, he fires blessed bolts. And you're not a follower of Bahamut. Yet it seems you weren't burned by an oath or anything, just marked by the quarrel itself. Your blood dispels ilmaurte and protects you from divine magic?" She asked, her soft blue eyes sparkling with curiosity.

"I'm a monk. There's no way I'm protected from divine magic, my entire practice is devoted to it," McKenna replied somewhat defensively. "Maybe Bahamut decided to go easy on me, I dunno."

Seth was studying her with that look again- the one he liked to save for when she reached the edge of some kind of identity crisis. She rolled her eyes to avoid his searching gaze, returning to the subject at hand.

"Anyways, we fought the ilmaurte and we seemed to destroy them- at least, we have no reason to believe they rematerialized. And our friends mentioned on their travels from the west, they saw towns that seemed… ghosted. Burned out, or simply abandoned."

"Quite a few towns have quested raids against this scourge. There's been no change then?" added Seth.

"No," answered James. "The horde has only grown larger. Luckily, less organized. But since you left the Guild of Tooth and Claw has been hard-pressed to even keep them out of blessed towns. At least, that's what they say. There seems to be a necromancer behind it."

"So they're finally acknowledging that option," McKenna interrupted. "And the ilmaurte have been here this long…"

She shivered, recalling the feeling of souls sliding past hers in the valley pass.

"There's no other alternative," responded Seth. "Necromancy is the only magic that can wield the ilmaurte, short of the goddess Atosa. What we don't understand is who's doing it."

James cast another glance at McKenna and shifted uncomfortably.

"Well, Lianor thinks it's the ilvir," responded Katherine, swirling wine in her glass.

Seth scoffed. "They would. Nobles like to pit us lesser beings against one another to hide their own questionable misdeeds. But the ilvir would know if it were Atosa releasing the ilmaurte. They've worshiped her for centuries. Why would they allow refugees in their forests if they started this in the first place? I don't see them benefitting from this. Only the aesir."

"Nobles? You mean, magistrates?" McKenna asked in confusion.

"No, the nobles of Lianor. You've never heard of them? They sailed over from who knows where, settling in Lianor as it was built. They brought Sanct Germain - and excessive amounts of gold. It's like the biggest event in aesir history," answered Katherine quickly. "You didn't know about it?"

McKenna shrugged helplessly. "I always wondered

why asafolk had two gods. I didn't realize Sanct Germain was so... new."

Katherine blinked. "Err, this was like a hundred years ago. Though I guess to a duergi," she tilted her head thoughtfully as she studied McKenna, "that may seem like yesterday."

Sipping at her drink, McKenna was too deep in thought to catch her comment. "So then Golden Eye - is a Noble's guild? How does that even work?"

"Golden Eye's basically their attempt to assimilate. They revolutionized our economy, our social structure, everything. The plains people are pretty plain farmers, not so far descended from the ilvir, and between the Hops guild to the north and the Builders' in the south, we all tended to lead the same kind of life, share the same level of culture. Without a guild, who would take them seriously? They came in and gentrified with a vengeance, and they all but rule Lianor now."

"Tooth and Claw just... let that happen?" questioned McKenna.

"Tooth and Claw wouldn't exist without the nobles. They were a bunch of overgrown goblins with big sticks compared to the Lianor elite."

Katherine ignored the sounds of outrage that came from her companions. "What? It's true. Bahamut was sick and tired of the dick-waving contests that kept happening between Wheelspoke and Dragon's Hill, and began the prophecies of paladins to recruit us both to the guild and stop our constant warring with each other." The noises of outrage and effrontery grew louder, but she continued to ignore them; McKenna, though listening intently, had to stifle her laughter in her palm. The aesir guilds had always carried with them an aura of mystique and invincibility; it surprised her to find out they, too, were as fallible as the race they served.

"Anyways, that made it pretty easy for the guild to fall under the influence of the nobles, especially once they took up residence in Lianor. The guild's might and supremacy definitely flourished, but..." she trailed off, absentmindedly tracing the runes surrounding the scar on McKenna's arm, "it came at a cost."

"There's a reason we were able to work with the other races before, and suddenly... err, stopped," chipped in James.

McKenna inhaled sharply, nostrils flaring in an attempt to overlook the implications in James' statement. Seth, however, came to her defense immediately.

"Those pathetic cowards sit in their ivory towers and dictate how the rest of us get to live our lives. Tooth and Claw poisoned their own mead trusting and kowtowing to them like they do," he hissed angrily.

James leaned into his friend, his eyes narrowed as he replied, "You need to keep your voice down, here. We've all adopted the party line, because it's simply too dangerous to do otherwise. But," and he slipped a scroll into Seth's lap, "there are other parties we can hear from."

Seth pocketed the document in one quick fluid motion just in time. The holvir had finished singing, so the bar around them had gotten quieter. A few black stares directed at Seth meant recognition they couldn't exactly afford.

"You shouldn't come home anymore," whispered Katherine, her voice tight. McKenna caught a glimpse of excruciating heartbreak cross James' face and the squire's arm flexed. Despite her distaste for the man and the strange tension between them, she couldn't help feeling a little sorry for him. Seth put a hand on his and let out a sigh.

"Thank you, for what you told us," replied McKenna. She scanned the bar quickly and saw that Ginni and Tjen had vanished completely. The bartender caught her gaze and nodded, tight-lipped, towards a door behind the bar. Her eyes bespoke thanks as she realized he'd helped them disappear.

She felt an aching dissonance in the discord of the room's aura. Several tables were full of hunched figures- their sympathy intermingling with the sense of their fear. And yet others- louder, larger, more imposing- simmered with wrath. For once McKenna thanked her un-duerglike appearance. It was probably the only thing keeping them from being immediately accosted by these xenophobic patrons.

Suddenly the barkeep materialized at their shoulder. "We're closed for the night," he stated loudly, grabbing their mugs and gesturing them towards the door. McKenna, realizing his intervention prevented a more violent outbreak, offered him another smile of mute thanks. His adamantine gaze softened almost imperceptibly as he turned from them to take a seat with James and Katherine, who ducked their heads in whispered conversation.

Not eager to make more enemies of the patrons still present, Seth and McKenna slipped from sight and made their way through Wheelspoke's darkened town square.

"I can't believe they just turned on you like that. I know you and your mother have your differences, but you're still her son- shouldn't they respect you in honor of her?" said McKenna when they were finally safely on their own.

There was an edge to Seth's voice when he finally responded. McKenna recalled the look on James' face, but waited in silence for him to speak.

"My mother is the reason I left the guild. She knows it, and she pretends to feel guilty for it, but she made her choice just the same."

McKenna looked at him confusedly but didn't interrupt.

"Our village didn't have to succumb to the rules that Tooth and Claw were enforcing. We could have stayed vigilant and protected the refugees, but my mother… she believed them. She believed she was establishing our family's might and my position, my future as the Grand Master of the Tooth and Claw. But she was wrong."

"She what?" asked McKenna, slowing her pace.

"The ilmaurte are indiscriminate in their attacks, burning towns and scattering our people to the four winds. Their advance kept getting worse and worse. Ginni and Tjen only confirmed what I've known for some time - whole villages, cities even, razed and defenseless survivors left to fend for themselves. The forest guilds, like Hand Over Fist or Moonbow, have acted to protect their people, since Meliamne has managed to escape the scourge's advance. Lianor has suffered the fewest casualties, and therefore the guilds and the nobles are our strongest force in the realms right now. Instead," he seethed, almost too angry to finish his sentence, "instead of offering refuge while our neighbors rebuild, they're treating it as free recruitment. Opportunity for evangelism. Join the Noble's guilds - or die."

McKenna recoiled in shock. Illusen, Hanthor, the northern towns, almost all Beausun's civilization, already worshiped Bahamut- but they generally avoided the guilds, refused the patronage of the larger cities to the south, and willingly maintained trade and relationship with the durgir. To the west, cities like Ljotebroek led similar lives free from such structure, allowing their citizens to practice their worship as they chose so long as they offered the same discretion to their fellow citizens. Clearly, it wasn't even just a question of religion. They had to adopt the rules, the hierarchy, that the guild enforced. "Abandon their culture, their way of life, in exchange for protection? What kind of false choice is this? What happens if they refuse?" *What kind of gods allow such heresy?*

"We cast them out. Bar our gates. Make them face the wrath of the ilmaurte horde, or waste away on the plains, or take the long and mostly perilous journey to the forests to throw themselves at the mercy of the ilvir." His face hardened as he spoke.

"And it happened to Wheelspoke?" whispered McKenna. "Refugees came *here*, and their neighbors, their fellow aesir, denied them?"

"The home of the child of prophecy. The stronghold of our family, the most powerful and influential and long-lived followers of Bahamut in all the realms. How do you think it went?" he spat. "My mother tried to convince me it was for the greater good. That my future was to

uphold the might of our guild- that regardless of their
circumstances, it was my duty to evangelize them one
way or another, and that the will of gods forced them into
their situation in the first place. She nearly manipulated
me into thinking that it was my only choice, but I made a
different one. I left."

*A perfect town. A perfect image. All for the glory of an aesir
dream. A son cast into darkness, a husband buried in ignominy.
Was the price of security ever too high?*

"But Arya," argued McKenna, "surely she must be
aware?"

"My sister doesn't know anything. She is under the
impression," irony dripping from the word, "that my
mother did all she could to persuade me to stay; but in
the end, I was too stubborn and heretical to listen."

"This doesn't make any sense to me," McKenna
muttered, her head swimming from everything that had
just happened, that he'd been telling her. "Durgir are
straightforward. We don't speak in riddles, we don't lie to
each other, to our families least of all. Why would she do
this to you? To her daughter?"

*And we just left her there. That poor girl. Stuck in her
brother's shadow, trapped under her mother's thumb, locked in
a bubble of a world where nothing is ever out of order.*

"Do you see where we are? Who these people are?
They're asafolk, like us. They live and they fight and they
die; their loyalties are limited. Whoever shows the least
weakness, offers the strongest protection- that is who they
rally to. It's that simple," he responded.

"Durgir raised me, not asafolk, and we don't treat one

another like this," she countered, ignoring the expression on his face and the dangerous implications of his choice of words. "Sure we fight, but ultimately we all work together for the common good, and let each other find our own ways of happiness. And I'm still a durgi," she said simply.

"Yes, but you weren't born one," Seth insisted.

"It's not about the identity I was born with!" She shouted in frustration, her fury at his insistence unleashing a torrent she wouldn't control. "It's about the identity I chose. I thought you of all people would be able to understand that- you, who walked away from the identity forced upon you since your people decided you had a talent."

Seth recoiled, shock on every line of his face. Then suddenly the force of his anger collapsed, and he leaned heavily against the ramparts surrounding the village, a weakness she knew without words that he'd never indulged in before. The hands that covered his face had been offered to her in friendship, the person who knelt before her had offered her a respect and a dignity she little expected in this strange and convoluted world. Wordlessly, she took his hand and held it in both of hers, hoping against hope she hadn't just destroyed every ounce of faith she'd built with the rogue, but unable to let him continue to allow the failed expectations of others to hold him back.

To her relief, he didn't disappoint her. "I'm sorry. You're right," he said quietly. "No one has ever seen that in me before. They all think I abandoned them out of weakness. Even my sister, try as she does to hide it, is disappointed because her brother, the child of prophecy, is nothing but a rogue and a callous deserter banished from his home and condemning his family to idleness and danger. No one has… recognized that it was the death of my soul, my very being, to continue to tread that path. I… thank you."

All we ever need is a little faith in one another. A little kindness.

"Seth, you don't owe anyone anything. Least of all those who would take from you without giving in return," she replied in a measured tone. "I'm on this quest because I'm trying to find my place, my purpose, and my direction beyond what I've already achieved. If I were meant to be there, among the durgir in the mines of Mount Oer, I still would be - but I'm not." She squeezed his hand again, drawing his eyes to hers. "You made the same choice. You faced the purpose you devoted yourself to for so long and saw it wasn't enough. You have every right to be here, every right," she said passionately, mesmerized by her own daring, "to get from this life all that you are strong enough and deserving enough to take. I promise."

As she spoke, she felt again that powerful ache of pride for the warrior who stood before her. He honored his god with every fiber of his being despite losing everything. She remembered James' stricken look as Katherine told them to leave, the pain and confusion of his father's last moments, the desperation in Arya's voice as they left her with her mother- and knew there wasn't a single aesir in all the realms with better conviction or sense of righteousness than this one. For a moment, she understood the race's general sense of superiority. Such a person as this couldn't be found among any but theirs.

"That's not true either," muttered Seth, reading in her face the words unspoken. "The durgir have a perfectly good example right here," he complimented, squeezing her hand as he smiled up at her.

She blushed and rolled her eyes, resting a hand on his hair. "Come on, we should go find our mounts. And our friends." She tugged him back to his feet and together they walked, disappearing into the dark night.

XX

Hand In Hand With Destiny

The plated glass of the scrying bowl reflected a gruesome sight. Wave after wave of refugees flooded the plains of Beausun; a desperate, shapeless horde aiming directly for the high impenetrable walls of Lianor. Thousands, from the ancient and venerable wielding farm tools to scrubby youths who had yet to initiate into life's greater challenges, covered league after league of prairie, fear lending wings to each stride.

"I see Makarh's rumors paid off, Razan," cooed a sultry voice seated before the bowl.

Razan curled his lip in distaste at the silken woman who addressed him. Gems dripped lasciviously from every inch of her, shining brightly against the darkness of her feline visage. At his expression, her blood red lips parted in a coquettish grin. Yes, the Lady Lilithen Astore wore her beauty well. Something, thought Razan with disgust, he hoped she'd stop flaunting at her dispassionate son.

"I hope you found your payment… satisfactory," he replied, words dripping like venom from his mouth.

"Oooh, deeply, deeply so. Are you looking for a little brother? Or a sister, perhaps?" She snickered at the disgust on his face. "Forget I asked. Only one of you is needed anyways."

Razan snorted, shooting a malevolent look at his shameless mother. "Now what is that supposed to mean?"

"Just that, despite your best efforts, you may not turn out to be such a disappointment after all."

Without giving him time to digest the comment, she laughed again and turned back to the image in the scrying bowl. "So, what is the point of driving all these impoverished miscreants here? Have they exhausted the ilvir of Meliamne already?"

He scanned her languid form, debating whether or not he would answer. Truly he couldn't trust the cryptic and mysterious cult of Naszer to which their family belonged with any kind of truth, but the very chaos they represented served as a perfect disguise. A twisted, parasitic growth that hid in the bowels of Lianor's esteemed church of Sanct Germain; they walked the knife's edge of obliteration from the lawful realms by simply hiding in plain sight. Well known to be in thrall of the daemoric powers of the Abyss, goodly clerics often sought the wisdom of Naszer's highly trained sorceres to track the hellspawn that roamed Faie in order to obliterate them.

Yet somehow, these goodly guilds always managed to turn a blind eye to the source of the hellish beasts.

"Doubting the presence of my philanthropy? You wound me, Lady Astore," mocked the assassin. She simply shrugged and reclined. Her son's dealings almost always bored her.

"The nobles of Lianor are desperate to control the bounties of Beausun. It's no secret. What they can't keep in their coffers, they can always collect in taxes," his glance narrowed in in her direction, curious to see how enthralled were the easily manipulated clergy of Lianor's principle gods, and through them, the eager nobles of the coastal city whose entry into Faie had been as sudden as it was violent. "The hardy asafolk of Beausun's limitless plains have found their own way to the gods, and their own economy, and ignore the salvation and protection offered by our greater ones. So it seems they just needed a little more... persuasion."

She laughed outright at her son's graceless confidence.

"The advance of the undead is no myth, no rumor. You think you know every secret, Razan, but indeed the daemor to whom your princess trusts her plans are indiscreet," she responded, her seductive drawl grating on his ears.

He knew she expected a reaction at reference to Katarin, but his expression remained impassive. Instead, he simply watched the scrying bowl, realizing his own fabricated explanation struck closer to the truth than he first realized. Lady Astore had been almost too eager to assist with such a inane request. At first he assumed the woman had simply been eager for an excuse to engage with Makarh, but now he wondered uneasily how deep her cult's involvement with the scourge defiling Faie really went. Turning back to regard his mother, he forced the concern from his mind. Her glittering eyes matched the onyx beads at her throat, and she used them like weapons to parlay with her son. She settled back into her couch, languidly fixing her attention to him.

"But perhaps you are right. The guilds care little for Faie's sister deities, or the healthy trade with lesser races that leak gold from aesir pockets. Where awe of great and goodly deeds do not turn the hearts of men, fear must take its place instead," she said bluntly. "Abyssinians are too unwieldy; to release one with the hopes that a hero questing in the might and name of his god will destroy it is a dangerous strategy. How much easier," she gestured laconically, "to release death upon the land and both literally and figuratively chase these heathen souls into the church?"

"What control have the clerics of Sanct Germain or Bahamut over Atosa's realm?" he challenged.

"None at all, my volcanic son. But where there are advantages to be taken, it behooves them to strike when the iron is hot."

Razan wondered if his mother had discovered McKenna's surprise existence. Lianor knew better than to take arms against the ilvir of Meliamne, and accusing their beloved princess of such crimes would draw down their wrath in an instant. To that end, he questioned his mother further, toeing a fine line of intrigue even as he spoke.

"And the cult of Naszer has been whispering the secrets of stirrings in the undead to the ears of the goodly gods, have they?"

She snickered to herself, still refusing to meet his gaze.

"Who listens to daemor? The undead are stirring, whether from Atosa's disappearance or from the feckless proddings of that child whom the tiresome ilvir hail princess."

Tingles of suppressed magical energy coursed through his veins. It had been like this always. He, refusing every bait she threw, and she, calculating and disdainful, mocking the way her rebellious son chafed against the bonds of his fate. Almost he thought she had let him escape all those years ago. A test, to throw him upon the tender mercies of their heartless world in the expectation he would either die, or finally manifest the innate talents of his daemoric ancestry to claw his way free.

He hated the thought he was no more than a puppet, no matter how many years and leagues he put between him and his accursed family.

"The Third Sorcere is no child," he spat finally, sick of Lady Astore's vague words and keen to deflect her sinister curiosity from Katarin. "The Guild of Moonbow recognized her right to ascend in the place of Atosa, not more than a tenday ago." The riposte of her candid gaze fell harmlessly upon him, and he matched the lilac silence of her eyes with the bloody glow of his own.

"She aspires to goddesshood, does she?" Lady Astore seemed to find this highly amusing. "And what is the point to goddesshood if one's worshipers don't recognize them?"

The horde appeared, surging after the exhausted refugees. Leagues still lay between them, but no measure of mortality can forever escape the dead.

"So the little princess will wield her almighty rule over death, annihilating the undead and freeing the sufferers who beat in futility against the barred gates of

Lianor." No sound escaped the scrying bowl, her voice simply narrated the images that flashed before him. "Dramatic, but effective."

Each word flicked like a whip against the raw of Razan's soul. Something was missing. The irony of his mother's voice, which he usually tuned out, whispered life into every misgiving the assassin had ever experienced during this whole endeavor. His loyalty to Katarin remained so devout due to her absolute lack of such insidious intrigue. She stood a foil everything he had left behind with his horrible family. The murder of a rival, the assassination of a clan that threatened war-these were duties he accepted in his line of servitude to the Guild of Moonbow. But the implications made by his mother were far, far worse. To be manipulating the homeless, wandering undead into a direct attack upon the defenseless citizens of Faie just for recognition was a level to which he firmly believed the sorcere would never stoop.

"Your daemor don't tell you everything." He scorned her insinuations and, with a sweeping bow, left the apartment.

"Hmmm, my hopeless child, and your lover doesn't either," the Lady Astore whispered to his retreating back.

XXI

A Heritage Unknown

"That was fast," giggled Ginni from a branch upon which she and Tjen perched above a cheerily burning campfire, not far along the forest path. "I assume you two forgot to tip the barman."

"House T'ssama pays Domhnall's rent." Seth's reply was curt. "But he did us a favor, that's for sure."

"You can thank us for that," Ginni said sweetly. "We warned him about you being here. Though you'd think a bar owned by your family would know better than to kick its Lady's son out. That's just bad business."

In response to the disgusted sound Seth made, Tjen pushed Ginni out of the tree before lithely dropping to the ground themselves. "I hope you learned something worthwhile," they asked as Ginni dusted herself off in a huff.

"We learned that between undead hordes and power-hungry guilds, I'd rather face the former," McKenna responded, her teeth on edge.

Seth snorted and the tension in the little clearing suddenly dispersed. Ginni just rolled her eyes; another musical huff belying her annoyance.

"They meant about the mirror. Gods bedamned-anything that can throw Seth like it did piques my interest," she reminded them cheekily.

McKenna drew it forth as Seth reached into his pack and pulled out the journal. She cast an uneasy glance at their surroundings, but the holvir had chosen their rendezvous well. They were distant enough from Wheelspoke that no marauding sentry could accost them, and yet still within fair enough boundaries of aesir settlement that would protect them from anything else. The rain, which had been sputtering determinedly throughout the day, caught itself among the branches and leaves overhead and hissed against the smoldering logs of the holvir's fire. Its soft, shy whisper did its best to deaden the sounds around them, offering cover from any unwelcome listener.

Such as the one disguised in the trees above.

None but Razan could command the dappled shadows of leaf and cloud enough to escape the sharp notice of Seth's trained eye. Nor did he mean to betray his position just yet. His motive, parallel to Katarin's assignment, was to try to come to an understanding of the kind of individual this surprise twin sister professed to be. His belabored spying so far had discovered no ulterior motivation to her avowed one of questing enough to grow a beard. Beyond that, her motives stumped him. The woman showed absolutely no curiosity toward her fabled history, no interest into the rights behind her strange delivery as a babe to the durgir who'd raised her. It baffled him to see her so completely devoid of any desire to understand who she was or where she came from. Her utter surety in her upbringing as a durgirn monk of Malfaestus brooked no disagreement.

And the discovery soothed a measure of his heart the assassin almost didn't recognize.

If McKenna, bless her innocent soul, could so fully and completely escape the shadow cast by her birth and her mother's legacy, could not Katarin do the same? Katarin was an exceptional sorcere in her own right. A powerful motivator, inspiring loyalty and devotion in the most aloof of all the races who roamed Faie. What good would goddesshood do her that decades of service upon the altar of her guild couldn't? Out of loyalty, he had assisted with the necessary dark deeds that accompanied her ascension. Serving Katarin with ungrudging, unquestioning devotion lent color to the assassin's shadowy life. He studied his hands, so skilled with blade and passionate in holding the jewel of his heart, and wondered suddenly where his place would be once Katarin has assumed her godly mantle.

The thought spurred him to rash action. He dropped, suddenly, silently, into the little gathering below.

A sabre point pressed against his breast and the blade of a guisarme scratched the stubble at his chin. He smiled disarmingly.

"Don't worry; though I know who all of you are, it's an advantage I don't mean to take of you for long." Extending his wrists in proffered peace, he knew the band wouldn't kill him immediately.

"Wait, I recognize you! You're the... uhm. Well. That guy... you didn't exactly give us your name, but we know you!" Ginni dithered excitedly, a hand on Tjena's shoulder. "Tjena, see, we... oh heck."

Tjena chuckled incredulously. So did Razan. The muscles on Seth's and McKenna's face didn't crack.

"Razan Astore, of Onyx Blade," spat the rogue, without lowering his weapon.

McKenna tensed to Seth's tone, confused by the conflicting emotions among her party. "Forgive me if that still doesn't mean much," she offered candidly, her staff raised level with his throat.

"The humble guildmaster of an even humbler guild, good duergi," he offered with a courtly nod and a smirk. "And, if I may be so bold, a loyal bondsman to your own dear sister."

McKenna's eyebrows shot up. "Sister? Are you crazy? I don't have a sister."

Seth put pressure on the point above Razan's heart. "I would choose your words more carefully, assassin," he hissed, anger kindling in every word.

"Oh? Is it possible you don't know in whose company you are, paladin of Bahamut?" he laughed, his hands still in the air in surrender.

McKenna tossed Laghrusse to the ground in disgust. "Asafolk, I swear by Malfaestus… what exactly is going on? Why are you here? Have you been following us?"

"Hmm, how long do I have to answer those incredibly loaded questions before your champion skewers me as much with his blade as he's been doing with his eyes?"

McKenna narrowed her own at the unexpected

interloper, then whispered a quick prayer. The runes on Laghrusse fired suddenly, in a pattern that flickered too quickly along the shaft to be comprehensible. She looked at Seth.

"My belated thanks to the Magis- I normally couldn't work that spell by myself even if I had a week to prepare. If he makes any move with intent to harm, my blade will slit his throat."

Seth grimaced, but trusting the monk's infallible connection with her god, sheathed his sabre in one quick motion. Crossing his arms, his eyes fixed to the assassin in a look that would ignite the soul of a lesser man.

Razan simply laughed again.

"There, that's something more hospitable. My thanks to you, good monk. Now, about your sister-"

"WHAT sister?" she interrupted exasperatedly.

"Princess Katarin, Third Sorcere of the Guild of Moonbow," muttered Ginni, suddenly sure of McKenna's dubious ancestry.

Seth narrowed his eyes at the holvi. "How did you know?"

"We're bards. We know stuff. Also, we met her. Briefly. That's where we met this guy too. He showed us the way, then kind of just, vanished. We never did say thank you... I guess we owe you one for that! Thanks," Ginni curtsied prettily at the assassin.

"Don't thank me yet," he replied cryptically. "But yes, Katarin is indeed my employer, and it is she who seeks you. However, I am far more dispensable, and easier to send across the country."

McKenna stared blankly between him and Seth. She fixed on the latter. "You know about this? How is it even possible?"

Seth sighed. "I tried to warn you. You just told me it was a metaphor."

The word rang in McKenna's memory. A metaphor…

She laughed outright.

"Okay, you all are completely crazy. You think I'm some kind of… of goddess?"

"Her child, actually. Mortal, but with perks," a flashing grin accompanied the assassin's tongue-in-cheek jibe.

"Perks…? Perks like…" McKenna trailed off, her gaze drawn to the smear of blood that still stained the mithril blade.

"Like power over the dead, for one thing. An attunement to those who have slipped the bonds of mortality to meet their immortal maker. Oh, and probably the possession of a priceless artifact- a mirror, with wondrous and untested powers,"

No one in the clearing moved a muscle.

"Well, I seem to have struck a nerve," he remarked flippantly.

McKenna's whole being sustained a shock to

which she had no armor. Flashes of memory flitted before her- adventures in the mines after disembodied voices, ducking under every doorframe of the durgirn stronghold by age eight, scrying Seth's dead father in the mirror. And a lurking silence in the edge of every durgirn voice when she petitioned for her beard quest. None of them had ever said she wasn't a duergi.

But then, had any ever said she was?

"While you puzzle that out," offered Razan, "I thought I should answer the rest of your questions. I have indeed been following you- truly, it's just my job, and I'm very good at it, so don't be offended- and as for what is going on, I had hoped you'd be able to tell me that."

A low growl emanated from Seth, whose entire body had taken the rigidity of stone. McKenna wondered what went through his mind to incite such tense rage. Razan noticed as well.

"Your friend here seems to think I'm implying too much. I guess I should back up. You are all aware of the ilmaurte pestering the goodly folk of Faie. They've been the talk of the realms for quite some time now- accompanied, it seems, by talk of a mysterious young woman who claims to be a durgirn monk appearing in the realms with uncanny powers over them. Surely a strange coincidence-"

"How dare you," roared Seth. The sabre thrust toward Razan's heart met the sparks and adamantine of the assassin's own blade, moments before striking flesh.

"Wh- Seth! Are you kidding me?" cried McKenna, reaching down for Laghrusse. Ginni grabbed her wrist and yanked her hard to the ground, just in time to dodge a crossbow quarrel that whizzed past the locks of her hair and narrowly missed grazing Razan's cheek.

"Sorry, McKenna, but I really don't think you should get in their way." Ginni had a wild light in her eye, but McKenna caught the tone and remembered how often she'd read the histories of asafolk and their strange, unaccountable affinity for duels of this nature. She squinted accusatorially at her holvi friend.

"Ginni. Don't tell me you're enjoying this."

"What?" she countered innocently. "It's kind of hot, don't you think?"

Tjena snorted in disgust, then slid down beside Ginni as a shower of sparks, the remains of their magical fire, sprayed over the little audience as the fighters whipped viciously through it.

The bright embers peppered Seth's armor, clattering harmlessly against the mithril maille. He slid backwards, dragging a boot through the thin silt that dusted the forest floor. Parrying a lunge, he flicked the bold assassin's strike wide, but didn't press the offensive. The weight of Razan's blade sliding along his own gave him a measure of his prowess, but he knew a bait when he saw one.

Razan too had stepped back, nimbly whipping another thrust toward the paladin's throat. A sharp scrape rang along the intercepting blade, and this time forced the assassin to dodge a counter. McKenna could barely follow the swordplay- the blades that flew through the air were a blur, the arms extended that controlled them moving with power and grace in movements too quick to anticipate.

With a hiss, Razan drew back, running the edge of his short cloak along a fresh cut along his cheek. "Not the face, you know better than that- no point."

"This isn't a duel and your guard was down," returned the paladin.

Razan dipped quickly, tucking into a roll while scooping a handful of smoldering ash and tossing it viciously at at the rogue's unprotected eyes.

"What- I can't see!"

"Sounds like my advantage then, not yours."

Razan choked out a laugh, while dodging as Seth's vicious saber stabbed repeatedly at him. Though Seth pressed forward, the assassin managed to hold his own, parrying with sword and dirk while Seth blinked rapidly to clear the dirt from his eyes. Suddenly he struck out at the paladin's unguarded hip, exposed by a too-long strike at his opponent. The paladin's maille turned the sharpness of the blade, but the strength of the thrust was enough to throw him off balance.

Razan turned his attack for a downward blow at the paladin's exposed neck- a trick he forgot he'd already tried once, in a similar battle not too long ago against the fierce warrior. He grinned ruefully as the paladin's heavily studded fist struck out at his forearm, and winced as the blow nearly broke his arm. *Every time, Razan. Get good already.*

The hit almost caused him to drop his sword. He took a leap backwards, putting distance between himself and the prone paladin. As Seth rose, the venomous malice in the look he bore struck the assassin almost as hard as the punch did.

Razan had longed for another duel with this one, ever since their first meeting- a battle brought to pass by the rise of the daemor Makarh. Though both sought a quick despatch of the bloodthirsty daemor, Razan chose to focus more on the glory of defeating Tooth and Claw's greatest champion in combat.

Seth, prepared for a battle with a daemor that would nearly send his soul to the Abyss, had no time for those games.

Finally the quixotic assassin snapped. What right of superiority did this man have, after all? To look at him with such spite, such passionate fury, ignited a rage within Razan's breast; a call to challenge that grim look of righteousness and to humble the paladin once and for all.

The din became deafening. Both favored light blades, but the clangor of each rang through the clearing like the clash of a dozen battleaxes. Sweat ran into their eyes while dirt and ash clung to maille, to cloth, to bronze skin and black. They met with a fury and separated in a rage, and for minutes McKenna sat staring, dazed into inaction by the display.

She realized with a start the noise would begin to attract more unwelcome visitors, and uneasily peered into the gloom among the low, scrubby trees surrounding them. All lay still and quiet, save for the two violent combatants, but they really weren't far from Wheelspoke. At any moment a sentry or late-passing farmer could encounter them. As she looked back toward Seth and Razan, the former threw down his saber and punched another studded gauntlet toward the latter's stomach.

He managed to turn just in time, but the hit landed on the elbow of his already injured arm and Razan felt the fingers go numb, then drop the sword they held.

"Okay, enough!" she shouted, and Laghrusse spun through the air to slice between the battling figures, the force of the impact knocking each back from the other.

"Are you quite done?" she seethed, eyes crackling in dangerous fury.

"Spoilsport," muttered Ginni. Tjen flicked her ear and she yelped, sticking out her petulant tongue.

The fury of the gazes of each would have annihilated anything caught in their crossfire. These two antagonistic spirits could barely tolerate each other's existence. The decisions and the paths of each, and how they travelled them, were too close for comfort. Each saw in the other an image of what might have been. Powerful families, chosen for greatness, and yet walking away in disgust from those who would use and abuse them for greater gain. McKenna honestly found it hard not to empathize, but the wanton violence she would stop at all costs. She addressed Razan, with less venom, and greater curiosity, blended in her voice.

"You first. I have some questions, and you can't answer them if Seth's knocked your lights out."

Razan, gasping heavily for breath, narrowed his eyes, but smirked. "I would hope you do," he said, lowering his blade and exhaling slowly, "and I will do my best to answer."

Seth grunted, but favored the assassin with no further attention. He stood and shook the dust from his garb, then sheathed his blade in disgust and left the clearing. Realizing she'd get no contribution for good or ill from the paladin, McKenna turned her attention back to Razan. "Let me see if I have this straight. I get to find out I'm the offspring of Atosa, a goddess most faiefolkr don't even remember, just in time to be accused of unleashing an undead horde? Somehow, I feel you can do better than that," she quizzed, her uncanny amber eyes boring into his bemused ones. She noted they had a strange shade- the color of dried blood, like the mark upon her blade.

He shrugged, still panting. "Stranger things have happened. Of course, most faiefolkr- yourself included- didn't even know of your existence. But it seems you've been making quite a name for yourself. You're kind of…" he scanned her massive form, "hard to miss. So it seems all anyone knows, is that for reasons unaccountable the goddess Atosa has gone silent, and allows the undead to walk free alongside a child whose existence has been for so long buried in myth."

"Now hang on. You've spiked your own guns there, my friend," piped up Ginni. "Maybe no one knew about McKenna, but they do know about Katarin. Especially the fact that she's a child of Atosa. Why isn't she being accused, when by your own admission she has just as much claim to her throne?"

He regarded the holvi with a pensive expression, choosing his next words carefully. Tiny bards spread tall tales, after all.

"Katarin is Third Sorcere of Moonbow. It's because she is recognized that none would bother to accuse her. She has always been the next in line to assume the birthright her mother left her behind to claim. In fact, the realm of Meliamne proclaimed not too long ago

that, should her mother not return to fix this problem
of wandering souls, Katarin would assume her mantle
and become the shepherdess. Katarin has worked, and
waited," he suddenly became vehement, "for her entire
life to prepare herself for this moment, though she knew
not when that time would come."

"But an upstart, hidden sibling," murmured Ginni
thoughtfully, "would think to challenge her sister, you're
saying? By somehow destroying the gates of death and
releasing them upon the land?"

"Your words, not mine," he countered with a cocked
eyebrow.

"Does that always work for you, Razan? Putting
words in someone's mouth so you can pass the blame for
their being said?" snarled Seth, suddenly returning to the
clearing and the conversation.

"You would know, paladin," countered the shameless
assassin.

McKenna ignored them. "But Atosa," she said in
confusion. "Where is she? Where could she be?"

"Who knows? She is gone, that is for certain. Leaving
a perfect opportunity for battling out any sibling
rivalries," he offered unhelpfully.

"That's absurd. McKenna just wants to help folks,"
challenged Ginni. "You wouldn't want to… what did
he say… 'assume your mother's mantle' and become
Goddess of Death, right?"
"Not in a million years," she said, her eyes locked
with Seth's. She thought she had mastered the emotions
his face could show, but they hid from her now. "All I

want is a beard."

Razan's inscrutable eyes glittered like the dance of light on the edge of mithril. "Are you absolutely sure about that? You would never take up arms against your sister? Even if it meant having the power to restore the balance of life and death in your hands?" he prodded.

She hesitated. "What do you mean?"

"You say you want to help faiefolkr. Wouldn't reversing the tide of the horde's march, restoring their spirits to the realm of death, and saving the denizens of Faie make you the greatest hero of all?"

"Enough!" shouted Seth. He was trembling. "You come here weaving your false stories- I know your games of intrigue, assassin. We'll have none of it."

Ginni looked curiously at Seth. "Should be McKenna's decision, honestly. Not sure what she owes you- OW!" Tjena stomped on the careless holvi's foot. "What? I'm not wrong."

McKenna's heart gave a queer beat. Everything she had known, believed about herself, had been a lie- worse, a half-truth, burying the secrets the durgir hadn't cared enough to share with her under layers of who they expected her to be. What did she want, anymore?

"Well, I wouldn't take too long to think about it, my good McKenna of Clan Hammardin. Your mother is missing and your sister is waiting- and this is where I take my leave."

The assassin spoke so nonchalantly the sudden crack of his transportation globe startled them all. Before anyone could react, he vanished.

Laghrusse flashed, but remained motionless on the floor of the clearing.

She felt a gaze upon her. Tjena, their unseeing eyes locked on McKenna's face, looked troubled, almost apologetic. She wondered what the holvi was thinking-then wondered why she was so senseless to everything she'd just discovered.

A child of the goddess Atosa. Abandoned by her mother, raised by durgir who barely even recognized Atosa's divinity. Who had accepted the babe unquestioningly despite that, and raised her as one of their own.

One of their own. But she wasn't. And that was more painful than any other thought.

Suddenly McKenna's guisarme sparked, a rune marked to return the blade to its master's hand firing. She didn't need Seth's sudden unsheathing of his hand crossbow or the gasps of the holvir to know that deep in the gloom, surrounding them, lay in wait the very scourge she had just been challenged to control.

And they lay in wait to feast.

XXII

Pain In The Aftermath

"You know, a break for like five minutes from this nonsense would be super appreciated right about now," Ginni murmured exasperatedly. She motioned to Tjena, who dumped the contents of a small pouch onto a pile of dead leaves. Ginni whipped out a flint and with one quick, sure stroke sent a shower of sparks over the lot. In an instant, a fire burst to life, scattering the shadows that hid the shambling undead.

Their ghastly, ghostly faces were no less repulsive than on the outskirts of Ljotebroek. Aesir, ilvin, orghi, duergi- the corpses lacked such defining characteristics. The barely faiefolkr shapes reeked of decay and otherworldly horror. Bile rose in McKenna's throat. She stood paralyzed, even as the click of a crossbow quarrel whizzed past her and struck its mark.

The bolts slowed the ilmaurte to a crawl- but still, the dweomer animating them proved more powerful than those blessed strikes. She watched in horror, unable to move, even as the nearest swiped a scabbed hand at her face. Seth swore under his breath, mounting Kurya and yanking the stationary monk out of their direct line of advance, before continuing along the line and firing more bolts as he called down blessings to aid in their battle.

Power over death. She had power over death, over… this. This was death and she stared it in the face. Revulsion poisoned every thought, every motion. The bards' heartfelt tones wavering through the air, building a wall of purity the ilmaurte couldn't easily penetrate, did nothing to clear the monk's hateful thoughts. She retched, putting a hand to her stomach and to her soiled mouth.

"McKenna!" screeched Ginni, releasing a strike of fierce sound against the undead that moved to take advantage of the prostrate monk. Tjen coaxed a complex little medley from their instrument, bow flying over the strings as they clenched their teeth in concentration. Ginni's focus reverted, training every note of her pure, sweet voice directly at McKenna's form.

There were voices clawing at McKenna, aching moans that grasped with an energy undeniable. Wistful, hopeless, dangerous, appalled, vehement. *Why must we die, only to become this?* What blind, vengeful gods allowed this tragedy? For these souls finally at rest, weary of the world, forced to return and, blind to the glories of life, rise again and seek revenge against those who enjoyed the blessings they no longer shared?

Her vision, blurred by tears, slowly registered the effect of the holvir's song. The ilmaurte, unable to advance but unwilling to retreat, swarmed and clawed at the air with nerveless fingers. Seth swept to and fro upon Kurya's back, keeping the monsters at bay with crossbow and saber, chanting loudly and desperately for a blessing to sever the dweomer and dispel the undead. Though his divine power had grown undeniably stronger, Bahamut had no domain over death, and Atosa's silence proved more powerful than her influence.

Reaching down, Laghrusse's sturdy length made its way into her hand. She flung a lackluster strike across the chest of the ilmaurt nearest, its body disintegrating at the mithril blade's lightest touch. The runes on the shaft lay mute, unresponsive to the wielder who could no longer reach her god. Malfaestus had no more domain over these monsters than Bahamut. The springy coils of her hair crackled with energy sourced directly from the depths of her own soul, of her heritage first unknown, then denied. The severed soul of the undead, quivering in place where its destroyed body once stood, let out a cry of release almost as pure as the notes from Ginni's song.

Seth and Kurya had retreated to stand before the holvir, unsure of McKenna's next move. He wanted with all his heart to rush in and save her, but he couldn't deny the deathly power that emanated from her. Wave after wave, it plucked the edges of his soul as though to pull it from his own being. The embattled and embittered warrior had, in moments dark and overwhelming, longed for death as an escape from a life that seemed to have lost its direction. But the draw of this, the blood of the immortal goddess unleashed, was a sensation he'd never felt before. He held back, knowing that any closer step would be toward an inescapable death.

He cast a despairing look at Ginni, who maintained the strength of her song without a single broken note. She too gazed at the glowing figure before them, outlined as though by fire amid the crowd of undead. Tears tracked silver trails down her face, the desperation of mourning she couldn't avoid, at the thought of losing her friend to these fiends. Losing the one person in all the realms who saw them as equals, who truly believed these people who walked so long in the shadow of the soulful beings deserved their own place in Faie's sun. Would she turn to the dead, would she seek the power of the goddess who had abandoned her?

Seth put a hand on the holvi's shoulder, needing the warmth of her friendly touch. She smiled at him and laced her fingers with his. Perhaps together, her song and his devotions could reach the monk, remind her of the home, and friends, and family who believed in her.

What would her mother do? McKenna thought wildly. What had her mother *done*? How could she endow two mortal children with godly power that they may never learn how to wield? It was hateful- it was unfair- it was a destiny she neither asked for nor sought. She felt unclean, separated forever from the beings with which she shared this wonderful world. With a gesture as though washing her hands she tried to shake the energies clinging to her, flinging them free to settle in the trees, the dirt, the sky above.

Freed souls grasped her outstretched fingers.

She saw tiny, gossamer threads clinging to her fingertips, each one aligning with a stationary undead figure. Whispering along the bright strands were stories, memories, laughter; unbearable sadness, and incendiary anger. At one point each thread had tethered a soul to a mortal body. Throughout the history of the races that populated Faie, its soulful creatures had lived, animated by this mysterious and otherworldly and tangible magic that she now held with her calloused fingertips and wound around her pale palms. She tugged lightly, drawing them closer. With an ungodly wail, the undead corpses severed from their souls disintegrated, dissipating into the night. Into a darkly dissolving cloud of vapor the advancing horde vanished, until there was nothing left but these shimmering threads weaving a ghostly pattern before her.

Atosa is gone, they seemed to whimper unhappily. *Once you free us, we are doomed. The Doors of Death are closed, we can't get in.*

McKenna looked helplessly over her shoulder at the party huddled by the dying fire. She knew they could do nothing; that despite the companionship they shared, she faced this alone.

Tjena stroked the bow along the instrument, drawing forth a sound that jogged Ginni's memory.

"Urtha. We have to get the souls to Urtha. The orgir are shepherds of the dead. That's what Urtha was telling us."

McKenna's face brightened, then fell. "But how do I carry them?" she said, casting a forlorn look at the souls, leylines tethered to her by the lightest touch.

"The mirror. Show them the mirror," answered Seth suddenly.

McKenna eased the mirror slowly from its pocket, holding it out to reflect the light of the moon and the cloud of shimmering souls. It flashed silver, then gold with their incandescent glow. She could hear them; a whisper that rose to a din, the mournful voices of these stolen souls, the sounds of the undead raging against the summoner who controlled them, and desperately pled with the one who seemed to carry the touch of their goddess. As they slowly drifted into the mirror, she framed a promise in her heart. The balance would be restored. She could not deny her heritage, not if it meant she had the power to save them, to send them back to their final resting place. The runes around the mirror sparkled briefly, then in a moment all went dark and still.

"Huh. Well, I guess it worked," offered Ginni.

McKenna turned in mute inquiry to the gathering. Tjen set their instrument down and held out their arms, and she swept up the little holvi in a fierce embrace, sobbing uncontrollably.

"I- never want- to hear the word *hero*- ever again," she gasped through tears. Ginni wrapped herself around the monk's legs, and Seth laid a hand on her quivering shoulder.

"Of course not. We're all just trying to make our way, just ordinary faiefolkr on extraordinary adventures," soothed Ginni.

McKenna turned a tearful, agonized gaze toward Seth. She expected to see fear, doubt, confusion written on the rogue's face, but it was as ever an enigma.

"My sister can have this, whatever it is. I want none of it." Her vow echoed clearly though the still forest. "But if she doesn't stop whatever curse has been unleashed upon the realms, then I swear I will."

Out in the dark night, Razan's bangles chimed once, twice, thrice. With a triumphant grin, he vanished.

The fingernail of a new moon rose into the sky, casting a mournful glow over the exhausted party. Ginni had rekindled the fire and held McKenna's hands as close to it as they could get, chafing them with her own little fingers to draw forth the warm lifeblood that had left when she touched the freed souls. Seth held the mirror in one hand and the battered notebook in the other, his brow furrowed in intense concentration. Tjen leaned listlessly against McKenna, humming a soft tune while drawing their bow gently across the strings of their powerful instrument.

"How did you know?" She whispered softly, turning an almost fearful gaze upon him.

He put the journal down, forcing himself to look at her instead. The depths of a curious sensation filled her being when she stared into his eyes as she recognized within them a warmth and a sympathy they normally lacked.

"I guessed, at first. But then I saw the mirror, and…" he pointed at the curious runes along the bottom edge, "you said you could read these?"

"Well… kind of. I mean, in Common it just says 'Yourself', but that can't really be all of it. And they're, well…" she stammered, realizing for the first time that she had never actually translated them before because they weren't written in any language she'd ever studied. "They're fuzzy," she finished lamely.

"They're not fuzzy, McKenna. This is true Celestial." He pointed at a loose leaf page tucked in the journal that seemed to swim before her eyes, the lines drawn upon it shifting as soon as she focused on any one of them. "This is a codex handwritten by Nahariel, one of the most powerful and accomplished paladins of Bahamut to ever live. His first, actually, who had sworn devotion to the dragon and helped him become a god. My father had the only copy to ever exist. He won it in a competition with the Lord of Dragon's Hill. Not even our Guild has a full codex, because no aesir hand on Faie can transcribe them. Only another Celestial can read these runes," he replied, grabbing her hand to place it on the edge of the mirror. She looked at the word again, the same swirling uncertainty surrounding a clear and comprehensible meaning.

"Your aura is unlike any other I've ever seen.
You appeared out of nowhere, claiming the ancestry
of the durgir, yet you radiate the Celestial power of
the pantheon. I tried to tell you, but…" he trailed off,
unwilling to force her to confront the dissonance that
rattled her being.

*I told you I was a duergi. Insisted in no uncertain terms
that I knew exactly who I was. Defied you for a weakness you
have always been strong enough to admit.*

As a look of uncertainty screwed up her normally
confident features, he suddenly leaned forward and put a
hand to her chin, turning her to look at him.

"McKenna. You also carry with you the blessings and
oath of Malfaestus. Your clan, even the strangers we met
in Ljotebroek, they all recognized his calling within you.
You can be both," he said softly, an encouraging smile
lighting up his face. "You are both god and duergi. And
I think you, of anyone, knows the power of choice, to
choose the path you follow."

She sighed and laughed. "Now, why does that sound
familiar?"

*Of course he's right. We both get to choose our path, with
every new day and every next step. How lucky I am our paths
run together, then, rogue.*

He stroked a thumb along her cheek lightly, then
picked up the journal and tucked it back in his pocket. As
he did so, a small scroll fell out.

"Huh. What's this?" He studied it for a moment, then
brightened. "Oh, it's that note James gave me. Should I

read it?" he offered to McKenna, studying her face.

"Honestly, it can't be worse than what we've already heard tonight, can it? Not like my dad's a daemor or something," she joked, smiling at him.

He was glad to see the monk's spirit returning to her. The experience had left a ghastly tinge to her normally warm, dark complexion. Even now in the moonlight her skin had a translucent quality to it that made him uneasy. But the holvir beside her were no novices to the persuasion of emotion; the same power that could turn a room from xenophobic disgust to incredulous and candid delight easily manipulated the dread sadness that clung to McKenna as they sang softly.

He spread out the paper, sharing McKenna's lap. Across the top was a brief greeting, but further down, Seth saw what had made James so discreet about sharing it. "The Guild of Golden Eye is now in open league with the Cult of Naszer. Why doesn't THAT surprise me," he scoffed. "But Tooth and Claw and Golden Eye have been at daggers drawn since the beginning of time, why would-" he trailed off, continuing to read to himself.

McKenna waited, while he silently browsed the missive. Realizing she'd get nothing more from him for some time, she rolled her eyes and turned to the holvi. "Ginni, could you possibly tell me who the Cult of Naszer is?"

"Not really. There are rumors, sure, but they're pretty mysterious. Mostly because the rumors are that they... err... consort with daemor," she replied pensively.

Tjen snorted. "That's an understatement."

"Don't be filthy."

McKenna watched them volley bemusedly. Seth was still embroiled in the paper, his head in his hand.

"They're just a weird cult, based in Lianor, like the guilds are. I don't see what they have to do with the Guild of Tooth and Claw, to be honest. Unless the guilds are proposing some kind of truce, to face the undead horde. But once the Doors of Death are fixed, they'll go right back to rivalry. It's in their blood," Tjen carried on the train of conversation, ignoring Ginni.

"When you say in league with…" prodded McKenna, "you don't mean they actually like, ask them to set daemor loose on Faie or anything, right??"

"Not usually. Naszer has a… reputation… for being able to do that, but if it were true, they would've been wiped off the map by now. The rumors may just be due to their family's ability to control daemor. 'In league with' probably means Golden Eye is using Naszer to seek out any that have snuck onto the Material plane so they can find them, kill them, and banish them. Abyssinians are tricksy creatures. If they don't want to be found, you will not find them. But Naszer has an uncanny communion with the Abyss. So they're being kept around for the sake of hunting them down, I expect."

The firelight flickered across their faces, and McKenna recalled again the daemoric presence in which she'd once stood. Sparks, manifesting a baleful grin before disappearing in smoke, made her shiver.

"But what do daemor have to do with anything?" she mused. "If it's the Doors of Death that let free all the undead-"

"I knew it," Seth interrupted, smacking the paper. "A powerful necromancer. This must be the Lich King. Not many know the true history of the Cult of Naszer," and he pointed to a footnote scrawled neatly at the bottom of the scroll, "but it is said they formed to summon him, a great undead god. He's not bound by the same laws as daemor, either; he may not have a corporeal form, but now that his essence has been called to existence he can insinuate himself almost anywhere, and influence the minds of anyone willing to let him in."

"Corporeal form? What do you mean?" Ginni asked curiously.

Seth pondered how to answer that for a moment, staring into the fire. "When a sorcere summons a daemor, they can draw forth its actual, physical form. But the Lich King... isn't a daemor. I think the best way to describe him is that he's... an idea. A powerful idea able to control souls, reanimate the dead, and defy the very laws of life. But an idea is just that," he shrugged, holding his hands out as though to touch the air, to grab from it the very form he was attempting to describe, "it's just thought. He doesn't exist except in the power of those who would defy the laws of life with him, defy the balance and order of the magic that lays within the realms. He must be using Naszer to manipulate the guilds into all this frenzy, to disguise his return; while they feign ignorance, and feed the guilds just enough information to face off against the ilmaurte without any chance of destroying them. There's no telling how long he's been here, biding his time while massing enough followers and enough strength to trap Atosa and unleash death."

Fear gripped the monk as she looked into the lightless eyes of Tjen curled up beside her. Could this idea have already grown in strength enough to be behind the march of the undead? Or kidnapped Atosa, holding her hostage against his own rise?

"You think the guilds don't know? That Naszer is hiding the truth?"

"I think the guilds, with the nobles instigating them, are too busy taking advantage of this opportunity to care. I told you, they've been denying the ascent of a Lich King. It's much easier to hang the blame on Atosa's disappearance, the abdication of a *lesser* god, and use the undead's advance as a way to showcase their own might and fill their coffers by offering protection at any cost. On top of that, with two of Atosa's children supposedly battling it out to replace her…" he trailed off.

"He'll be able to remain in the shadows, growing in power. Waiting for his perfect opportunity to strike."

They all went silent for a moment, the cool sweet air of night whispering words unspoken among them. Tjen huddled closer to McKenna and the monk wrapped an arm around them.

"But what about you two? If it truly is the source of the Lich King's power and the souls he's stolen who lie in wait at the bottom of that chasm, is it safe for you to go back there?"

"We have no choice," Ginni spoke with an adamantine edge alien to the softness of her voice. "We have to cure the blight. The Lich King couldn't control us before, so, you know, hopefully we'll get away a second time."

A sudden realization startled McKenna. "Wait a

minute. You said you met Katarin. You met my sister. Is she the one who said she could cure Tjen?"

"Yeah. But I swear, any idea of you two being related didn't occur to me until like, just now!" Ginni squawked, flailing her arms. McKenna laughed, settling the little holvi with a stroke to her tousled curly hair.

"Hmm. I just wonder if she was telling the truth. If she knows about the Lich King, or if she'd do anything about him if she did." McKenna put her chin in her palm, puzzling out this mysterious twin sister she'd suddenly discovered.

"Ginni and I have our own reasons for thinking she told the truth. As for the other stuff, I guess we won't know until we see her again," Tjen shrugged, summarily dealing with any doubt posed by the monk.

"We promised to accompany you, and I stand by that promise," Seth spoke with a warm light in his eye, not owed completely to the dwindling remains of the fire.

"As do I," echoed McKenna, with a soft squeeze to the holvi's shoulders.

Ginni peered at her with a curiously empathetic expression. "Are you sure? If it's true, and the Lich King is really there, holding Atosa hostage… what will you do?" she asked, with her uncanny knack of giving voice to words left unsaid. "You just learned of your heritage, and you are worried it will undo you 𝓲and the goals you set yourself. Do you owe your mother anything?"

McKenna thought about that for a moment. She thought about Seth, crusading alone against the ilmaurte though severed from his family and the guild that would exploit them. She thought about Yori and Michelle, holding fast against the growing horde in the town they built from nothing and refused to watch burn. She thought about the restless, mournful souls trapped in her mirror, and the rest, lost and tortured in the grips of an unnatural and hellish necromancy. Tjen's sight, Arya's thwarted dreams, the betrayed gods whose guilds acted in their name and not their faith. All these pointed to a single purpose, one for which she felt, subconsciously, she had been fitted since birth. A preternatural calm settled over her heart. She looked up and caught Seth observing her with a fiercely guarded expression.

She smiled and knew her answer. Neither of them needs seek the Lich King alone.

"Together, then? Come what may?" She knew he'd read her mind, as a smile of soft sweetness crept across his face.

"Together. We will seek and destroy the Lich King, and restore Atosa to her throne," she replied, with a bright grin and a cheer from the holvir.

What more could a hero ask from her party? She may still be beardless, but this had turned out to be one hell of a quest.

XXIII

The Friends We Made Along The Way

The day, soft and pearl grey, began to take fire by the light of the rising sun. A cacophony of colors, radiating iridescent throughout the heavens, lit all below with a flawless golden glow. Divine light bathed each face upturned in solemn rapture; the light that even the gods cannot keep wholly from their mortal subjects. In a brief moment, they were all Celestial, all immortal; a reminder that the true divinities of the land of Faie are and always will be her creatures and the souls that traverse upon it. McKenna, all vestiges of her brush with her immortal heritage removed, felt cleansed as never before by such a radiant morning. She brushed a hand along the runes inked upon her flesh. Her kinship with her god, though briefly dormant during their last battle, returned in full as in forgiveness for weakness she couldn't control. Her discovery may have called into question the heritage she had so unconditionally accepted and identified with, but her loyalty to her divinity remained stalwart.

And, to give him credit, Malfaestus recognized her regardless.

The party regained the western cardinal road leading from Wheelspoke. Their journey passed mostly uneventfully, though it soon became obvious they were swimming upstream from the few parties of travelers upon the road. All they encountered spoke of the advancing horde, deeming them nothing short of crazy for heading toward Naijor and certain doom.

"Hang on for a moment, I just have to finish this," Seth paused for a moment, scribbling furiously.

McKenna pulled up, confused. "Finish what?"

"A letter I'm sending to James," he replied offhandedly, then darted away.

When he returned empty-handed, she looked around searchingly. "Wait. Where did it go?"

He jabbed his thumb over his shoulder, peering quizzically at her. "Right... over there, McKenna, what are you looking for?"

She was scanning the sky, a hand shading her eyes from the glare of the sun. "A raven, or something? Don't you need one of those to send letters?"

He blinked, and his tone quivered as he replied. "What... year do you think it is, McKenna?"

"I don't know!" She said defensively, "I've always read asafolk send letters by bird or whatever, is it magic now? Do you-"

The sound of pounding hooves interrupted her. A decently-dressed aesir, erect upon the back of a hale brown horse, thundered past them and pulled up briefly beside one of the curious poles she'd noticed that marked every so many leagues along the road. He tapped expertly at the side of it, and with a metallic clang a drawer full of tightly furled scrolls and folded envelopes popped out. Tucking them quickly into a sack, the lad whistled and his steed took off again at full speed.

"Wh- who was that?! Where did he go? Who... did you see that?" She cried, whipping around in place on the back of her mule, staring first in disbelief at Seth, then Ginni, who simply watched her dumbfounded.

"It's called *post*, McKenna," Seth finished, sternly martialed tones betraying his desperate desire to laugh.

"Post," she mouthed silently. Her incredulity proved too much for the rogue. He broke out into deep, hearty laughter that echoed across the prairie.

"McKenna, you are a gem," giggled Ginni, biting her lip in an attempt to control her own laughter.

In the evening they found surprising shelter. A party of durgir, heading back from a fruitless rendezvous to the few ghost towns that lay to the west, had a makeshift encampment set up along the main road and hailed the approaching party heartily. Ginni and Tjen, confident in the safety afforded by the militantly defended camp, wandered off to chat with a couple of other holvir hangers-on who had joined the convivial durgir.

A familiar face called to McKenna from a mess tent.

"Eh! Garble! That be ye, then?" She cried in recognition, grasping his outstretched hand joyfully. Despite her identity crisis, she slipped with ease back into her duergi mannerisms.

"Hail, monk! Won' Pabble be glad we saw ye! Come 'n sup, for sure'n we've both tales ter trade!" He replied, and McKenna ducked behind him under the low-hanging flap of their mess tent.

Seth couldn't relieve the tension that settled upon him at the sight. A certain rigidity always characterized his demeanor, but the past few weeks had introduced a softness more notable as its absence intensified. A bevy of durgir, bearing the mantle of Clan Hammardin, gathered around the engaging and imposing form of McKenna. They weren't fully capable of completely obscuring her from his view, but they did their best for all that.

The motive for the discomfort, though internally ignored and would be patently denied, should have been clear enough. One couldn't quite call it jealousy, because jealousy implied an ill intent and unwarranted level of possession that Seth had never and could never assume over the monk. The knotted tautness in his gut and the swooping adrenaline that erratically flatlined into a chilling emptiness more accurately represented fear than any other of the quantifiable emotions. No, perhaps the motive lacked clarity after all. For it wasn't her safety he feared. These were her brethren, these were her friends.

Finally, it dawned on him. He feared her loss, not by attack or kidnap, but simply from her desire to return with her kin to the home she left before she joined him. He tried to shake the feeling. She owed him nothing, not her company, not her strength in battle. To lose his reserve over the thought of losing her disrespected not only their friendship, but her autonomy, and he would rather face the Lich King himself than admit such weakness.

Meanwhile, had he been able to employ the uncanny ability to read her mind that had often discomposed her, his musings would be far from their current strain. She, while surrounded by some of the closest bondsmen she'd known since infancy, found herself suffering from incredible and almost unbelievable anxiety. As the durgir brumbled about veins of ore struck and deals made with their ilvin foils to the south, McKenna's newfound understanding of the races and her experiences among them rendered their discussion almost incomprehensible. One of the women made a crude remark about the structure of ilvin households and McKenna felt cringe enter as iron into her soul. Who were they, that thought they could sling such scurrilous stones within their own fragile glass houses? She caught herself frowning and tried to smooth the wrinkles from her expressive face before they suspected her discontent. Luckily, they were all too engaged in one another to notice. And not a single one spoke of the ilmaurte, despite their camp being full of refugees. Almost as though the struggles of these non-durgirn societies meant nothing to her kin. They would help as far as they could, if they happened to stumble upon the opportunity, as if the faiefolkr were no more than animals left out in the rain.

She wondered how best to bow out of their company, and made a mumbled excuse involving more alcohol, something she knew wouldn't face question from the group. Sure enough, she encountered barely a glance and acknowledgement. It was almost frustrating. She was on a beard quest, after all. She should be an object of interest, of envy.

Traditions die every day, it seems, she thought despairingly as she made her way through the crowded pavilion.

Suddenly she could sense a presence of familiarity and comfort. Looking through the camps dotting the hillside, she spotted Seth's spare form reclining in the shadows looking much as he did the first time she'd seen him. A shy smile lit up her face at the memory, and she unhesitatingly made her way towards him.

As she approached, he shifted a bit closer toward their fire and made room for her. Pulling a flask from his pack, he emptied the contents into her outstretched mug. She sank with a grateful sigh cross-legged beside him. Sensing him trying to surreptitiously gauge her expression, she knew he'd read her mind before she had to explain herself.

"Penny for your thoughts?" he quipped anyways, borrowing Ginni's pet expression. She smiled ruefully back at him, before pensively swirling the contents of the mug as though it could spin the right words for her.

"Sometimes we move on from our friends," she said haltingly, a quiver in her voice. "But… I've no idea how to even begin to do that. Am I now an outcast from my people? The only life I've ever known?"

The look on his face startled her, and then she realized what she was saying. Here was a man who, whether willingly or no, stepped away from his own heritage fully with the knowledge that he could never return. While it was true that her people honored McKenna's quest, she knew deep down that the true nature of a beard quest was not to return triumphant. If your better self could not be found in the mines, among the family and friends you'd always known, a quest to seek it would only serve to enhance the differences between oneself and one's kin. If she couldn't find her beard among the durgir, finding it out here in the wider world meant she really might be a part of it after all. She no longer belonged to the dim, smoky halls of Mount Oer.

The thought shocked her nearly to tears.

"We're always told that dealing with death is the hardest," he mused, gazing into the depths of his own draught. "I don't know if I quite agree with that. Losing a way of life is difficult, it's true. But it's nothing to the pain and discomfort of birthing a new one."

She bristled at his casual tone, still wracked with anxiety from her encounter with her kin. She took a drink as though to wash the irritation down, but it lingered still.

"So what do I do next? Mourn my dead and move on?" she replied, an edge to her voice whetted by her own insecurity. "How do I even begin to do that?"

He sighed, still unable to look at her. He could hear the pain in her voice, and he knew he couldn't handle seeing it in her face. Or worse, the wish that it represented- the wish that she could return to that life, and leave the rest of them behind. "If only I could answer that. But you do realize who you're talking to, right?" he replied, a self-deprecating grin curling his lip.

Tension racked her form. It had been some time since she'd heard him use that tone and her insecurities mounted. She bit her lower lip involuntarily and turned away, not sure how to respond. Suddenly a hand gripped hers and, looking up, she saw the tawny fire of his eyes focused with such intensity she could almost feel the warmth of his gaze. It thawed the frost biting her heart, almost as quickly as it had descended, and she managed a watery smile.

"I shouldn't have said that. Almost implying I haven't found a life worth living- that's not true," he stammered, not breaking eye contact. "I just find it difficult… to put to words the journey I've been on."

His palm remained pressed against hers, as he drew a long breath. Desperate at this point to answer the pleading cry he sensed in her soul and remembering the difficult and painful road he had walked alone, before she had entered his life with her ceaseless joy and desire for adventure.

"Our life is just a cycle," he continued, taking her hand. "So you take that next step, allow yourself a healthy grieving period for what you leave behind, and also prepare for what is to come." His eyes finally raised to hers as he spoke, trying to give words to the lessons he'd spent so long learning. "We must know the grief is pure and not allow regret to tinge it or spoil its cleansing power. Give it a wholesome, healthy mourning. Season it with thankfulness and nothing more. I haven't reached the point yet where I anticipate the future, McKenna," his voice, eager, and determined, soothed her. "But now the fallout has cleared, I can see what's left and I… I'm surprised by the results. By a shining light at the end of this godsforsaken tunnel."

He petered off and she laughed. The self-deprecation had transmuted into a purer tone of fervor, stifled by his indecision and therefore responsible for his inaction. They had somehow reached the same crossroads; the two of them, outcast from their society, both sought new purpose. She felt lucky they could do so together.

"I am ready for it! We are no longer as strong only as our greatest weakness. We are greatness itself," she declared, her face flush and aura glowing with glorious purpose. The beauty of her noble soul, shining forth as it did, stunned Seth.

"You have a partner for your adventures, come what may," he said, with depth of feeling hard to mistake.

The pair leaned into one another, staring into the studded horizon misted by smoke and spark of flame. While she desperately wanted to maintain their moment together, the mystery of the mirror nagged at her, the only key to this strange and new identity she found herself faced with.

"Can I… I don't really know how to use this, but I want to see if I can get to know it," she turned toward the rogue, pulling the mirror into her lap. She feared seeing distrust or misgiving in his gaze, but he met her with thoughtfulness, and an almost eager spirit that matched her own. "Maybe it can answer these nagging questions that plague us both."

"You think your mirror shows the past?"

"No, Seth," she said calmly, holding the hands that held the mysterious object between them. "I think my mirror shows the truth."

Seth contemplated that, not wanting to spoil the moment they'd been sharing, but knowing beyond anything that the truth is exactly what he wanted this woman to know. The truth about him, the truth even he had been too blind to see.

XXIV

The Missing Battle

As his thoughts took form shapes began to swirl in the mirror, clearer even than the ones that appeared when McKenna had accidentally scried the portrait of Seth's father. She leaned over but cast a concerned look at Seth, wondering if he meant for her to see what it showed. The depths of his golden eyes spoke a plea, a quiet desperation that, if she would, know and judge what truths he had to show her. The emotion shocked her, but unwilling to resist and push the man further away she took a deep breath and settled in place, letting her mind step away from its grip on reality and slip slowly into the suspension into the past offered by the images in the mirror.

A paladin, equipped in full battle armour, kneeling before a wizened old woman seated upon a golden throne.

"A daemor genirae? To the North??"

"You don't have to repeat me, Seth," she replied querulously, then softened at the expression on his face.

Fresh off the victory of a tourney, and I have to send him out with Gareth and that band. And I can't even blame the gods for this - their silence speaks volumes.

"The last thing I want is for you to be away from the guild in a time like this," Elgitha, the Grand Master of

Tooth and Claw, whispered, steepling her fingers before her face in concentration. "But I have no one else to send. A genirae could destroy an entire city in the blink of an eye and we have no time to waste. I don't know how one escaped to our plane, but I promise I will make it my solemn duty to find out," she assured him, as a myriad of emotions crossed his face.

Implications can always be made at times like this. Another joust, another huge expense on the part of the nobles. And barely any of the stands filled. The faiefolkr were drifting further and further from the protection of the marble city; the awe it inspired fading, like their faith in the guilds.

I swear to the gods, if Golden Eye is playing another one of their stupid games...

Seth bowed, fixing his expression so it communicated only the solemn loyalty he felt for his guild master, and honest faith he had for his god. His own accomplishments meant nothing in the face of such danger, and he focused all his considerable confidence on the woman who sat before him. "I care not for games, Grand Master, you know that. If you tell me to fight, I will fight. Master Gareth and the apprentices..." he trailed off, knitting his brows in concentration, "it will be an excellent exercise for them, in teamwork and in concerted battle. Gareth and I can lay aside our differences. Besides, I think he came off rather well in the last joust-"

She snorted loudly, cutting him off. "You just keep your eye on that one, you hear me? Don't worry about the guild. Lianor is safe, so long as I sit here. But whether they recognize us or not, the cities in Beausun need our protection. We can't let them suffer for our hubris."

A silence hung in the golden air. Light filtered through high windows, glowing on Elgitha's throne and on the brow of the goodly paladin who knelt before her. Heroes were made of stuff like this. The Cathedral was built for such tableaux, such displays of loyalty and righteousness.

But there were corners in the cathedral which even the brightest light could not illuminate.

Almost as soon as they left the high walls of Lianor, Seth could begin to feel the daemoric energy leaching the brightness from the sun, the colour from the trees. Barely a twoday's ride from the marble city. *Where do they keep coming from? How can we not sense the portals opening?*

"I suggest we split up. Surround the beast before it advances," Master Gareth, astride his dappled destrier, spoke with confidence as they came within sight of the Abyssinian aura pulsing upon the plains.

Kurya, Seth's own golden mount, curled his neck slightly, lowering his proud head while refusing to break eye contact with the master paladin. At their side, James stood impassive behind a massive shield, built to cover both squire and rider. Neither looked at Seth, but wondered what his response would be.

Sensing their trepidation, Seth swallowed frustration as it bubbled to the surface of his calm demeanor. *We have to trust one another. There is no evidence against Gareth - my feelings are not facts. Without trusting him, how can I know he will trust me?*

"Agreed. Take the vanguard north, circling back toward Lianor. I will make my pass south, with James," he pointed his sheathed saber toward a narrow track that led through a copse of trees; clearly an old orgir trail, long abandoned, as the paved and protected roads that passed through Lianor and Wheelspoke grew in popularity and ease of use.

Gareth nodded grimly and, with a shout, wheeled his steed around and broke off with the three novitiates who accompanied them to battle.

"You still trust him, then?" James remarked incredulously, exchanging glances with Kurya. The horse snorted through his teeth.

"I have no reason not to. Grand Master Elgitha has granted him this quest, same as myself. He fights with honor and loyalty to our guild," Seth admonished. "Rumors are just rumors, James; we are no better than the cowards who start them if we choose to believe and perpetuate them."

"Rumors always have a root in fact," James muttered under his breath. And in his defense, the fact that all seven paladin Masters who accompanied Gareth on his last quest had gone missing was a pretty damning one. The lone paladin had returned, inches from death, unable to name the being that attacked them, unable to even recall the fate of those who rode with him.

Yes, damning was an understatement.

"We all know the risk of battle. As a squire, and not one initiated in our guild, I don't expect you to understand it," Seth replied over his shoulder as they moved deeper into the forest.

"Hop off your high horse, then," spat James. He hated when Seth got like this. "You think that signet ring on your finger means you know danger better than anyone without it? Stop protecting Gareth just because he bears your same title. The man is twisted, his followers are barely aesir, and he's been caught more times than I can count sneaking around Golden Eye. He's a noble-"

"He's a Master, James," Seth barked, sliding off Kurya's back to face his squire. Almost he regretted it. Seth wasn't short, but James towered over him anyways.

"Come on now, Seth. It's not a reflection on you. There's bad eggs in every batch. Just because you're both Masters doesn't make you beholden to his behavior. It just means you have to work twice as hard not to imitate or defend it," the squire spoke mildly, lowering the shield he carried.

The paladin sighed in disgust. How could he make anyone understand that this wasn't a competition. This was his identity. Failure to achieve the ideal meant annihilation of everything the man understood about himself, and his place in the world.

James watched him quietly, then hoisted his shield back up and continued along the narrow path. *I'll let him figure that out. He's been drawing away for weeks now, and I don't know what-*

A sudden darkness descended, swallowing him where he stood.

"What the- James!" shouted Seth, who watched in horror as his partner disappeared. A deep, grating laugh filled the trees.

"Sorry to break up your lover's quarrel," a voice echoed from the canopy above, "but we have some business to attend to, and I'd rather even the odds in my favor."

Kurya reared, and with a sharp scream struck a hoof out into the blankness before them. With a keen wail and a blinding flash, the chameleon spell broke and revealed the speaker- a tall, angular man with laughing eyes the colour of dried blood.

"Razan. Of course you would be here," Seth spat, twisting his own wrist to activate an oath preventing the assassin from simply restoring the spell.

"Are you implying I have the power to sustain a daemor genirae? You give me far too much credit, Paladin," he replied with a fiendish grin.

"You may not, but you know what they say about the apple not falling far from the tree," the paladin returned, focusing on summoning spells and blessings to his aide.

A groan met that remark, the assassin rolling his eyes expressively. "You're behind the times. As if I have any involvement still with the Cult of Naszer, or their protectors. No, I have bigger dreams than that, my friend."

A sudden spark of light struck the assassin, who barely dodged in time, whipping out a globe of darkness that teleported him away from the spell's area of effect. Now it was Seth's turn, to slide the saber at his side from its sheath to his cheek as the assassin's blade sliced toward it.

"Are you going to try and sell me the same story, then? That your cult simply 'found' this daemor too? I'm not dumb enough to swallow that," he hissed as he pushed the assassin back, legs planted firmly and blade drawn parallel to his body, defending from any angle of attack.

"It's not my cult. I'm merely a spectator, just like your precious Elgitha," Razan responded, his arms held high and dancer's legs planted loosely to balance the blade above his face, leaving his torso wide open in an attempt to draw Seth into an attack.

"Spectator… we're here to destroy it, to clean up the mess your hellish family keeps making. Now what did you do with James?" Seth whispered, dropping another blessing meant to draw forth the aura of any hidden being, friend or foe.

All he saw was a deep, impenetrable fog that descended, surrounding them closer even than the boughs of the trees overhead. *Of course. He must have activated a dampener spell as soon as he cleared James' shield. I'm an idiot.*

"Oh, you know, I don't actually know where these portals go," he replied laconically, twirling two of the globes of darkness dexterously between his long black fingers. "He could be back in Lianor, at the bottom of a well, anywhere really that isn't here."

He uses those for transportation, I know it. James must be back outside the copse. It's the nearest point we were before we entered the dampener's range. I hope he takes the north road with the others… he's smart enough to know better than to enter a Fog.

"Anyways, he's not interesting, and I don't waste time or words on those who don't interest me," the assassin continued. "What exactly do you hope to accomplish here? Your precious Grand Master has already lost seven of her champions. What was she thinking, sending her brightest on such an obviously doomed mission?"

"Shut up, Razan. Loyalty may be a foreign concept to daemor, but I'm not here to teach it to you," Seth snarled. With a lunge, he leapt onto Kurya's back, hoping he could call down a blessing strong enough to part the Fog.

No answer met his call.

"Who do you think summoned this hellbeast in the first place?" Razan jibed, continuing to dance around the paladin.

"I'll not play your mind games, assassin," Seth spat in response, slowly dancing Kurya backwards in an attempt to break from the man's advance.

"You're already a fool. You don't have to be an idiot," he snapped, whistling to draw the fog tighter around them. "You hide behind that Elgitha woman and the bright star of your own faith, while everyone around you plays a deeper game."

"Shut UP!" cried the exasperated paladin, realizing there was no escape from this battle even as he heard the cries and shouts of his squad further up ahead, as they faced off against the daemor genirae without him.

The only way through the Fog is through Razan. If I force him to retreat, the dampener spell will dissipate. Of course, that's what he wants... but there's no other option.

He slid off the horse's back, and activated a dweomer on Kurya's bridle. The horse disappeared in a dazzling flash of golden light.

"Impressive. Too bad it doesn't work while you're on him - what kind of half-useful gift is that?" Razan chided.

Seth responded with a wild slash of his saber, smashing so forcefully against the raised sword held by the assassin he felt the reverberation up to his elbows. Metal screeched against metal as the two combatants matched their strengths: Razan to defend, Seth to strike. A perfect match, physically impossible, but there are exceptions to even the most strict of rules. Both their eyes widened at the realization, and both shifted simultaneously to a new angle of attack.

Not a single opening could Razan find in the paladin's expert defenses. He noted the fine maille draped across his chest, immaculate, and humming with a faint spell. *No strike has ever landed on that armor. How is that even possible?*

Meanwhile, Seth was analyzing Razan's own minimally clothed form. *Not a scar, not a mark, on an inch of flesh. He doesn't even wear armor. And yet some still say the blood of Naszer is pure. Only a daemor could be so impenetrable.*

They stood, measuring one another, men of reputation almost as much as of action. Though Razan had drug himself up from the slime and gutters of exodus from his family, here stood his foil, a glowing, glorious hero who refused to acknowledge the inevitable betrayal promised by his own. He took an experimental step, and met the ringing mithril of Seth's blade. Another quicker motion garnered the same result. Measured, erratic, accelerated, or paced, the two warriors simply could not break the mastery of the other.

I feel sorry for him. Stupid of me, really, for he would never extend the same pity to me. Of course I can't beat him. Not when part of me wants him to win, to spite them all. Razan breathed deeply, his eyes glowing now, a deep blood red.

This man could've been a powerful warrior, a hero of Faie, and yet he chose to become this instead. I'd almost feel sorry for him if I weren't so disgusted at his lack of discipline, or of purpose. Seth stepped back, his golden eyes focused, betraying no emotion.

"This won't be our last battle," promised Razan. He knew what awaited the warrior outside that fog. Time to see if the gods would undo the machinations of man. Before Seth could react, he whipped one of the portals from its globe and disappeared.

As the fog began to clear, the hulking ferocity of the beast loomed into sight. Not a single warrior stood in battle before it. The sounds of battle had all been a spell, Gareth's troops probably long gone back to tell of the sad demise of the Champion of Wheelspoke. The genirae's evil grin revealed teeth that would slice effortlessly through the paladin's armor, four muscled arms that could crush him to dust.

A trap.

The towering mass of daemor stood twice again as tall as Seth and ran four abreast of him. A miasma, deathly energy that clung to creatures from the Abyss, left a halo effect killing all the vegetation surrounding and leaving an almost crater-like depression around the beast.

No cover. Damn. Seth whistled, and with a shrieking whinny, Kurya materialized beside him, almost immediately shying away from the hulking form before them. Mounting his horse brought him barely chest level. And perfectly within range of all four curled fists.

He could feel the daemor's aura begin to drain him. Of energy, of vigour, of simple viability. A sense of despair descended, almost immediately. *A daemor genirae. I have to fight this creature alone, when it has defeated legions of warriors like me. What's the point.*

Kurya reared up suddenly, a fierce bundle of sinew and muscle, forcing Seth to break from those thoughts of dread and instead focus on keeping his seat.

"Steady! What in the gods-" he began to chastise, before the horse turned an intelligent eye on him, demanding the paladin's attention, recalling the man to the hero he was that could so mount such a glorious steed.

The moment proved well-timed. Seth snapped back to martial alertness just as the genirae, mouth in a wide grin, swung one of those boulder-like fists. Pirouetting in place and dodging the attack, Seth slung his hand crossbow out of its holster, sliding several bolts doused in blessed water into its waiting barrel. Firing them off with one hand while directing Kurya with the other, the paladin regained his posture, quickly assessing the battleground upon which he found himself.

The genirae hissed as the blessed bolts found their mark. "Insolent. They send only one of you, when Makarh was promised a feast." He struck a blood red palm against the wounds, and with a metallic ping the bolts fell to the ground from the rib cage in which they'd been lodged.

"It will take only one of me to slay you where you stand, daemor," countered Seth with confidence, drawing himself up and radiating with the aura of his chosen god.

Makarh chuckled, the sound rasping against both man and horse. "Foolish, indeed. You'll not survive even the Abyss long. And I assure you, you will find my home before I do."

Summoned straight from the depths of the Abyss. But how did he end up here? Seth wondered, while keeping Kurya alert, prancing along the blackened soil well out of reach of the monster's fists.

He called down a quick spell, an oath to reveal magic traces. A powerful one, needed to break through the fetid magical aura that saturated the space around the daemor. However, Seth's oaths commanded greater presence than most and he could see, faintly distinguished in the black miasma, the traces of a portal. His eyes widened in fear at the realization.

Called forth by a sorcere strong enough to survive the encounter, and then transported without any sort of magical chaperone, or holding dweomer? No one controls this beast any longer. Any summoning bond they may have held is long gone now, severed by their own stupidity. What in the blazes were they thinking?

Suddenly the paladin had an idea. One he realized had almost no chance of working, but put into action anyways. The edge of despair was beginning to work on him again, but he ignored it, turning all his focus instead to a binding oath.

As soon as the spell began to manifest, Kurya whinnied concernedly. Binding oaths were meant for goodly creatures, a mutual agreement as much as magical compulsion. There was no way in any of the planes of this life or the next that the genirae Makarh would simply acquiesce to a binding oath. Instead Seth channeled every ounce of magical energy into compelling the beast, forcing his essence to succumb to the greater power of the paladin's heroic might.

It would have worked.

It should have worked.

Makarh swung a clawed fist directly at Seth's unprotected face, knocking him flying from Kurya's back.

It didn't work.

He took shallow breaths, shock recoiling every nerve from the pain. Curled in fetal position, clutching his knees to his chest, head spinning from the blow. The sky was beneath him, the ground above. A dazzling flash, a piercing whinny; Kurya had… doubled… in size? The divine steed matched every blow of the daemor's fist with a vicious slash of his ferocious hooves, and Makarh hissed in anger and frustration as the horse danced with lightning speed around him, protecting his fallen master.

Bahamut. You didn't send me alone into this after all. But we need more. I… are you even here?

He stumbled to his feet, rubbing the heel of his hand across his cheek, dazzled by the bright blood smeared across it. Eddies of magic dissipated from his open palm, the blessings he'd called down weakening in the face of this seemingly invincible foe. Golden eyes narrowed, focusing on the distracted genirae as it lunged one way and the other to try and pulverize the prancing horse.

It was a trap. I'm meant to die here. Did Elgitha know? Did James know?

The despair clutched at the fibers of his being. Luckily he hadn't even the presence of mind to notice at this point.

Am I a fool?

Saber unsheathes. Mithril glinting in the vestiges of light that breaks through the pulsing miasma as it grows deeper, more impenetrable. The man becomes a pure martial spirit, a fiend almost in his own right, to face against the dread Abyssinian. Kurya, dazzling, but unable to bear a rider so distant from his god. The Abyssinian turns toward him, that vile grin growing ever wider.

"You could be a daemor genirae too. I see now the strength you hide, cowering behind golden gods too far from heroes to hear their cries. Lay down your weapon."

A command. A smirk hitches itself to the corner of Seth's mouth. So much for binding spells, so much for blessings, so much for greatness. *A monster from the pits of the Abyss expects me to bend the knee to it. A single betrayal brings me to this? Am I truly so weak, so expendable, after all?*

"I will not succumb so easily as that," he hissed in return, and began a deadly dance of his own, blade swinging with light fluidity, whipping at every opening. Makarh actually found himself hard pressed to block each strike, the stinging slap of mithril dragging at his daemoric essence.

I refuse to die here.

The fighter increased his speed, nipping with greater dexterity deeper and deeper into Makarh's mottled red and black hide. The beast roared in fury, unable to dodge both the flailing hooves of the magically enlarged horse and the keen bite of the saber that seemed to move faster than time itself. But Seth knew he'd have to take a greater risk if he had any chance at all to strike the heart of the beast, collapsing its corporeal form and banishing it back to the Abyss. The smirk widened to a grin. Greater risk is all Seth knew. Greater risk, time and again, pressing the boundaries of his abilities, crashing over each and every line drawn around his limits. This may be his final step, the one that managed to meet him to a wall insurmountable even to this hero, who for so long hadn't met a foe worth standing against.

The Champion of Wheelspoke took a deep breath and leapt with a thrust, extending his whole body, toward the heart of the daemor. He felt all four of those powerful arms wind around his torso, threatening to crush the very life from his bones; the sharp ridges of teeth slice through the soft flesh of his cheek in a desperate attempt to rip out his throat; the piercing claws that gripped shoulder, rib cage, anything to stop the blow that angled perfectly into the beast's seething, rage-filled heart.

I may be a fool. But dammit, I'll be a daemor-slaying fool.

He didn't lose consciousness until after Makarh, with a feral scream that shook the very ground they stood upon, evaporated into a clap of fiery ash as his essence was banished from Faie for a hundred years or more.

The mirror swirled into darkness, and McKenna blinked, refocusing on the pale hands clasped in her own. With a start, she looked up, expecting to see the same livid, bloody face that had just faded from the silver glass.

She saw only Seth's pensive, thoughtful golden eyes. And a white scar burned into the bronze flesh of his high cheekbone.

"You survived that? How… how is that even possible?" She whispered, incredulity nearly knocking the wind from her.

"Kurya. I thought I'd abandoned my god. In fact, I pretty much decided I had to. Despite that, Kurya remained by my side, and the binding spell he shared with me soon restored me to myself. Healing… well, I've always been good at taking hits. But as soon as I realized what happened, I knew I could never return to the guild, or my old way of life," he replied, measured tones surprisingly calm. McKenna realized with a start that this wasn't the first time he'd relived these memories.

He must carry them with him, see them every time he closes his eyes, knowing no moment of peace unbroken for the darkness and despair of his past. How could anyone survive that? How could anyone continue to live?

"You… are much stronger than I took you for," she stammered bashfully, not really knowing how to face him now that such a wall had come down.

He carefully set the mirror down and took her hand in both of his. "There are secrets, mostly of pain endured, that we share with no one else, for fear that pain will drive them from us. For fear that our spirit will dissolve in the face of what we have endured, for the wedge it places between us and those who have never faced such tragedy. I have carried those secrets for long enough," and he sighed bitterly, then smiled in relief, as he realized she hadn't removed her hand from his grip.

She nodded, still uncertain of what to say. "What… well, what happened next? If you couldn't go to the guild, what did you do?"

He took a breath. "I went home. I sought an audience with my mother, told her of the guild's betrayal, and how they left me for dead. She… well, she thought it would be a wonderful opportunity to… accelerate my ascension to Grand Master."

The monk let out a noise somewhere between a roar of outrage and a hissing shriek. "What? She expected you to… to challenge Elgitha?"

"Probably. Maybe not in so many words. When I told her I believed Elgitha had nothing to do with it…" he swallowed, then repeated his mother's parting words to her disgraced son.

"Of course she hid the truth from you. She needs you just as much as you need her, and if you knew the truth, you'd fall apart, just as you're doing now."

"She easily bought into the guild's garbage about the undead being a holy visitation among the heathens and nonbelievers. It's not a far cry to assume she thought my mastery over Makarh meant I too had passed some arbitrary test, ready to enforce the might of our guild, for the glory of our god."

He looked past McKenna, into the horizon, into the distance of a memory that he had long fought to suppress. The woman hesitated, desperate to hear more, but not confident that she had warranted such a deep trespass into the man's confidence.

He is who he is now. That's what matters, really, not the past. As long as we have a future to look forward to, and as long as he knows he can trust me, to either keep silence or confidence, whatever he needs. What more could I ask, really?

She noticed him studying her, and she raised an eyebrow at him quizzically, challenging that inscrutable gaze of his. They remained silent, until a musical voice over their shoulder broke into their reverie.

"Wow. That was one hell of a flashback," the little bard said as she flopped gracefully beside McKenna.

"Ginni... how long have you been there watching?" She returned, a bemused grin softening the worry that had wrinkled her face.

"Oh, the whole time. Sorry, was I not supposed to be?" Ginni took a bite of an apple, shifting her attention from McKenna to Seth unabashedly.

"Most *innocent* bystanders tend to announce their presence," Seth replied in amusement, tousling the bard's long auburn curls.

"I'm a holvir. No one notices us anyways," she shrugged, offering another apple to Seth, who took it with a grateful nod. McKenna and Tjen, who had followed behind Ginni, exchanged glances and shrugged at their friend's brazen shamelessness.

The moment passed. The mirror, unassuming, inconsequential, reflected a moon waxing full on the horizon and the lighthearted friends who sat around it, ready to face whatever truth awaited them so long as they could face it together.

XXV

Oases And Orgir

"You'd think with how easy the orgir found us that one time, we shouldn't be struggling so much to find them now," grumbled McKenna.

Wandering around the seemingly endless savannah occupied the past few days of the party's progress. McKenna, though having spent the better part of the past solstices traveling, still couldn't begin to grasp the vastness of Faie. The mountain she called home towered above all, reducing anything near it to microscopic perspective. But these interminable stretches forced a new perspective on her idea of the landscape. And it was so empty! They still distanced the Naijor by dozens of leagues, and yet not a single town, settlement, or camp passed them by.

"Why is it asafolk choose to remain so close to the sea?" She questioned Seth, realizing the sparseness of the surrounding area was exclusive to the western regions. The coast, and the plains that rolled inland from it, housed the majority of the race's civilization.

Atop Kurya's back, the rogue gave her a thoughtful look before answering.

"The nobles came from the sea," he started to explain. "There have always been folkr- all kinds- on Faie. But with the nobles came most of aesir civilization, our culture, and the strength of our gods. Even our wealth," he muttered under his breath. "Lianor is a testament to the vast prosperity that the nobles heralded, a city built from marble, the streets paved with stone, and every window a pane of shimmering crystal. Most of our people, if our histories are to be believed, relied on basic subsistence or the good nature of the orgir and ilvir to survive before they came. With their gold and their ideas of society, we've managed to build greater cities, guilds, and laws to protect ourselves and improve our welfare."

Ginni snorted gently under her breath. Sensing the quizzical look McKenna cast upon her, she rolled her eyes. "Lianor nobles didn't build it all themselves. Hand Over Fist designed that city, and they were the first guild to exist on Faie, before even the nobles came. They benefited from other races too. Durgir, ilvir, even holvir. In fact, there are still holvi members of Hand Over Fist. At least, there should be," she trailed off uncomfortably, remembering the ghost towns scattered across the southern plains. "And were it not for the Bristendine durgir and Sun ilvir of Gamorre, the marble stone used to build Lianor's wall would still be uncut lumps of rock in a Gamorran quarry. No, the nobles didn't bring culture, so much as they brought the idea of success and glory no matter the cost."

Remembering what Katherine had said of the slowly splintering alliances among the races, McKenna realized that must have been the missing catalyst. Instead of the slow, but natural growth of the realms and its denizens, these nobles brought with them cataclysmic progress at the expense of its trust and unity. She cast an uneasy look at Seth, whose mouth was set in a grim line at the bard's offhanded dismissal of his people's heritage.

"I think you should cut him some slack, Ginni," she said, elbowing the holvi and nodding over her shoulder at the rogue. "That was generations ago. He can't be held responsible for history he had no control over, and it looks like he's since been doing his best to make reparations for it."

"Hey, I thought you were on our side!" She pouted, turning an accusatory face to the monk.

"I'm not… there shouldn't be sides in this, you know," she replied slowly, watching Seth's figure silhouetted against the sun. "There's an evil loose in this land, and I'm going to find out a way to stop it. All I want to know is whether faiefolkr intend to fight with us, or simply flee. *All* faiefolkr, Ginni," she spoke with emphasis. "Not just asafolk. They may be responsible for this mess, but as much as they need to acknowledge and take action against it they need the forgiveness and the acceptance of the rest of us to help them. Or else they will never come to learn to bridge the gap."

Chastened, the little bard settled back against the monk, and they continued in silence along the undulating dirt road that wound deeper into the savannah toward the desolate wastelands of Naijor. McKenna assumed asafolk avoided settling the land because of its inhospitable nature, or infertility, but the many oases popping up proved that wrong.

It was at one of these oases, that they met Urtha.

She sat beside the gurgling spring as though she'd been waiting for them the whole time. As they approached, she uncoiled her legs and arms with a stretch, beckoning them forward almost impatiently. Her feral beauty entranced the monk, with her severely cropped hair and leather tunic made from the hide of some carnivorous beast that she'd outsmarted and slain.

A thin trail of smoke curled from the pipe clamped between her full lips and large, sharp teeth.

"You have learned perhaps, that when orgir do not want to be found, they will not be. A lesson many asafolk, who demand everything of the realms they can, find hard to remember." She ruffled Tjen's fluffy strip of hair in greeting and winked chummily at Ginni. But to Seth and McKenna she remained stern, implacable.

"We thank you for greeting us, Shepherdess," greeted McKenna, looking away from the orgirrin chieftainess as was etiquette. To presume upon the eyes, where orgir believed the soul lived, proved a grievous affront.

She harrumphed again and tapped her pipe, then reached a long finger out toward McKenna's face. "Daughter of our goddess, for so I see you are. My eyes wish to look upon Atosa's, if I may."

McKenna turned her head with a small smile. Urtha stroked her cheek fondly, incapable of completely hiding the joy and reverence she felt at meeting this half of Atosa's immortal soul.

"It is long, too long, since the eyes of my people have gazed upon any so fair as yours. And your companion, too," she nodded at Seth, who studied the ground between his feet. "Though his eyes look not upon the goddess in such reverence, in his heart I see humility. You are welcome this night."

He bowed his head in thanks, and they progressed toward the small camp Urtha prepared. A cheery fire, plush carpets of moss, and sizzling game enhanced the refreshment of the oasis.

"Urtha," Ginni, not wasting any words with their mysterious hostess, began, "we need your help. You told us the shepherds for souls had lost their souls, right? Well, it looks like McKenna... ah, found some."

She beckoned for the mirror, and McKenna handed it over, slightly reluctant to relinquish the treasure. To her surprise, Urtha refused to touch it.

"Have you learned what this mirror is, child?" she spoke sharply. "Many years has it been in your possession. Enough to learn its truth, I am thinking. Perhaps I am wrong?"

She shook her head. "I lost it. I don't know where it's been hidden, but at the beginning of my travels I...it... well, we were somehow reunited."

Urtha waved an impatient hand. "That is irrelevant. You have carried it with you, and you should be knowing what it does."

The monk's grip tightened on the mirror's frame. "I managed to... to collect the souls that whoever is controlling the undead used to ensorcel them. They're in here, they asked me..." her voice broke, but she cleared her throat forcefully and continued, "they asked me to help them. To keep them safe until they could return. We hoped... we hoped you, the orgir, would be able to send them home."

McKenna trailed off as Urtha shook her head, denying her request before she'd even finished. "We cannot get to the Doors of Death, as neither can these souls. That which sets them free bars us also from it."

Learning the convoluted history of the mirror simply

wouldn't be enough. They still had no idea how to use it. McKenna cast an agonized glance at Seth, even though she knew it was just as much a mystery to him. Urtha knitted her brows, shifting her gaze between the two. "I see. You have not understood the mirror yet. You are running out of time. Let us hope this aesir is faster than durgir, who look upon each day as nothing but a single grain of sand in a limitless hourglass. Meanwhile," she leaned in toward Ginni, taking a bite from the spitted meat, "little bards, I wish to hear again your songs."

Ginni nodded, and leaning against Tjen, began a soft ballad about the adventures on which they'd been since departing from the orgir tribe. Journey after journey and day after day unfolded in her sweet song, while Urtha reclined against a moss-covered boulder and absently smoked her pipe. McKenna listened with half an ear, trying to tune the song toward unlocking the mystery of the mirror. Now that she knew the secret behind her strange existence, the fact her divine mother left such an inscrutable object in her infant care frustrated her. What was the point? Was this a test?

Her masses of coppery hair, her clear amber eyes. The swarthy skin colored deeper than the mountain she mined. A flash, of amethyst and ebon scales...

"Nature. It's true nature," Seth blurted unexpectedly. "The runes, they say "Your Self", but what it really means is one's true nature. This mirror," he said, lowering his voice reverently, "do you think this was the mirror Atosa used, in the legend? To return from mortal to immortal deity?"

Urtha chuckled, purple smoke issuing from her lips. "Aesir are indeed, much faster than durgir."

The stroke of Tjen's fingers upon their instrument came to a slow halt, and Ginni's voice transitioned from musical to inquisitive. "True nature, huh? How is that any different?"

"This mirror…" Seth scrutinized the shimmering bit of glass laid in McKenna's lap. "It doesn't just reflect what's in front of it. It can unlock the true nature of the one who holds it. It can… can scry any aspect of someone, something, and reveal that to the bearer. And doing so unlocks the bearer's ability to access that, whatever it is. When you saw my father…" he trailed off.

"Your father was already dead. What I looked at was a portrait. But the nature of the man never dies. And it showed me the truth, after all," she said softly. "It showed me his genius, not his madness, and it showed me his pride in his son and not his despair at himself. He may not have even known himself how he felt, but the mirror saw it anyways."

Seth stared at the mirror, a look of clarity tinged with pain on his face. She wondered if he'd known of his father's deeper beliefs; she wondered if he endured the treatment of his abandonment of the guild as a sort of self-inflicted punishment for the betrayal he felt from his father's death. She slowly slid her palm over his clenched fist and gave it a little squeeze.

"He saw you. He knew you would do better than he did. That despite not being strong enough to endure it himself, he left behind a man who could. The strength of your nature gave him the courage to escape his pain. Courage," she emphasized, looking into the stricken face of the fighter, "courage, not inadequacy. Not fear."

She could feel, by the pulse racing in his palm, that he

heard and trusted her.

"When you gaze upon the mirror, what do you see?" Seth returned, casting a fierce look upon McKenna.

"I..."

She thought about all the times she'd looked into the mirror. A bare, stubble free face. A callous youth unworthy to strike the iron within the mountain. She didn't know what she could see, because she never bothered to try and look for what was there. Only for what she expected to find. She took a deep breath and, maintaining her grip upon the fingers Seth laced with hers, peered with eyes newly focused into its depths.

"When I look into the mirror," she began, chanting the runes that became clearer, as she learned to accept her identity, and accept the immortal blood that flowed within her.

"De aso mal'dhenna mak lahde."

The Celestial words flowing from her tongue tasted strange, but familiar.

I see my true self.

Two babes, side by side. One ghostly pale, the other dark and warm. A woman held them close, a woman with unassuming, but clearly aesir, features. A clarion call- the woman, in a swirling shaft of light and sound, assuming a true immortal form almost too painfully beautiful to look upon. The anguish and heartbreak she felt upon leaving them, mirrored in the hearts of her children; a desperate wish they could join her. A gangly youth in a library, already a head taller than her master beside her, ruefully rubbing a chin that lacked the whiskery coverage of her brethren. But day after day, and night after night, yearning more deeply for adventure than for the beard it should bring. The softness of a spirit, hovering almost protectively around her; the harshness of the difference that estranged her from the kin among which she grew. The moment when decades of study and indecision finally crystallized itself into a single, glorious purpose to quest, to adventure, to become a hero. To do good in a world that seemed to either resist the march of progression or accelerate it beyond control at the expense of its denizens. She felt a warmth of recognition, a humility and a painfully poignant sense of contentment, wash over her.

"It's not about the beard," she looked up, locking eyes with Seth. "It's not about my identity, about who I was before or who they expected me to be. It's about my choice. It's discovering my ideals, my focus, my drive to continue and live my life, *my* life, to its absolute limit."

The little gathering grew quiet. Urtha looked at the faces of each, and then stood gracefully before the fire. She puffed upon her pipe, and the plume of smoke took the shape of a dragon roaring with lifelike vigor.

"You see now the road before you. Orgir never tell what we know. We do not trust, we are fearful. But times are changing. You are a hero," she said, speaking to McKenna with reverential grace, "and you will deliver us from the evil which will walk among us. We cannot see him, he cannot see us. We are protected by the grace of Kumbo and his promise to Atosa. But we know he is here. And he will stop at nothing, *nothing*, to flood the world with the death and decay he so revels in. What a world is this? We wonder. It may be nothing better, but it is what we choose. If he takes away the power of our choice," she finished, tapping out the pipe and grinding the embers beneath her foot, "we are nothing. Worse than dead."

She laid a hand on the holvir's heads briefly, and with a smile, bowed to McKenna and vanished into the night.

"That was an… experience," Ginni, wrapped protectively in Tjen's arms, shivered and smiled. "She said you were a hero, though. That's nice, right?"

McKenna couldn't answer in so many words. The exchange left her shaken, but resolute. To make a declaration, even if only to these three, her closest friends, could change her intention. She needed time to understand her next steps.

A new, and powerfully magnetic, expression lay in the depths of Seth's golden eyes. She met his look with a crooked smile. "What, are you thinking about worshipping me now or something?"

"Hmm. Or something," he joked back. McKenna could only be thankful he pledged to adventure by her side. The feelings that dawned, too direct to be mistaken, had soothed a measure of her own heart as yet untouched and unknown. If Urtha had meant for her to discover the true nature of those unspoken whispers, she knew she had done so. To travel beside him, to harmonize with the song of his soul, was the single point upon which her world revolved.

Even if that road led them straight through the door

to Hel.

XXVI

A Dance With Death And Destiny

Another few days of travel led the party, finally, to the outskirts of the tribe's settlement. About half a league away, Ginni and Tjena came to a halt.

"We're still banished, after all. You two should continue on and visit the village. Our Pasha, Oyewolo the Elder... he'll listen to you, McKenna. You have a way with you, you're so charismatic."

McKenna snorted at the look on Seth's face. "What, and I'm not?" he scoffed.

"Seth, I love you. Please don't make me answer that," replied Ginni.

"And you're sure we can't come with you? Seems unfair that we escort you this far, and yet you have to do the dangerous bit on your own." The rogue couldn't keep the concern out of his voice entirely.

"Well, we did it once before... what's the worst that could happen?" Ginni shrugged nonchalantly.

"Yeah, I mean, you can really only go blind once," muttered Tjena.

McKenna and Seth looked at each other and dissolved into laughter. Ginni huffed and rolled her hazel eyes. "You know, I hope he eats you this time. Now come on, this should only take a few hours at the most. Wole should know some more history of the chasm. And he may even have seen anyone coming or going since we left. If we're not back by morning, send a search party."

They waved the holvir off, then turned to make their own way toward the village. It was the first time she'd been alone with the rogue since the beginning of her journey, and McKenna began to feel a shyness she almost couldn't explain away. Seth, erect upon Kurya's golden back, stared directly ahead toward the horizon. McKenna couldn't muster the courage to break his reverie, so the journey was a silent one. What had come over her?

The sight of figures flitting to and fro upon the path distracted her. No form of sentry or gate barred their entrance. The village simply sprang into being before them. Chickens squawked as children chased them through the dirt, past shanties built from the bamboo-like wooden reeds that grew in the marshes and white mud plaster. Almost every facade before them bore a mural, a painting, or other such work of art. McKenna felt her heart race as they turned the corner and faced a low wall covered in incredibly detailed and realistic renderings of the ilmaurte. Music, fading in and out of windows and winding through narrow alleys, permeated the entire space. The variation should have been a cacophony, but somehow all the different instruments and singers blended together in a soulful melody.

Of middling size, the settlement seemed to showcase the determination of the holvir race to struggle and endure. That they could scratch this incredible beauty and hearty viability from the dismal and dangerous waste stood testament to such. And they all seemed… happy. Just plain joy that ran deep, wells of cheerfulness without any intention of running dry. It reminded the monk of Ginni's delirious nonchalance at their meeting, and her glowing charisma regardless of what character she stood before. Being among her kin helped the monk understand the personality of her friend a lot better.

"I've never seen so many holvir in one place," Seth remarked. "I didn't know they built societies like this one. Usually you catch a few banded together here and there, but so far as I know, there's never been any such thing as a camp - let alone a village of this size."

She hearkened to the awed tone of respect used by the rogue. "Perhaps it's easier for them to abide with the other races in smaller parties, but they still have a shared heritage and a shared history. I'm glad, even if it is in such a desolate wasteland, they can find the joy in society with their brethren."

"I think so too. But I hope when this… is over…" he hesitated, looking around at the dried, barren grasses and the crumbling, leaning shanties, "we can bring them closer. I know this kind of life isn't by choice, it's by force. We forced them to this extreme, and…" his eyes flashed, "we owe them better than this."

The monk nodded with a smile, happy to see that Seth had taken her desire to heart. To unify the folkr of Faie, instead of continuing to excuse their poor treatment of each other as insurmountable differences.

Most of the holvir they came across gave them a wide berth, not meeting their gaze, dancing around them as though they weren't there. The village had a single authority figure and until he greeted and assessed the nature of these visitors, the little citizens simply treated them as part of the scenery. However, McKenna could sense they were being almost herded in a specific direction, and she dismounted alongside Seth to follow the trail subtly laid out to them. As they turned the corner, they met an eccentric sight.

Dancers, spinning wildly in cloaks of dry reeds and vines, whipped through a clearing nestled amongst the cozy shanties. The hollow sound of drums and wooden pipes echoed within McKenna's breast and she gasped in delight at the wild display. Quite a crowd had gathered to watch the dance, and on the other side of the clearing a small group surrounded a single figure who sat raised slightly above them. The figures seemed like nature come to life, whirling wildlings of dancing mania that swept through the air and across the ground, bare and flat under the pounding of their feet. They moved with the grace of the wind that flowed across the prairie, undulating waves of gold and green beneath the lavender of a twilight sky. McKenna and Seth stopped in their tracks, arrested by the magic of their display.

And it contained, literal, magic - though the holvir were barred from the divine power that Faie's pantheon shared with the rest of its inhabitants, the runes upon McKenna's skin and along the shaft of her glowing guisarme shivered and sparked in response to the ebb and flow of natural energies generated by the dance. As she relaxed into a standing meditation, attuning herself to the source of the strange energy, she recalled the waves of power commanded by her bardic friends and their music. How had she never noticed it before? How could the holvir work such magic without a god?

Kurya's tailed swished against her, dragging her consciousness from its meditation. The horse's head dipped before the tribe's pasha seated upon the dais, his intelligent gaze meeting the holvi's own. A divine beast, willed into being by the great god Bahamut, recognized the careful and equitable energies that lay within these native folk who grew from the ground, blossomed from the trees, flowed from the river Styckes itself.

The dance slowly petered out, the final beat of the drum echoed throughout the clearing, and the holvi upon the dais rose. His features seemed typical of the race. Only his age singled him out. Holvir had no longevity to speak of, even by the standards of the short-lived asafolk, yet the one who stood seemed as ancient as the realm itself.

McKenna looked slightly confusedly at Seth. She had no idea what the proper greeting for a holvi leader would be, and she could have kicked herself for not bothering to ask Ginni or Tjena before splitting up. Seth, however, stared directly ahead at the ancient elder. Then, with a smile and a low nod, he advanced closer.

"Greetings Oyewolo, Pasha of Padfoot. We come to ask you for the gift of your hospitality, and we thank you for the display we've already been graced with. McKenna," he motioned the monk forward and she stepped toward him, "and I have been travelling with some members of your own tribe. We seek your wisdom and ask your guidance in ridding our land of the scourge that defiles it."

The wizened little Pasha made no response. McKenna bit her lip, wondering if they had somehow offended the inscrutable holvi. She chanced another glance at the Wole's face, and stifled a shocked gasp.

His aged eyes were full of tears.

"You have come among my kin with requests, you say," he spoke in a low tone, but with a clarity and purity unexpected in so old a person. "Requests, when those of your nature would take with demands. We could not deny you anything you wished to have of ours. Your strength and the gods in whose light you walk are too great for us to defy. But yet, you asked."

McKenna covered her mouth in distress, then kneeled in order to level her amber gaze with his piercing blue one. "We come before your people in utmost humility and goodwill. I am a duergi, and our people do not cross often, it appears. But I have since learned of your treatment at the hands of those who walk these realms as you do, and I vow," she said, her voice breaking, "I vow with every ounce of my being to change that."

This drew murmurs from the little crowd around them. The greater folk of Faie, helping holvir? They shrugged their shoulders. Surely times were changing after all.

The Padfoot Pasha put out a palm and rested it upon McKenna's forehead. "Duergi you are not, but believe you, I will. You are welcome to our family, and I hope the friends who found you," his voice softened slightly, "are not so far behind."

"Do you know the two who travel with us, then?" asked Seth.

The murmuring of the crowd around them grew louder. Several holvir wiped tears from their eyes, and one patted the back of another who sobbed against his shoulder.

"We did not want to lose them. They were our brightest stars," he responded, gazing off toward the heavens as though to see them sparkling above. "We cannot change our nature, we cannot change our ways, for to do so would mean death. But the banished pair, they are honored above all others, and we would do anything to have them back among us."

"We couldn't follow them on the rest of their journey," Seth continued, "but we know where they are. Tjen won't be cured until they return to Meliamne and the sorcere who offered a cure. But will you allow them to receive the blessings of their people, and embrace their homeland once more? We all seek the Lich King, whose appearance has caused the blight upon them and flooded the realms in such danger. Once we destroy him, perhaps the curse upon your kin will be lifted?" he spoke hopefully.

Wole put a long finger against his wrinkled cheek, deep in thought. "I do not know," he sighed, with a shrug. "But there are many unknowns in this unknowable world. We either take risks and fail now, or we stay static and fail later. My people," he said, waving his arms out toward the gathering, "will you allow our brave adventurers to return home, knowing the risk?"

The silence resonated for a moment, then a small voice broke through it.

"Please, heroes," she said, staring beseechingly at McKenna and Seth. "Please bring back our Ginni and Tjena."

The rest of the tribe broke into a similar clamor and plea, the sounds mingling into music and developing into a slow, mournful ballad carried by the whole village.

The Padfoot Pasha put a hand over his heart and stood, motioning again for silence.

"Who am I to ignore the pleas of my people? If you can bring them home, we will welcome them. And now," he said, settling back into his seat and signaling for assistance in caring for the horses and drawing up cushioned seats for the travelling pair, "we must discuss what is known and unknown about the treacherous Likirricanthe."

As they talked, the tribe set up a communal feast, mingling their cooking with song and their dishes with dancing. The holvir favored rich broths poured over the grains that throve in the hardy climates of the savannah. Their gardens were small, but grew with the abundance and vivacity of the holvir who tended them. Knowing what she did about the affinity between holvir and their Faie Mother, it finally made sense to the monk how the holvir managed to survive so long at the edge of the world. They focused on the wonders of nature, on the land and the flora growing upon it, seeking no beauty of gold or of deed but simply what they could do to make the ground more fertile and the waters more sweet.

She blew softly on the contents tipped by one of the holvir into her clay bowl, savoring its aroma. Beside her, Seth absently scooped mouthfuls from his own bowl with a piece of flatbread in his hands, listening intently to the Pasha. Most of the younger holvir scurrying around them cast wide-eyed glances at the sight of their great Pasha bowed in deep conversation with a paladin. Or at least, a man who bore the aura and the armor of one. Catching McKenna watching, one grinned sheepishly and shrugged, as if to say, *we've never been visited by one of your kind, and yet here are two of the greatest among us like equals, eating our bread and listening to our words.*

It seemed the one thing holvir never stopped doing was moving. As the day yawned into darkness, the bustle grew more and more boisterous. A bonfire took the place of the cauldron from which they had feasted, and small groups and couples swung merrily around it to the tune of the curious instruments their brethren played. McKenna watched them in awe, until Seth stood and bowed deeply before her, extending a hand.

"Care for a dance?" A vivacious smile flitted across his face, the infectious result of the holvir's personalities around them and the golden glints of firelight that danced in her copper locks. She grinned back and grabbed his hand, stepping into the gathering of swaying figures.

They wove in and out together, the martial training of each imbuing a sense of grace and rhythm to their movements. No whirling creatures of grass and grain; the melody was charming, light, refreshing. They hovered around the edge of the clearing, watching almost as much as dancing. The shyness McKenna had felt earlier evaporated, whisked away as quickly as their swirling steps.

"Now this is relaxing," she said comfortably, staring into the depths of the sparkling night sky above her, so like and yet unlike the first she'd seen upon leaving the mines of Mount Oer. "I think we earned this, don't you?"

"You're telling me. I've been so focused on protecting myself since leaving the guild, and there wasn't much relaxing while I was in it, to be honest. It's been years since my last dance," he replied, twirling her expertly.

"Hmmm, it's been quite a bit longer than that for me. Dancing is too frivolous for chapel… and durgir, come to think of it. I probably haven't danced since before I started my novitiate over fifty years ago.

Seth blinked, stunned. "You're uh, you're how old now?"

McKenna pondered for a moment. "A hundred and four? Or maybe, nine? Uhm, I lost count."

The rogue's jaw dropped. "What?" laughed McKenna. "How old did you think I was?"

"You've been alive for over a century, and yet you had no idea you were part Celestial?"

"Oh my gods, Seth. I was raised by durgir. They don't die unless they're killed. What was I supposed to think?"

He laughed helplessly, and pulled her closer as the music became slow, quiet, melancholy. Suddenly, McKenna couldn't help feeling nervous. What did this aesir think of her? Was she really so strange, so uncanny? Did she truly have a place among these faiefolkr she had newly met?

"Does it make you uncomfortable?" she said softly. "Is it too difficult to travel with, to have a companion with such an identity-"

He cut her off by placing both hands on her cheeks, and stared with an intensity that merited his slow, deliberate movement. He gave her all the time in the world to deny, to step back from what she knew she wanted more than anything. The soft touch of his lips upon hers. As his first venture was met with complicity he pulled her closer and matched the force of his gaze with a ferocity of passion that left her breathless. She didn't know what it was to love someone until this moment, to feel such love and compassion from him.

When they finally broke free, she laughed breathlessly and lowered her gaze. "That's a no, then."

"That's a no, McKenna," he replied, with a hand cupping her dimpled chin. He stroked her sable cheek, flush with the emotions and passion his caresses fired within her. She placed a hand over his, glorying in the sensation of the way he held her. Together they stood, the lights of fireflies and sparks swirling around them along with the remaining couples on the dance floor. Death had no place here, among the glories of the living, the bright spirits that they were. Duergi, monk, goddess - woman, she realized, as she felt the warmth of his touch, and the depth of his desire. Come what may, they would hold each other close for this golden moment the gods had gifted them.

XXVII

The Price Of Ambition

He arrived in the darkness, stepping softly through the chambers lit only by the glow of a dying fire. Katarin, her long, lithe, stately being slung listlessly into a divan, stared unseeingly into the glow of the ember's depths. He'd never seen her like this, so quiet and almost melancholy. His princess, who always knew her status, her power, and her future. He crept up and laid a hand softly upon the crown of her head.

She relaxed perceptibly under the unexpected touch. Only one hand could ever caress her like that, and though out at her own bidding she long ached to feel it again. A sigh broke free from her tightly pursed lips, and he took the opportunity to scoop her up and cuddle her against his chest.

"Sweet princess, what lays you low? The reward for your ambition is so close at hand. After these long, long years of preparation, you will finally achieve your dream." He planted a kiss on the nape of her neck.

"I'm tired, Razan," she spoke quietly, almost fearfully. The weeks of waiting and scheming wore down her resolve, and as she grew closer to her ascension she felt almost an ebbing power escape her, leaving a vacuum in its wake. Today she had done little more than lounge on a sofa, unequal to any exertion or communication. She was glad the guild master returned. Glad to rest against the heart beating in his chest.

Beating for her.

"What good am I really?" she wondered out loud. Never before had she suffered such doubt and confusion in her normal confidence and bravado. "All this… did I truly earn it? Is it mine, my own accomplishment, or is it just the gift of the luck of my birth? What distinguishes me from anyone else who covets such power?"

He didn't know how to respond right away. The surety, the upright nature of the durgirn monk who shared this heritage, had given him hope that Katarin's own ambition in the name of her mother might be misdirected. He often wondered whether Katarin sought greatness because she was expected to, rather than her expressed motivation of actually wanting to.

"Katarin. Look at me," he said suddenly, putting a hand on her chin and tilting her face towards him. Her cheek gleamed palely in the moonlight, but at his touch a faint blush of rose spread across her features. "Everything you are, everything you have done- these are your gifts. Whether born some holvir spawn out in the middle of the bogs or princess descended from immortals, the things you've done with the gifts you have are your own to claim."

Power that filled her from birth found expression at her lightest thought. Scores of Masters and novitiates past had died for a fraction of what she commanded without effort. She regarded the man before her, aesir, or so she thought, who had clawed his way to this position hand over hand, throwing down those above him to be trampled beneath his feet. Next to her, and to the centuries-old Grand Master Mistmoon, no one wielded more power, commanded greater respect. And yet here he was, below her still, subservient, proving the truth of his words. She should deserve it all.

"I've chased these dreams for so long. I've forgotten what a moment in time feels like." A halfhearted smile drew itself up to to the corner of her mouth.

An invitation? He thought to himself. It had been so long since they'd felt the pleasure of one another. Since the White Solstice, she'd been wrapped in single minded purpose, and he in performing her every bidding. She smiled wanly at him, but he hesitated, savoring the sight of her languid form, as close to submission as he'd ever seen her. He wanted nothing more than to hold her, to drink in her sight, her smell, her sweet and silvery form. Wondering what she'd do if he approached her, hesitantly, he leaned in to brush the nape of her neck with his lips.

She sighed, her body arching toward him. With the utmost control over every single motion, he continued to caress her, reaching into her heart and filling it with his own. He wanted to fill every inch of her, absorb her soul and carry it with him into the eternity of the afterlife.

She rose, meeting him with every touch. She whispered his name in his ear and it electrified him, this perfect woman, this glorious soul. For the moment, she was his. For eternity, he was hers.

To hell with mutual benefit, to hell with ambition. My whole life I've been running to escape my destiny. I will find it here. No matter the cost.

Dazed and breathless some time later, he turned toward her, admiring the silky skin that shone silver in the moonlight. He dragged a finger along the ridge of her hips and she blushed, pulling lightly at the locks of his hair. Though her spirits seemed higher than when he first encountered her, he could tell a lingering sadness still lowered upon her. Watching her silently as they dressed, he quickly determined how best to restore her to herself.

"Come on, Princess," he cocked his head with a smirk, grabbing her hand and pulling her urgently. "I've got something you should see."

"Razan, where in the world are we going?" she spoke weakly, but made no move to deny him.

"Just follow me, and I won't spoil the surprise," he said, as he led her from the tower to the forest beyond.

Gleaming lights met her bemused gaze. So close to the Solstice, the Moon ilvir bustled in preparation for their quarterly sing. Red Solstice, heralding the turning of the leaves, and the turning of the year. A magical celebration honored by every race across Faie, though in ways best suited to each. She could almost laugh at the faces of asafolk staring around at the sight of lithe, nimble figures flinging themselves through the canopy, alighting the souls of starflowers among the boughs of the tall stately trees. Somewhere in the distance she could hear music, the low, coaxing tones of a harp accompanied by the treble and bass of the flexible voice of their city's fledgling Choirmaster.

"No one can hold a candle to Marvel," Razan commented ruefully, as he detected the faintest weaknesses in the otherwise clear, clarion pitch that floated through the effervescent forest.

"He was Choirmaster for so long," she replied, a heaviness on her soul as she thought of the departed

Master. Marvel Whispermane had led the people of Meliamne, in song and in society, for centuries. It was said the power of his song had helped called down the immortal soul of Atosa herself. Fewer, and more carefully guarded whispers, had rumored it was his seed who sired her immortal children. Certainly it was true he had carefully raised the precocious princess left with the ilvir, all the way up until his death.

"Hmm. Yes, but I think the ilvir have also… forgotten their place, somewhat," he said, casting a look at the marvelous towers that rose from the forest floor alongside the ancient trees among which the people of Meliamne had for so long made their homes. "The Guild doesn't see it so much as they should; the realm moves on, and molds their culture to more closely emulate the asafolk."

Katarin shrugged. "Can you blame them? Their goddess forgets them. Just as the asafolk grow restless while the scourge advances, so do the ilvir grow impatient with the death that makes its way through the sacred groves of life they so assiduously protect."

"I can't blame them, but I can bemoan the loss of our old way of life." Change was inevitable. Adapting to it was what made the assassin so powerful. But even he struggled with the pace at which the world was moving.

Unable to resist the draw of the music, Katarin followed Razan as they made their way towards the palace and the source of the sound. A large, open pavilion, scattered with flowers and figures born forth by a similar pull, flowed with the graceful song and dance of the people of Meliamne. Razan bowed deeply and, granted with the boon of her hand, drew her into the glittering, shifting throng.

"I forgot... how close we were to the solstice," she murmured, her head resting gently against his chest.

"You've had many things to distract you," he said, revolving her slowly amid the other dancers. Many bowed at the sight of their princess, and as their generous appreciation filtered into her perception she began to feel her spirits lift.

"Oh, Razan, why must life be ever like this? Why can we not enjoy the moment for what it is?" she spoke with a resigned edge to her voice.

Razan didn't respond for a moment. "You have the choice, Katarin," he said slowly, clinging to his princess tightly, "the choice to make what you will of what you have. We both are gifted with so many years before us," he spoke soulfully, feeling the gem of his heart resting so close to him, "why should we not use them to make our own way?"

She sighed listlessly. The vacuum of energy, the clamorous voices, had not returned yet to deaden her fears or her discontent. What if Razan was right?

A shower of starflowers descended; scattered on the evening breeze. A cheerful cry rang out from the figures revolving on the platform, lifting into glorious song that matched the resonance of their souls. It was so easy, she thought to herself. So easy to be loved and admired like this.

Easy, but worthless.

She stepped back from Razan's grasp, tense and aloof. He dropped the hands that had held her, staring concernedly at the rigid woman. She saw the confusion flit across his face, but it had no effect on her. What right had he to tell her how her life should be lived? What did he know about the destiny that hemmed her in on every side, that forced each step in line with how she should act, how she should feel, who she should be?

"I want that mirror, Razan," she whispered, the venom in her words cloaking the nakedness of her spirit, retracing the steps toward intimacy to which he had betrayed her. "You will never understand. I am nothing like my sister. She is weak, worthless, and a fool, and she will never have what is mine."

He stood looking at her, dumbfounded. Turning on her heel, she disappeared into the crowd.

In his empty hands, a starflower fell, its petals limp and lustrous.

———

A watchful, unseen figure loomed on the edge of the wastes. The music from the holvir camp, so like and yet unlike the music that filled the groves of Meliamne, echoed hauntingly in his ears. He remained cloaked by the uneven terrain, standing still in the shadows of the titanic cliffs that sank below the surface of the desert boundary. Hovering on the edge of life and death, battling with the desires of his heart and his determination to submit. To free himself from the passion threatening to undo him.

Razan bowed to no mortal. The enigmatic man represented the textbook definition of neutral chaos - serving himself above all others, and serving those who interest him next, regardless of the machinations of anyone around him and finding pleasure only in uncertainty and disorder. Nothing entertained him more than upsetting schemes and plans that weren't his own, just for the fun and novelty of seeing things blow up and watching people scramble to restore them. Were he an introspective sort of person, he would probably have recognized that tendency arose from the narrow restrictions of his upbringing, and his violent and volatile desire to avert his supposed destiny at any cost. However, introspection was definitely not Razan's forte. He preferred action first, consequences later.

She needs that mirror to assume her mother's mantle. If I let them go, and they somehow find and restore Atosa, she'd never forgive me. But what if I brought it to her and made her see herself? What if I could prove to her she's stronger than ever a goddess could be?

The tiny figures of the approaching holvir bobbed along the trail. Razan wondered idly what they were doing here. By their own admission, they were banished from their homeland, and Naijor definitely wasn't a pleasure destination. Making himself as subtle as a whisper and as unassuming as a shadow, he drew nearer to them, hoping their conversation would aide his plans.

"Whew, do you remember it being this deep last time we were here?" Ginni was saying, as they came within earshot of the hidden assassin. She looked over the vast expanse carved into the desert waste before them, wavering on the horizon and looking more like a painting than a real place.

"Well, considering I can't see it, I can't answer that," Tjen replied, somewhat breathlessly.

"Oh. I guess that… yeah. Okay fair," the bard subsided, as the two made their way along the narrow path.

The sheer cliffs dropped directly into the fathomless gorge below. No track lay beside or into it; at least, not one that a common mortal could traverse. The holvir sought a tunnel, carved by one of the smaller brackish streams running lazily into the larger river Styckes. In a pit, nearly invisible due to the reeds and brush that lay around it, they found the same path they'd followed that had first led them to that dark courtyard below.

Curiosity piqued, the assassin noiselessly followed. Attuned as he was to the Abyss, and the horrid creatures that lay within it, he wondered with a shock how the duo could be so inured to the miasma that surrounded them as soon as they entered the tunnel. He could feel it, pulsing like a living creature, sliding against the sinews of his soul and pulling at those energies he sternly suppressed- the daemoric ancestry he had run from for so long. Part of him wished to flee; leave the holvir to their fates. But he realized he had no other way of approaching the rest of the party and stealing that mirror without their aide. A black globe rolled between his fingers, a quick getaway. He whispered an enchantment into the bangles upon his wrist, a binding spell that would tie the bard's mind to his without her knowledge. Until he understood their motives, he chose to remain hidden, following them at a distance close enough to learn the truth of their journey.

Luckily, Ginni made his wait fairly short. "Finding a trace… what the heck is a trace, anyways? This pouch she gave us doesn't have anything in it."

"Seriously? You've been carrying it this whole time and you didn't realize it was empty?" Tjen asked incredulously.

"I... I forgot I had it, actually. I kind of just... remembered," she replied uncomfortably.

The two were silent for a moment. "Now you mention it... I never really thought about it either. Not til you brought it out just now," Tjen's voice grew concerned in the darkness.

A sudden light illuminated the space. The bard had scooped a handful of lightfire from their pocket and lit it in the palm of their hand, to help their partner investigate the questionable item gifted them by the enigmatic sorcere. There was another pause.

"Do you think she tricked us? Pretty elaborate trick, if you ask me... what could she want us here for? If there's no way for us to find what she needed, what is she expecting us to bring back?" Ginni asked, a sense of desperation tinging her normally lighthearted lilt. The bard didn't know how much longer her partner had before the blight utterly destroyed them; she didn't know what she would do if that time suddenly ran out.

"Hmm. Try singing. Maybe we can-"

A sudden roar cut them off, a deep, guttural sound that could only belong to one type of beast. The stuff of legends, the wildest, largest creature to walk the Material plane.

The roar of a dragon.

"Faie Mother preserve us, that was absolutely not here last time," Ginni wheezed.

"Do you think it eats holvir?" Tjen squeaked, the light

in their palm flickering as they shook in place.

"I think it eats *everything*, Tjen. But what is it doing here? Dragons can't live underground. They- what was that?"

Razan's sudden appearance cut her off mid sentence. Dropping the enchanted globe and ringing his bangles together with one deft twist of his wrist, the three were spirited from the tunnel, back out into the endless night.

"Holvi Ginni, you are bound by my spell to know my thoughts, but not my face," he chanted quickly, so only the bard could hear him. With another chime of his bangles, he knocked Tjen senseless. The binding spell would only work on the one of them, and he couldn't risk the blighted musician overhearing him and disrupting the spell.

"What was that?" She responded fuzzily, attempting to focus on the man standing before her.

"That was a dragon. Why it's there… well, I hope you can tell me that," he responded through clenched teeth.

"Huh. She never mentioned a dragon. She just wanted to find the trace," Ginni answered, compelled to honesty by the spell. "I dunno if we found it… but I…" she shook the pouch at her hip, and suddenly it jangled, like it was full of small stones and metal. "Hang on. That was empty."

Razan snatched it from her and dumped its contents on the ground. Runes, and a diminutive brazier; the basic components of a summoning. The assassin was no sorcere, but even he could see the runes were all wrong for the summoning of an Abyssal creature.

If he were a necromancer, he'd recognize the runes were meant for summoning death from Hel.

"Where is the mirror of Atosa?" He asked, his heart sinking within him. *I have one chance to get that mirror. One chance to save her from this horrible fate.*

"Uhm, McKenna has it, last time I… checked…" she trailed off, still blinking and rubbing her eyes, desperate to shake the spell and understand what she was saying and who she was saying it to.

"You need to get me that mirror. I promise your consort no harm, but only if you bring me the mirror of Atosa," he spoke firmly. *A dragon. A dragon guarding the Doors of Death.*

"Consort? Tjen? Wait, where's Tjen- where are they? What have you done with them!" wailed the bard helplessly.

"Not your concern right now. You bring me that mirror, I give you both your freedom," he hissed.

The little holvi shook her head, as though trying to clear it, but compelled by the binding spell she turned and marched back along the path towards the settlement.

What was she planning? the assassin thought to himself, debating whether or not to dive back into the tunnel and see for himself the dragon trapped within the gorge. Sending holvir to prepare a summoning- holvir couldn't abide divine magic. It would probably destroy them before they even lit the flames of the brazier. She must have known that… which meant she also must have known about the dragon deep in the bowels of this crater cut into the wastes. Did she set it there to guard death until she could replace her mother? Had that been her use of the genirae Makarh?

Wouldn't my mother be proud, he thought with disgust. *Played for a complete fool. Well, Princess, two can play at that game.*

He scooped the runes and the brazier back into their pouch, tying it negligently to his belt, and swept back along the path.

XXVIII

The Spirit In The Mirror

As the dancers began to disperse, the Pasha beckoned them over. He seemed perturbed.

"One of the villagers just came back from the border of the wastes and spoke of a strange presence. It did no harm, but he said it seemed almost to cry for help. I shouldn't ask you, our guests, to face this unknown danger. But I think your mirror can help. Maybe this spirit has more answers for you than I did."

Suddenly nerveless fingers clung to Seth's; but McKenna shook herself sternly and summoned a confidence and tranquility more fitting to her vocation. He had turned to look at her, mute inquiry in his face. She wished she could thank him aloud for doing so, instead of assuming she would be willing to face the mirror again regardless of the cost.

He's learned a lot about sacrifice, I think, she thought as she pulled out the mirror, holding it delicately while peering into its endless depths.

No answer would find them here; she realized she would need to seek the spirit within the wastes. Seth found the villager who had discovered the presence and, together, they followed his directions into a scrubby dead wood that lay between the village and the wastes.

In sharp contrast to the abundance of life that lay

within the confines of the tribe's settlement, everything outside it lay dead, desiccated, and absolutely silent. Far off in the distance, they could just make out the sharp relief of the moon's light reflecting off Styckes as its oily waters sank into oblivion below a massive gorge. Somewhere deep within that fathomless crater, their friends had disappeared. McKenna felt a keen stab of refreshed fear as she realized the fate they'd been left to.

"I'm thinking Ginni's request for a morning search party may end up turning into a moonlight one," Seth muttered, sensing the fear radiating from the monk. "I couldn't leave them in there alone all night either."

The monk cast him a look of approbation, thankful he would share her worry instead of mock her fear as being unfounded. "This is… strong magic," she pushed the words through the dryness that caught in her throat. "There is a presence here, but I can't see beyond the miasma." The light on the river water caught her attention again, and suddenly she asked curiously, "What… is that place?"

He studied her for a moment, seeing the glow of the undulating river reflected in the depths of her amber eyes. A halo of celestial aura surrounded her, a reminder that she belonged to more than just this world.

"Styckes is the lifeblood of Faie. At least, that's what the orgir believed, and the orgir have lived here longer than anyone. And where life goes, death follows. Styckes brought the souls from across the realms home to their final resting place. It's said that Styckes feeds the Doors of Death."

The Doors of Death - another metaphor? Or another legend based in truth? She wondered idly. "So… why did it dry up? Where did the river go?"

"As the old gods withdrew from their people, their legends seemed to go with. Atosa was never a very strong deity even at the height of her power and influence. She always felt overshadowed by her sister, and neither of them really did much to stem the tides of change, when they finally flowed across the land."

Atosa tried to turn mortal, turn her back on the pantheon, on the domain and the people who needed her. She had been ready to give up everything to save herself, to feel love and need within the mortal realm. Only the desperate plea of her sister changed that desire, returned the goddess to the role she felt as restricting as a prison.

"Do you think… Atosa turned Styckes? Hoping that perhaps, with the advance of the new gods, and the new civilization, she could finally… pass on? Return to mortality, and live a fuller life than the one she suffered as a goddess?" McKenna whispered, trying to come to terms with the actions that led to her abandonment.

"No one really knows. I only know this much because my father, much to the disgust of my mother, often spoke to holvir, the only people who have lived here longer than orgir. He listened to their stories, and not just the ones about asafolk. Whenever a roaming party would stay in Wheelspoke, he'd often either sneak out himself or send someone he trusted to find them safe shelter and a fair pay. In exchange, they were more than willing to tell him everything they knew about Faie's history, and all its people, without the bias asafolk liked to cast on it. But holvir care none for deities," he said with a wave of his hand toward the little settlement, "and honestly, I can see why. Time and time again, magic and gods forced them further and further from the societies they helped build. They knew the stories the orgir would sometimes share, the riddles hidden in half truths that few could ever understand. My father, and other likeminded people, pieced together what they could understand, but of course, in deepest secrecy. You can't tell nobles, or the people who cling to the hems of their golden robes," he scoffed, "that their influences led to the destruction of the realms they pretended to save."

Join us or die. This land does not belong to you, this land belongs only to the mighty. Durgir, unwilling to fight, burying themselves deep where Faiekind could not reach them. Ilvir, unlikely to descend from their bowery treetops, making halfhearted gestures of alliance while turning a blind eye to the slowly creeping destruction. Holvir and orgir, unable to challenge the invaders or defend their homeland, pushed inch by bloody inch into the wastes. Unnecessary, unimportant, unworthy. And now a scourge, that fed upon the disarray, that found its source of power in the very imbalance caused by such a shift in magic.

"And I remained buried, all this time," she seethed inwardly. "Thinking I studied the glory of our noble pantheon, yet blind to the people who abused its powers. I thought my quest would help me get to the place that I worked so hard to find, but now I'm realizing I've just marched with military precision the paths that have been laid before me. None of these accomplishments are really mine. They belong to… to someone else."

Suddenly she stood, currents of devoted serenity ebbing around the roaring waterfall of hurt and confusion that flowed within her. Taking deep, measured breaths, reaching for the peace and tranquility of Shav'asana, her divine center, she turned with clear eyes and a calm brow toward her companion.

"Alright. That's enough feeling sorry for myself for one day, I think." He opened his mouth as though to contradict, to justify her feelings, but she lifted a staying hand. "No, really, it's not in me to fight this anymore. I watched you suffer enough," she smiled, putting a hand on his shoulder, "but I can just move past it. My god honors me," she spun Laghrusse idly, the runes sparking solemnly in agreement, "but honestly, each step I take from here on out is my own. This may have been a destiny drawn without my consent, but now I see it for what it is, and I can choose it."

Her face shone with radiance. Even in this lifeless desert, even though the celestial power within her bowed to the great mysteries of death, she still stood resplendent of life, glowing with ambition. The warmth of love still lit its roseate shade upon her damask cheek as she looked at him, fresh from the battles of his own heritage, his own failures. To be a hero was to be more than simply alive. Stories are not written about those who fail all the time. They are written about those who succeed against all odds, those who sacrifice peace for greatness. No matter who told their story, no matter how many mistakes they made along the way, they would continue to pursue the highest, and they knew they would find it beside one another.

"You really are a wonder, you know that?" Seth replied, pulling the monk to his side. "It took me the better part of a year to come to terms with what I dealt with, and you just did it in all of a few moments."

"Discipline, what can I say. Seems despite all your 'chosen one' and 'champion of Wheelspoke' and 'Bahamut's brightest follower' nonsense, you clearly don't know anything about good old fashioned discipline."

He laughed, nuzzling her ear, and she leaned into his embrace. *Terrible setting for romance, really*, she thought to herself as her lips sought his. *Yet I think it kind of suits us.*

They approached the gnarled wood described by the villager, almost tiptoeing through the eddies of ash and past blasted trunks of twisted trees. The aura of death, an almost pulsing and oppressive atmosphere in its strength, saturated the land upon which they stood. She could only begin to imagine how strongly it emanated within the gorge itself, and began to feel herself drawn forward towards it. Taking half a step, she suddenly returned to herself and her focus.

They soon discovered any fear of misinterpreting the holvir directions had been unfounded. The essence he described permeated every inch of the brittle woods. The very fibers of her soul felt plucked by the mournful energies surrounding them. Even Seth seemed affected—he stood closer to her and, seeking comfort, slipped a hand into hers. She squeezed it reassuringly, holding the mirror forth in the other while training her senses to focus on the ethereal spirit. This was a wholly new experience; scrying first a portrait and then a living, breathing being bore no comparison to trying to draw forth the hovering energies that manifested just out of reach of the material plane.

"I don't know how to call to you, spirit; I... I'm new at this. But I want to help you. If you trust me, show yourself, your true self, in the mirror."

A swirling purple aura surrounded her. Through her lips a whisper, words unspoken for a millennia, reverberated in the night air.

"Asone mal'dhenna mak lahde"

The mirror glowed a bright, silvery blue. In a couple moments, she began to make out the face and figure of a man reflected back at her.

"When I used the mirror to scry your father, I couldn't talk to him," McKenna said to Seth nervously. "Do you think I can communicate with this spirit?"

He drew in a breath, but smiled at her. "Trust yourself. Try to reach in and summon the same energies you used to contact those released souls. I won't let you go too close to death," his hand tightening in hers, "and together, maybe we can release him."

McKenna nodded, taking a deep breath and focusing not on the figure before her but the aura of the spirit itself. Her meditative practice bore her in good stead. Slipping into the mindset necessary to attract that which rested not on this plane proved far easier than she expected. She breathed carefully, then let her voice carry into the darkness.

"Spirit. I am the daughter of Atosa, and I hold the mirror that can speak the truth of your nature. With her blessing I will guide your soul through Hel, once this unfinished business to which your spirit clings is complete."

It seemed to be the right call. As her voice faded, another one rose to meet it, much like the conflicting whispers she felt as she separated the reanimated corpses from their hostage souls. Yet this time, McKenna could focus on one, the one whose voice she summoned, and the one whose essence was strongest in this dead and dismal wood.

The man in the mirror spoke, a tremor and a fervor in his voice. "Another child of Atosa. But she does not lie, this one. Our goddess has many mysteries indeed. And why her children must be at odds, we witches will never learn."

"Witches," whispered Seth as realization dawned on him, "does he mean the witches of the Ward?"

With his words, a cacophonous shriek caused McKenna to nearly drop the mirror. She winced, biting a lip and sucking in her breath to stifle the cries that did not know how powerfully they assailed her.

"I don't know who they are, but I think you might be right," she replied through gritted teeth as the wailing subsided to a mournful sigh.

"They're a cult that follows Atosa, one of the ancient aesir tribes who lived here before the nobles arrived. Instead of following the gods the nobles brought with them, they retreated, like the orgir, to the wilderness. No one's heard from them in years… most tales told of them as disappearing into the wastes of Naijor."

The spirit, still trapped in its mournful dirge, seemed unlikely to either rebuke or corroborate this tale. She frowned, acknowledging he rest of what the spirit had said. "Children at odds?" McKenna looked at Seth, raising her brow. "I've never even met my sister. Why would I be at odds with her?"

"You say you seek to restore my spirit to the afterlife," the spirit replied dolefully, the quivering wails of his voice finally subsiding back into intelligible speech. "Yet it was your sister who trapped me, who trapped all of us, here in limbo."

Both McKenna's eyebrows shot up. Seth, keeping one hand in hers, wrapped the other about her waist as though to brace her against a tidal wave. And not a moment too soon. The spirit, overwhelmed at the presence of his beloved goddess and desperate for release from the tethers of the Material plane, poured forth a deluge of otherworldly energy that nearly washed her soul away.

She saw a stunning darkness, tasted the coldness of mithril and the warmth of blood in her open mouth. She felt the agony of watching her brethren fall to hidden swords, one by one, around her. The tightness of her chest, as she gasped out a prayer- "Atosa's will"; the keening wail of souls torn from their slowly expiring bodies as they wound tightly around her own. The figures with their dancing blades she couldn't recognize, until the dagger slid from her throat and its possessor, a man whose face and figure she recalled in an instant, stood before her.

Razan, the assassin who found them in the forest and unveiled McKenna's heritage- his eyes, the rusty color of dried blood, lit in a daemoric frenzy.

She gasped, through the choking blood that stifled her. Before the grip of death closed upon her, she could see, in the same brittle wood that they stood now, a range of ilmaurte. Their morbid forms were ready, waiting to descend upon the death surrounding the massacre.

"McKenna! McKenna, monk of Malfaestus, you must open your eyes!"

Something was shaking her. *A dragon?*

"McKenna, please, please come back, please!"

A dragon. And a tiny fairy.

"I think she's breathing. Yes, she's definitely breathing." The tiny fairy laid its hands on her breast, then her forehead. The lightest sounds, like the softest breeze rippling across still water, filtered through her head, her limbs, the gash at her throat. She took a tepid breath, expecting to feel the same choke of blood, but she breathed freely. Suddenly she shot up in a panic, gasping at the freshness of the air around her.

Arms held her tight, and in her lap rested the curly hair of her friend, Ginni. Seth was beside her, pale and shaking, but still alert.

"Ginni. What? Did you make it back? Where are we? Where's the… mirror…"

Ginni held up the enchanted object. It no longer glowed, but when McKenna took it she could feel the thrum of magic that told her she had somehow acquired more souls. She remembered the sensation of all the dead witches binding together and understood.

"This soul… he knew the truth, the truth about Atosa, the source of all this death, and… and my sister…" she covered her mouth, her eyes filled with tears.

A flash, of amethyst and ebon scales. Deep within the heart of the gorge, an immortal spirit trapped within a mortal form.

"Who did you see, McKenna?" Seth's soft, concerned tone calmed her. She took another ragged breath and leaned into his embrace, while keeping a hand on Ginni and the mirror in her lap.

The slow inevitable rise of mortal woman to immortal goddess. The pale twin who shimmered in moonlight, calling down the gifts of her heritage in order to destroy her mother and steal her throne.

"I saw Razan. He and his band, they hunted down the witches and… and killed them. I think they challenged Katarin, and so she… she had them murdered."

Razan thought I wished to challenge my sister. Would he have killed me, too?

She recalled the haunting undead figures within the wood, and shuddered violently, expecting to see them materialize and attack at any moment. The saturated aura of death oppressed her, stifling almost every sense. She felt tainted; separated as if by a barrier from the mortal, hearty forms of her companions beside her. They belonged to the land of the living. They need not answer the insistent call that pulled her immortal soul toward its destiny. She suddenly felt horribly, painfully alone.

"Katarin. She's a sorcere, and she's a daughter of Atosa. I can't believe it. *She's* the necromancer. She's the one who's been releasing the ilmaurte."

She is half of me. I control this as much as she does. Have I released death upon the land? Has my existence caused this terrible rift?

The memory of souls she'd met, without knowing what power it was that drew her to them, haunted her. They should have passed on, and yet by her voice, and her hand, they remained tethered to this mortal world.

Was it possible she could be responsible for this?

Ginni clutched tighter to McKenna, and a look of shock distorted Seth's features.

"But why? Why would she do that? What about the Lich King?" He knitted his brows, too many ideas to track scrambling his speech.

"I don't know. Maybe she's using him. Maybe he's using her. But wouldn't it make sense?" she seethed, suddenly furious with her sister, with her missing mother, and with the weakness she felt in her own bones, "To discover you have a convenient sister to pin the blame on, while you continue to release a seemingly sourceless and uncontrolled horde on the realms? To send your lackey to track down that sister, and try to trick her into betraying some kind of power over death?"

Seth's grip on her tightened. "The ilmaurte. They attacked us right after that, right outside Wheelspoke. Those woods are crawling with sentries. I bet Razan set the horde on us so they would see you use your power, or use this mirror, and keep the deception going. They don't really care where the ilmaurte are coming from," it was impossible for him to keep the rage out of his voice, "as long as they keep doing their dirty work for them, driving the uninitiated into the arms of the guilds. But if there have been rumors that the guilds are responsible for the horde, they would jump at the chance to spread the word of an unknown child of Atosa, spotted controlling ilmaurte outside the goodly town of Wheelspoke."

The thought rendered McKenna too angry for words. To think that her name would be tarred by this falsehood annoyed her beyond expression.

All the monk had ever wanted was a damn beard.

He could see the train of thought as it crossed her expressive face, and the nagging dread that haunted her in her quivering fingers. He put his hands- warm, rough, alive- on either side of her face, and forced her gently to look at him.

"None of this is your fault. You are a victim to circumstances beyond your control, beyond any mortal control. You are not responsible for the mother who abandoned you, or the sister raised without you. I..." he trailed off, speaking gently, "the durgir should never have lied to you about the truth of who you are. They all did you a great disservice, and this world owes you so much more than that."

She nodded weakly, stretching her hand out towards Ginni, who gripped her fingers tightly. She looked around her again and frowned. "Where's Tjen?"

Ginni lifted her head. "They're... back at the village. I... made them stay behind, when we were told where you guys had gone."

McKenna nodded absently, still in the throes of her brush with death and anger at her sister. She continued to focus on her breathing, marshalling her thoughts into disciplined order and meditative prayer. She felt the soothing effects almost immediately, the power of her devotion lessened not one iota by the discovery of a new celestial allegiance. Her durgirn family may never have told her she descended from a goddess, but Malfaestus always knew, and accepted her homage regardless. She owed the god much for that.

"...it would be like her to have an evil twin, wouldn't

it? She's so good, after all," Ginni was saying to Seth, while McKenna's measured breathing restored her focus to her immediate surroundings. Seth smiled at her, the warmth of his relief clear in the sparkle of his golden eyes.

"Knowing McKenna, too, I'll bet she's ready to go after Katarin and force her back into order. I wouldn't want to be on the receiving end of any sibling rivalry with her- would you?" Seth bantered back.

A smile wavered its way onto the tired woman's face. "I seem to have a lot on my plate, don't I? Destroy the Lich King, find Atosa, restore the balance between life and death, champion the holvir, and go bully my sister into being less of a heinous witch."

"Didn't you just say you get to choose your own path now, monk?" Seth chided gently, amusement clear in his golden eyes.

"I absolutely choose this path. All of them. In fact, I really should write this down."

"I'll make a song for you. I'm good at that," added Ginni with something of a smirk.

"The world is in danger, all of Faiekind is in danger, and we are only so strong together as we can be individually," McKenna continued, overwhelmed by truth.

"Don't you have that backwards?" Seth asked confusedly.

The monk laced her long fingers, staring at her skin's slow ombré of darkness that blended to a lighter peach upon her palms. All the old wisdoms had always been called into question by the inquisitive and forward-thinking monk. "No, see," she explained, "everyone thinks they can make no difference, because they see only what could be accomplished by greater people, by movements they aren't a part of or changes that have yet to happen. But I think it's better to focus on what you can do, even if it means acknowledging you are only a single entity among voiceless millions. The smaller things you do will grow, and those around you will see that and be inspired by it and so make that change themselves. We expect a catalyst, we think we are worthless without one. But we are the catalyst. We are the change. If I have to be the first to do it," she declared, with a sparkle in her eyes, "then I will do it with every ounce of magic I have in me."

Though many should have heard her speech, her only audience were the companions beside her and the ancient creaking of the dead forest in which they rested. After a moment, she sighed and rolled her eyes before reaching out her arms to Seth, who braced and lifted her up off the floor of the haunted wood.

"Let's start with saving the world, and then we can worry about all that other stuff later," he said, planting a surreptitious kiss on the tip of her nose. McKenna blushed, flustered that he would be so affectionate before their garrulous friend. In fact, she was surprised at the holvi's silence, until suddenly-

"Wait, where did Ginni go?"

XXIX

The Rise Of The Lich King

Razan returned from his reconnaissance to see Katarin restlessly pacing the lengths of her chamber. He watched her lithe form retreat and advance, not wanting to interrupt her musings in such an unpredictable state.

"You better have a good explanation for why you had my sister and her mirror in your grasp and yet just let them go," spat Katarin, suddenly turning about to face him, her rigid posture glowing with wrath.

The force of her speech made him reel, and he wondered how she even knew about his encounter with her sister. He saw the scrying bowl behind her, and wondered with unease how well his own cloaking spells had managed to outwit it. His bangles would have alerted him if he'd been spied on by such a device.

His bangles were powerless to the ever-watchful eye of the dead.

She wondered if he'd answer her honestly, but if she were honest with herself, she really didn't care. Single-minded purpose strangled her passion and a dull headache distracted her focus. The magical solstice's restorative power fell dull upon her desensitized skin, unable to penetrate the deathly aura that encased her like a shell. His silence began to provoke her, and she scoffed, waiting with crossed arms for any kind of response.

Thinking quickly, he assumed his normal charming grin. If she continued to blind herself, stubbornly under the impression he remained oblivious to her schemes, he would work to keep up the charade.

"I had to find out where they were going. And I couldn't get close enough to strike, not with that damned ex-paladin there. But don't you see? This is the perfect opportunity. Guarding the Doors of Death is a feral vicious dragon. Your sister seeks to close it. Let her face the monster, who can destroy her and the mirror in one breath," he explained, slowly advancing amid her ceaseless perambulations.

An inexplicable sneer crossed her face, one the assassin didn't know how to interpret. Her actions were so dismissive, and he felt none of the warmth and quiet pensiveness from their earlier encounter. A madness, a frenetic energy, crackled around her, stunning him.

Continuing to look beyond him, she answered slowly, almost mockingly. "What if McKenna knows how to use the mirror? You need to go there and assure its destruction. Throw them in Styckes for all I care. We cannot leave any of this to chance!" she cried, furious that he would so nonchalantly disobey her commands.

"Use the mirror?" He asked confusedly. "Use the mirror on the… dragon…"

He trailed off, realizing with a start just who that dragon was. Atosa hadn't simply disappeared. Katarin must have summoned her, kidnapping her own mother and trapping her in this monstrous form, hiding the goddess in plain sight.

How could he be so blind?

Seeing in the taut, arrogant figure before him all the seething manipulations he'd spent so long desperately trying to escape from, he desperately clung to any shred of hope that the woman within this towering pillar of icy disdain could still be saved.

He felt the power of her gaze as she summed him up, saw the way the dawning of his understanding began to effect the way she viewed him. It wasn't flattering. The corners of her mouth were downturned, she had a hand on one of those full hips, and an air of contempt that enveloped her entire mien. Of course, she would have directed it at any who tried to stand in her way, but Razan had always been above that; able to access an inner echelon of her personality that hid within the thorny, impenetrable armor of absolute assurance and disdain for others. Assuming an air of bravado, he pushed the revelation from his mind, trying to think quickly, desperate for a way they could both escape.

"Come now, Katarin, you know I'll see this through to the end. When have I ever disappointed you?" he scoffed, raising a hand to her pale cheek.

She slapped him.

"You go too far, assassin," she seethed, her beautiful face contorted in a mask of sheer malice. "I am the Master here, and your Princess. I allow you license to control your pitiful party of rogues, but your duty is to me and me alone," she hissed, eyes narrowed in contempt.

His swarthy face paled. Never before had she

commanded his obeisance like this. Without warning, the devious voice and wicked eyes of his mother assailed him. The violent aura possessing the sorcere clashed violently with his own, almost as repugnant as a rotten stench. He was a child again; standing before the warped gate that opened a portal into the Abyss. The fibers of his being dragged themselves away from the vestiges of his naked soul, draining his essence, drawing him toward a fate worse than death for any mortal. The clerics surrounding him bowed before the daemoric power he exuded. He wanted none of it, rebelled against it. But one cannot rebel against their blood, the nature of their heritage.

Why would her aura recall these fiendish horrors? He searched the face that he had watched over for decades- observed in every dancing light and every creeping shadow. The woman who stood before him seemed as one possessed.

Then it struck him, like a physical blow. She *was*.

His mother's words suddenly possessed a clarity he'd previously denied. The wandering undead, the kidnapping of Atosa, the allegiance of daemor; all of Faie seethed and churned with a deadly curse that had been almost a century in the making. Katarin was simply a pawn, a victim, to the manipulations of a being whose power knew no bounds. Abyssinians and the dead. Only one could have such insidious sway over both realms.

As far as he ran, he could not escape the trappings of fate, the insidious clutches of a family whose lust for evil and chaos threatened the very stability of the plane they resided on.

I do not belong to them. I fled from it, and yet no matter how far I ran, my path led me here, a fate worse than death. He calls for me too, desires the soul that belongs to the Abyss and the mortal form that walks the goodly realms of Faie.

The Cult of Naszer finally reached their god.

"The Lich King. It's true then? He's returned?" he whispered through clenched teeth. She didn't hear him, but with a deft chime of his bangles the truth appeared before him.

He gripped the pouch left behind by the holvir couple, suddenly incredibly thankful that he chose to intercept them before they ventured any further into the chasm. But how could he stop this woman from finishing what his fiendish family had begun? Avoid the fate that wound itself tightly to this borrowed soul, this immortal body, and save them both?

"You sent the holvir there to summon the Lich King. Do you even realize what you have done?" he breathed, still in shock at the discovery.

Whispers drowned out his words, rising like a cacophony in the sorcere's brain. A throbbing headache formed over her temple, but she simply dismissed it as easily as she dismissed him.

They told her what to say, words rising as easily as smoke from the pyre. She didn't flinch. "He is a tool, an aide to restore me to my rightful throne." The whispers grew louder, forcing her to close her eyes, measure the words as carefully as possible. "He cannot usurp my rule. He... has no corporeal form."

Of course he doesn't. There's only one he could possess.

"It is not form he seeks, Katarin. He's just a spirit, he's just an idea, he can control without one," he insisted, trying to brush the poisonous intrusions from her mind. Even his magic failed him. As though she lay wrapped in an impenetrable cocoon, he could not reach the mind that he so long admired, nor the heart he thought he held. "He will use you, he has been using you. And when he has destroyed Atosa he will destroy you too!"

She swept away toward the scrying bowl upon her dais, dismissing the accusation. Misgivings arisen were swiftly quenched by those subtle manipulations that had influenced her since time immemorial. She flatly refused to believe Razan would know anything more than she had chosen to tell him; in her hubris, she truly believed the guild master, smitten by his infatuation, remained completely under her thumb.

His heart sank within him. He knew the truth better than she even could. The Lich King's realm was none other than that of the despised Abyss, plane of the denizens of pure chaotic evil. While a sorcere as talented as Katarin could summon and master even the largest daemor, her goddess-given powers were nothing in the face of the disgraced Celestial of Necromancy, the Lich King.

A wave of nausea rolled over him as he wondered how long she had been possessed. Surely since the disappearance of Atosa. But before then? Memories like incandescent motes flashed forth of her carefree and precocious childhood, her inquisitive and licentious adolescence, her autocratic and embattled adulthood. How could he have missed it?

An attack of sudden doubt stunned him, as he realized the truth, the nature of their relationship. He loved her, this woman who stood before him. Had loved her since first laying eyes on her, a fledgling princess upon her flower throne, so many years ago. And yet, was it truly her, he loved? How much of her nature, her spirit, had the Lich King consumed? The thought of their bodies entwined, in the throes of passion, mated in body and soul, filled him with revulsion.

He was no better than his accursed mother. He made love with a daemor incarnate.

All this passed in an instant. She had already turned from him, back to the scrying bowl, trying to find the charm the holvir should have placed by now but unable to see anything lurking in the black depths.

"The Lich King is no pawn, Katarin." An edge of desperation lent itself to the assassin's voice, hoarse, unaccustomed to pleading. "He is a being of unknown power, a hellish creature that feasts on the discord of the planes and drains the magical energy of any being he can cling to!" She turned to regard him, and he could see in the depths of her amethyst eyes the faintest flicker.

Was it misgiving?

"Let me bring you the mirror," he continued. "You can use it, you can save yourself-"

"There is nothing I need saving from!" She hissed angrily, clawing the stone desk with sharp nails in her rage. "We've been over this time and again, Razan. This is my destiny. My future, my purpose."

She's completely mad. How far has he gone, how deeply has he penetrated that lovely mind, that powerful soul? Do I stand any chance at all?

In the scrying bowl, the dragon uncurled from the cavern floor, rolling the length of its amethyst scales and yawning, revealing rows of metallic black teeth and a curled, forked tongue. From shoulder to tail, the dragon stretched over three times the length of a normal aesir, and a sinuous neck held its imperious head almost as high as the multistoried clock tower that stood in Ljotebroek. A curious, pulsing light emanated from behind it and a lurid red and black cloud of otherworldly ash sank into the pit from a ledge above.

Katarin scanned idly for the brazier the holvir were meant to place, but it did not appear. The nudging of the insidious presence that compelled her insisted she simply had to set up the summoning circle herself.

"Hmm… the holvir never appeared. No matter; I can accomplish their errand on my own," she murmured, then turned and caught Razan regarding her. Unable to interpret the complexity of emotions hidden in the man's dark eyes, she grew cold, dismissing him snidely. "What, you're still here? Will you finish what you started and retrieve my mirror, or will I have to do that myself as well?"

The assassin wondered if he could walk away. But a measure of the man's loyal heart refused to deny her anything. He thought quickly. Perhaps if he got the mirror, he could get Katarin to use it to free herself from the Lich King's clutches. Despite his earlier doubt, he knew the woman he loved still existed, in some measure, beyond the Lich King's control. He would do anything to restore her, or he would see them both through the fires of the Abyss himself.

He bowed deeply, not bothering to answer aloud, and

then vanished in a flash of black smoke.

She turned away from the scrying bowl, a sudden empty feeling knocking her breathless. For the first time, she sensed the presence dividing her mind. The thoughts she always attributed as her own, took a form and desire apart from her. But with the disappearance of the assassin, with the retrieval of the mirror so near, she couldn't focus on this discovery. In a moment, she was again overwhelmed by her single-minded purpose. She whispered a quick spell, opening a planar gate into the chasm, and stepped through to light the pyre through which her all-powerful master would be summoned.

The Lich King must rise.

XXX

Come What May

"Ginni? Ginni! Ginni, where did you go?"

They tore through the woods, searching distractedly for their missing companion. Seth, prayers mingling with his shouts, tried to illuminate any life that stirred in the dead wood.

A dim silhouette of gold flashed through a thicket of brambles. McKenna raced toward it, ignoring the thorns that snagged on her skin as she dug past them. But the figure trapped in the thicket wasn't Ginni. It was Tjen.

"Tjen? What are you doing here?" She pulled the holvi free, while they looked around delirious and disoriented. Seth doused his hand in an elixir and placed his palm on Tjen's forehead.

The holvi stirred weakly at the touch, and their expression shifted back to normal. "Ginni… where's Ginni? She… we… we were heading toward the chasm, but Ginni was strange, and she… I ended up in there," they pointed forlornly at the dark brambles. "It's all hazy… we went into the tunnel and we heard a… a dragon…"

Seth blanched. "You heard a what?"

The little holvi nodded with conviction. "Yes. A dragon. Ginni and I… we're bards. We can recognize any sound, even if we've never heard it from the source before. Only one creature can move the very land with its roar, and that," the very air seemed to shrink from their lungs as they recalled the noise that forced them to flee, "is a dragon."

The party grew quiet amid the swirling eddies of fear, shock, and disbelief that surrounded them. Undead hordes were one thing- dragons, quite another. In the entire history of Faie, as they knew it, only one dragon had ever freely walked the realms, and he became a god. It seemed unlikely this dragon had come from the same place, especially in secret, and found itself trapped beside the Doors of Death.

Kneeling beside the shivering holvi and putting a hand on their shoulder, Seth drew a breath, trying to calm both himself and his shaken companion. "Do you remember what brought you here? After seeing the dragon?"

They screwed up their face in concentration for a moment, but shook their head sadly. "No. Everything after the dragon is a blank. I... the blight may have..." they shrugged their shoulders confusedly, unwilling to face how close they were to a cursed death.

"And Ginni, she was with you? Before you lost consciousness?" McKenna asked gently.

"I think so. Yes, she must have been. But I can't... can't remember anything after the roar."

Shuddering, the bard clung to McKenna, unused even for a moment to being apart from their spouse, and still reeling from the effects of the curse and this new spell. McKenna looked concernedly at Seth, then frantically began patting the pockets of her cloak.

"The mirror. The mirror, it's gone. She must have taken it, but… where could she have gone so quickly? She was right here!"

Seth studied the wood and began to trace symbols in the air with his fingers. McKenna laid a hand on the shock of hair that lined the crest of Tjen's head, trying to soothe the holvi into a measure of composure while the rogue worked his oath.

"That bastard," he said suddenly, stooping to pick something off the ground. It was a small, rounded piece of glass- the remains of a shattered orb. "This is an Onyx Blade spell. They used these pestilential orbs of summoning to slip between planes and travel any distance they want in an instant."

"Onyx Blade? You mean… Razan was here? But why?" Frustration keyed into every pitch of the monk's voice. McKenna hated being so in the dark about these powers she supposedly had, the mysteries surrounding her heritage, and most of all, the enhanced importance of that stupid mirror. She knitted her brows, recalling the holvi's ballad they had sung upon meeting for the first time.

> *"A mirror, by ilvir in secret held*
> *The corporeal gift of body meld*
> *For three days and nights did Atosa gaze*
> *Until a mortal form for her would raise"*

She whispered the words under her breath, while staring at the concentrated look on Seth's face. She saw a flash, of ebon and amethyst scales, and the runes carved along the bottom- *What do you see in a mirror? Your Self.*

"Seth. That mirror. It can restore Atosa. It's the mirror she used to create a mortal form for herself in the first place. If she gets ahold of it, wherever she is, she can be restored to goddesshood. They stole it so they can destroy it."

She knew I had the mirror all along. She didn't send Razan to test me. She sent him to steal it. And to think I actually pitied her.

Tjen gulped, placing a quaking hand upon McKenna's knee. "The dragon. The dragon wasn't there before. Urtha said something, that on terms not her own Atosa has returned to mortal form…"

A flash of ebon and amethyst scales, the smoke of a pipe roaring with lifelike vigour.

"Atosa is the dragon."

A deep sense of betrayal settled on the monk, weighted by the realization she had lost yet another family. This new heritage, recently discovered, now composed exclusively of some crazed power-hungry sorcere who had kidnapped their own godly mother and turned her into a monster to usurp her power. *And to think I gave the durgir flak for sending me out into the world naked. They're positively saints in comparison.*

"Seth, what in the world is the point of even having a family if they're going to do things like this?" She asked, laughing weakly in the face of these baffling and unavoidable truths.

He gave her a look; one she'd grown quite used to by now. "Why else do you think I would be hiding out in a bar playing drinking games with strangers as far as I could get from my own?"

What am I saying. I haven't lost a family at all. My family is here, with him. Has been, since we toasted that first cup of mead.

"Pfft. I can't believe you tried to convince me you let me win. When this is over, we're going for a second round," McKenna threatened. She had no intention of succumbing to the despair threatening to consume her. To do her justice, the company she kept made it easier than it might have been. The glowing aura of the man beside her soothed the monk's soul and feverish restlessness. This loss would not cast her adrift; not while she had him to moor to.

A low vibration, the heady thrum of ancient and evil magic, reverberated throughout the clearing, emanating directly from the gorge. Tjen began to shiver, and McKenna placed a calming hand upon their brow. The holvi recognized no god; but the soothing energies she applied were powerful enough to reach them anyways.

"Tjen, I'm sorry, but you have to take us there," the urgency rang in Seth's voice. "Razan must be taking the mirror to the Lich King. If it can restore Atosa's mortal form, there's no telling what it can do for his."

"We'll find Ginni, and the mirror, and stop them. We'll save her," McKenna held the little holvi's face in her hands, staring into their sightless eyes, "I promise."

Tjen nodded, and led them on to the pit beside the gorge. A faint smoke- black, tinged with red- had already begun to leak from it. Swallowing hard, McKenna dispelled a blessing of protection over her party, hoping

the god to whom she had devoted her life, her soul,
and her heart would see them and grant them the same
strength in the face of this universal foe. Together they
plunged into the heart of Faie, the chasm that bordered
the realms of life and death.

Determinedly plumbing the depths of the seemingly
bottomless gorge, they snuck quietly along the fictile
corridors, unconsciously tracing the steps the holvir
had made so long ago. Tjen, guided by uncanny muscle
memory and determination to be reunited with their
better half, set the pace within the labyrinthine depths.
They concentrated only on the path to Razan and his
captive, Ginni.

McKenna and Seth paced behind, struggling to
keep up with the holvi's frantic momentum. McKenna
felt uneasy. Her durgirn upbringing attuned her to the
strength of stone and she could sense the rock in the
cavern was weak, loosened both by the constant tremors
that rocked the chasm and the breach between the plane
of the living and the dead.

"Why is it like this? What are these tremors?" She
nervously touched the walls of the cave, trying to feel the
spirit within the rock.

A clamorous cacophony nearly knocked her from
her feet. The walls were saturated with death. The souls
that could not enter Hel's portal, and the ones that
had slipped free when their guardian disappeared, all
hovered intangibly as near to the entrance as they could
get. Without the mirror, she had no way to free them. She
slammed a fist against the wall in frustration.

"They're trapped in there- trapped in the here and
there, neither here, nor... there!" She babbled angrily,

confused by the energies around her.

There were thousands, thousands of homeless and tetherless spirits locked within the porous stone. Suddenly the sheer volume of roving undead made sense. The difficulty in necromancy came from the power needed to summon souls used to reanimate corpses. Corpses were plentiful; souls, less so. But with such a bounty here in the chasm, sustaining an army of undead would take little more than the magic required to bind the soul to the body and the body to its master. The implications were exceedingly dangerous.

"That must be the source of the tremors then. There's too much frenetic energy in this place. Disturb them, and the whole thing comes down." Seth took her hand, holding it gently and dusting off the gravel that clung to where her knuckles met the rock wall.

"Wait. Did you see that?" She pointed to a flash at the end of the corridor.

The three of them bolted, careening to a halt at the edge of a bridge suspended across a deep gorge. Thunderous rumbles, different from the roll of the rock and sediment surrounding them, emanated from its depths.

"Do you think..." Tjen shivered, pointing to the darkness below.

A screech of metal rang out, louder even than the groan of shifting rock. McKenna spun in place, throwing out an arm to protect Tjen and drawing forth Laghrusse in one swift motion, but Seth had been faster.

"Razan! This is madness, and you know it!" He

shouted into the assassin's face, dexterously turning the battle away from the edge of the gorge to give McKenna and Tjen time to cross the gorge and find the path that descended on the other side.

"You don't know anything, rogue," Razan spat viciously. Tired of games, tired of chivalry, tired of willful ignorance. He would either find victory against this challenger, or go down fighting. *There are worse ways to go,* he thought to himself, as the smoke rising in the gorge began to fire in his soul, bringing forth that bloody light to his daemoric eyes.

Without pause, McKenna and Tjen sprinted across the narrow bridge. Though desperate to turn back and fight alongside Seth, the path simply wasn't wide enough to allow for the swing of her staff. She watched uneasily as the combatants pivoted along the perilous cliffside, Seth trying to use the battlefield as a means to keep his opponent too distracted to be deadly.

Razan was alive to that strategy, though. With vicious and powerful strikes he forced Seth along the treacherous walkway, taking the advantage of space for movement from both of them. That bloody light grew brighter with every thrust, and a shriek of triumph made them flash as he whipped his sword across Seth's face, narrowly missing his throat but sending forth a spray of blood from his jaw that peppered the walkway.

The paladin's focus seemed trained exclusively on maintaining his footing, and preventing his adversary's advance. Very few of his strikes were aimed anywhere other than where Razan's blade struck, and though McKenna knew the latent strength that lay within him, she knew also that his god couldn't reach him here to give him the edge he needed to overpower his foe.

Meanwhile Razan's power seemed to grow, his thrusts quicker, his movements more timely and graceful. The smoke from the chasm grew thicker in the air, obscuring McKenna's view of the two and at times blotting them out almost entirely. Oddly, though Tjen had covered their mouth with their tunic and seemed to draw breath with difficulty, the air and energies within it didn't disturb McKenna other than to make the hairs on her arm stand on end and the runes on her skin crackle with currents of power.

Is this dragon breath? Or a daemor miasma? I sense the powers of death even beyond the souls trapped in the walls, but-

Without warning, she felt a strange surge of energy, then the blood drained from her face. She had an instant to act. Whispering a prayer to Malfaestus, she grabbed Tjen and threw herself into an alcove. Just before a terrific jolt racked the chasm and tore apart the bridge upon which they battled, followed by a stream of deathly fire that flooded the gorge and for a moment burned the fog away.

When the dust from the rubble cleared away, McKenna saw the walkway the combatants stood upon had been utterly demolished. Her crouched form rested at the utmost edge of that which had broken apart, and over that edge…

"SETH!" she screamed, flinging herself at the rocky precipice.

He had dug finger and nail into the shelf of rock that jutted from the decimated ledge. McKenna could just reach him. Her adamantine grip locked upon his wrist, preventing him from slipping into the blackness below.

A low roar could be heard, roiling from the rift amid plumes of smoke and sparks of fire. Any descent into that inky morass almost certainly meant death. Each corded sinew of muscle tensed at the thought, fingers tightening upon the only lifeline to which he clung.

An agonized glance cast over her shoulder saw Tjen, knocked senseless, lying in a heap out of reach. She cried out in frustration. While she may have been able to stop Seth from falling, she couldn't lift him out on her own strength. She had no idea whether Razan had perished to the cave-in, or if he escaped and lay in wait to strike her at her weakest.

The paladin's aura blazed forth, drawing her attention back. She could barely see him; any attempt to dash away the tears that blurred her vision could loosen her already tenuous hold. But somehow the brightness of his aura soothed her, reminded her that though the mortal body may suffer the immortal soul it carried would always stand forth in greatness and nobility.

"Come what may?" his tortured eyes, revealing the true expression of his heart for the first time, locked with hers.

"Come what may," she whispered back, emotion choking sound from her throat.

Their fingers slipped apart and he disappeared into the black.

The dragon's roars drowned out her cry.

She dropped beside Tjen, quickly applying pressure to their temples to draw their senses back to life. As the dazed holvi came to, they took off down the corridors, McKenna subconsciously following the trail of life that lit the way to her missing holvi companion.

"She's close," whispered Tjen, too senseless to realize Seth had disappeared. Every breath they drew grew more and more ragged, and McKenna could sense the slow deterioration of the light of life that kept them aloft. That acrid smoke, rising ever more thickly, carried with it a sort of cursed energy that Tjen, blighted as they already were, hadn't the strength to fight.

Slowing down, McKenna held the holvi's face in her hands for a brief moment, searching deep within the immortal soul she knew lay within her. Decades of devotion to a god, learning the magic of the domain he controlled, taught her what to look for, and she whispered an oath to Atosa. Breathing ancient Celestial words onto Tjen's upturned face, she infused them with a strength to repel the spectre of death that loomed over them.

She couldn't cure the blight, but she could fight death.

A huddled form down a dismal corridor caught her attention, and she cried out in relief at the sight. It was Ginni, the holvi captive. McKenna and Tjen quickly changed course to seek out her little companion, desperate to save as much of her family as she could from the looming specter of death that haunted the mighty rift. She breathed easy; the holvi no longer carried the mirror, but she was still alive.

"Tjen, do you know another way out of here?" McKenna asked, while dousing the bard in fresh water and probing the nature of the spell Razan had placed to try and revive her. Ginni's eyelids fluttered and she murmured softly, smiling at McKenna's touch.

"'Knew you'd save us," she whispered, struggling to
sit upright.

"We can find our way out. Are you... will you...
where is Seth?" Tjen responded, realizing suddenly
the emptiness where once the presence of the paladin
occupied.

"I need to save my mother, and put an end to this,"
McKenna, wincing, chose to answer only the first part of
the question. "Leave now. Find your people and warn
them that if I fail, they need to go to Meliamne and beg
the ilvir to put a stop to Katarin's madness at any cost."

The hair on the back of the monk's neck stood on
end; danger lurked in every corner of this cursed place.
Standing shakily, the two holvir gazed for a moment at
their friend- a simple durgirn monk, who stood before
them now nearly engulfed in the simmering and godly
power of death.

"He's... gone, isn't he?" whispered Ginni, as she saw
the smoke rising from the chasm, and the silver trails of
tears upon McKenna's face.

Another roar shook the cavern. Another wail of
tortured souls grated against their ears. Even the bard,
mortal as she was, could feel and hear their doomed cries.

But she knew McKenna's heritage gave her an
advantage no one else had. She shook the monk's hand,
tearing her from her dreadful reverie. "I know it's not too
late. Seth believed in you. He knew you had the strength
to do this. Find the mirror, and save her. Save them all,"
she sang, with a wide sweep of her hand that seemed

to dispel, for a brief moment, the dim smokiness and illuminate the souls that haunted the space, waiting for salvation, desperate for release.

You're the daughter of Atosa, the bard's eyes seemed to say. *You are a goddess, and a mortal, and yet you saved us, the weakest and the lowliest. If you can save us, you can save him.*

They turned and crept through a crack in the wall, leaving the demigoddess behind to face the peril of her unknown heritage.

The air was full of that fetid red and black smoke. It dimmed her vision, and she could feel her calling weakening, the blessings of her god dimming as though muffled by static. A dread heaviness sank upon her soul, a daemoric presence that whispered every dread, every misgiving the monk had ever faced. How did it know her better than she knew herself? How could she think to face such a being, the true Master of Death, that not even her mother could oppose?

Though the smoke had dimmed her connection to Malfaestus, she still felt the draw of the bond she had forged with Atosa. Through it, she could sense Razan's presence. It seemed he had survived the heaving tremors.

At all costs, she had to prevent him from bringing that mirror to Katarin.

The keening wail of trapped souls showed her the way. They recoiled in pain at his presence, the daemoric energies slowly awakening in his blood causing chaos in the planar rift. Arcing threads of light glowed through the stone, synapses firing erratically, chaotically; each one sent a flood of memories, fragments of ghostly conversation, and overwhelming emotion she could feel deep within the soul that threaded itself throughout her own form.

For an instant, silence descended like the empty vacuum of space. In one moment the cavern seemed full to bursting with more than it could hold; in the next, she walked in a fathomless and empty space, no footsteps but her own. The dichotomy of her own existence saved her. Any mortal tossed so freely between the boundaries of the Material plane and Hel would have been lost forever. But she took a deep breath and summoned another oath, drawing herself up and arcing Laghrusse above her just in time.

Razan, taking base advantage of her preoccupation, emerged from the shadows that hid him in order to strike.

His sword came down in a mighty arc, ringing against the polearm whipped up to block it with such force they nearly felt the ground crack beneath them. McKenna trusted the blacksmith's spells imbuing Laghrusse with infallible strength, and used the muscles corded from years in durgirn mines to push back hard against her foe. Out of the corner of her eye she spotted the mirror strapped to the harness he wore bound across his chest, tucked under his vest.

"Why must you fight like this!" she cried. "This is not your battle, it is my sister's and mine alone!" She swung the guisarme in an attempt to sweep him off his feet, but he dodged nimbly away.

"Ah, but you see your sister pays me to fight her battles for her. Her strengths are better for other tasks," he chided. That bloody cast to his eyes had spread through his face, bright red and black veins scrolling across the once comely visage.

He must've used one of this stupid globes to transport from the cave-in just before the bridge dropped. I'll make him regret that.

Their weapons wove and cracked in a deadly dance, he unable to penetrate the wide guard of her long polearm, she too devastated and weakened by the energies raging both outside and within to do more than keep him back. Each sword stroke clanged against the magical weapon, but while they drew him no closer neither did they diminish his taste for her blood.

"My sister is callous and a thief, and she has no more right to that mirror than I do. You're a fool if you think she'll give you anything for a job you'll never succeed in finishing!"

He snarled viciously, a dirk in his left hand complementing the sword balanced lightly in his right. He moved as though the two blades were ten. But McKenna, nothing daunted, maintained the distance between them that rendered each of his strikes meaningless. Her own friendly spars with Seth along the road, the training and dedication to perfecting her body and her control, and above all, the Celestial power she finally recognized and allowed to flow through her stood her in good stead. Like a magnet drawn to his blades the shaft of the guisarme raised to block each strike, repelling them with strength imbued by the power of the glowing runes carved along it. Each parried strike drained the assassin of more and more strength, as though instead of fighting against a single adamantine pole he assailed the cold impenetrable walls of marble that surrounded Lianor.

Not even the paladin fought like this, he found himself

thinking. The monk's aura glowed, refusing to dim even in the murky smoke that suffocated their tunnel. She moved with rapidity, with ease even, her bare feet shifting along the smooth stone floor, toes balancing every inch of her massive frame as it wove and danced around his blades. The copper coils of her hair fairly crackled with energy, and though he knew the woman had just watched her partner perish, nothing distracted her from the singleminded purpose before her. Defeating him, and saving her friends.

With an upward swing containing every ounce of strength her body possessed, she managed to thrust Laghrusse between those flashing swords and whipped them from Razan's grasp. Without pausing, she twisted her pole and snapped a blow with the blunt end to his ribcage, knocking the air from his lungs and the ground from his feet. He hit the ground so hard the mirror went flying, spinning across the floor and out of his reach.

Blood-red eyes met amber. Though lost in her identity, the clarity of her purpose suddenly illuminated the murky chaos that lurked within the man's tortured soul.

She knew the price one had to pay for passion. She could see with vital lucidity the passion that drove this man to madness.

"And you are a fool if you think my sister's love is worth your life," she spat, kicking his blades into the gorge where she had watched her own love fall.

Razan blanched, realizing the truth of her words and of his own defeat. He felt a pouch behind his back and gripped the orb-bound spells tightly as McKenna advanced on him. Doubting not that she'd slay him then and there, putting an end his mercenary pursuit, he whipped the globes free and a flash of darkness pulled him from her path.

She watched him disappear without a blink.

A silence descended, brief and eerie. Blood pounding in her ears and her slow breathing were silent sounds indeed compared to the ring of battle and the thunder of a dragon's roar. She picked up the mirror and took a deep, measured breath as she approached the yawning void torn into the ground before her. For a moment she could close her eyes and imagine herself back in the quiet High Road, alone but for the whisper of wind in the trees and the bubbling of water in the valley river.

Save them all.

McKenna winced into a half grin, and, without a single backwards glance, stepped over the edge.

XXXI

Through The Doors Of Death

"What? Why did you leave! She has the mirror!" shrieked Katarin as the globe's spell resolved and Razan appeared before her.

He gazed at her impassively, McKenna's words warring in his breast. He had nothing left to fight, and was unable to face the fact he'd met his match in both sisters. He waited, aching to see a relenting light dawn in Katarin's eyes.

He waited in vain.

"You fool! Without it, the Lich King is finished, and everything I fought for goes for naught," she cried, turning towards the scrying dish in desperation at the roaring dragon and the holvir fleeing the gorge. The goddess Atosa had not yet been restored, but she sensed the weakness of her hold over the Lich King's army, both trapped in the walls of the chasm and advancing across the plains- as though the necromanced souls could feel the power of their former deity returning, severing their hold on this plane and allowing them to dissipate in relief.

"I should have known better than to trust your ability. There's only so high you can reach, after all," she murmured indifferently, already losing interest in the tortured man at her feet.

"You call me a fool, yet we both knew I would fail to destroy the mirror, or your sister," he replied in a low tone. "She is, after all, a Celestial like you-"

"She is a *mortal*!" retorted Katarin, the edge in her voice sharpened by the draw of the Lich King's daemoric power.

"She beat me and she took it," he spat into Katarin's livid face. "But if we can't destroy the mirror, then it's time to simply destroy them all."

A gleam, the pyre's light flaring off a ceremonial dagger, flashed into Katarin's eyes. She blinked, and suddenly he could see a very honest look within them. For years he had devoted almost every beat of his immortal heart to evoking that look, hoping he could win along with it the vitality and love of Katarin's mortal soul. Never again would those shining violet eyes caress his form in the throes of passion, and never again would his own crimson gaze hold hers in a union of truth only they two could know. There was only one way to save her, save her soul from the vile clutches of the vile Celestial who clung to her.

He had nothing left to fight, but everything left to give.

In one swift, powerful motion he swept the dagger from its perch and plunged into the pyre, dexterous hands so skilled with the blade carving a path deep into his chest, through flesh, through rib, into the heart so callously denied by the woman he bled before. The heart, given wholly and freely first to she who had wrested it from his chest with her flawless determination and imperfect trust. And then, once denied, a heart given broken to the Lich King, who would consume it in his wrath. Summoning the fiend's spirit was one thing, but this, providing him with the means necessary to create a corporeal form, giving him access to the one being in all of Faie who could host such a creature, would grant the Celestial more power than anything else. And, Razan hoped, would free the woman whose soul he would do anything to cleanse from the Lich King's mighty grip.

A heart is nothing, he mused as his life was drawn from the vigor of his frame to the pyre's enchanted flame.

Nothing.

Around Katarin, the chamber became suddenly airless. She knew in a second what Razan had done. Unable to retrieve the mirror and restore her to herself, he had only the recourse of sacrificing himself in her place; giving the Lich King a corporeal form, that his control over her mind may finally be destroyed.

Suddenly, the voices within her went silent, snuffed in a single swift motion as she watched the only love she'd ever known perish before her to suffer a fate worse than death.

The two laid entwined on a couch, tucked away in the high tower. It was the eve of her ascension to Third Sorcere of the Moon, and Razan had brought congratulations in the form of his lithe figure and comforting passion. It was midnight on a solstice gathering and he'd brought a bale of glowing starflowers. To shine among her hair, was all he remarked. It was the stroke of his blade, piercing the heart of a rival who threatened her, the mithril pendant, restored by his hand from the one who had stolen it long ago. It was an escort to the place of her childhood, a starlit night spent dancing among the trees, a princess again among her people.

It was the light that died in his eyes, as her heart throbbed with the strength to banish the possession with which the Lich King held her to the deepest plane of the chaotic Abyss

Too late to save him, too late to save them both.

With a roar and a flash he was gone, and there, in the pyre, stood the Lich King.

He seemed a being made from pure, inky blackness. An ephemeral shine, light cast from an otherworldly source, lined his features; faiefolkr, yet alien in its sheer chaotic aura. He held out an arm, examining each finger slowly and delicately, then cast a dubious glance over the sorcere. She had fallen where she stood, the snap of his possession from her mind rendering her unconscious and barely alive. He turned away from her insensate form, back to the pyre.

The souls trapped in the rock surrounding him shrieked and writhed in agony at the sight. Tremor after tremor racked the courtyard as he reached a hand into the dying embers and pulled forth a scepter. With a wave, the souls grew still. An eerie hush almost painful in its deathly silence descended.

"Now," the depth of his voice pierced the stillness of the space, "for Atosa."

—

The sweet decay of rotting dirt and ash of dragon's breath filled the air that rushed past McKenna's swiftly plummeting form. She reached out, grabbing for something, anything, to slow her descent. Quickly she felt a pull, a shift almost in her gravitational field, as she continued to drop into the chasm. The tender touch of a million souls clung to her, arresting her momentum and preventing the same fate to which she watched Seth succumb. As the canyon floor finally rose up to greet her, she dropped almost nimbly down and rolled to disperse her energy.

Her gaze locked to the being before her. Honestly, she probably couldn't have looked away if she tried. The monstrous dragon, her scales, her deadly spines, the shine of adamantine teeth, the gleam of those amethyst scales, mesmerized her. She had never seen anything so beautiful. She had never faced anything more deadly.

With a mighty roar that shook the cavern, the beast challenged this wild interloper, daring her to approach. No flicker of recognition; no intimation that the dragon had ever been a being of soul, and flesh, and magic, like the woman who faced it.

A fight. I have to fight a dragon.

As she began to chant, drawing down blessings to imbue her with the strength and protection necessary to face such a foe, the dragon thrashed angrily, energy dancing like water upon each shivering scale. It braced for attack, slamming its spiked tail against the ground, and again against the wall of the cavern, drawing forth the moans and shrieks of souls trapped within it.

At least I'm not naked this time.

A bright flash envelops McKenna. Her flesh attains the strength of mithril, her eyes glow along with the runes

flickering in patterns across her skin and the shaft of the
weapon she draws up, slow, languorously, as though to
engage the beast in a dance instead of a battle. Nothing of
her mother looks out of the beast's eyes; no godly grace
emanates from its massive bulk. Just a feral shriek and a
foreleg capped in razor sharp claws, reaching to shred the
woman where she stands.

McKenna moved with lightning rapidity. She swung
around the shaft of Laghrusse, bracing the mithril
polearm against the stone floor and using it to vault over
the dragon's strike. Time and again the beast swings
its massive claws in an attempt to grasp the deftly
maneuvering monk, each missed strike driving it more
and more wild with anger. In frustration, it lets loose
a wave of fire that breaks along the wall of protection
erected around her; a shining globe transfixed to the
glowing runes upon her sable skin.

Malfaestus has always been stronger than fire.

The dragon breathed its hottest, but nothing could
penetrate the protections that clung to McKenna as
closely as she to her god. As the dragon's breath began to
fade, a smoke trailed behind the fire, a cloud of death, its
inky purple blackness threatening to suck the life from all
it touches.

It settled on McKenna, severing the connection she
had called down from the pantheon. It should have
ended her life, too. But the soul dedicated to Malfaestus,
the Forge's Hammer, the Secret Keeper, belonged also to
realm of death. The crawling miasma cannot command
that nature which controls it.

Her aura glows silver, brighter as the dense smoke
attempts to dim it. Its paralyzing touch slowly evaporates

around her, receding, retreating, leaving her standing a pillar of righteous fury, a true demigoddess of death. As it recedes the runes flicker to life again; as it dissipates, the monk, after so long ignorant and so long in denial, comes into her full heritage.

"I could kill you with a single touch," she whispers to the dragon. It roars again.

Dragons don't speak Celestial.

Instead they begin another deadly dance. The dragon's claws are powerless against mithril, and their ringing screech against the empowered guisarme chimes like bells and echoes up the chasm's stone walls. Souls pour from porous recesses within the rock, surrounding the combatants, a haunting ring of specters, spectators, who wonder what outcome each wants.

Would the child of the goddess of death seek her mother's throne?

A snap of the dragon's vicious maw, a parry that rang out against the bloodstained blade.

Has Atosa tired of her immortal reign? Will she seek the gift of life again?

The monk weaves in and out of teeth, claw, spine, tail. Incandescent wave of shimmering scale. The souls that stand in audience ripple silently, the shockwave from each empowered strike so strong it touches even their immaterial shapes.

McKenna's voice is full of song, her eyes full of light, the blessings of her god surrounding her and the power of her heritage shining from within her. Her heart is locked in wordless anguish. She knows the shape that lies still in the gloom. She knows that of all the spirits who silently watch, the one who matters most is no longer there. Finally, with a call to the heavens, a fearsome cry that possesses all the mortal power of the duergi and immortal power of the goddess, she forces the dragon to recede, to coil upon itself in submission, to face destruction, defeat, death.

Atosa's eyes, those same amber orbs that looked back every time she glanced in a mirror, lock on hers. Facing her mother, even in this form, nearly overwhelmed the monk. She couldn't break their shared gaze. She knew somewhere in the dusty dimness lay the crumpled form of Seth, and to see him would undo her entirely. Holding the mirror out, she spoke the runes Seth taught her to recognize, calling to her mother with the flow of a language she'd never learned but instinctively belonged to her, was a part of her heart and soul. Each word seemed to come from an untouched well within the woman's very being, bursting forth through the dam of everything behind which she hid her nature. Could she have seen her own aura, it would have dazzled her. The gloom of the cavern scintillated with her glorious, righteous beauty as she called to the immortal spirit of Atosa locked within the heart of the fearsome dragon.

"I have come to seek you out, mother. I'm sorry for making you wait so long. I was angry that you left me, I was angry that you left me to learn for myself who I am. But I... am thankful, too," she chanted, tears spilling golden tracks down her cheeks. "Thankful after all that you let me forge my own path. You may have thought you had no other choice. But at least you gave me the power to make mine."

She laid the mirror before the dragon. "This is your

realm, not mine. I do not want your throne. I ask that you return to it. Please," she pleaded. Death had done her no favors, had taken that which she wanted more than anything else. "Restore the balance of life and death."

A million motes of light, drawn to her powerful aura, gathered to settle on each of the dragon's scales, on her horns, clinging to each tooth and nostril and the full length of her entire monstrous form. The souls, who so desperately desired release, swirled free from the mirror and joined the lights. The very walls of the gorge sang, shone, softened as the trapped spirits pleaded with their goddess to return.

A chime- a high pitched, clarion call- a flash of the purest, most dazzling light. As it faded, McKenna could make out a new form.

"You're… you're tall."

McKenna clapped a hand over her mouth. Did she really just say that out loud?

The woman before her smiled, soft lines creasing her nearly translucent face. She seemed made of starlight, or the shadow of the moon cast upon snow. She held out her hands to McKenna, who took them, trembling.

"Daughter. It's been so long."

The monk smiled amid her tears. "Mother, welcome back. I'm so happy to meet you."

They stared at one another for a moment, but suddenly Atosa's form flickered, brightening and then dimming almost imperceptibly.

"He has risen," she said quietly, recognizing the draw of power as her adversary assumed his corporeal form. "You cannot fight him. You are a mortal. I hope you don't… resent that," murmured Atosa.

"Not for a minute. I have friends…" McKenna choked, remembering the price of mortality, "family, who I want to live, and fight, and die with. Only mortals can be so blessed."

Atosa closed her eyes, as though to bask for a moment in her child's aura. The souls who restored her form still hovered adoringly, clinging to their beloved goddess.

"You can bring him back, you know."

A dry sob racked McKenna's form. She hadn't been able to look at him. Through eyes blurred with tears, she could just make out his recumbent form.

"What… do you mean?"

Atosa paused for a moment. "I must face the Lich King alongside as many gods of the pantheon as I can get to join me. He is a being that exists only in the vacuum I created, when I became mortal all that time ago. He will insinuate himself into more hearts, more minds than your sister's, and he will unleash an army of hell and daemor upon this land. But you, child, you have another journey before you." She pointed toward Seth's body, through the protective haze of souls that hovered around it. He glowed with their light almost as strongly as his aura did in life.

"And you need your sister." She frowned suddenly, and a bevy of souls congealed, then vanished. In a moment, they returned, carrying the limp form of

Katarin.

The sorcere moaned as Atosa passed a gentle hand over her face, and ran fingers through her moonlight hair. "She is free from his poisonous intrusion. I know it may take time to trust her, but you must. Together only can the two of you journey through the Doors of Death, to bring back the souls you wish to save."

"But mother-" McKenna felt a vice grip her throat, her chest.

"No buts," said the goddess, with a smile. "You are a great hero. You will succeed, as you have done here. And you can use the mirror," she said, holding it out to her, "to keep track of the friends you leave behind."

McKenna looked into the glass. She saw Tjena with their head in Ginni's lap, looking around and blinking rapidly.

"The blight! It's cured?" she gasped as the realization dawned on her.

"Yes. Love is a powerful force. The Lich King isn't strong enough to keep hold on hearts so pure as the two those carry. Especially now that he's shifted his focus to those weaker and easier to control."

Atosa put a hand on McKenna's cheek. A small contingent of souls soaked into the wall, and glowed. The outline of a door, lined with runes, appeared before them. An ungodly wail rocked the chasm as it took shape, and a small frown formed between the goddess's eyes. "Oh, he didn't like that," she sighed to herself.

The Doors of Death had opened once more. Souls

drifted through the open portal, pausing to bask beside their goddess for a moment before passing through into the realm beyond. McKenna stared in awe at the sight; a glorious glowing beacon into a strange, shifting plane that seemed to resonate with music and magic. The Afterlife, the portal to Hel.

Katarin stirred, then rose slowly, blinking in the shifting gloom.

"Perhaps this will teach you not to abuse your power, next time," Atosa addressed her sternly. Katarin covered her face with her hands and wept silently into them. McKenna stepped away, allowing them to speak with one another, and crouched near the figure she both loved and feared more than anything else in the world.

His face seemed peaceful, content even, graced with the touch of a god. She stroked a lock of hair from his forehead. A faint glow of gold lined his form, traces of the aura not so easily extinguished by the severance of an immortal spirit from its mortal coil. Hope still remained. She reaches out to spirit and fire, feeling the intangible souls that slid between this plane and theirs. The strength of her celestial heritage guides her pull- the brightness of his aura, the nobility of his shining soul, meets her trembling grasp. He smiles at her, trusting her, knowing she will not leave him to wander long.

Behind him, nearly dazzling, is the form of a great, golden dragon. Bahamut will not let his bravest warrior go so easily into eternal night. She meets the dragon's gaze, and he bows to her- to her, a simple durgirn monk.

The scene dissolved, and she found herself again with his lifeless body in her arms. She bit back a cry of excruciating pain, instead rising to meet her sister.

"Katarin of Moonbow."

"McKenna of Hammardin."

They faced one another, tracing invisible similarities, measuring the might of the other like wary predators. Both appeared so different, though a weary sadness seemed to cling to each. Before their mother, before the realm they shared with her, they could little acknowledge one another and their antagonism faded to nothing.

Perhaps they are strangers. Perhaps they are known to one another more keenly than they know themselves.

The two women stared for a moment. Twins, with figures and natures as alien as any could be. United by a single purpose, a shared goal, they turned and, together, stepped through the Doors of Death.

Thank You For Reading!

Looking For More
Iron Breaker Books?

www.ironbreakerbooks.com

www.ingramcontent.com/pod-product-compliance
Lightning Source LLC
Chambersburg PA
CBHW031112160726
47991CB00004B/1343